The Traveling Consultant

The Traveling Consultant

CHRIS BRYDA

PALMETTO
PUBLISHING
Charleston, SC
www.PalmettoPublishing.com

Copyright © 2024 by Chris Bryda

Paperback ISBN: 9798822968134
Hardcover ISBN: 9798822963399
eBook ISBN: 9798822963405

Contents

Authors Note

Chris Bryda is the author of two novels and is currently working on a third. His novels include *The Grudge List, The Traveling Consultant*, and, coming soon, *The Willow Brook Murder Society*. He is retired from the software consulting business that he operated for twenty-four years. When he is not authoring books, Chris is playing golf and riding his racing bike on the Swamp Rabbit Trail. Chris lives with his wife Deborah in Greer, South Carolina.

* * *

I did in fact travel across the USA and several other countries engaged with business executives to make them more efficient in a competitive environment. I am grateful to those clients who gave me an opportunity to demonstrate my skills and add value to the organization while they were on their journey. I hope the readers enjoy this story, which is a complete fabrication and whose characters bear no resemblance to anyone living or dead.

Enjoy the read. And thank you in advance for spending time with James Crowley as he travels the countryside and avoids the land mines.

PalmettoPublishing.com
chris.bryda@icloud.com

Chapter 1

James Crowley was looking for work once again. He had just finished a twelve-week project in Iowa for an agriculture business. An extension was not offered by the current IT director. The reason given for the short-term assignment was that they only needed a little push on the project and not a long-term resource. James knew this was a bullshit answer and the director was just covering his butt.

The consulting world is a strange business. Some employers are in a hurry to hire you as a consultant, and others take their sweet-ass time. It all comes down to the burn rate, the amount of cash that the project is hemorrhaging on a monthly basis. The higher the rate, the quicker the director wants the implementation to be finished. When this happens, all hands are on deck and consultants make a fortune.

* * *

He started the search all over again by logging onto the Dice and LinkedIn websites. Hours and hours of searching for another gig were expended to get to the next project. His Westies Champ and Abbey were by his feet as his fingers did the walking on various websites. After a few hours, the dogs wanted to go out and play, so a break in the action was taken. He would get some fresh air, play with the dogs, enjoy the sunny day in Fallbrook, California. Since the casita was right next to the yard and completely fenced in, the dogs would be safe to wander. You just had to watch out for roaming coyotes. The warm sun felt good on his face as the cell phone started to ring.

* * *

"Hey, James, how are you?" said Bill Hogan.

"Not bad. What's up, Bill?"

"Hey, I got a line on a project in Pittsburgh. You interested?"

"Well let me look at my schedule?" James said.

"This guy I found wants an assessment."

"An assessment?" James asked.

"He wants the two of us to put together a project plan to implement the Enterprise Software package. They just bought the software, and they need consultants to implement the plan."

"Then what does he want the assessment for?"

"I think he wants the assessment to interview the two of us and then maybe hire us."

"What kind of details can you share with me?"

"He will give us a flat $5K for a two-day assessment plus travel expenses to Pittsburgh, where their corporate office is."

"When does he want you and I out there?" James asked.

"He would like to see us next Wednesday and Thursday."

"That's kind of short notice."

"I know, but he is willing to pay for it."

"Are you sure about this one, Bill?" James asked.

"Yes, I am sure. Can you put the assessment together from a prior project, as well as a PowerPoint presentation for the two of us, for next week?" Bill asked.

"I have a couple of canned presentations already prepared. I'll need to change some of the details, and then we can be off to the races."

"Great. I'll confirm with the guy."

"Who is this guy, and what is the company name?" James asked.

"The vice president of the Butler Energy Corp. His name is Ted MacDonald."

"So we have to up front the travel expenses and then submit them to the company?"

"Yep. I know this is less than ideal. But it's work," Bill replied.

"OK, I'll take a chance with you, Bill. I am between projects right now anyway."

"One more thing, James: I'll be there for just one day and not two. I have something to take care of on Thursday of next week."

"So you're going to leave me to do the assessment by myself the second day?" James asked.

"Yep. I talked with Ted, and he is OK with me being there one day and you for two days. You know I am the technical guy and you're the project manager and financial guy."

"Bill, you're doing it to me again—signing me up for something I know little about."

"James, you will be fine. Ted seems like a real nice guy. What's the worst that could happen? We only get the assessment and no other future work?"

"It could be worse. We do the assessment, give away the project plan, and get stiffed for the travel expenses," James said.

"You are always a worrywart. You need to trust people more, James."

"When you're out of work, you need to watch your pocketbook, Bill. You don't get unemployment benefits when you're a 1099 consultant. Remember?" James said emphatically.

"Just put the assessment together and I'll confirm with Ted MacDonald that we will be on-site at his office next Wednesday and Thursday."

"OK. But if this thing goes sideways, Bill, I will never forgive you."

"I have a good feeling about this one, James," Bill said.

"Call me later in the week when you have more info on the particulars. But I'll book the flight for a Tuesday evening arrival; the meeting starts Wednesday at eight a.m."

"Sounds good, Bill. I'll talk with you later in the week," James said as Bill hit the end button on his cell phone. Then James added, talking to himself, "What did I just sign up for?"

* * *

James went back to the casita to start on an assessment package for the Butler Energy Corporation using the current version—10.0—of Enterprise Software. He had done twenty projects with full implementations over the past fifteen years and could put assessments together in his sleep. It did not take long to copy an old client plan and change the name to Butler, and then poof, the assessment was ready for refinement. Champ and Abbey were at the door once again and wanted to play in the yard. A dog break was always a good thing to do, and they did not want James to work. So once again it was back out to the yard for playtime with the Westies.

It was a sunny day in January; the temperature was seventy-five degrees and simply perfect for anything outdoors. Next week Pittsburgh would be in the twenty-degree range and would require a winter coat, which would need to be pulled from the storage closet, along with gloves and a hat. *Why would anyone want to live in Pittsburgh?* James thought to himself.

Wait till he told his wife that he would be traveling east next week. She would not be happy about the trip. But work was work, and consultants had to go wherever the clients asked them to go.

Chapter 2

Frank Browning, an Enterprise Software Corporation sales representative, walked into the office of an IT department vice president named Ted MacDonald on Monday morning. Frank was a seasoned closer for the company and was extraordinarily successful in selling additional software to clients that did not need it.

Frank knocked on Ted's office door and was met by Charlotte Webb, an office manager.

"Hi. I am here to see Ted MacDonald for a meeting at nine a.m.," said Frank to the pretty young woman at the desk.

"Hi. I am Charlotte Webb, executive secretary for Mr. MacDonald and our CFO Mr. Tim Murphy."

"Hi, my name is Frank Browning, with the Enterprise Software Corporation."

"Ted has been expecting you this morning," said Charlotte.

"Thanks. Which office is he in?"

"Ted's office is on the left. We don't have the nameplates up yet. We are still organizing the office space," said Charlotte. "We just took over this space in the office building, and we need to get a little bit more organized."

"Growing pains for a new company are always a welcome event," Frank replied.

"Ted is still on the phone so you will need to give him a couple of minutes to finish up a bit of business."

"Sounds good, Ms. Webb. Thanks."

"Please call me Charlotte."

"Sure thing, Charlotte. That is a beautiful name."

"Thank you, Frank."

Frank noticed that she did not have a wedding ring and was stunned by her beauty. He looked at her; she was a gorgeous blonde with blue eyes and a fantastic hourglass figure of 34-28-32.

"I am jealous of your husband," said Frank.

"Oh. What do you mean? I am not married."

"I was just admiring your beauty. You're a knockout. If you don't mind me saying that."

"Thank you, Mr. Browning," Charlotte replied.

"Please call me Frank."

"Please call me Charlotte."

"Can I buy you dinner sometime?"

"You are very direct, Frank."

"I am just mesmerized by your beauty. I'll apologize in advance for saying that and being a little forward."

"Well, thank you." Charlotte was blushing. "All of the men here in the office are married, and a good man is hard to come by."

"So dinner tonight? You can pick the place," Frank said.

"Well, let me think about it while you are having your meeting with Ted."

Just then Ted opened the door to his office and walked over to Frank.

"Hi, you must be Frank Browning." He extended his hand to Frank for a handshake.

"You must be Ted MacDonald," Ted replied. "Please call me Ted."

"Please call me Frank."

"Charlotte, I'll be in a meeting until ten a.m. Please don't disturb us unless it is absolutely necessary?" Ted asked.

"Will do."

Ted closed the door behind Frank as they entered his office.

"Did you get a chance to look over the proposal from Enterprise Software Corporation?" Frank asked.

"I did. It looks a little bit high," Ted replied.

"Oh. What part is high?"

"The whole quote is high."

"We can find some ways to trim the costs."

"You can remove the Enterprise consulting for the implementation cost. I will plan to hire a full-time project manager for that piece of the plan. You can also remove the cost for the technical consultant. I'll plan to hire this one as a full-time resource as well."

"Ted, that's a big chunk of the project," Frank replied.

"Yes, I know. You have the Enterprise consultants at $225 an hour, and I can get them for $100 an hour."

"Our consultants know the product and the best way to implement the software."

"This is not my first rodeo," said Ted. "You guys make a bundle on consulting services. I'll let you make some money on us. But I will not let you rip us on this project. Your software is a tier-two product at best, and you're charging tier-one, Oracle prices."

"I am sorry you feel that way," replied Frank.

"Cut the bullshit. Give me your best quote on this software purchase, and you have a deal. Otherwise, I can go buy another software package from somebody else."

"I will need to rework the numbers and get back to you."

"That's fine. I'll be here till Thursday, then I'm out for a few days."

"Can I get back to you on Tuesday, same time in the morning?"

"I can pencil you in for nine a.m. on Tuesday," Ted replied. "Come back with your best number, or you will not get the deal."

"I'll need to talk with my management about what we can do."

"That would be fine. I'll hold the nine-to-ten-a.m. slot open for you on Tuesday."

"I will come back with a better quote for you then."

"Make sure you sharpen your pencil. Our plan is to buy up to ten businesses and create a huge company. So what you lose on the initial quote you will make up on the back-half volume."

"Can I ask, What do you expect the final user count for ten businesses to be?" Frank asked.

"A projection of the user community would be about two to three hundred but not initially. We would ramp up to that number and would need to phase the user count in as we buy the businesses."

"Can I ask how long this will take?" Frank asked.

"That all depends on our CFO and his vision."

"So you need Enterprise to be flexible in this quote?"

"Exactly," Ted replied. "You be flexible with us, and we will definitely reward your company with a juicy deal."

"OK, I'll go back to my management with this information, and we will sharpen our pencil for you."

"Thank you. I appreciate your sincerity and look forward to working with you and your company."

"I want to thank you for this opportunity. We will not let you down. Give me twenty-four hours to see what I can do."

"I have another meeting in ten minutes, so I need to run. I'll have you coordinate with Ms. Webb and work out any details with her."

"Thanks, Ted. I'll check with her as I leave," Frank replied.

Ted opened the door and shook Frank's hand as Frank exited.

"Charlotte, can you take care of any arrangements that Frank needs and schedule another meeting for Tuesday at nine a.m.?" Ted asked.

"Yes, I'll take care of that for you," Charlotte replied. Then she said to Frank, "So I need to reschedule the meeting for nine a.m. on Tuesday?"

"Yes, that would be fine." Frank replied before adding, "Can I buy you dinner tonight?"

"You are pushy."

"Is that a yes?"

"Well, I do need to eat tonight."

"You pick the place, and I'll treat you to a nice dinner."

"Well, OK," said Charlotte. "Say, seven p.m.?"

"What's your address?" Frank asked.

"I can meet you at your hotel, in the lobby," Charlotte replied.

"Are you sure? I can pick you up."

"No. I'll meet you in the lobby of your hotel."

"I'm staying at the Palmer, down the street from your office."

"Yes, I know where it is. I can meet you there at six thirty. I'll make a reservation for seven at Frank's Italian Restaurant."

"Sounds good. See you then and thanks."

"Until tonight," Charlotte replied.

As Frank left the office, Charlotte started to think, *Will he play ball with me or not?* That was the question she would have to figure out at dinner. Then she would put her plan with Frank Browning from the Enterprise Software Company in motion.

Chapter 3

Charlotte arrived at the Palmer Hotel, which was only a few miles down the street from the office, at 6:30 p.m. She walked into the lobby, and there was Frank Browning in a nice sport coat and pair of slacks just waiting for his date. She strolled into the lobby in her red cotton dress with a low-cut blouse to show off her beautiful breasts. Several of the men in the lobby were doing a double take at her appearance as she walked by.

"Hello, Frank. How are you?" Charlotte said.

As Frank turned around, his mouth dropped. "You're beautiful."

"Thank you."

"Are you sure you're not married to someone?"

"What are you talking about?"

"You are drop-dead gorgeous. How can you not be married or in a long-term relationship?"

"Well, I am not. I told you: all the men in the office are married or engaged, and there are really no good single men around. Thanks for the compliment."

"Are you ready for dinner?" Frank asked.

"Yes. I am starving."

"Well, then let's get going." Frank extended his elbow out for Charlotte so he could escort her to his car. She tucked her arm around his as they walked out of the lobby.

Frank's Italian Restaurant was just a few minutes away in the downtown area of the Coraopolis business district. The eating establishment was well known and had the best Italian food for miles around.

The reservation was for 7:00 p.m., and they arrived a few minutes early. The restaurant was not terribly busy for a Monday evening; the hostess seated them immediately as they came in the door. Frank had his doubts about the evening, and the lack of patrons was not helping to ease his concerns.

"I know what you're thinking," Charlotte said as they sat down.

"What was I thinking?" Frank asked.

"The restaurant is empty—how good could the food be, right?"

"Were you reading my mind?"

"I assure you the food here is really good. Just give it a chance."

"OK. What is their specialty?"

"The fettuccini, bolognese, ravioli, and lasagna are their four best dishes. They make them all from scratch."

"You have obviously eaten here before," Frank said.

"You bet. This is my favorite Italian restaurant in Coraopolis."

"Let's get some wine. A Chablis or a Chianti. Any suggestions?" Frank asked.

"The Chianti is really good here," Charlotte replied.

When the waiter came to their table, Frank ordered two glasses of the house Chianti. The waiter said that was a good choice and left to get the drinks.

"I am so glad you came out for dinner with me, Charlotte. I was going to have to eat alone tonight because your boss asked me to come back on Tuesday for a follow-up meeting."

"Were you not going to stick around tonight?"

"No, I was supposed to be in another state with a different client."

"So Ted messed up your schedule?" Charlotte asked.

"Yes, he did."

"He does that. You know he is the boss."

"Well, he is my customer and not my boss. But the customer is always right. So here I am in Pennsylvania for a second day."

Just then the waiter brought two glasses of Chianti to the table and then darted away as if the restaurant were busy. He mumbled that he would be back to take their order in a minute.

"Here's to a new client." Frank raised his glass and toasted toward Charlotte.

"You have not gotten the sale yet, Frank," Charlotte replied.

"I will get it from Ted on Tuesday."

"He is a tough cookie."

"I'll make it a sweet deal for him."

"How do you intend to do that?" Charlotte asked. "Ted is looking at another software package. You do know that there is competition?"

"I did not know that. But thanks for telling me," Frank replied. "Can you tell me who it is?"

"I am not sure who it is, but I know their number."

"Can you tell me what it is?"

"Well, I could, but then you would have to do something for me."

"Anything. Just tell me."

Just then the waiter came back to get their orders for dinner. *What bad timing that waiter has,* Frank thought as he pulled up the menu and started to look it over.

"Ladies first," the waiter announced.

"I'll have the lasagna with meat sauce and a garden salad with ranch dressing," Charlotte said to the waiter.

Then the waiter turned to Frank, who said, "I'll have the same as the lady."

"Very good," the waiter said as he scurred away from the table.

Charlotte just smiled at Frank as he was puzzled about what she had just said. Was she trying to help him get the deal, or was she just playing with him?

The waiter dropped off the bread and a plate of butter. As he walked away, Frank pressed Charlotte. "So how can you help me if I help you?"

"Let's enjoy our dinner, and we can talk more about how each of us can help the other later tonight."

"Later tonight?" Frank asked.

"At your hotel," Charlotte replied with a smile.

Frank smiled. "You don't waste any time, do you?"

"No. I don't. My daddy taught me that when I see something I like, I should always go after it."

"You're an interesting person, Charlotte."

"Because I am a little bit forward?" Charlotte asked.

"I am used to being the one that's forward."

"Well, let's see how this evening goes."

The waiter came by to deliver their salads, and the conversation just dried up. Shortly thereafter the lasagna was delivered to the table piping hot. As Frank forked a piece of his entrée, his taste buds were shocked.

"This is really good."

"I told you Frank's was the best in town," Charlotte said.

As they finished the meal, Frank was feeling rather good about his date. *A nice blonde, a nice meal, and a new customer. What more could a guy ask for?*

* * *

After dinner Frank drove Charlotte back to the Palmer Hotel, where her car was and where he was staying the night. As he exited his car to open the car door for Charlotte, he asked her, "So what did you mean by the comment about helping me help you?"

"You have a room here, right?" Charlotte asked.

"Yes, I do."

"Do you want to find out?"

"Yes, I would like to find out."

"Let's go back to your room."

The two of them walked into the hotel through the side door so as not to arouse any suspicion from the front desk. The key card was used to open the side door, and up to the third floor they went. His room number was 307, just off the stairwell and at the end of the hall.

As they walked into the room, Frank asked once again, "How can you help me get Ted to sign?"

"I know his number—what he is planning on spending for the software," Charlotte replied.

"But where do you come in on this deal?"

"I'll get you the deal if you get me seven percent commission on the project."

"So you want a commission on the quote?"

"Yep. Don't you get ten percent commission on your quotes?" Charlotte asked.

"Well yes, that's my normal number."

"So you will get three percent of something instead of ten percent of nothing."

"That's a high price to pay for a deal," Frank replied.

"You also get one more thing."

"What's that?" Frank asked.

Charlotte started to take off her dress. She unzipped it from the back and let it fall to the floor. As Frank looked at her body, her gorgeous body, a 34-28-32 hourglass sculpture, he just said yes.

"You have to do this my way," Charlotte said.

"Whatever you want me to do, I am yours," Frank replied.

She helped him take off all his clothes and slowly walked him over to the bed. She grabbed her purse and pulled a few toys from it.

"Are you OK with this?" she asked.

"What do you have in mind?" Frank replied.

"A little bit of bondage, if you don't mind?"

"No. I don't mind."

She proceeded to pull out her favorite toy, the Scarlet Couture Bond to Surrender Cuffs. One for the right hand and one for the left hand. As she wrapped his hands, Frank just smiled. Then a chain that extended to the wrists was applied to the right and left bedposts. A lock was placed on the cuffs, thereby restricting Frank's hands from any movement. Two more chains were applied to the right and left footposts and just left on each corner.

Another favorite toy of Charlotte's, the Scarlet Couture Spreader Bar, was pulled out. The left cuff was strapped around his right ankle. The right cuff was strapped around his left ankle. The chains from the bottom bedposts were locked to the cuffs with a small lock. Frank was completely immobilized by the 110-pound blond beauty.

"Are you still OK with this?" Charlotte asked Frank once again.

"Sure. I underestimated your passive-aggressive nature."

"It's just what I like."

She pulled two more items out of her purse: a squeeze bottle of chocolate syrup and a can of whipped cream.

"What's that for?" Frank asked.

"You will see in just a minute."

As Frank was lying there on the bed, he was thinking about what he had gotten himself involved in. Was she a crazy person that craved sex or the sexual conquest of random guys? Either way he was enjoying the show and did not have any problem with being bound to a bed in a hotel room by a blond beauty. She squeezed chocolate syrup on both of her breasts, then sprayed a little bit of whipped cream from the can on top of the syrup. Just before she mounted him, she asked him the question.

"Are you going to get me the seven percent commission?"

"Can you do five percent instead?" Frank the bound and helpless salesperson asked.

"No, it's seven percent or nothing." Charlotte jumped on him and slammed her breast into his mouth. "Do we have a deal?" she asked once again.

"Yes. We have a deal. Seven percent commission," Frank replied.

Charlotte went wild as she undulated up and down on Frank. She pressed her breasts into his mouth so he could lick up the syrup and whipped cream. She knew this one was hers. She controlled him, and he would give her what she wanted: a 7 percent commission on the deal.

After Charlotte was fully satisfied and Frank was spent, she got off of him and unlocked the cuffs. She was happy with her trap. *One of many deals to be made*, she thought.

"I underestimated you, Charlotte," Frank said.

"I get what I go after," Charlotte replied.

"You do indeed."

"Did you enjoy our evening?"

"Yes, I did. But at what cost?"

"Just a seven percent commission. That's all."

"Does this entitle me to a return trip?" Frank asked.

"That will be subject to discussion and negotiation at a later date," Charlotte replied.

She moved away from Frank to put her clothes back on so she could get home for the evening. As Charlotte left Frank on the bed, she gave him one more look. "Don't forget the seven percent commission."

"You did not tell me the number."

"It's $125,000 for the deal," Charlotte said as she left the hotel room. "And don't forget I get seven percent."

"Yes. I remember, Charlotte."

Frank lay in bed and contemplated what had just happened. He had been taken by a beautiful blonde who had thrown her body around like a sledge hammer and trapped him in her web. How could he explain this to his manager? He had to give up 7 percent to get a 10 percent commission. Was that a fair deal? *But the sex was fantastic. So maybe it was worth it,* he thought as he justified the adventure.

Chapter 4

Ted had scheduled an appointment with a second manufacturing software company for Tuesday at 8:00 a.m. in the Coraopolis office. This one was the Ask Manufacturing Software Corporation, and the salesperson was Mark Wagner. He wanted to get a second bid rather than just buying the Enterprise Software Corporation off the shelf. If there were at least two software companies bidding for the project, he knew the final numbers would at least be competitive.

Mark showed up early at Ted's office on Tuesday, a full fifteen minutes before his scheduled appointment. As Charlotte arrived at her desk, she could see that a gentleman was waiting, and all the doors were still locked. As she opened the office vestibule door that led into Ted's office, she asked the man standing in the hallway, "Are you here to see someone today?"

"Yes, I am. My name is Mark Wagner from the Ask Manufacturing Software Corporation, here to see Ted MacDonald."

"I am Charlotte Webb, executive secretary for Ted MacDonald and our CFO Tim Murphy. I handle both of their affairs."

"Nice to meet you, Ms. Webb."

"Thanks. Please call me Charlotte."

"Thank you, Charlotte. When do you expect Mr. MacDonald?"

"He should be here any time," Charlotte replied.

"Mr. MacDonald asked me to meet him here at eight a.m. sharp."

"I am sure he will be here shortly. Can I get you a coffee while you wait?"

"No thanks."

Charlotte saw the wedding ring on his finger and knew this one would be harder to trap than the last guy, who was single.

"You sure I can't get you a water while you wait?" Charlotte asked.

"Well OK, a water would be fine," Mark replied.

As Charlotte got him a bottle of water, she bent down to give it to him and display her cleavage in the purple dress she was wearing. She caught his look and knew he was interested.

"Here is your water, Mark."

"Thanks, Ms. Webb."

She saw him look at the finger where her wedding ring would be; she was almost there with the hook.

"I am sorry, Ms. Webb. It is Ms. Webb?" Mark asked.

"Yes, it is 'miss.' I am not married, if that is what you were wondering."

"A pretty woman such as yourself must have a lot of guys."

"Sadly, no. I work here, and all of the men here are married or engaged. A good man is extremely hard to find."

"A good woman is hard to find as well. I am so happy to have found my wife in college, a few years ago."

Just then Ted MacDonald strolled into the office. Charlotte knew that this one was not going to play ball with her. She would have to discredit his proposal or find some way to make his quote uncompetitive. She was not going to try and sleep with this one or play her games. He was married, and those types were hard to bend her way.

"You must be Mark Wagner?" Ted said.

"Yes, Mark Wagner from the Ask Manufacturing Software Corporation. I have your service quote and would like to go over it with you."

"Come into my office, and we will discuss the quote." Ted pointed to the open doorway. "Tell anyone who is looking for me I'll be in a meeting until nine a.m.," he said to Charlotte and closed the door.

"Here is the service quote for the software purchase," Mark said as he handed Ted the proposal.

Ted thumbed through the five-page quote and scanned the last page.

"So the purchase cost of the Ask Manufacturing Software is $135,000 for one hundred users?" he asked.

"Yes, that is the quote for the purchase cost without consultants, as you asked for on Friday," Mark replied.

"That's your sharpest number?"

"That's the best number I can give you for one hundred users."

"You seemed to have sharpened your pencil from the $200,000 initial quote."

"I am not making much on this deal."

"Well, let me think about this for a couple of days."

"When should I call you back on this quote to follow up? Monday?" Mark asked.

"Monday would be fine," Ted replied. He then got up and opened the door to show Mark out of his office.

"Thanks for the opportunity to quote your business, Mr. Mac-Donald," Mark said.

They both shook hands, and Mark left the office with an unsigned quote.

"So you did not like that guy?" Charlotte asked.

"His number was too high," Mark replied.

"Can I ask, What was his number?"

"His service quote was $135,000 for the software package," Ted replied.

"Wasn't he lower than the other one?"

"Yes, the other guy was at $200,000 but included a lot of consulting hours in the proposal. I hope he comes back with a better number."

"Which one did you prefer?" Charlotte asked.

"Either one would work, but I think the Enterprise Software Version 10.0 would be a better fit for us."

"You had me set up a nine a.m. follow-up meeting with that other one today, right?"

"Yes, with Frank Browing, the guy who was here yesterday."

"OK. I'll keep an eye out for him, Ted," Charlotte said.

A few minutes before 9:00 a.m., Frank Browning walked into Charlotte Web's office. His eyes caught her eyes, and he was still just mesmerized by her beauty. She was wearing a purple dress and showing a lot of cleavage. He ran through in his mind that the woman in front of him had been all over him in bed last night; he just could not stop thinking about her.

"Good morning, Ms. Webb," Frank said. "I have a nine a.m. meeting with Ted."

"Good morning Mr. Browing. Yes, I see your appointment. Ted is just finishing up on a phone call. I'll let him know you're here."

"Thanks," Frank whispered toward Charlotte. "Is the number still $125,000?"

Charlotte replied, "Yep."

"Thanks for last night," Frank said.

"You're welcome. Don't forget the seven points," Charlotte replied in a low whisper.

"It will be a night I will not forget."

"I'm glad you had some fun."

Just then the door opened and Ted motioned Frank to come into his office.

"Charlotte, I'll be in a meeting until ten a.m. Please don't disturb us unless it is absolutely necessary?" Ted asked. Then he closed the door behind Frank and they both sat down. "So what is the updated service quote?"

"I can go to $125,000 with no consulting hours on the project," Frank replied.

"Is that the best you can do?"

"That is the best pencil-sharpened number, Mr. MacDonald."

"Well, I guess we can take that."

"Do we have a deal?"

"Yes, we have a deal."

"Can you sign the quote?"

"Sure." Ted signed and dated the quote to buy Enterprise Software Version 10.0.

"Thanks, Ted. I appreciate your business."

"When can we get the software loaded?" Ted asked.

"I will need a day or two to turn the deal around."

"So by next Monday sound good?"

"That should be fine. It's Tuesday—that gives me three business days to get the wheels turning on this deal," Frank replied.

Ted got up from his desk to open the door and escort Frank out of his office. Frank followed and shook his hand as he left with the signed quote in hand.

He passed by Charlotte's desk and said, "Thank you and have a nice day, Ms. Webb."

"You're very welcome. It looks like your meeting with Ted was very productive?"

"Yes, it was. Ted signed the quote."

"How nice. So you got the deal?"

"I got the deal," Frank replied.

As Frank exited the office, he was thinking to himself. *What did I just do? I let this 110-pound, blond, 34-28-32 hourglass figure of a woman manage my deal, and I gave away a seven-point finder's fee from my ten-point commission. At least that is how I will put it down on my tax return.*

Chapter 5

James Crowley finished the project plan assessment for the Butler Energy Corporation late in the day on Tuesday. This was a comprehensive plan to implement the Enterprise Software Version 10.0 package and detailed out the steps to be followed, along with dependencies, to get the business on the software. All in all, the project plan was a six-month proposal that had extraordinarily few company specifics. This was a general hook to get the client and demonstrate to them that the consultant knew what he was talking about. This project plan was to be used to present to the executives what could be achieved if they executed it against a time table. The plan would be put forth as a starting point after an initial assessment and review of the business objectives with the managers. An iterative process would be used to ask questions and propose general answers as more information became available. James knew that the plan he prepared would be changed and modified many times before the new client signed off on the proposal.

* * *

James traveled from his home in Fallbrook to the San Diego International Airport, bound for the Pittsburgh International Airport, on Tuesday night. He made a reservation at a local Hilton just outside the Coraopolis airport location for Tuesday and Wednesday nights. This way the drive to the Butler Energy Corporation office on Wednesday morning would only take a few minutes. He did not want to be late for a new client, and staying close to your client was a normal ritual in his line of work. He would try to catch up with his friend Bill Hogan in the morning over breakfast and go over the proposal.

* * *

James worked out in the hotel gym, showered, dressed, and then went to the lobby for breakfast. He hoped to bump into Bill so he could go over the plan before springing it on the new client. But Bill was nowhere to be found. James called him and did not get any answer on his cell phone. Now he was beginning to worry. Bill was a bit of an odd duck, and sometimes he did not show up on time. So James decided to just go over to the Butler Energy Corporation and ask for Ted MacDonald.

He drove over to the office, which was just down the street. It was close to 8:00 a.m. when he arrived; that was the scheduled time for the meeting. There was no sight of Bill Hogan. James started to worry once again. Standing a colleague up in a meeting with a new client was not a good idea, and James would never forgive Bill for this infraction. As James walked into the inner office on the first floor, he stopped at the desk of a gorgeous woman.

"I am looking for the office of Ted MacDonald," he said.

"Do you have an appointment with him?" the woman asked.

"Yes, I do."

"Are you with the Bill Hogan team?" the woman asked.

"Yes. Bill Hogan and I are here to have two days of meetings with Ted MacDonald."

"Come on into the office. I'm Charlotte Webb, executive secretary for Ted MacDonald and our CFO Tim Murphy," Charlotte said.

"Oh, you have two executives to take care of?" James asked.

"Well, not really two. A lot of the time they are not in the office."

Just then Ted's office door opened, and Charlotte walked over to Ted.

"The second person for your eight a.m. meeting is here. A Mr. James Crowley," Charlotte said as Ted walked over to shake James's hand.

"So you made it?" Ted asked.

"Yes. I did. I flew in from San Diego last night."

"Come into my office so we can get started. Bill Hogan is already here."

"Thanks, Mr. MacDonald."

"Please call me Ted."

"You're the vice president of IT here at Butler Energy Corporation?" James asked.

"Yes, that is correct," Ted replied.

"Should I hold all your calls until your meeting is done, Mr. MacDonald?" Charlotte asked.

"Use your discretion. If someone needs to talk with me, you can interrupt," replied Ted.

Ted proceeded to close the door and motioned to James to have a seat. Bill was already sitting in the other chair and extended his hand.

"Good to see that you made it to Pittsburgh," Bill said with a smile.

"I was telling Ted that I flew in from San Diego last night so we could get an early start on the assessment this morning."

"Well, let's get started. What do you need from me, James?" Ted asked.

"I have the assessment printed out and on my laptop. Which method would you prefer?" James asked.

"Can we do both?" Ted replied.

"Sure. I'll fire up my laptop and display it on that wall. You can follow along with the paper copy or the Microsoft Project Plan software," James replied.

For the next few hours, the three of them went over the assessment plan line by line. Ted asked many questions, which James and Bill answered as best they could with the limited information that had been shared by Ted. Late in the morning, Ted abruptly stopped the meeting. He pulled out a nondisclosure agreement (NDA) and had James and Bill sign on the dotted line. It was clear that Ted wanted to share the vision of the company but could not until both consultants signed the document. This was a normal business operation in the consulting world: most consultants were required to sign NDAs before any work could be done for the client. After all, the consultants were privy to the inner workings of the business and could be construed as insiders. So a liability of nondisclosure was a practical way of doing business.

Once the NDAs were signed, Ted opened up about the vision of the company. The president and CFO wanted to buy ten related businesses in the oil and gas environment and put them under one company, thereby making a big company. The big company would go public, and all the investors would make a bunch of money. At least that was the plan according to Ted. He had worked with this same president and CFO before, and they had done this same business package a few years back. The investors made a lot of money on the prior deal, and they were anxious to do it again.

Right around the noon hour, Charlotte walked into Ted's office with lunch. An assortment of small sandwiches were on a tray along with bottled water and assorted beverages.

"I thought you three might be getting hungry," Charlotte said.

"Thanks, Charlotte. I do not know what I would do without you," Ted replied.

"You boys have to eat something, so I am just glad to help out," Charlotte replied and then left the office.

"She really takes care of you, doesn't she, Ted?" Bill asked.

"Charlotte has been with the CFO for years. She takes care of the two of us very well," Ted replied.

"Can we eat and talk?" James asked Ted.

"Let's just eat. We have plenty of time," Ted replied.

The rest of the afternoon was spent going over the project plan and how the software was going to satisfy the companies' goals of putting ten smaller companies together into one giant company. James could tell that Ted was getting extremely comfortable with him and Bill and that a consulting deal with the Butler Energy Corporation was in the making.

At 4:00 p.m. Ted had to go to a meeting; James and Bill were told to hang out in the conference room. At about four thirty, Charlotte walked into the conference room and said that Ted was going to be tied up for the rest of the day. A request to come back the next day at 8:00 a.m. was passed along to them.

"I will return then," James replied.

"Unfortunately, I will not be able to meet with Ted on Thursday," Bill informed Charlotte.

"OK, I'll let Ted know," Charlotte said.

"Thanks. I'll see you in the morning." James started to pack up his stuff, then left the conference room.

Chapter 6

James Crowley came back to the office of the Butler Energy Corporation on Thursday for round two of the assessment planning and to finish up the marathon of meetings. Since the first day had been successful, James was not sure how he was going to fill the day. Ted had taken in the presentation on the first day and had agreed to the project plan in principle. However, there were a lot of details that needed to be filled in. James was hoping that select team members would be introduced so he could ask a lot more questions.

The integration of a business using Enterprise Software Version 10.0 had lots of perils and pitfalls for anyone using the package. The key was to ask the right questions of the team and then configure the software for optimal performance. James, as a consultant, prided himself on being very skilled in the art of implementations. He could cut through the crap and ask the hard questions to get most teams to be productive using the software within the first thirty days of going live. He had a good feeling about this project but was uncertain if he was going to have enough answers from the team to work past Thursday. Ted would hopefully be able to answer any open questions at the end of the day.

James arrived a few minutes before 8:00 a.m. at Charlotte's inner office. She was there at her desk and was dressed in a red silk blouse and blue cotton business skirt. He was thinking to himself, *How the heck could this woman still be single?* She was a beauty. She appeared to be 110 to 115 pounds, 5-foot-4, blond, blue eyes, with a 34-28-32 hourglass figure. *Whoa, what a knockout,* James thought to himself. If he wasn't already married, he would make a play for this gorgeous woman. The thoughts were put aside—he knew that the assessment, not Charlotte, was where he needed to focus his attention.

"Good morning, Charlotte. I am back to see Ted for round two of the assessment project," James said.

"You will have to park yourself in the conference room today. Ted has a few meetings with some suppliers, and he will need his office for those meetings," Charlotte replied.

"Will Ted be meeting with me today?"

"I think he wants you to meet some of the team members that you will be working with."

"Working with?"

"Ted wants you to meet some of the accounting staff that will be working on the implementation."

"Working on the implementation?"

"Didn't Ted tell you that he extended you for the project? Along with Bill Hogan," Charlotte replied.

"No, he did not."

"Sorry about that. He asked me to draw up the engagement documents for you and Bill for a six-month contract arrangement."

"I am extremely pleased that he wants to contract out the two of us. I guess I must have done a good job on the assessment plan yesterday."

"Ted told me that he was impressed by the two of you. He said you seem to be the right guys for the project."

"Well thanks, Charlotte."

"You're welcome, James."

"Is this why Ted wants me to meet with the accounting staff today?" James asked.

"That's correct. Ted wants you to get started ASAP. I'll introduce you to the staff that works here in this office and the people Ted wants on the project."

"I am going to have a lot of questions for those team members."

"I am sure they will give you the answers you're looking for," Charlotte replied. "You can head to the main conference room. So set up shop there, and I'll parade the people in and out of the room."

"Sounds good, Charlotte. You're the boss."

"Well, thank you. That's exactly what Ted tells me."

"Good minds think alike. It could be the mold we are made of."

"You and Ted are going to work really well together. You will like the way he gets things done."

"I'll go set up in the main conference room."

"I'll plan for lunch so you can eat with Ted there. Will that work for you?" Charlotte asked.

"That would be nice. Thanks in advance."

"You're welcome," Charlotte said as she walked into Ted's office. Once she had stepped in, she asked Ted, "I set up James Crowley in the main conference room. Is that OK?"

"Yes, that will work," Ted replied.

"When that guy gets here at nine a.m., let me know?"

"That would be Peter Hamilton from Peterman Trucking— your scheduled appointment."

"That's right. I forgot his name."

"Is he the guy we are buying all those trucks from?" Charlotte asked.

"Yep, that's the guy. We are going to spend millions on those trucks."

"I'll let you know when he comes into the office."

"Thanks. You're terrific."

Charlotte left the office and closed the door behind her.

Peter Hamilton showed up at the desk of Charlotte Webb at exactly 9:00 a.m., on time.

"I am here to see Ted MacDonald for a meeting at nine a.m."

"And your name is?" Charlotte asked.

"Peter Hamilton from Peterman Trucking."

"Let me check with Mr. MacDonald to see if he is ready for you."

"I hope you don't think this is too forward, but what are you doing for dinner?" Peter asked abruptly.

"I don't even know you, Mr. Hamilton," Charlotte replied.

"Call me Peter, please."

"Peter, I don't even know you."

"Well, let's have dinner and you can get to know me."

"Let me think about it."

Ted had just walked out of his office and saw that Peter was with Charlotte and they were chitchatting. "I am ready for you now, Peter," Ted announced to the two of them.

Peter walked with Ted into his office.

This meeting between Ted and Peter from Peterman Trucking was to secure at least 10 heavy-duty water trucks with a capacity of at least 4,000 gallons. The asking price was $180,000 per truck. But Ted was looking to shave a few dollars off of the purchase price. These trucks would be used in the first acquisition business that the Buter Energy Corporation was planning. As Peter reviewed the proposal with Ted, the question was asked.

"Is this your best offer?" Ted said.

"For brand-new heavy-duty water trucks, $180,000 is our normal selling price," Peter replied.

"But we are buying ten this time, and I will be buying more in the next round."

"Well, I will need to see what I can do to get the price down."

"When can you refigure the pricing?"

"Can you give me a day to get back to you?"

"Sure. Can you come back on Friday?"

"Say, nine a.m.?" Peter replied with a nod of his head.

"See you on Friday," Ted replied.

Ted led Peter out of his office. As they passed by Charlotte's desk, Ted asked her to set up a follow-up appointment for 9:00 a.m. on Friday with Ted once again. He then left Peter with Charlotte to make the arrangements.

"How long do you think you need for this follow-up meeting on Friday?" Charlotte asked.

"A half hour should be enough time to present the revised contract."

"So I'll block out nine to nine thirty."

"Thanks. You still interested in that dinner appointment?"

"Well, a girl has to eat."

"How about I pick you up at seven p.m. and take you to dinner? Your choice."

"Can I meet you at your hotel?"

"Sure. I am staying at the Pittsburgh International."

"I know where that's at. I'll meet you in the lobby at six thirty."

"Sounds good. You pick the restaurant and make the reservation."

"I can do that. See you at six thirty," said Charlotte.

She saw dollar signs on this one. She knew that this purchase of trucks was the first of many and if she could hook this guy, it would be a big payoff for her.

Chapter 7

The parade of accounting people through the conference room that day was exhaustive. James had asked so many questions and received so much feedback that he didn't know where to start processing it all. The controller, Jean Roberts, was the most informative of the bunch. She had provided some real facts and figures on the first company the Butler Energy Corporation was planning to buy. The company was Barron Water Hauling Corporation and was owned by Barron Roberts and Jean Roberts. It had been around for a long time and was passed down from the parents of the Roberts family to the two living kids. This company serviced the oil patch of customers that needed water hauled to their oil wells being drilled for the production of oil. It was located in the town of Morgantown, West Virginia, in the middle of the Utica and Marcellus basins in the oil patch. The company had 100 customers, 500 vendors, 50 employees, and 10 old water trucks. The financial numbers for fiscal year 2023, as obtained by Jean Roberts, showed the following: $50 million in sales, $6 million in accounts receivable, $1 million in accounts payable, and $1 million in inventory.

These were the facts and data that Jean Roberts was willing to share. But James knew there was more information about this company that was about to be acquired. The two owners were being offered a noncompete agreement for three years after the smooth sale of the company to Butler Energy Corporation. There was also an earn-out agreement after the sale. This was a common practice so owners could not set up shop around the corner and torpedo the sold business by stealing the customers. James was happy that he was getting the core questions answered; this would help him with a smooth implementation of the new software.

Since this was the very first company being transitioned to Enterprise Software Version 10.0, the existing QuickBooks version would be allowed to expire and no renewal was to be offered to that vendor. The owners were so comfortable with QuickBooks and what it could do that when they heard it was not going to be used, they were shocked. In their thinking, they had business software that met their needs, so why would anyone want to use something else? James knew what the new management wanted to do. They would use Enterprise Software Version 10.0 to scale the business upward to $250 million in sales, a task that a QuickBooks software program would have difficulty achieving. The QuickBooks software was designed for mom-and-pop operations and was really not scalable. The Ted MacDonalds of this world knew what they were doing, and it did not include entertaining any thought of using QuickBooks for any of its acquisitions. They needed robust software that was scalable and grew with the aggressive business purchases that were planned for the next three years.

James finished up all the interviews and meetings and was exhausted. He had a ton of notes, and he needed time to write them all up before he had a conversation with Ted MacDonald to determine the next steps. He was also curious as to when Ted was going to have a conversation with him about the six-month agreement that Charlotte had mentioned to him.

James had packed up his computer at 4:30 p.m. and was done for the day. Just at that moment, Ted MacDonald walked into the main conference room.

"James, I am so sorry about what happened to you today. I had a series of back-to-back meetings and could not change my schedule to spend more time with you."

"That's quite all right, Ted," James replied.

"Did Charlotte tell you of my plans for you and Bill Hogan?"

"Well, she said that you wanted to sign us up for a six-month engagement."

"Yep. I liked what you and Bill showed me yesterday. I felt a good feeling that both of you know what you're doing and that you two would be good to have on our team."

"Thanks for the vote of confidence," James replied.

"Are you and Bill available for a six-month project?"

"I just finished a project a week ago, so I am available. I'll need to check with Bill to see where he is and get back to you."

"Can you call him right now?" Ted asked.

"Let me call him on my cell phone."

Bill answered on the third ring.

"Hi, Bill. I need to put you on speaker. I have Ted MacDonald in the conference room. He wants to talk with us both at the same time." James proceeded to push the speaker button and place the cell phone on the table.

"Hi, Bill. This is Ted MacDonald."

"Hi, Ted. Sorry I could not be there today," Bill replied.

"No problem. Listen, I have to talk fast. I have another meeting in a few minutes, but I want to get this going right away," Ted explained. "I want to sign you both to a six-month agreement for setting up the software and bringing these businesses onto the platform. You interested?"

"Sure," Bill answered, and James nodded his head.

"What will it take to get you both to sign for a six-month gig?" Ted asked.

"I am available," Bill said through the speakerphone.

"And you're available, James?" Ted asked.

"Yes, I am."

"Then it's done," Ted replied.

"What is our rate?" James asked.

"What do you boys get normally?" Ted asked.

"I normally get $90 to $100. Bill?" James asked in front of Ted.

"How about I give you both $105 per hour, but then you're exclusively on this project—no other customers?" Ted asked.

"I am good with that rate," Bill replied.

"I am good with that rate as well," James added.

"Done. I'll have Charlotte put the agreements together for you both to sign, and we can get started in earnest."

"The travel expenses are above and beyond the consulting rate, right?" James said.

"Yes, the travel expenses are passed through to the company. We will reimburse you as if you're an employee. But you will be a 1099 contractor. Does that work?"

Bill and James both agreed to the new arrangement. The contract rate would be $105 per hour plus travel expenses. Ted would be their boss in all matters on this project. He would approve of all weekly time submissions and expense reporting.

"Listen, I am late for another meeting. Do we have a deal?" Ted asked. Bill on the phone and James in person said yes as Ted exited the conference room. "I'll have Charlotte coordinate the details with you both on Friday," Ted added, then exited the conference room in a hurry.

James took Bill off of the speakerphone. "You good with this deal?" he asked.

"Damn straight. I told you I had a good feeling about this one," Bill replied.

"So far, so good. But I have a nagging feeling that Ted was not telling us all that we need to know."

"Have you ever had a client tell you everything?" Bill asked.

"No. But we need to go into this thing with our eyes wide open."

"We can do that. We just need to watch each other's back, if you know what I mean," Bill replied.

"OK. Here we go. Talk to you on Friday when I get home. I am flying out later tonight."

"Sounds good. Have a safe flight," Bill said.

James ended the call and put the cell phone into his bag.

* * *

James had a four-hour flight, but due to the time change, he was picking up three hours. So his flight out of Pittsburgh International Airport would depart at 7:00 p.m. Eastern time and arrive at San Diego International Airport at 11:00 p.m. Eastern, but with the time change, it would be 8:00 p.m. Pacific time. It would be a long night after working all day for his new client. Friday would be a welcome rest for a tired consultant.

Chapter 8

The Pittsburgh International Hotel was a mile from the airport on Old Mill Drive. This is where Peter Hamilton said to Charlotte that he was staying for a few nights. He had business in the Pittsburgh area and was trying to coordinate the active leads on new customers for this trip. Ted MacDonald was one of those prospects, and the Butler Energy Corporation could be a juicy contract. He had put forth a quote to Ted for ten heavy-duty water trucks at $180,000 each. But the customer was not satisfied with the initial price. There was room for Peter to lower the price if he knew that this contract would generate residual business. Reducing the price on the quote meant that all future sales would be negotiated lower based on volume. So Peter wanted to make sure he started with a large number on the first order. Then as time went on, the price would slide down, but the maintenance deals and extras could easily make up for any margin hit on future sales. This was Peter's plan of attack with most new customers. But one thing he wasn't expecting was Executive Secretary Charlotte Webb and her plan.

It was almost 6:30 p.m. on a Thursday night, and Peter had to hurry up to make it on time for Charlotte in the lobby. He knew that she would be prompt but did not know what to expect of this evening. Charlotte was a stunning beauty, and Peter was captivated by her gorgeous body. *I wonder if she will sleep with me*, he pondered.

Peter arrived in the lobby of the Pittsburgh International but saw no one in the area. He sat in one of the comfortable lounge chairs right outside the restaurant connected to the lobby. The restaurant was affiliated with the hotel. The name on the side of the wall was the Pittsburgh Chop House. Their specialty was seafood and steaks. As Peter looked over the menu under the glass box on the wall of the entrance, Charlotte strolled into the lobby. She was stunning in a full-length red cotton dress that showed off her cleavage. Her full-length winter coat was open and displayed her 34-28-32 hourglass frame in perfect form. The high heels must have added another three inches to her five-four height. She was a knockout. As Charlotte got closer to Peter, he stood up and just smiled.

"Good evening, Ms. Webb."

"Good evening, Peter. I told you to call me Charlotte."

"Let me try that again. Good evening, Charlotte."

"Well, good evening."

"That is a beautiful dress you're wearing."

"Oh, this old thing. It's just something I threw on for our dinner."

"Well, you look gorgeous in it."

"Thank you. You must say that to all the women you meet?" Charlotte said.

"No, I do not. You fill that dress out perfectly," Peter replied.

"Oh stop, you're making me blush."

"What can I say? You're an attractive woman that I would like to get to know."

"I would like to get to know you as well."

"So where did you make our reservation?" Peter asked.

"At the Pittsburgh Chop House," Charlotte replied.

"Here at this restaurant?"

"Yes, right here. They have fantastic steaks and great seafood dishes."

"Shall we go in?"

"Sure. Can you take my coat?"

"No problem." Peter took Charlotte's coat as she twisted away to reveal her full figure in the red cotton dress. "You're a knockout."

"You told me that already."

"I just don't know why you aren't married to some guy already."

"I told you: I work with a bunch of married executives, and a good man is extremely hard to find."

"They don't know what they are missing here."

"Can we go eat? I am famished," Charlotte replied.

They walked into the restaurant.

"We have a reservation for seven p.m. under Peter Hamilton," Charlotte told the hostess at the front door.

"Yes, I see it. A table for two," the hostess replied.

"Do you have a table in a quiet place?" Peter asked.

"Yes, we have a very private table for two in the far corner of the restaurant," the hostess said.

"That would be nice. Thanks," Peter said.

Peter and Charlotte were seated in a very private alcove of the restaurant off of the kitchen hallway. Unless you knew the layout of the place, you would not be able to see the patrons that were dining in this spot. When the waiter noticed the table was filled, he brought over two waters and two menus.

"Hi. I am Antonio, your waiter tonight. Can I get you two started on drinks?" he asked.

"I'll have a Malbec," Charlotte replied.

"I'll have a Gentleman Jack and Coke," Peter replied.

"Very good. I'll be right back with your drinks, and I'll give you some time to look at the menus."

The waiter came back with the drinks in a few minutes and then proceeded to take their order. "What would the lady like tonight?"

"I would like a garden salad with ranch dressing, and a petite filet mignon, medium well, with a fully loaded baked potato," Charlotte said to the waiter.

"Sir, for you?" the waiter asked.

"I would like the twenty-four-inch Porterhouse with a fully loaded baked potato. Oh, and a salad with Thousand Island dressing." Peter responded.

"How would you like that prepared, sir?"

"Medium well would be fine."

"Thanks. I'll get these orders to the kitchen right away."

As the waiter walked away, Peter shouted to him, "Take your time. We are in no hurry."

Charlotte and Peter talked the whole time during the dinner. They enjoyed the salads, the steaks, and the baked potatoes. They spent a great amount of time talking about Ted MacDonald. Charlotte was sure he was fishing for what Peter's bottom number was on the new trucks. So she thought it was time to play the game.

"So, Peter, what is the real reason you asked me to dinner?" Charlotte asked.

"Well, I thought if I took you out, I could figure out what Ted's number was."

"Ted's number?"

"What Ted is willing to pay for the trucks before he goes somewhere else."

"Why do you think I would tell you that?"

"I was hoping to soften you up and maybe throw you a finder's fee to get Ted's business."

"A finder's fee? You mean, like a commission?"

"Not exactly. I have some room in my contracts to pay a small fee to anyone who has helped me land a new contract."

"How much are we talking here?" Charlotte asked.

"So you're interested?" Peter replied. "Between one and three points on the Butler deal."

"That's all?" Charlotte asked.

"Well, I can go to four points. But that is stretching it."

Just then the waiter came to the table to clear the dishes now that the meal was finished. Peter motioned to the waiter for another round of drinks with his glass and two fingers held up in the air. The waiter understood and did not say a word. A few minutes later, he returned with another Gentleman Jack and Coke for Peter and a Malbec for Charlotte.

Peter had to excuse himself from the table. "I'll be right back. I need to go to the little boys' room."

This was the excuse she needed. Her purse was retrieved, and the bottle of Valium powder was removed. Two pills were crushed into powder ahead of time and placed in a small vile. The vile was poured into Peter's drink. A quick stir of the glass, and the powder disappeared into the alcohol. Since the Valium was colorless and odorless, the victim would never know what hit him.

Peter returned from the bathroom. The check had arrived in his absence.

"The waiter left you that," Charlotte said.

"Thanks. Can we finish our drinks before we get out of here?" Peter said.

"Sure. I was thinking about what you said. You know, the finder's fee."

"It is sort of like a commission."

"Maybe I can help you out. But the finder's fee has to be seven points."

"I would like to have Ted's business, but I can't go to seven. I can only go to four."

Peter paid the bill with his credit card and waited for the waiter to come back with the slip. The waiter returned, the slip was left, and they exited the restaurant.

"Thank you for a nice dinner," Charlotte said as they walked into the lobby.

"You're welcome. Want to come up for a nightcap?" Peter asked.

"You want to know what Ted's number is?" Charlotte asked.

She knew she had only a few minutes before Ted would be slurring his speech and becoming impaired. She would need to get him to his room so she could immobilize him and have her way.

"I sure would," Peter replied.

"Let's go have that drink."

"My room is on the fifth floor, number 507."

As Peter and Charlotte rode the elevator up to the fifth floor, he appeared to be a little dazed. She grabbed his elbow and held him steady. They made it to the room, and he opened the door with his key card. She walked him to the bed, where Peter started to say he was really feeling the alcohol. So he sat down on the bed to steady himself.

"I am feeling really tired all of a sudden."

"You must have had too much to drink. Good thing you're not driving."

"You're even more beautiful than before." Peter was getting frisky.

"Can we work out a deal on the finder's fee?" Charlotte asked.

"What did you have in mind?"

"How about seven points and…" She paused.

"Seven points. That would cut into my commission base," Peter replied.

"I can make the extra three points worth it."

"I don't know about that arrangement."

"This is what the other three points gets you." Charlotte unzipped her red cotton dress, and it fell to the floor. She was standing there in her red bra and red panties. Peter was just smiling ear to ear. She was a gorgeous woman, and she was taking advantage of him. As she straddled him on the bed, he knew it was over. She had won, and he had lost.

"Do I get the seven points?" Charlotte asked once again. But this time she was taking off his clothing. He seemed to be all butter fingers, and none of his fingers were working.

"So we have a deal?" Charlotte asked for the third and final time.

"Well, I guess so," Peter responded.

That's when she knew this was going to be a little bit tricky. He would be dazed by the effect of the Valium for another fifteen minutes or so, and she had to act fast. The toys came out of her purse. She started to move around the bed with the fun chains, which were fastened to the four posts of the bed. They were extended at a forty-five-degree angle for hooking up to the arms and legs. Then the Scarlet Couture Bond to Surrender Cuffs were wrapped around the right and left hands. A lock was fastened from the cuffs to the extended fun chains. Peter's hands were now fastened to the toys and partially pinned down. The Scarlet Couture Spreader Bar was pulled from the purse. The ankles left and right were wrapped and extended in the prone position. The fun chains were fastened to the cuffs with a lock on each ankle. Charlotte's toys had worked once again, and she was happy with the result. He was now the property of Charlotte Webb, one powerful young woman.

As the Valium was wearing off, she could tell he was coming around and becoming a little more aware of his surroundings.

"Charlotte, what's going on here?" Peter demanded.

"We are having a little bit of fun tonight," she replied. "We are having a business meeting, and you just agreed to a seven-point finder's fee."

"No, I didn't," Peter replied.

"Yes, you did." Charlotte took her cell phone and started to take some pictures of Peter bound on the bed, helpless and vulnerable.

The pictures would be edited later in case Charlotte's face was in any of the shots.

"Hey, that's not fair," Peter shouted.

"I just want to make sure I get my seven points. A little bit of insurance in case you renege on the deal."

She placed the cell phone on the nightstand and took off her remaining clothes. As she mounted her next victim, Peter, she could feel him inside of her.

"Now do we have a deal?" Charlotte undulated up and down on Peter. Higher and higher, harder and harder, until Peter finally agreed.

"Yes, we have a deal," he shouted.

Charlotte was happy to sign this one up. This vendor would be a big one, and the residuals for seven points would be nice to have. She figured about $10,000 per truck was hers—that was an excellent payday.

"You did not tell me what Ted's number is," Peter said as she was taking off the toys.

"He is willing to pay $150,000 per truck," Charlotte replied.

"I can make that work."

"Including my seven points?"

"Including your seven points, Ms. Charlotte."

"Thanks, and nice doing business with you."

After Charlotte put her clothes back on, she exited the room as quietly as possible. Peter knew he had been taken by a gorgeous woman and it had cost him a great deal to get the future deal with the Butler Energy Corporation. And he knew he could not tell a soul about any of the details of the sexual encounter that had just happened to him.

As he rolled over in the bed, alone and still groggy, his thought to himself was *What the hell just happened?*

Chapter 9

Friday at the office was going to be a busy day for Charlotte. A number of meetings were scheduled all day, and she would be running with Ted to most of them for support. The CFO Tim Murphy was off on a vacation day with his family, so the interaction with him would be minimal.

The first meeting was at 9:00 a.m., with Tom McFaden, the local insurance guy. Since Tim Murphy was on vacation, Ted MacDonald offered to take care of him in his absence. Tom showed up promptly at the inner office where Charlotte was sitting behind her desk.

"Hi, I am Tom McFaden, here to see Tim Murphy at nine a.m.," he said.

"Tim Murphy is out today. You will be meeting with Ted MacDonald, our vice president of information technology, instead."

"Thanks, Ms. Webb."

"Did you forget our little deal?" Charlotte asked.

"Don't know what you're talking about," Tom replied.

"Our seven-point arrangement?"

"I did not like that arrangement, so I changed it."

"You changed it?"

"Yes, I changed it to zero."

"You didn't tell me it was changed."

The door opened, and Ted extended his hand to Tom.

"How are you, Tom?"

"Fine. And yourself, Ted?"

"Just great. Come into my office so we can get started."

Tom McFaden from the Great American Insurance Company went into the office of Ted MacDonald while one Charlotte Webb was fuming. She had made a deal with this guy several months ago, and he had reneged. The insurance he had sold to the company had been around $200,000, and her seven-point cut amounted to zero. Now he was here to sell some additional insurance for the executives, and she was going to get zero once again. She was not a happy camper, but she put it out of her mind for now. She had some follow-up work with the two consultants that Ted had asked her to take care of.

The standard consulting agreement for Bill Hogan and James Crowley was compiled from the template files that the Butler Energy Corporation had approved from legal. The individual names were placed in the contracts and sent via email to Bill and James to sign and return. The contract's initial duration was six months, with possible renewals if both parties agreed. Bill Hogan was in the Eastern time zone and James Crowley was in the Pacific time zone, so Charlotte was hoping to get both signed and on Ted's desk by the end of the day. If either one delayed or wanted their own legal department to review, this would not get done till Monday.

Charlotte had taken care of just about everything on her morning to-do list when Ted's door opened around 10:00 a.m. and Tom McFaden exited.

"You will send me the paperwork on the executive insurance, and I'll get Tim Murphy to sign it on Monday?" Ted asked.

"I'll take care of this later today so it's on your desk by Monday morning," Tom replied.

"Charlotte, can you put a reminder to watch for this insurance package from Tom on Monday morning?"

"I can take care of that."

"Thanks for your business, Ted," Tom McFaden said as he exited the office. "Good day to you, Ms. Charlotte," he added as he left the office.

Charlotte did not even get a chance to talk with Tom to dig a little deeper into why he had reneged on the seven-point deal. She would have to confront him later tonight to get an answer.

"Did you get those consulting agreements out to the Bill and James?" Ted asked.

"I sent the standard agreements to them about an hour ago," Charlotte replied.

"Thanks. I really need these two guys to start in earnest on this project."

"Can I ask you why you hired these two consultants?" Charlotte asked.

"Sure. They are a bargain. The Enterprise Software Corporation wanted to charge $225 an hour. These guys are a steal at $105 per hour. And I can make them exclusive to Butler for the duration of the project."

"I see. So you will get them hooked on Butler and then hire them as company employees?" Charlotte asked.

"Exactly right. I'll convert them from consultants to employees if they prove themselves. This way we get the best of both worlds. They are a knowledgeable resource for the software, and we try them out to see that they are a fit for our organization."

"That's why you're a vice president, Ted."

"Thanks for that vote of confidence."

The rest of the day was a drag. Nothing else was going on; it was a Friday. Charlotte thought about how to handle the McFaden situation. The more she thought about it, the madder she got internally. She couldn't wait till quitting time. She was determined to get even on this one. An example would need to be made, and an agent of Great American Insurance Company would have to pay and pay dearly.

* * *

Charlotte knew where Tom McFaden might be on a Friday night. He would be at the local bar, the Steel Salon on Mill Street and Fifth Avenue in Coraopolis. This was a place that Tom had mentioned many times while he was under Charlotte's spell earlier this year. This was his favorite watering hole. She thought she would take a chance and see if Tom would be there tonight.

Charlotte walked into the Steel Salon around 6:00 p.m., after work, and sat down at one of the tables near the bar. As luck would have it, Tom McFaden was already there at the bar with a drink in hand. She noticed him staring at her, noting that she was alone. He was curious. So he walked over to Charlotte and asked her, "Do I know you? Charlotte?"

"You must be mistaken. My name is not Charlotte; it's Mary."

"My name is Tom McFaden. You look like Charlotte Webb."

"I have a sister, and her name is Charlotte. My name is Mary Webb."

"Hi. I'm Tom McFaden. I just saw your sister earlier at her office."

"Nice to meet you, Tom," Mary said.

"Who are you waiting for?" Tom asked.

"I am meeting someone tonight. First date. I am not sure what he looks like."

"Can I keep you company till he gets here?"

"Sure, but don't stay too long."

"Can I buy you a drink?"

"Sure. I'll have a glass of Chardonnay."

Tom went to the bar and got her a glass of house Chardonnay.

"Here you go. One glass of Chardonnay."

"Thanks."

"You two look a lot alike," Tom said.

"We are twins. Charlotte is blond, and I am a brunette."

Tom was thinking to himself, *Can I get lucky and sleep with the second twin, who is as beautiful as the first?*

"How long have you been waiting for your date?" Tom asked.

"About thirty minutes so far," Mary replied.

"I think he stood you up."

"You are right."

"Can I take you out for dinner instead?"

"I don't even know you, Tom."

"Well, that's what dinner is all about. Getting to know each other."

"How about another fifteen minutes, and if he does not show up, you can buy me dinner."

"Sounds good."

Mary knew that the date would never show up because there never was one. A few minutes later, Tom motioned to Mary.

"Looks like he is a no-show," Tom remarked.

"You win, Tom. Let's go have dinner," Mary said.

"I know a place near the airport that has great steaks. It's called the Pittsburgh Chop House," Tom said.

"I am not familiar with that restaurant."

"I have eaten there once before. It's a nice place for steaks and seafood."

"I am very fond of seafood. Steak, not so much."

Tom was thinking to himself, *How is this possible? Two gorgeous girls. One that likes steak, a blonde. One that likes seafood, a brunette. How lucky can one guy get? Will she sleep with me?* That was the question he would be asking himself during dinner.

"Do you want a ride, or do you prefer to take your car?" Ted asked.

"I'll follow you to the restaurant."

* * *

Tom drove a little on the slow side to make sure that Mary was following him. He did not want to lose her and the opportunity to sleep with the second sister. The drive to the Pittsburgh Chop House was only about fifteen minutes in light traffic. A reservation on a Friday night would not be needed. As they got closer to the restaurant, there were few cars in the parking lot. So Mary parked at the edge of the lot; it was her plan to draw him to a remote place. She faked a little car trouble to draw Tom to drive over to the spot.

"Having trouble, Mary?" Tom asked through the rolled-down window.

Tom drove up to her car and got out. He opened the passenger side door and asked, "What's wrong?"

"I am not sure. I think my car died," Mary said.

As Tom reached over the center console from the passenger seat, she let him have it. The two prongs on the Sabre stun gun were pushed into his stomach, and the trigger was pulled. His body gyrated like a flapping fish out of water for about fifteen seconds. As he collapsed on the passenger seat, she hit him again. Another fifteen seconds with the Sabre stun gun. He was completely immobile, the way Charlotte/Mary liked her men.

She acted fast by placing his body in the passenger seat facing forward. Put his seat belt on. Cuffed his hands behind the seat with a pair of chrome-plated police-style handcuffs. A ball gag was inserted into his mouth and wrapped around his neck. This one was now hers. He was motionless and still dazed from the stun gun. As a precaution, she hit him again for another fifteen seconds with the Sabre. She got out of her car and went over to his to turn the car off, lock the doors, and take his keys for later. The passenger door of her car was closed, and she drove off with one immobilized man in the passenger seat.

* * *

Where to dispose of this one was the next pressing issue on the agenda, along with how to finish him off. She was happy to have a small SUV with tinted windows so she would not have to worry about any motorists looking into her vehicle to see a restrained passenger with a gag in his mouth. As she drove out of town, she zapped her passenger with the stun gun to keep him passive and quiet many times.

At one of the deserted rest stops along the highway, she finished him off. She had a pillow in the back seat, which she placed over his nose and mouth. It only took a few minutes before he was completely suffocated; the gag in the mouth helped. After the lifeless body of Tom McFaden lay slumped in the passenger seat, she headed back on the Interstate 70 headed west. Her destination was the Winding River Canyon, located between the border of Pennsylvania and Ohio along the interstate. A deserted stretch of road was found, and a deposit in the canyon was made of a lifeless Tom McFaden. He was pushed over a cliff into a one-thousand-foot drop.

The seven points on this deal would never see daylight. But then neither would Tom McFaden, who had cheated Charlotte out of her promised payday.

Charlotte knew that there would always be men who got in the way of her goal of being financial independent. This was a world driven by the opposite sex and she wanted to control her own destiny.

Chapter 10

James Crowley arrived at his house in Fallbrook at 2:00 a.m. Pacific time on Friday. There was a mechanical issue with the flight connecting out of Houston International Airport that had caused a three-hour delay. James was tired and was not expecting to work on Friday. So he took it off and ignored his email inbox and slept in. He ran some errands during the day, but the phone keeps ringing even if you try to plan a day off. He looked at the phone late in the afternoon and he recognized the number; it was Bill Hogan.

"Hey, did you see the email that we have a six-month contract with Butler?" Bill asked.

"No. I did not. I got home late in the a.m. and needed to get some sleep and run some errands today," James replied.

"Plane issues?"

"Yep. A three-hour delay out of Houston, and I am beat today."

"Well, that assessment went well last week with Butler. Ted MacDonald wants us for at least six months."

"I'll take a look at the agreement and send it back to Charlotte or Ted," James asked.

"I'll do the same," Bill replied.

"Looks like we are working together once again."

"Yes, we are."

"When do we start?" James asked.

"Looks like ASAP."

"Do we know Bill if this is an on-prem, off-site, or cloud installation?"

"No, I don't know. We will have to ask Ted the next time we call him."

"We kind of need to know that to get started," James said.

"Let's call Charlotte. She may know the answer to that question," Bill replied.

"I bet that she knows where all the bodies are buried at that company."

"What do you mean?"

"She is a gorgeous woman that appears to turn men into jelly when they are around her."

"I kind of felt that way when I was around her," Bill said.

"Are you going to have trouble with this client? You're already acting like you're horny for this woman."

"I'll try to keep it in my pants, if that is what you're asking."

"Bill, don't do anything to screw this up. I need this project and the paycheck."

"I know," Bill replied.

"Can you call either Ted or Charlotte and find out about the installation?" James asked.

"Sure. Let me get off this call." Bill hung up with James and dialed Ted's cell. But there was no answer, just voicemail. He tried Charlotte on the main number. Nothing but voicemail again. Bill texted James and let him know that he would try later in the day to get the answer.

Later in the day, after a bunch of errands were completed, James had a chance to open the email from Charlotte on the consulting agreement. It basically said that the consultant and Butler Energy Corporation were entering into a mutually exclusive agreement for a duration of six months with an option to renew by both parties. Since Ted had mentioned that the Butler Energy Corporation was planning on combining ten companies into one mega company, this could be a multiyear deal worth a whole lot of money. Would this include Bill Hogan and him? That was a question that the little voice inside him was asking. Could this be the goose that laid the golden egg? Would he be on easy street for a while instead of moving through a series of twelve-week engagements with dead ends? He signed the agreement and sent it back to Charlotte via email. A thank-you from Ted MacDonald was received within fifteen minutes; James was surprised.

Ted had also requested a quick fifteen-minute meeting with James and Bill over the phone. They all got on a conference call and started to discuss the next steps. The plan was for them to come to Coraopolis the following Monday to do the detailed planning on the project. Ted was going to call all the other Butler team members to join them for that week so the whole acquisition strategy could be put in motion. Ted wanted his two new consultants to meet the executives as well. He wanted to show them off and assure the executives that their goal on the planned timetable would be executed. Ted had a significant bonus riding on this project, which the consultants did not know about.

James asked Ted about next week's plan and what he wanted him to do, and his response was to just get the project plan ready to go for the following Monday. This was also when they would find out that Ted had contracted out with a back-office hosting company called Blue Point Hosting. They specialized in discreet hosting in the downtown Pittsburgh area. They would be loading the software from Enterprise Software Corporation next week, so by the time James and Bill hit the ground in the office the following week, the software would be waiting for the consultants to start configuring.

* * *

Back in the Pittsburgh office, Ted needed to get Tim Murphy to sign the new executive insurance agreements by Monday morning.

"Hey, Charlotte, did you see the new insurance agreements from Tom McFaden this morning?" Ted asked.

"I did not get anything from Tom McFaden this morning," Charlotte replied.

"Can you call him to see where the documents are?"

"I'll try to get ahold of him or his office."

"Thanks, Charlotte. You're the best."

Charlotte knew she was not going to get ahold of him because Tom was no longer with the living. But she would try his office to see what they had to say. There was no answer at his office. She relayed the message to Ted to let him know. He asked Charlotte to try again on Monday or Tuesday, but she knew it would of course be a futile exercise to talk with a dead man.

Charlotte thought to herself, *That's what happens when you cross this bitch. I always get my seven points.*

Chapter 11

James Crowley had a new boss, and his search for another gig was done for now. During his conversation with Ted on Friday, he had agreed to spend this week off-site putting together the project plan for the acquisition of the first company using Enterprise Software Version 10.0. Since it was the first company, with more to come, a bit of proper planning had to be done. The configuration planning would have to accommodate folding at least ten companies into the software structure. Since Blue Point Hosting was being used as the back-end magic box, scalability would not be an issue. More blades or servers would be attached as needed to accommodate the companies being added to the network as each acquisition was completed. So the first target was a QuickBooks back end, and this would be an easy conversion.

* * *

Champ and Abbey had just woken up and wanted to go out for their daily ritual in Fallbrook. James was so accustomed to getting up early with the Westies that the luxury of sleeping in was not an option. Once the dogs did their business, it was time for breakfast. Their internal clocks told them and their owner it was time to start the day. Just as Champ and Abbey had finished their breakfast, it was time for James to get his. But a cell phone call would change that.

The phone rang, and it was Ted MacDonald.

"Hi. Is this James?" Ted asked.

"Yes, this is James. Hi, Ted. What's up?"

"Hey, I need you to change the project plan for our first acquisition."

"Change the project plan? What do you mean?"

"We kind of have a situation that we need to address rather quickly."

"What is the situation? Can you provide some details?"

"We thought we had a six-month window to get this first acquisition on the software, but we don't."

"How much time do we have?"

"We have a little over sixty days to get the company off their old system and on the one we just purchased," Ted replied.

"Ted, that's a tall order. The quickest implementation and conversion takes about six months on this new software," James commented.

"Well, I am going to ask a favor here. You and Bill need to do it in sixty days. Can you two work out the details so it can be accomplished?"

"I'll need to work on this right away with Bill and put an accelerated plan together for Monday."

"Sounds good, and thanks. I knew I hired the right team on this one. Don't let me down."

"I'll do everything in my power to get this done," James replied.

"I will make it worth your while," Ted said. "You know, if you two prove yourselves here, we will have at least nine more companies we want to integrate. And you two could get all that business."

"I appreciate this opportunity to show you that Bill and I can take care of this project for you."

"I am counting on it."

"Again, thanks for this opportunity, Ted."

"You're very welcome. Sorry to call you so early on the West Coast. I know it's a three-hour difference. I hope I did not interrupt anything?"

"No, I was up already. My Westies like to get up early."

"Westies?" Ted asked.

"I have two Westies. A boy, Champ, and a girl, Abbey. They are wonderful dogs. They also keep each other company and sometimes get in trouble."

"Who takes care of them while you're away?"

"We found a sitter here locally, a young girl who just started a business taking care of dogs, and she does a wonderful job. Unfortunately, she lets them sleep in her bed at night when the two of them are at her house. They are spoiled rotten. But they are our kids."

"You don't have kids of your own?" Ted asked.

"No, we do not have any kids."

"I have one, and she will be going to college soon."

"That is an interesting age."

"She is a handful. And she is my special little girl. Although, she is no little princess anymore."

"Well, I am sure you will watch over her when she goes away to college."

"I sure will. Hey, I have to run to a meeting. So redo the plan for a sixty-day bare-bones implementation. If you have to cut some corners, do it. I'll catch up with you and Bill later in the week." Ted ended the call before James could say goodbye.

James decided to call Bill's cell and let him know of this development. It went straight to voicemail. "Bill, call me when you get this voicemail. There has been a development on the Butler project."

About fifteen minutes later, Bill returned the call.

"Hi, James. What's up?"

"Just got off the phone with Ted MacDonald, and he has accelerated the project."

"What?" Bill asked.

"He is cutting the time from six months down to sixty days to implement the first acquisition into the software purchased."

"We have never done a go-live project in sixty days."

"I know. It is going to be a rocky road to get one done this fast."

"Can we pull this off, James?"

"I'll need to rework the project plan from the ground up. I'll need at least this week to put it together for Monday. I hope we can do it."

"We can do it. We will just have to move anything in our way to phase two after we turn it on," Bill commented.

"OK, will do. By the way, Ted inferred that you and I will get the other nine projects if we do a good job on this one."

"He actually said that?"

"He told me just before this call. If we do a good job here, we are a lock for the future business."

"Then let's kick some ass here," Bill shouted.

"OK. Let me get to work." James hung up the phone.

He had some doubts about this accelerated project plan. He had never turned a company on in sixty days and was feeling an immense bit of pressure all of a sudden. The gears in his head were moving as to what he could do and what would have to be pushed to phase two of the project. A complete rework of the project plan would be necessary. This would take at least three to five days to complete. The week was going to be a long slog, and he needed to clear the decks of any interference. The casita would be a perfect place to hide out and compile the plan.

Chapter 12

Barron Roberts and Jean Roberts were sitting at the local Starbucks in downtown Morgantown having coffee and an impromptu meeting. They were going over some details on selling the family business to the Butler Energy Corporation. They really were tired of the business and wanted to get out from under the weight of what the father and grandfather had built over one-hundred-plus years. They both had their sights set on a home in the warm sun of San Diego, away from the harsh winters of Morgantown.

"Sister, you need to clean up those four customer accounts and the four vendor accounts before we sell the company, right?" Barron asked.

"Yes, I know. All the balances need to be reduced to zero by collections or payments. The information for the eight names better not be converted when the Butler team gets here," Jean replied.

"Can you somehow delete them when you're done?"

"I don't think the software will let me delete them, but I can turn them to inactive so they will not become part of the conversion list."

"That should work."

"Whatever we do, Brother, those four customers and four vendors better not show up on any lists."

"Agreed."

"I'll take care of that when I get back to the office."

"Thanks, Sis. We are in this together."

"What about the retention clause and earn-out clause?" Jean asked.

"We are going to have to figure this out as we go. Maybe do a lousy job of running the business after Butler acquires it and then let them fire us both. I don't think you and I want to stick around for the three-year term they want us to sign. Do you?"

"No, I think they will figure out that we juiced the sales and expenses within a year."

"That's kind of what I was thinking, Sis."

"What happens if they find out what the real numbers are?" Jean asked.

"We will be long gone, in California. They will not want to sue us because it would be really bad publicity for them and their public shareholders. They would have to admit that the mom-and-pop business they put into their corporate enterprise was a sham."

"You really think so, Brother?" Jean asked.

"Yep. We just need to cover each other's backs here and take it one day at a time."

"What about this meeting next week in Coraopolis with the consultants to start the implementation process?"

"We will deal with them as they request the conversion data, and you and I will need to scrub the files before we send them in," Barron replied. "Can you work on those AR and AP records?"

"The accounts receivable companies—Argonaut Corporation, Anco Corporation, Challenger Corporation, and Falcon Corporation—need to be inactivated as customers. The vendor companies—Argo Enterprise, Aspen Enterprise, Eagle Enterprise, and Monitor Enterprise—need to be inactivated as suppliers," Jean commented.

The two siblings of the Barron Water Hauling Corporation had concocted this scheme to inflate the revenues by pushing an additional $20 million through four fake customers and four fake vendors. That brought last year's apparent revenue up to almost $50 million. All eight of these companies were DBAs of the Rainbow Water Hauling Corporation, which was a shell company to handle the revenues and expenses outside of the Barron Water Hauling Corporation. The intention here was to launder money legally and inflate the sales of the sending corporation. Since the Butler Energy Corporation did not know about the shell company, this was not part of the acquisition and therefore not on the radar of the team. If the consultants got a little bit nosey and wanted to convert all customers and vendors from the past two years, they would find these connections. So Barron and Jean had to filter all the data files and never give direct access to anyone from the Butler team to the QuickBooks software. They did not want anyone poking around and were determined not to give access to anyone.

"Hey, Brother, I forgot to tell you: the renewal for the Quick-Books Enterprise Edition comes due March 31. I told Ted Mac-Donald about this, and he said he was going to talk to the team about accelerating the acquisition timetable."

"That could work to our advantage. We tell them that the software expires, and they will want to move up the window," Barron replied.

"I need to get those four vendors and four customers wiped out first."

"Put them in the next check run to wipe them out."

"OK, that's what I'll do."

"Let's get back to the office, Sis."

"We have had a long coffee break, Brother."

They left the Starbucks in their own cars and headed to the office through the little town of Morgantown.

Chapter 13

Tim Murphy the CFO had a busy day on Tuesday. His calendar was completely booked with suppliers selling him stuff for the business. Since Butler Energy Corporation was a new company, they needed everything. Charlotte had seen a lot of vendors visit Ted MacDonald and Tim Murphy in the past couple of weeks. This one was in advertising, and he was here to see Tim.

Promptly at 9:00 a.m., a gentleman showed up at Charlotte's desk.

"Hi, gorgeous. I am here to see Tim Murphy, your CFO."

"You are?" Charlotte asked.

"Rick Samborski with Pittsburgh Advertising."

"I have seen your billboards. They are kind of cute."

"You're Charlotte Webb, right?"

"That's me."

"Tim told me to see you first thing on Tuesday morning."

"Yes, I see that you are on his schedule."

"What if I weren't on his schedule?" Rick asked

"I would have thrown you out on your ears."

"A beautiful woman like you would throw an honest working guy like me out?"

"You bet," Charlotte replied. "If you're not on my boss's schedule, you don't get near him."

"Well, that is good to know. Doing anything for dinner?"

"Rick, I don't even know you."

"I'm a very likable guy."

Just then Tim buzzed Charlotte on the intercom. "Is my nine a.m. appointment here?"

"Yes, he is here. A Rick Samborski from the Pittsburg Advertising Company."

"Send him in, Charlotte, and hold my calls for the next hour."

"Will do."

"You can go right in, Mr. Samborski. Tim will see you now."

"Please call me Rick. Dinner tonight?" Rick whispered to her as he went into Tim's office.

"Talk to me when you get done with my boss," Charlotte replied.

Rick went into Tim Murphy's office to try and sell him on all kinds of advertising: media, print, newspaper, billboards, whatever he could get him to buy. Rick was only interested in local billboard advertising. Since this first acquisition was local to the Morgantown area and the oil patch nearby, he felt this was the best media for now. Rick of course tried to sell him on more, but Tim was not biting. He said maybe later, if these targeted ads worked. They agreed on a five-billboard ad campaign in the Morgantown area for now.

Tim opened the door and told Rick to see Charlotte as he asked, "Charlotte, can you get the Pittsburg Advertising Company set up in our system with Rick Samborski as the contact?"

"Yes, I can get his supplier information and activate his AP account," Charlotte replied.

"Thanks, Tim, for your business. I'll earn it," Rick said as he walked over to Charlotte's desk.

"Charlotte will take care of you for now. I am late for another meeting. We will keep in touch, Rick."

"Thanks, Tim. It will be nice working with you and your team."

Charlotte pulled out the vendor setup form for Rick to fill out and handed it to him.

"You will need to fill this form out so we can set you up properly in our system," she said.

"I can do that. Dinner tonight?" Rick asked.

"Boy, you are pushy."

"It's just dinner. You can pick the place, and I'll pay."

"I wouldn't have it any other way. How about the Pittsburgh Chop House by the airport?" Charlotte asked. "They have great steaks and seafood."

"I know where that's at. Sounds great."

"I can meet you in the lobby at six forty-five, and I'll make a reservation for seven."

Rick left the office in the morning, and Charlotte ran all day—meeting after meeting after meeting. She had a tough time following Tim. He was like a whirling top with all the people he had to see. Finally, the day was over. It was time to go home, change quickly, and then go off to the Pittsburgh Chop House.

* * *

Charlotte arrived right on time, at 6:45 p.m., in the lobby of the restaurant. She had changed into her full-length red cotton dress that showed her cleavage very well. An open coat exposed her gorgeous body as she walked into the lobby. Rick saw her come through the doorway and was shocked at her beauty.

"Can I take your coat, Ms. Webb?" he asked.

"Yes, you can. Please call me Charlotte." She let him grab the coat as she twisted out and her hourglass figure was displayed.

"You are gorgeous, Charlotte."

"Why thank you, Rick."

They went into the restaurant and were greeted by the hostess.

"We have a reservation for two in the name of Rick Samborski at seven p.m.," Charlotte said.

"Oh yes. I see it. Right this way." They were seated by the hostess at a cozy table for two.

No sooner had they sat down than the waiter dropped off two glasses of water and two menus. "What can I get you two to drink?"

Charlotte asked for a glass of Chardonnay, and Rick asked for a Scotch and water. "I'll get your drinks and come back to get your order for dinner," the waiter said as he walked away.

A few minutes later, the drinks arrived via the bar runner. The Chardonnay was placed in front of Charlotte, and the Scotch and water was placed in front of Rick. Not a word was spoken by the runner.

The waiter arrived just a few minutes later to take their orders.

"What would the lady like tonight?" the waiter asked.

"I'll have a garden salad with ranch dressing; the petite filet, medium well; and a baked potato."

"What would the gentleman like tonight?"

"I'll have the same thing the lady is having."

"So, two of the same," the waiter announced and then walked away.

"So, Rick, what did Tim buy from you?" Charlotte asked.

"He bought some billboard ads, and that was it."

The salads arrived, and they continued to chat about Tim. Charlotte could tell that he was not successful in selling a whole line of advertising, but with time more business might come his way.

The entrées arrived a little later, and the steaks were done to perfection. The conversation went on and on about their backgrounds, work, and light topics with no substance. Toward the end of the meal, Rick ordered another round of drinks. Like clockwork, he had to excuse himself to go to the men's room. This is when she pulled out the vial of Valium from her purse. She mixed it into his Scotch and water and stirred it vigorously. Rick came back to see that the second drink was there, along with the check. The bill was paid as they both enjoyed their drinks.

Charlotte knew she had only about fifteen minutes before the Valium started to take effect, so she had to act quick.

"You want to get a nightcap?" she asked.

"Sure. Where to?" Rick asked.

"I got us a room here at the hotel."

"Why, Charlotte, you were reading my mind."

"I have a business proposal for you."

"What did you have in mind?" Rick asked.

"Let's go up to the room to discuss."

They both walked out of the restaurant and went to the elevator bank, up to the fifth floor, room 507.

Just as they got into the room, Rick started to slur his words. That's when Charlotte knew the Valium was kicking in. She walked Rick over to the bed to sit him down.

"So what's the business proposal?" Rick asked.

"What kind of commission do you get on the advertising?" Charlotte asked.

"I get a flat fifteen percent on all new business. Why do you ask?"

"How about you give me seven points, and I'll get you more business?"

"A commission on my commission?"

"Yep. A finder's fee."

"Well, that means I get eight points and you get seven points on the new business."

"What's wrong with that? I can steer you all the business from the Butler Energy Corporation. It's a good deal."

"Well, that cuts into my margin a lot."

"You also get this." Charlotte unzipped her red dress like before, and it dropped down to her ankles. Her glistening body was displayed, with a red bra and red panties, and she could tell that he was interested.

"You are gorgeous." Rick smiled.

"I know. Do we have a deal?" Charlotte started to remove Rick's clothes. Then she removed her bra and panties and straddled him on the bed. "Do we have a deal?" she asked once again. But this time she had mounted him, and the Valium had fully kicked in. Charlotte owned him for a few more minutes.

As she rode him to her delight, he yelled out, "I'll give you seven points."

Charlotte went wild, and Rick almost passed out. She thought about breaking out the toys so she could take some pictures, but it was not necessary. She might have mixed up the dosage on the Valium and put too much in the bottle. Rick was like a jellyfish. She reached for her cell phone and took some pictures anyway. These were just in case he reneged on the deal. She did not want to repeat the unfortunate incident with one Tom McFaden, which she had been forced to deal with in an unfortunate way.

She got dressed after she was done with him and had to wait almost an hour before he came around. The dosage was indeed too much, and she made a mental note to lighten up on the amount for next time. They both exited the hotel and went their separate ways. Rick was not sure what had happened this night, but he knew he had had a good time with a gorgeous woman.

He was caught in Charlotte's web.

Chapter 14

Nina Charles was the accounts receivable manager for the newly formed Butler Energy Corporation. Her job was to collect from the customers as fast as possible and to do credit checks on all potential customers for the company. Once credit was established, Nina would figure out what the credit line for each prospective customer could be. If you extend out the right amount of credit and the most favorable terms, you will get lots of customers. If you extend out the wrong amount of credit, then you get deadbeats that borrow your money and waste your time in collection calls. Those deadbeats tend to go bankrupt and never pay you back. So Nina was always on the lookout for bad credit risks.

Nina was training a new person today: the Butler Energy Corporation had hired Karen Rogers as the cash applications analyst on Monday. This was Nina's very first employee, so she would have to spend some quality time with her. Karen's primary function was to apply the cash to the customers' accounts, handle customer inquiries, and back up Nina when she was out of the office visiting customers.

One of the daily tasks was to apply the lockbox cash from the Wells Fargo Bank Pittsburgh branch. The bank provided a daily list of all the cash deposits along with the backup documentation that was received. The Wednesday morning summary was from the Tuesday close of business. A summary of $58,750.00 and ten checks with details were provided from the bank to the Butler Energy Corporation in a PDF file. Nina was going to walk through the process of cash applications to the customer accounts with Karen and then move on to other activities for her to perform.

As Nina reviewed the details from the bank, a single check stood out as not one of Butler's checks. This check was made out from the Enterprise Software Corporation, and the payee was Charlotte Webb. The amount of the check was $8,750.00, and the notation on the check line was "comm." The bank had deposited this check into the Butler Energy Corporation account by mistake. The other nine checks appeared to be proper and had customer balances that could be verified and credited against. Nina would have to call the bank and get them to reverse this check and redeposit it into the proper account.

She dialed the Wells Fargo Pittsburgh Office and got the customer service person that handled their account. "Hi. This is Nina Charles at the Butler Energy Corporation. I need to talk with you about a check deposited in our account in error."

"What is the date, check number, payee, and amount?" Customer Service Agent Mary Banks said.

"The lockbox summary was from yesterday, the check number is 100756, the payee is Charlotte Webb, and the amount is $8,750.00," Nina answered.

"Yes that is not a check for the Butler Energy Corporation," said Mary.

"We need to get it out of our lockbox receipts from Tuesday."

"You can issue a check to the payee on the check, or we can debit your account on Wednesday to reverse the transaction," Mary said. "Which way do you want us to proceed?"

"The check is payable to one of our employees here at Butler, so let me ask Ms. Webb what she wants us to do."

"OK. Just call the branch with what you decide so we can properly credit Ms. Webb's account. I do see that a Charlotte Webb has an account with the Wells Fargo Pittsburgh branch, so we could just make a transfer instead of the debit to your account," Mary replied.

"Let us verify that this is the same person. She is in our office today. I'll get back to you later in the afternoon."

"Nina, that would be fine. Just let us know, and I'll place this deposit transaction on hold until you do."

"Thanks, Mary. I'll call you back later today."

Nina hung up the phone, and she wrote herself a note on a yellow sticky note: "Charlotte Webb, $8,750.00 from Enterprise Software Corporation."

Nina finished up with the nine checks with her new employee Karen by going through the complete process and the follow-up of where to put the cash receipts documents on the network drive. The electronic documents from the bank were stored on folders that Nina had created for herself and her one employee and for the Butler Energy Corporation.

Nina had a nagging feeling about the stray check made out to Charlotte Webb. The amount of $8,750.00 was a large amount, and she did not know what to think about it. Was there something going on that she was not aware of? Was Charlotte involved in something? All kinds of questions were swirling around her head.

Later that afternoon Nina walked by Charlotte's desk. She needed to clear this transaction off the lockbox receipts for Tuesday.

"Hey, Charlotte, got a minute?"

"Sure. What's up?"

"We got a check from Enterprise Software Corporation in the amount of $8,750.00 made out to Charlotte Webb; it was deposited to our business account in error on yesterday's cash receipts."

"It was deposited into the Butler Energy Corporation business account with my name?"

"Yes. Wells Fargo made a mistake."

"Oh, that is the finder's fee they said they were going to share with me if they got the Butler business."

"Well, the bank has the deposit on hold for now. They want me to release it so they can transfer it to the proper account."

"I have an account with them. You can just have them transfer it to my account there," said Charlotte.

"OK. I'll tell Mary Banks to redeposit the check into your personal account."

"Thanks. I'll make sure I chat with them to get the account right on their end."

"I'll call Mary and put this through."

"Thanks, Nina. Sorry for the trouble."

"Oh, no trouble."

Nina got back to her desk and called Mary Banks. The check was debited to the Butler Energy Corporation and credited to Charlotte Webb's personal account at the same bank. Nina had thought to herself that Charlotte was entitled to a finder's fee if she did in fact recommend the software company to Butler. But this just did not seem right in her mind. She thought about asking somebody at the company, but Charlotte reported to the vice president of information technology and the CFO. Who would listen to a newly hired accounts receivable manager? Nina just pushed the thought into the back recesses of her head and forgot all about it by the end of the day.

Charlotte thought about the encounter with Nina and about the check from Enterprise Software Corporation. The salesperson Frank Browning had sent the check to the wrong account, and Charlotte felt exposed to someone finding out about her little criminal enterprise. She decided that making friends with Nina would be the best way to cover herself in the future. She laid out a plan to embrace Nina and make her part of her enterprise.

If she would play ball with her.

Chapter 15

James was working on the Butler Energy Corporation project plan on a warm, sunny Wednesday. He had to find a way to squeeze six months of work into two months of activities. This was a tall order since the software that had been selected required a lot of configuration and testing. Just as James was getting into the groove, the cell phone rang. The number was from the Coraopolis area and he knew it was someone from the Butler Energy Corporation main office, so he picked up the call.

"Hello. This is James Crowley."

"Hi. This is Ted MacDonald."

"Hi, Ted. I did not recognize the number."

"I'm calling from the office in Coraopolis."

"Oh, you're in the office this week?" James asked.

"I'll be here through Thursday, then out on Friday."

"What do you need this morning?"

"We talked about the plan. I just wanted to know how it was going and if you're going to be ready for the team on Monday."

"I should be ready for the team. But I have some concerns," James said.

"What concerns?"

"You requested that I change this implementation plan to a sixty-day quick-start approach. If we do this, there are things I will need to cut out and put in phase two of the project."

"That would be fine. I have no issue with a two-phase approach," Ted replied. "However, we may have to consider a forty-five-day timeline."

"That means that we will be using a lot of the standard functionality to get this thing off the ground. The reporting with the Butler logo could be an issue as well as this is a customization that is massaged early in the project. This sometimes causes grief for the client because the software is designed to be modified out of the box. The user community sometimes complains about the lack of flexibility."

"Well, I can have a chat with my team and advise them that a sacrifice will need to be made but that there is room for changes in the post-go-live phase."

"Ted, that's what I was hoping you would say."

"This is not my first rodeo, if you know what I mean," Ted said.

"Thanks, Ted. I just want to make sure your expectations are met and that we do not leave anyone behind."

"If for any reason you run into an issue, I will be a bull in a china shop. I can be the blocker if you need one on this project."

"I appreciate the assistance and understanding."

"Something else I need to tell you."

"What's that?" James asked.

"We have the second acquisition target on the table."

"You guys don't waste any time. Can you tell me anything about it?"

"No, I cannot say a word for now. It is still a secret, and we cannot release anything to the public or the internal team, including you and Bill."

"Should I consider a corporate structure with multiple companies or multiple sites? This is a question I need to get cleared up with you this week," James said.

"Could you go into some detail on the differences between site versus company?"

"I have done multiple engagements with a site or a company approach. A company approach would require the user community to log into each company when they need access to transact in the book of business. A site approach would allow all users to have access to all sites with one user account. The company approach uses a three-digit alpha code, like BEC for Butler Energy Corporation, whereas the site approach uses a three-digit numeric code as a segment in the general ledger book."

"Can we use one server for both approaches?" Ted asked.

"Yes, you can. But to do your business justice, the accountants need to make the call on this at the very first meeting."

"Which method would take longer to implement?"

"The company approach would take at least three to six months to put together."

"Then we should plan for the site approach."

"OK, Ted, I'll plan for a site approach, and this will be the first meeting with the accountants on Monday in Coraopolis."

"Agree. I need to get them to weigh in on the decision. They, and not the IT department, will drive this bus," Ted said.

"A typical structure would be a site followed by a department followed by a natural account for the general ledger structure. So an example would be 100.100.1000, where the first segment 100 is the site, the second segment 100 is the department, and the third segment 1000 is the natural account."

"James, this is Greek to me. I need for the accountants to decide this."

"Well, Ted, I have a leg up on them. I am a CPA by profession. I crossed over into IT because I found that most accountants could not speak IT talk."

"I knew I hired the right person for this project."

"You're kind of getting three people for the price of one: a CPA, an IT professional, and a project manager all rolled into one," James said.

"Don't be asking for a raise just yet," Ted said jokingly.

"That was not my intention. I just wanted you to know that I can help you with this project and I enjoy being all three of these people rolled into one. Sort of a jack-of-all-trades."

"I like that analogy."

"I also want you to know that this will be my twenty-first implementation using the Enterprise Software Corporation's product. So I have a little bit of experience in optimizing it for the user experience."

"That's good to know."

"Are we starting on Monday at eight a.m.?" James asked.

"Yes. Plan to get in Sunday night if you don't mind."

"I'll plan accordingly. So meetings will kick off at 8 a.m. Monday in the Coraopolis office?"

"Absolutely. See you on Monday. Thanks for all your attention on this. I have to run to a meeting." Ted hung up.

James thought that this project could be a fun one or it could be a major pain in the ass. Either way, he was going to try and have some fun putting it together.

Just then the Westies were whining to go out for a potty break. So it was time to take some time out in the warm Fallbrook sun.

Chapter 16

James got on the phone after the Westies' potty break. He needed to have a conversation with Bill and tell him that Ted had
changed the plan to a forty-five-day implementation.

Bill picked up on the second ring.

"Hi, James, can I call you back in a little bit? We are in the middle of this install on the server, and the software is throwing a fit."

"Are you at Blue Point Hosting?" James asked.

"How did you know that?"

"Just a hunch. Call me back later today. We have a few things
to go over."

"Give me about an hour."

"Sounds good." James hung up the call and went back to the
project plan.

* * *

Back in the Coraopolis office, Ted was wondering what happened
to the insurance information that the agent was going to deliver
on Monday. It was now Wednesday, and there was nothing in the
inbox. Ted went outside his office to Charlotte to see if he could
get an update.

"Charlotte, did we get the insurance package from Tom
McFaden?"

"I have not seen or heard from that guy since we saw him on
Friday."

"I wonder what the heck has happened to him. Did you try his
office?"

"His office does not answer. He could be a one-person operation."

"I guess that is possible. If you don't reach him or his office by this Friday, can you find another insurance broker for our executive insurance program?" Ted asked.

"I'll get started on it Friday."

Charlotte knew that if Tom or his office was not responding, the chances of someone picking up his work were slim to none. She knew better since the last person to see Tom was of course her. Calls to find additional insurance agencies that handled executive insurance would begin on Thursday. Waiting till Friday did not make any sense.

* * *

Bill finally called James almost two hours later. He figured the installation was not going well and to bother the technical team when they were doing this activity was not a good idea. The cell phone rang, and James picked it up on the second ring.

"Hi, Bill. How are you?"

"Just ducky. What's up, James?"

"I wanted to make sure you knew that Ted had changed the timeline from six months to forty-five-days."

"Yes. I know. That's why I am in downtown Pittsburgh today at Blue Point Hosting. We are trying to get the Enterprise Software Version 10.0 installed on the server. Ted instructed me to take charge of this activity."

"He is not wasting any time," James said. "He did not tell me that fact when we were on the call earlier."

"The guy is all over the map, if you ask me," Bill replied.

"So you will be done by Friday on this install?"

"No. We are trying to finish it today so I can go home. We have been at it for two days now."

"What's causing the delay?"

"It seems that there is a .NET piece of software that needs to be loaded along with a Microsoft license that is causing a conflict. The guys here have never dealt with this issue, so of course we have to call technical support. These two pieces needed to be on the server first, and the Enterprise Software would be third."

"Do you think that Blue Point Hosting is the issue, or is it Microsoft or the .NET package?" James asked.

"I really don't know. But if we don't get the compatibility issue fixed, we could be in for a rocky start next week."

"I just wanted to make sure I caught up with you and told you that Ted changed the plan, again."

"Thanks for the update and the nudge."

"I started a list with phase-two items, and Ted said move anything onto that list that is in the way and don't worry about it."

"That will make our life a little bit better, but we have to come back to all the stuff that was pushed aside during the go-live while we are supporting the application. The shitstorm is just pushing it down the road."

"We can kind of manage this volume of work after we get the instance up and running," Bill replied.

"There is another problem staring at us down the line."

"What could he throw at us so soon?"

"There is another acquisition in the hopper, and Ted said he could not say anything to his team or us."

"Holy shit, we don't even have the software loaded and configured," Bill shouted.

"They kind of warned us that they would be acquiring up to ten companies and wanted them all on one box."

"Yeah, I know, but we need some breathing room."

"Well buckle up, Bill; it's going to be a rough ride ahead."

"We can do this. Think of all the hours. We get to bill them at $105 per hour plus travel expenses." Bill was clearly excited about this prospect.

"Let's just take this one day at a time. I am going to get off the phone so you can concentrate on the install and work with the Blue Point Hosting team."

"I'll call you later when it's done." Bill ended the call.

James went back to the project plan for configuring the software and the secondary activities of setting up the first company. The Barron Water Hauling Corporation was going to be the first business on the new box. Special consideration had to be made to be able to replicate up to nine additional businesses into the software platform for growth and scalability. He would have one shot at the target, and he and Bill had to get it right or suffer the consequences.

Chapter 17

The Coraopolis Borough received a call on Wednesday morning from Terry Sanders to report a missing person situation. He could not find Tom McFaden of the Great American Insurance Company. The last time he had contact with Tom was on Friday, and his voicemail was now full and not accepting any more messages. Terry had talked with Tom about the Butler Energy Corporation's additional insurance request on Friday and was in the process of underwriting the policy. Terry needed more information about the executives and some limitations on the information before the insurance could be sent up for documentation. He thought he would get in touch with Tom on Monday to finish it up, but his calls were repeatedly going to voicemail. So he became concerned that Tom had dropped out when he had not returned his messages by this morning.

Sergeant Gary Lange was the first to receive the call from the desk officer about the missing person complaint. He immediately turned it over to the investigation team of Officer Bob Glowicki and Officer Pete Piotrowski.

"Hey, guys, I have a missing person complaint from a Terry Sanders. Can you two go interview him and see what is going on?" Sergeant Lange asked.

"Sure. What's this all about?" Officer Glowicki asked.

"It seems that the boss of an insurance company, a Terry Sanders, can't get in touch with one of his employees, a Tom McFaden. He claims it has been a couple of days, and he is concerned that something has happened to him," Sergeant Lange said.

"We will go interview this Terry Sanders," Officer Glowicki replied.

"His information is on the complaint," Sergeant Lange said.

"Let's go, Partner. We have someone we need to talk with," Officer Glowicki said.

"Where are we headed?" Officer Piotrowski asked.

"We need to see a Terry Sanders at the Great American Insurance Company in downtown Coraopolis. The address is on the complaint," Officer Glowicki said. "The office is at the corner of Tenth and Broadway, just a short distance from the station."

* * *

The officers drove down to the office of Great American Insurance Company to interview Terry Sanders. They had called Terry and told him to sit tight so they could visit him at his office. When the officers arrived, Terry was waiting at the front door.

"Are you the officers I spoke with just a few minutes ago?" Terry asked.

"Hi. I am Officer Bob Glowicki, and this is my partner Officer Pete Piotrowski."

"Welcome. I am Terry Sanders, the one that called in the missing person report," Terry said. "We can step into my office to go over any information you need."

"Thanks, Mr. Sanders. What can you tell us about the missing person?" Officer Glowicki asked.

"Tom McFaden was working on an executive insurance package with the Butler Energy Corporation on Friday, and that is the last time I had contact with him on the phone."

"Can you tell me who he was meeting with at that company?" Officer Glowicki asked.

"He was scheduled to meet with the CFO, Tim Murphy."

"Thanks, Mr. Sanders. Anything else you can add?" Officer Glowicki asked.

"I did go by the house where Tom lives, and it was empty. Even the garage."

"Can you give us the address so we have it for our records?" Officer Glowicki asked.

"Sure." Terry wrote the address on a slip of paper and handed it to the officers.

"OK. We will do a follow-up with the last person who had a meeting with him," Officer Glowicki replied.

"The Butler Energy Corporation has an office just on the other side of the airport, at the intersection of Ewing Road and Cherrington Parkway," Terry said.

"Thanks, we will head out there now," Officer Glowicki said as they left the office of Terry Sanders.

* * *

The officers drove out to the office of the Butler Energy Corporation, located in the Cherrington Parkway Complex. They needed to interview the individuals that spoke with Tom McFaden last before he disappeared. They arrived at the main floor of the office building on Cherrington Parkway and Ewing Road. The marquee listed the Butler Energy Corporation as suite 100 on the first floor. They walked into the office and found Charlotte at her desk, as normal.

"Can I help you?" Charlotte asked the two strangers.

"We are here to see a Tim Murphy the CFO." Officer Glowicki pulled out his badge.

"Do you have an appointment?" Charlotte asked.

"No, we do not. I am Officer Glowicki, and this is my partner Officer Piotrowski."

"Can I ask why you need to see the CFO?" Charlotte said.

"We are trying to locate Tom McFaden, who was known to have visited a Tim Murphy last before disappearing. We need to ask Mr. Murphy some questions."

"Let me see if I can interrupt Mr. Murphy," Charlotte said as she knocked and then walked into Tim's office.

After a few minutes, she came out of his office and left the door open.

"Mr. Murphy will see you now. You can go in," she said as she closed the door behind them.

"Hi. I am Tim Murphy, the CFO of Butler Energy Corporation. What can I do for you?"

"My name is Officer Glowicki, and this is my partner Officer Piotrowski."

"What can I help you with?" Tim asked.

"Did you have a meeting on Friday with Tom McFaden?" asked Officer Glowicki.

"Yes. We had a business meeting; Tom was helping us out with some executive insurance packages."

"Is that all you two talked about?" Officer Glowicki asked.

"It was a short meeting, and that was it. He left my office, and I did not hear from him again. I asked my executive secretary Charlotte Webb to try and reach him on Monday and Tuesday, and she was unsuccessful."

"Do you know where he was headed after your meeting, Tim?" Officer Glowicki asked.

"No, I do not. Tom did not mention that he had any other appointments."

"Do you have any idea where he is or where he could be?"

"No, I do not."

"Thanks for your time. We will be going now. Here is my card. If you think of anything, give me a call. Thanks."

Glowicki and Piotrowski left Tim's office and the building. As they passed by Charlotte, they put two fingers to their forehead as if to salute her and said, "Good day, Ms. Charlotte."

"Any time. Come visit us again," she said.

As Charlotte watched the two officers leave the building, she thought about when they would find Tom's body. She was hoping it would be a while so the trail would go cold. One thing she remembered to do was to take Tom's cell phone and dispose of it at a rest stop along the highway. That way, if they were lucky enough to find the phone and then the body, they would not be able to figure out why there was a distance between the two. It would just lead to speculation and more dead ends.

Chapter 18

James had been working on the project plan for the Butler Energy Corporation for the full week. It was now Friday, and he had to be done so that he could roll this out on Monday. He was going to call Bill Hogan since he had not heard if the installation was done. He knew he was having issues with the technical server and the loading sequence of the software. This also needed to be done before they went into the configuration meetings on Monday. After he dialed Bill on his cell phone, he didn't have to wait long. Bill answered on the second ring.

"Hey. I knew you would be calling me this morning," Bill said.

"Were you successful with the install at Blue Point Hosting?"

"Yep, we finished on Thursday. A day later than I expected."

"That's horseshit if you ask me."

"I had to remain in Pittsburgh a day longer and extend my stay," Bill said. "This was a real inconvenience, if you know what I mean."

"But it's done now?" James asked.

"Yes, it's done. To access Enterprise Software Version 10.0, you will need a secure user account with Blue Point Hosting credentials first and then another user account with the back-end software."

"The user community is not going to like the double wall to get in," said James. "That will cause all kinds of help desk tickets involving access."

"Hey, James, we don't even have a help desk system for them to use. It's going to be you and me granting access with permission from Ted MacDonald."

"Do you know if Ted was planning for one? Do I need to ask this question to the team on Monday?" James asked.

"It will be fair game for the team next week."

"Is there anything you can think of that we may have missed in preparation for the meetings next week?"

"I think we are good for now. As long as you have the project plan set to go, I believe we should be ready."

"OK. I'll call Ted and tell him that we are ready," James said.

"See you on Sunday night at the hotel," Bill replied, then hung up.

James was going to call Ted to let him know that the plan was set, the software was loaded on the hosting platform, and the consultants were coming in on Sunday night. Just before he made the call, a news broadcast caught his interest. Since he was in the casita working, he turned up the volume on the TV. A breaking news report indicated that a Tom McFaden had been found at the bottom of the Winding River Canyon. This location was on the border of Pennsylvania and Ohio off Interstate 70. His body was found at the base of the canyon, one thousand feet beneath the road, and the authorities speculated that he had been there about a week. This individual was a resident of the Coraopolis area and had worked as an agent in the local insurance industry. No other information was available to the reporter. Any tips were requested to be forwarded to the Coraopolis Borough in Pennsylvania.

This was an odd development that James had stumbled onto. He thought it was very strange that he was hearing about an event happening to one of the residents of the Coraopolis area. The last time something like this happened was when a consultant was found dead in his home of an apparent heart attack. This person was a key member of the team when they were trying to do an implementation project in Buffalo Grove, Illinois. The official cause of death was a heart attack, but the whole team thought that the person died of mysterious causes. *Could this insurance guy be related to the Butler Energy Corporation? Could something nefarious be starting all over again?* James was asking himself questions that he could not answer. He was happy that he had steady work and was looking forward to spinning up a new instance of the software that he enjoyed immensely.

A Canadian manager a long time ago said that you need to find something you're good at. You need to do it well. You need to enjoy it. If you do, then the job you're doing will not be a job but a career.

* * *

James called Ted MacDonald at the end of the day on Friday. Since he was three hours behind, on Pacific time, he called at 1:00 p.m., which was 4:00 p.m. Eastern. Ted answered the call on the second ring.

"Hey. How is my favorite consultant?" Ted asked.

"Fine. I just wanted to let you know that we are ready for the Monday meetings in Coraopolis."

"That's good to know. Bill let me know this morning the work at Blue Point Hosting was wrapped up."

"That is correct, Ted. I caught up with Bill earlier, and he said it took an extra day but it was completed."

"There was a conflict with the licensing that needed to be ironed out. I knew I hired the right guys for this project," Ted said.

"We are happy you hired us as well. We will do everything within our power to get the project done as quickly and efficiently as possible."

"I am sure you two will do fine. Listen, I have to catch a flight in fifteen minutes. So I need to say goodbye until Monday."

"Ted, I am sorry I caught you at a bad time."

"No problem. See you on Monday morning at eight a.m. sharp."

Ted ended the call and was probably running to catch the plane home. James would have his turn to run through the airport on Sunday night.

Chapter 19

James Crowley had arrived on Sunday night at one of the local hotels a few minutes' drive from the Butler Energy Corporation's headquarters in Coraopolis. His plan was to get there early and get a good night's sleep. His plan also included getting up early on Monday to go through the project plan with Bill Hogan.

On Monday morning Bill could not be located, though. James had seen this behavior from Bill before and suspected he had been blown off once again. James was feeling a little bit let down by his partner in crime. He decided to just go over to the office and present what he had for the initial kickoff meeting. He was certain what was in the project plan was rock solid, and it would be filled in with additional information as the team members added their two cents.

James drove over to the parking lot of the Cherrington Office Complex, where the Butler Energy Corporation had its headquarters in rented space on the first floor. As he got out and grabbed his computer bag, he noticed Bill walking up to the office building from the same parking lot, just a few rows down.

"Hey, Bill."

"James, I see you made it in today."

"I thought we would go over the project plan this morning. What happened to you?"

"Sorry, dude, I slept in."

"What the heck am I going to do with you?"

"I trust you got the plan in order. Like you always do."

"Yes, the plan is ready. There are just a lot of holes that need to be filled in. Hopefully by all the team members we meet today."

"Well, let's get inside and meet everyone," Bill replied.

Shortly before 8:00 a.m. Bill Hogan and James Crowley showed up at the desk of Charlotte Webb.

"Good morning, Ms. Webb," James said.

"Good morning, boys. Please call me Charlotte."

"Let's try that again. Good morning, Charlotte," James replied.

"That's better. James and Bill, right?" Charlotte asked.

"That's correct," Bill said as he and James nodded their heads.

"You will be in the main conference room the whole week. I have it blocked out for your meetings per Ted's instructions," Charlotte said. "The room is at the end of the hall."

"Thanks again, Charlotte. Bill and I will go set up for the team."

Bill and James walked down to the main conference room and plugged in their computers to get started. The Wi-Fi credentials were listed on the whiteboard. There was also a projector, which James hooked up using the HDMI cable; he then tested the display. Everything was working as planned.

As James and Bill were setting up, Ted stepped into the room.

"Good morning, boys. Glad to see you both made it here on time and in one piece." Ted chuckled. "The team will get here in a few minutes. We will do introductions and then let Tim our CFO lay out the strategic vision of the company. Tim will bounce in and out as he has time to do so."

"You're the boss here," James said.

"We are going to move the schedule around a little bit. I hope you don't mind, James. I am sure you have a set routine, but I know this team and they have already been primed to go," said Ted.

"If you don't mind, I have some core questions we need answers to so we can get the project started," James replied.

"If they don't get answered by the team, then by all means ask them," Ted said.

It was a few minutes after 8:00 a.m., and Tim was running late. All the team members that had been asked to attend the kickoff meeting were in the main floor conference room. Everyone was engaging in a little bit of small talk while they waited for Tim Murphy.

Charlotte Webb walked into the conference room and said to hang in there as Tim was finishing up a call and would be there shortly. The initial noise got quiet when Charlotte entered and then loud again as soon as she left the room.

Tim reentered the conference room a little after 8:15 a.m.

"Thanks to all who have attended here today. What I say here does not leave the room. Understand?" Tim asked as he looked around the room. "We at Butler Energy Corporation will be building a giant energy services business to serve the oil patch areas in Pennsylvania, West Virginia, Texas, Oklahoma, Ohio, and other areas throughout the USA. We will be doing this by purchasing ten to twelve freestanding businesses and consolidating them into one mega business. We will streamline and eliminate all redundancies and significantly reduce our SG&A expenses, thereby saving the mega business a ton of money. We will be using one system as the backbone of this organization, and you all will contribute your talents and passions to make this happen. We have selected the Enterprise Software Version 10.0 package to accomplish this as the back-end solution. This software will save the company money by using a full integration software package. That in a nutshell is the vision. Now you all will need to make it happen. I'll turn this meeting over to Ted MacDonald, the vice president of information technology, and he can get all of us started on this journey." Tim finished his vision statement and turned the floor over to Ted.

"Thanks for providing us a sense of direction, Tim. We have reserved this conference room for all the meetings this week that will be necessary to get us started on this journey as Tim has outlined it," Ted said. "There are two consultants that will run the project for us. Let me introduce James Crowley, who will be the project manager, and Bill Hogan, who will be the technical support manager for the project. They will be asking a lot of questions of you all, and you all will be asking them a lot of questions in return. They are the experts on the software that we purchased, and they will configure it based on our needs and your expectations. Our first objective is to get the software up and running with the first acquisition we have in the hopper. But keep in mind we will be defining the structure so that ten to twelve business entities can be on the same platform. So when you think of your little world, make sure you consider the growth for the other businesses. Don't be shortsighted. Please consider the scalability and growth of this project. Tim did not share with you all, but we are trying to be a $500 million business within four years."

Ted concluded his comments for now.

"Can we do some introductions on the team members that have joined us now that Tim and Ted have made their opening remarks?" James asked.

"I'll start. I am Barron Roberts, the president of Barron Water Hauling Corporation."

"Hi. I am Jean Roberts, the controller of Barron Water Hauling Corporation."

"I'm Paul Meadows, the controller here at Butler Energy."

"I'm Shirley Moore, the accounting manager here at Butler Energy."

"Mary Thomas, the AP manager here at Butler Energy."

"My name is Nina Charles, the AR manager here at Butler Energy."

"Tim Murphy, CFO."

"Ted MacDonald, vice president of information technology."

"Thank you, everyone, for the introductions. Over the next couple of days, we are going to map out the strategy on configuring the software and then converting the first business, Barron Water Hauling, onto the platform of the Enterprise Software Version 10.0 package," James explained.

For the next hour, James presented the implementation plan to the group; very few questions were asked by the Butler team. At the end of the hour, when the PowerPoint slides were completed, the team started to ask the questions they had saved up. For the next two hours, the team peppered the consultants with questions and the duo of James and Bill did their best to answer them. The team was happy with the consultants' answers, and Ted MacDonald smiled as he looked at James and Bill. A thumbs-up gesture was given to both of them, and James said silently to Ted, "Thanks."

It was almost lunchtime, and the team members had been cooped up for nearly three and a half hours in the conference room. When Charlotte walked into the room with a lunch tray, the team asked if they could break for lunch.

Ted announced that lunch would be provided and that there would be a break until 1:00 p.m. James and Bill ate lunch in the conference room so they could answer more questions and eat at the same time. The questions were flying during lunch, and answers were provided without a hitch. There was a look from Ted to Tim that James caught out of the corner of his eye. Ted pointed to James and Bill while looking at the CFO, and he knew what that meant: Tim was congratulating Ted for the hire of the two consultants. This was going to be a good day to shine. James earned his money that day.

* * *

The team started back up at 1:00 p.m. in the conference room. Some of the team members had announced that a few issues had come up that needed immediate attention and that they would not be able to attend the afternoon session. So Ted decided to cancel the afternoon meetings.

"We will reschedule to Tuesday at eight a.m.," Ted announced to the team.

"We have enough to get started." James looked over to Ted.

"OK, you guys use this afternoon to get organized," Ted said.

"Sounds good," James replied.

"I have plenty to do," Bill said.

The afternoon was spent going over how to configure the software and getting ready for the site-versus-company discussion. The site approach would cut the time to implement the software down significantly and was approved by Ted. This was going to be sprung on the team on Tuesday morning. It was a fundamental decision that needed to be answered, and quick. The other decision was the GL segments structure. Once these two big questions were decided on by the finance team, the setup work could start in earnest.

Chapter 20

Tuesday was round two in the conference room with the Butler team. The same group showed up for this discussion. A few emergency situations had been handled the prior afternoon, and the team was now ready to proceed.

"Good morning to everyone, and thanks for joining us today. I guess I did not scare anyone away—that's a good thing," James said. "Are there any follow-ups from Monday?" He asked the group. All were silent.

"If there are no follow-up questions, then we will get to some of the discussion items on the project list," Ted said. "No objections here."

James started the presentation once again. The slide being displayed was a question on the site-versus-company discussion. After a thirty-minute discussion on the advantages and disadvantages, the team decided to use site as the primary factor. This would be easier to implement and quicker to configure. The next slide was a question on GL segments. An example was put on the board, with a site segment followed by a department segment followed by a chart segment. This issue took almost an hour to hash out with the team. But a decision was made to use a three-digit Site, a three-digit department, and a four-digit chart, with the period as the separator. This decision blended in very well with what James had done several times before. This was also a "best practice," which he pointed out.

The next slide covered the help desk point. There was no discussion there. Ted said the question would be handled at a later time. There was no staff to support this currently. James had advised the group that the consultants would normally do this in the beginning and then at some time the company would evolve and create a help desk team.

At this point it was 10:00 a.m. and everyone needed a break. So Ted advised the team to come back in an hour. "Check your email, take care of business, and see you all in a little while," he said, then asked, "Hey, James, did we get through the problem areas with the team today?"

"Those were the three hardest configuration questions your team needed to answer. Everything else is downhill from here," James replied.

"So we can cut this team loose for the rest of the day?" Ted asked.

"If I give them their assignments later this morning, then the afternoon will be an open session," James said.

"Let's do that. I have had a few comments that we are taking up too much of the team's time with these all-week sessions," Ted replied.

"You're the boss, Ted. We can be flexible, but Bill and I need to get the answers to start the configurations."

"Give the team their assignments when we reconvene at eleven a.m., and then we will cut them loose," Ted said.

The team gathered once again in the conference room at eleven. Ted made the announcement that all members would be assigned certain tasks to go and work on and then would bring their responses back to the consultants later in the day. Sort of like homework. This way the members could get some work done rather than sitting in meetings all day. James announced that he would be sending out requests to all and would answer any questions in regard to the information that was needed. He would be in the conference room the entire day if they needed clarification. They all agreed and dispersed to their respective desks.

"Don't forget Charlotte has set up a lunch for us in the conference room today. You can have lunch or be on your own. I'll leave it to you all to decide," Ted announced to the team.

"Thanks, Ted. I think we should have impromptu meetings for the rest of the week. This will allow Bill and I to get some work done."

"Sounds like a good plan," Ted replied. "If you're not making progress, let me know immediately."

"Believe me, Ted, Bill and I are not shy about that."

The rest of the day was left open, and both Bill and James sent out numerous requests to the Butler team via email. Some team members came into the conference room for a bit of clarification, and others were probably buried in work from running the business. Either way, the consultants were off to the races to start the configurations and setups for the new Butler Energy Corporation.

* * *

Just after lunch two officers appeared at the desk of Charlotte Webb.

"Hi again. I am Officer Glowicki, and this is my partner Officer Piotrowski. We were here last Wednesday to talk with Tim Murphy. Can we talk with him, if he is in today?"

"Let me see if he is available," Charlotte replied. "Can I tell him what this is about?"

"It is about the disappearance of Tom McFaden," Officer Glowicki replied.

Charlotte knocked on the door of Tim's office and then went in. A few minutes later, she returned and the door was opened.

"Tim will see you now. You can go in," Charlotte announced.

The officers walked past Charlotte and into Tim's office with a grim look on their faces. This made Charlotte wonder if they had found the deceased insurance agent already.

"Hi. To refresh your memory, I am Officer Glowicki, and this is my partner Officer Piotrowski. We are here to ask you some follow-up questions."

"Questions on what matter?" Tim asked.

"The body of a Tom McFaden was found on Friday at the bottom of Winding River Canyon. He had a note in his pocket with the name of Ted MacDonald and mention of a Friday meeting."

"Ted is our vice president of information technology," Tim replied.

"You told us that you met with the deceased on the previous Friday in this office," Officer Glowicki said.

"Let me check my schedule," Tim replied. "I was mistaken. I was off on that Friday, and Ted MacDonald met him in my absence."

"Can we speak with Ted MacDonald to ask him a couple of questions?" Officer Glowicki said.

"I'll have Charlotte bring him over here so you can talk with him."

Tim walked out of the office and went over to Charlotte's desk. "Charlotte, can you go and grab Ted MacDonald from the conference room? These officers want to talk with him and ask some questions."

"Sure. Give me a couple of minutes," Charlotte replied.

A few minutes later, Charlotte returned with Ted MacDonald and they both walked into Tim's office.

"Thanks, Charlotte," Tim said.

"No problem." Charlotte closed the door behind her.

"Ted, this is Officer Glowicki and Officer Piotrowski, and they are asking questions about the insurance agent Tom McFaden," Tim said.

"He was the guy I had a meeting with two Fridays ago when you were off on PTO. Then he disappeared."

"Well, we found him at the bottom of Winding River Canyon *dead*," Officer Glowicki announced.

"I had a meeting with him on that Friday, and he was alive then," Tim replied.

"Do you know of any reason why someone would want to kill him?" Officer Glowicki asked.

"No clue, Officer," Tim said.

"Tom McFaden was last seen here at Butler, and then he fell off the face of the earth, literally," Officer Glowicki said.

"He was working on some executive insurance packages for us, and that was the last I heard of him. When he left this office, he seemed fine," Ted said.

"I'll leave you with one of my cards. If you think of anything else that may be important to our investigation, please give us a call."

"I can do that," Ted replied and took the business card from Officer Glowicki.

The officers left, and Ted turned his head. "What was that all about?"

"I have no idea," Tim replied.

Charlotte knocked on the door and then entered Tim's office to ask about this last meeting.

"What were the officers asking about?" she said.

"They found Tom McFaden dead, and they wanted to know if we had anything to do with it," Tim replied.

"That man was here to sell us insurance. How could you two know anything about his business?" Charlotte asked.

"Well, Charlotte, it seems that Tom may have had an enemy or two looking to do him some harm," Ted said. "Let's all get back to work."

"Good idea, Tim," Charlotte replied.

She went back to her desk, and Ted MacDonald went back to the conference room. As Charlotte was thinking about the deceased Tom McFaden, she thought it was funny that the officers did not want to talk with her. She was safe for now. No incriminating clues pointed her way. She relaxed. She was happy with her handiwork in the disposal of one Tom McFaden.

Chapter 21

Wednesday was day number three in the conference room, but without the Butler team. The members were turning in their assigned homework tasks via email and only once in a while came into the room for discussion and clarification. James and Bill were happy with this situation; it gave them plenty of flexibility and time to get stuff done. Ted MacDonald stayed away and spent most of his time in his office taking care of business. Charlotte was the only person who popped in and asked if anything was needed. They were both grateful for Charlotte's admin presence since she knew everything about the Butler Energy Corporation team members.

"Did you boys need anything today?" she asked.

"No, I think we are good today. But thanks for everything. You have been a wonderful host," James said.

"Ted told me to take care of you two," Charlotte said.

"We appreciate it. Thanks, Ms. Charlotte," James replied.

Charlotte left the conference room, and James could see that Bill was watching her leave the room.

"That dress she is wearing is so revealing. Yellow is definitely her color," Bill said as he turned his head to James.

"Keep it together," replied James.

"I know. Keep it in my pants."

"Bill, don't make me bust your chops on that one. She is a beautiful woman, and you need to leave her alone."

"I know. I am just horny, and she is a fox in wolf's clothing."

"Don't screw this engagement up," said James.

They both went back to work with their heads down and focused on the screens of their laptops. The silence between the two consultants was so total that you could hear the birds chirping outside the window.

* * *

Ted MacDonald was on the phone with Rick Cook, the owner of the Cook Salt Water Removal Corporation in Carthage, Texas. He was discussing the QuickBooks software system that they were using to run their business. The license they had was scheduled to expire April 30 of the current year. Since the acquisition was going to close on March 31, the acquired business would go on the new software as of April 1. Ted was saying that this would be a tight schedule and there may be some bumps in the flip of the switch, but it was a doable situation.

"I have two very bright consultants that can get this done," said Ted.

"If you think we can pull this off, Ted, I'll cancel the renewal for QuickBooks and we will prepare for the conversion onto the new software," replied Rick.

"I'll need to have a conversation with the consultants to see if this timeline is possible," said Ted. "But first and foremost, the deal needs to be completed. Are all of the acquisition documents signed by you and your legal team?"

"I'll get them finalized by Friday and then return them to Tim Murphy," replied Rick.

"I think Tim will be out on Friday. Send the documents to Charlotte Webb and me," Ted replied.

The Cook Salt Water Removal Corporation would be the second business to be acquired by the Butler Energy Corporation. Tim had negotiated this deal with Rick Cook early in the week and wanted Ted MacDonald to go over the business system they were on just in case. Little did Tim and Ted know that the owner Rick Cook was holding a secret. He and his team were hauling a minimum of 300 barrels per truck and billing 350 barrels per truck to each and every customer in the oil field. In the salt water pulls, there was some oil removed, which was then skimmed and sold off, further padding the bottom line of the haul. There were no measurement devices on the 50 trucks that Rick Cook was using in his business, so there was no way it could be ascertained if a short haul was done. But the drivers in the trucks were using sight levels on the side of the truck to stop at the 300 number, thereby perpetuating the fraud.

* * *

Ted MacDonald got off the phone with Rick Cook and walked into the conference room, where two unsuspecting consultants were going to be the target of his next major acquisition opportunity.

"Hi guys, I need to discuss something with you two," Ted said.

"What's up, Ted?" James asked as Bill looked on.

"We have a major development in our acquisition strategy. Our next target is a business called Cook Salt Water Removal Corporation, located in Carthage, Texas. The deal is scheduled to be signed on Friday. The target date is March thirty-first, with an implementation on April first. They are on QuickBooks, and we will be pulling them off of this system ASAP."

"Ted, are you asking us to get the second acquisition online by April first?" James said.

"That's exactly what I am asking. Is that impossible?" Ted replied.

"Ted, Bill and I will need to work around the clock to make this happen."

"So it's possible?" Ted asked.

"Ted, this is a tall order. There is no one who could pull this off. But I think Bill and I would be willing to try."

"That's what I like to hear."

"What if we fall short?" James asked.

"I have faith in you two."

James had just signed up for an impossible task: two businesses to be loaded on the software, and the main system was not even turned on. This was a tall order; he had bitten off more than they could chew. Bill had commented to James that this was a no-brainer. But James knew better. There was so much work ahead of them that the task list just exploded. All James wanted to do was to go home and get away from the Butler Energy Corporation.

Chapter 22

Thursday was day four in the conference room, and all was quiet. James and Bill were working away as usual. Charlotte strolled into the room just after 8:00 a.m.

"Can I get you guys anything this morning?" she asked as she dropped off a carafe of coffee.

"Charlotte, you did not have to get us coffee," James replied.

"I just want to make sure you two were fully caffeinated and working for my boss."

"Thanks, Ms. Charlotte," said James.

"Please just call me Charlotte."

"OK. Charlotte."

She proceeded to walk out of the conference room, and that's when Bill erupted.

"That red dress on her is so revealing. She is a knockout. I bet she is a 34-28-32, if I had to guess," said Bill.

"Slow down, Mr. Horny. I am sure she has a boyfriend," replied James.

"What a lucky guy."

"Can we get back to work?"

The two consultants went back to work and were quiet once again. A few minutes later, a Butler team member came into the room.

"Hi. My name is Nina Charles, and I have a couple of questions," she said. "How do you intend to bring over the customer file from the first acquisition company? How will the balances be brought over from the old to the new system? I have more questions, but I would like to hear how you're planning on doing this conversion."

"Nina, we will pick a point in time in the month, and you will provide us a flat file with the customer data. We would prefer it in an Excel template or a CSV file format. We can work with either. The file will have the customer number, invoice number, the balances, and indicate if there are debit balances, credit balances, or any overpayments on the account. We will load the file using a tool that is provided by the software vendor. It is kind of Excel on steroids. But before we load the data files, we will need two prelim files."

"What prelim files are you referring to?" Nina asked.

"You will need to provide a file with the customer ID and the address information, including SSN number. You will also need to provide us with a terms file. We will load the terms file first, then the customer master file, then the customer data file, in that order," said James.

"What about the customer history?" Nina asked.

"We will not load that data. Since this is a new company, we are not concerned about the history and it will remain on the old system. This is the normal approach that we use when we convert old to new," said James.

"But what if I want history on these customers loaded? Can it be done?" Nina asked.

"Yes, it can be done, but we are very limited on time here."

"I understand. So you need at least three files from me?"

"Yes. The terms file and customer address information file right away," replied James. "The AR balance file later."

"When do you need the customer balances file?" Nina asked.

"It depends on when you want the data converted. As soon as this happens, you need to use the new system and not the old one. I personally like to do this at the end of the month or the fixed acquisition date. But you will need to tell me when this is. This is your decision to make," said James.

"OK. I'll need to get back to you on the exact date for the cutover," replied Nina.

"We will be here until Friday, so if you find out, let us know."

Nina left the conference room and mumbled that she would try to get the answer by Friday for all of the three files that needed to be converted.

Just as she was leaving the conference room, Mary Thomas, the accounts payable manager, walked in.

"Hey. I have a couple of questions," Mary said.

"Sure. What kind of questions do you have?" replied James.

"What exactly do you need from me and the accounts payable team?"

"We will need the active vendor file with information on the address and SSN numbers. We will also need the terms file for all the vendors. In a normal situation, we would also need a third file from you, the vendor balances file. But a decision was made to burn the accounts payable file before we convert. So the full vendor balances is planned to be zero," replied James.

"Do you mean that a final check run is required to zero out the vendor balances?" Mary asked.

"Yep. We are limited on what we are bringing over, and this is the fastest way to convert the business by start-up day," said James.

"What about the history of the vendors?" Mary asked.

"We will not be bringing this history over. There is not enough time in the conversion schedule to accomplish this task."

"But I need the history," replied Mary.

"You may want to talk with Ted about this issue."

"I'll have a follow-up conversation with Ted later today," said Mary.

"We would ask that you get us the terms file and vendor information file as soon as you can. This way we can start to load the data," James said.

"I'll work on that later today," replied Mary.

As Mary left the conference room, she started to mumble like Nina before her. James thought it was an odd thing that both the Butler team members mumbled as they left the room.

"They are just overworked," said Bill.

"It seems to be a theme around here," replied James.

James knew that the two biggest complainers were going to be Nina and Mary since they had the bulk of the data conversions. The only other team member that could be an issue was Accounting Manager Shirley Moore. Since the general ledger was not being converted, there was no conversion file to worry about; only a simple balance sheet of opening numbers was to be prepared, and this could be done with the copy function once the ledger was set up.

Later in the afternoon, Shirley Moore showed up in the conference room to ask some questions. The general ledger structure that had been decided on was a site, branch, and chart structure. So Shirley had to provide the values for each of the segments.

"Hey, guys, what do you need from me?" Shirley asked.

"Hi, Shirley. Good of you to meet with us," said James.

"No problem. I did not want to hold you up."

"We need the values you want to use for the site, branch, and chart segments. Once this is done and we get the final numbers, we will need the balance sheet values for each business we convert by the new general ledger account number. Then we will load these balances as your official balance sheet opening position," said James.

"So you just need the values to be assigned to each of the segments?"

"Yep. That's it. We normally would have a discussion on this with the users who would need to have an opinion on the final values," replied James.

"Users—there are only four of us right now: Paul Meadows the controller, Nina Charles the accounts receivable manager, Mary Thomas the accounts payable manager, and I," Shirley said.

"The accounting team has an opportunity to make the chart of accounts the way you want it. So, for example, assets would be a 1 followed by some numbers; liabilities would start with a 2; equity accounts would start with a 3; revenue would start with a 4; cost of goods sold would start with a 5; administrative costs would be a 6, 7, or 8; and other costs would be a 9. You have some flexibility here, and we want you to use a best practice when setting this up. It will make your life a lot easier later," said James.

"You just said a mouthful, James."

"Can we get the four people in the conference room and discuss this?"

"I think that Paul Meadows has a rather good idea on this. Let me go talk with him and get back to you."

"Sounds good. We need this decision right away. If I could get it by Friday before we leave Coraopolis, that would be most helpful."

"Let me see what I can do?" replied Shirley as she left the room.

"You pushed kind of hard on that issue," Bill said to James when they were alone again.

"You know me, Bill, I have to push the accounting team; otherwise this will languish, and you and I will be behind the eight ball. You remember I am a CPA, right?" James asked.

"Yes, I know. You remind me of that once per project."

"You need to know when to push the team on this. Otherwise, they will drag it out and make us late on the project plan."

"You know what you're doing here, so I'll leave it in your good hands."

"Thanks. Now let's get something done today. It's almost the end of the day," said James.

Chapter 23

Ted MacDonald came by the conference room at the end of the day on Thursday. He wanted to invite James and Bill out for dinner to talk with them and get a read on how this week had progressed.

"Hey guys, can we go out to dinner tonight?" Ted asked.

"Sure. What did you have in mind?" James asked.

"I know a great Italian restaurant in downtown Coraopolis that Charlotte recommended. I have been meaning to try it, but I needed some company. Tonight, you're the company. Is that OK for the two of you?"

Both James and Bill just nodded their heads.

"OK. So I'll meet you in your hotel bar after work for drinks. We can drive together to the restaurant," said Ted.

"What's the name of the restaurant?" James asked.

"Frank's."

"What time did you want to meet?" James asked.

"Let's say five p.m. Sound good?" replied Ted. "Now pack up and get out of here. I will see you then."

James and Bill abruptly ended what they were working on. They knew from past experience when the customer wanted to have drinks and dinner, it meant right away. Everything they were doing could wait. James was also thinking that Ted wanted to share something with him and Bill but was not sure of the signals that he was receiving.

* * *

James and Bill were waiting for Ted in the bar of their hotel as planned. They did not order anything, though; they were going to let Ted make the first move and set the tone for the evening. Ted arrived shortly after 5:00 p.m. and announced that they had to have a round of drinks to celebrate.

"What are you guys drinking?" Ted asked.

"What are you having?" James asked.

"I'll have a Gentleman Jack and Coke."

James and Bill nodded their heads and raised the three fingers. The bartender knew that meant three of the same. A few minutes later all three of them were having the same drink: a Gentleman Jack and Coke with a lemon twist.

"Well, we have something to celebrate. The Butler team likes you guys, and you two have lessened their fear that this acquisition is going to suck," said Ted.

"Suck. What does that mean?" James asked.

"You two have demonstrated that you know enough about the software that the Butler team can stay focused on the acquisition and its operations. The entire team has expressed that when you acquire mom-and-pop businesses and put them together, things happen."

"You mean the skeletons in the closet come out once a family business is acquired?"

"You hit the nail on the head, my boy."

"I can speak for Bill, and we have seen some weird shit happen when a family business has gone from one generation to the second generation and then the third generation sells out to a company like Butler," said James. "The accumulation of dark secrets, crimes, fraud, and waste are center stage, and sometimes it's an ugly situation."

"Well, I want you two to watch out for anything out of the ordinary and report any nefarious or unusual activities while you are working for Butler."

"Is this why you wanted to have drinks with us tonight?"

"No. I wanted to tell you that the Butler team likes you and they think you two are knowledgeable about the software and the acquisition process. They wanted me to pass on these concerns and comments."

Bill just nodded his head. "This is what we like to do," he replied.

"Finish your drinks, and we will head to the restaurant," said Ted.

The glasses were emptied and then placed on the bar.

"Let me get this," said Ted. "You can get dinner."

"So you get the small bar tab, and I get the big dinner bill?" James laughed.

"Yep. That's the rule." Ted smirked.

* * *

The three guys left the hotel bar and drove together in Ted's car to the restaurant. It was a rental car from Hertz, a Nissan Maxima, and fit three adult men extremely comfortably. The destination was Frank's Italian Restaurant in downtown Coraopolis. It did not take but fifteen minutes to get there with little traffic on the streets. Charlotte had earlier made a reservation for Ted at 7:00 p.m. He relied on Charlotte's good nose for sniffing out great places in the area to dine at. Since Charlotte was a native of the area and Ted was not, her opinion was high up there in his mind.

As the three of them entered the restaurant, they noticed there were not a lot of people eating dinner. This had Ted a little worried, but Charlotte had said this was her favorite restaurant for Italian food. As the evening progressed and they made it through the wine, salads, entrées, and deserts, the three men all agreed what a wonderful meal.

"Who recommended this place?" James asked.

"Charlotte told me to entertain you two here. It is her favorite place in the Coraopolis area," said Ted.

"We will have to thank her for the recommendation. The food was fabulous," replied James.

"The chicken Madeira was absolutely wonderful," Bill chirped in.

"My Bolognese was excellent," said James.

"My Veal was perfect," Ted added.

As the bill arrived, the waiter went to put the portfolio in the middle of the table. Ted grabbed it and said, "This one is yours, James."

"Can I put this on my expense report?" James asked.

"You sure can. Make sure you send it to me for approval," replied Ted.

"So we send all time sheets and expense reports to you directly?" Bill asked.

"Yes. You can coordinate with Charlotte and myself," said Ted.

As James took care of the restaurant tab, which was $350 with tip, Ted made the comment that they should go back to the hotel for a nightcap. It was only 9:00 p.m., so neither consultants had anywhere to go. Plus, they were passengers in Ted's car and really did not have a choice.

* * *

They arrived back at the hotel bar and immediately ordered three Gentleman Jack and Cokes with a lemon twist. The bartender said, "Didn't I see you three here earlier?"

"Yep, we are here for round two," Ted said. "Except this time, he is paying the bar tab." He pointed at Bill.

Bill looked like a deer in the headlights of a speeding car.

"What?" he asked.

"You're paying for this one," said Ted.

The three of them had a long conversation about life, experiences, backgrounds, sports, and everything else under the sun. James suspected that Ted was pushing them to see how far they could go before they broke. This was also an opportunity to ask a lot of questions of Ted about what was really going on at Butler.

The night progressed into a two-hour drink marathon with a bar tab of $200 including tip. This one was for Bill to pick up, and he was a little worried that he would not get reimbursement. But Ted would honor the expense reports submitted with no questions asked. They finally broke up and all three went to their respective rooms for a good night's sleep. A hangover for some might have been in the making, but only time would tell. Friday morning would be there fast enough for them to feel it.

Chapter 24

Friday morning in the conference room was a little bit rough for the consultants. Both James and Bill were feeling the effects of the drinking binge that Ted MacDonald had subjected them to the night before. James could not remember how many Gentleman Jack and Cokes he drank, but he knew it was too many. James could tell that Ted wanted to party by drinking the night away. Maybe this was a test to see if the consultants could hold their liquor, and maybe it was a test to see if they would slip in the presence of Ted. Either way both consultants were on guard for a loose lips approach and made sure not to offend the customer. They had seen this before—a customer who liked to drink while away from his home and wife. The manager was carefree and threw caution to the wind. But this was when the consultants had to be on guard. One wrong word, and you could offend the customer and get yourself fired from the engagement. Both James and Bill had been around the block on this and knew how to play the game. They were suffering this morning and would struggle through the day. Then they would go home and have a nice long sleep to get out of the fog.

Right on schedule Charlotte came in with a pot of coffee, just after eight o'clock hour.

"How you two holding up?" she asked. "Ted told me the three of you went to Frank's last night."

"Thanks for asking, Charlotte. But we went to Frank's between the drinking marathon at the bar," said James.

"So Ted took you out for drinks, dinner, and drinks?" Charlotte asked.

"You already knew?" James asked.

"I suggested it to Ted, to see what you two were made of."

"Did we pass?" Bill chirped in.

"You passed with flying colors," said Charlotte. "You two showed up here on time and in reasonably good shape."

"Thanks for the vote of confidence," replied James.

As Charlotte was leaving the conference room, Paul Meadows walked in.

"Hey, do you two have time to discuss the chart-of-accounts setup issue?" Paul asked. "Shirley Moore and I were going over this item on the list, and I need a little bit of assistance before I put the final numbers in front of you two."

"This is all you, James," Bill said as he walked away from the conversation.

"Thanks, Bill," replied James. "I can answer your questions, Paul. What do you need?"

"I have a chart of accounts from a previous company that I would like to use, but I need to make some changes before I give it to you," said Paul.

"This is your opportunity to make it yours. I suggest you and your team take the time to get it right and use the best practices approach. Your team will live and breathe this thing, and you need to own this decision," announced James.

"Can I give you the numbering of the site, department, and chart on Monday? I need some time over the weekend to carefully go through it?" Paul said. "I have a lot of stuff to take care of today, and I need a few hours of quality time to study the final numbers."

"If you need a few extra days, by all means take it. I can inform Ted, and I am sure he will be agreeable to changing the schedule," said James.

"Are we running behind because of the finance team?" Paul asked.

"Well, not really. This is an important decision, and you really don't want to mess it up. Sort of like measure twice and cut once, to use an example," said James.

"I'll get you the numbers by Monday," said Paul.

"That would be fine. There are plenty of things I need to do to get everything else set up. Are we still good with the site, department, and chart structure?" James asked.

"Yes, the structure is solid. I just need agreement on the numbering within the structure. That I will discuss with the finance team today. I am going to shoot for a target date of Monday to deliver the final numbers. Is that OK with you?" Paul asked once again.

"Yes, that will be fine. I'll rearrange my schedule for the configurations," said James.

"Thanks. I'll let you get something done today. Looks like Ted got you last night," Paul commented.

"What do you mean?" James asked.

"I know Ted took you out for drinks last night. You two look a little bit hungover this morning."

"It shows that much?" James asked.

"Ted does that to everyone, including the finance team. A word of caution—and you didn't hear this from me—Ted likes his time away from his home and family," said Paul. "His expense reports are an indicator."

"Thanks for the word of caution. He definitely can hold his liquor," replied James. "Do you know if Ted is hungover?"

"Nope. He is fine this morning," said Paul. "I was just in his office earlier."

Paul left the conference room and was mumbling to himself as he exited. James thought to himself once again that all the Butler team members appeared to mumble when they left the room. *Is this a trend, or is there something wrong with the Butler organization?* Only time would tell.

A little while later, Ted strolled into the conference room to see how the two consultants were getting on.

"Hey, guys. How are you this morning?" Ted asked.

"Just fine," replied James, and Bill just nodded. James went on, "Hey, I just had Paul Meadows in here a little bit ago. He said he would be delayed in providing the site, department, and chart numbering until Monday. I told him that was fine."

"Will this put us behind?" Ted asked.

"It just puts some pressure on Bill and me to get this to the finish line."

"I have faith in you guys. Just keep me informed if there are any roadblocks," said Ted. "Oh, and I don't like surprises, so make sure you give me adequate notice of any issues."

"That I can guarantee you," replied James.

"What time do you guys leave today?" Ted asked.

"I need to leave here by one p.m. to get to the airport," said James.

"I need to leave right around that same time," replied Bill.

"OK. If I don't see you two before you leave, safe travels," said Ted.

"You as well," replied James.

The rest of the morning went by uneventfully. No more visitors, with the exception of Charlotte. She strolled in late morning just to take a pulse on James and Bill.

"You boys doing OK?" she asked.

"Yes, we are. Thanks for the recommendation last night. Frank's is a great restaurant," said James.

"It is my favorite restaurant in Coraopolis," replied Charlotte.

"I have to tell you that when we walked into Frank's, there were not many customers."

"They do a huge catering and takeout business in addition to the sit-down style. They are always busy," said Charlotte.

"Well, the food was top-notch. Thanks again."

"You're very welcome," replied Charlotte. "I did not order lunch for you two today. So you're on your own. Is that OK?"

"Yep, that's fine. You have been wonderful this week. We could not have done it without your assistance."

Charlotte left the conference room, and James could see Bill staring at her as she walked out. Once she was out the door, Bill's comments came out.

"Those jeans on Charlotte are so tight. I wonder if she was a model at one time," commented Bill.

"Your lust for that woman is showing again. You're a pig," James scolded.

"I know. She is just gorgeous."

"So where are we going to lunch today?"

"I was going to work as long as possible and then eat at the airport."

"Well, then I am going to go get lunch on my own."

* * *

James was headed out the door for lunch and just happened to pass by Ted's office on his way out.

"Hey, Ted. I was just going to catch some lunch; do you want to join me?" James asked.

"Can I catch you next time? I have a call to make."

"No problem."

"Hey, since you're here, can I ask a favor?" Ted said. "Can you finish up the configurations next week on the software and start to demo it when you two come back the following week?"

"Ted, that's a tall order. I'll need to get the final chart of accounts from the controller on Monday."

"But you two can get it done?" Ted asked.

"Yes, Ted, we can get it done."

"When you come back the following week, plan to demo the software to the finance team on Monday."

"Can we schedule it for Tuesday just in case?"

"Well, OK. Tuesday will be fine. But make it happen, and do whatever you need to do. Cut some corners if you have to," said Ted.

"I'll inform Bill of this, and we will adjust the schedule accordingly."

"Thanks, James. I know I am pushing you a little bit, but we need to get this thing moving. There are a lot of things going on, and my boss Tim is counting on me to pull this off. I in turn am counting on you and Bill to pull this off. If you need overtime to get it done, I authorize whatever you need."

"We will get it done."

James left for lunch; he needed to clear his head. He was tempted to go back into the conference room and let Bill know of this recent development, but he was hungry and had to think about the conversation that had just taken place. Lunch had won out. He exited the building in search of a chicken sandwich.

* * *

After lunch, at around 12:45 p.m., James returned to the conference room for just a few minutes, and Bill was gone. He was going to catch up with him and relay the conversation with Ted. This would have to wait till later today or first thing on Monday morning. He knew what Bill would say: The demo would be all on him and he would assist but not be present. That wasn't his thing.

As scheduled, James packed up at 1:00 p.m. and headed for the airport. If he was lucky, a quick look for Bill before he boarded his plane would be successful. He wanted to share the conversation and the enormous amount of pressure Ted had placed on him to deliver to the Butler team.

* * *

James got lucky and saw Bill at the airport. His gate was five sections down, and he stopped to have the conversation.

"Hey, Bill, got a minute?" James asked.

"They will be boarding shortly, so yep," replied Bill.

"I just wanted to tell you about a conversation I had with Ted a few minutes ago. He wants us to demo the software on Monday of the following week."

"Shit, this guy doesn't waste any time. Can we be ready for that?"

"We have to be ready. He insinuated that there is something else going on and we need to be ready by that date."

"Can you finish up the configurations in time?"

"Well, I will do my best to get them done. Ted said to work overtime if necessary."

"I hate to tell you James, but this is all you," replied Bill.

"Yes, I know. The finance team is dragging its butt on the chart, and that is the biggest holdup. The controller said maybe Monday for the numbers."

"You will need to push him on Monday. But you have three hours extra when you get back. You're on Pacific time next week."

"Are you being cute with that comment?"

"Just trying to make a joke," said Bill.

"Hey, I got to go; they're calling my zone for boarding."

"Safe travels, Bill."

"Safe travels as well. Don't worry, we got this."

James knew that this project now rested on him and the software being fully functional by Tuesday of the following week. He had bought himself one extra day, and he was going to need those eight hours. The weekend would involve working and trying to get ahead of the shitstorm that lay ahead.

Chapter 25

This was the fourth week of this engagement with the Butler Energy Corporation, and the end of February was right around the corner. James was busy early on Monday in the casita making changes to the software. The templates he had used many times before had become an invaluable aid in replicating new companies with just a change in the name and other vanilla settings as well. There were over three hundred company settings that had to be touched to activate Enterprise Software Version 10.0. Some involved just a simple flag that had to be turned on from off, others a value that had to be decided and then set. All of these company settings were going to take at least three days to complete, and then allowing for two days to do some simple testing and troubleshooting was a must.

He was grateful that the casita acted as his sanctuary and that only the two Westies would interrupt the plan. Champ and Abbey always wanted to play and distract James from his work. Sometimes a distraction was welcome. But this week his wife was home, so the Westies stayed in the main house with only frequent visits. It was going to be rough to get everything done, but it was doable. The challenge had been set by Ted, and James had never turned on this system in less than six months. He had been given two months to turn on the bare bones and then place stuff in the parking lot for phase two after the go-live date.

James pulled out the template from a prior client and started the configuration process for Butler Energy Corporation. He carefully took screenshots of the Butler setups in relation to the template in one massive Word document. This could also be used in the future for other clients, with built-in slack time for billing purposes. He always wanted to underpromise and overdeliver, rather than the alternative. Clients always appreciated this strategy. This document could also be used as an interview form to go over with the Butler team on all the setups established; he would then allow them the opportunity to make a change if necessary.

James was happy with the progress during the day. He had made it through one hundred pages of the two-hundred-page template, and at that pace, he could be done in two days instead of three. The only nagging item was the chart of accounts, which Paul Meadows the controller had promised by the end of the day on Monday. At 1:00 p.m. Pacific time, James sent an email to Paul requesting the numbers and asked if he was having any delays on his end. There was no response from Paul, so James just continued on with the configuration checklist.

The casita door opened, and Champ and Abbey came running in to say hello with their tails a-wagging, compliments of his wife.

"Hey, can you take care of the Westies for a little while? I need to run out for an errand." Lynn asked.

"Sure," replied James.

The Westies were in the mood to play, so James stepped away from the desk and went outside to run around in the warm Fallbrook sun. Once playtime was over, Champ and Abbey came inside the casita and found their dog beds. It was now nap time for the Westies, and back to work for James.

At the end of the day, there was still no email from Paul Meadows on the numbers file. James had made it through 125 pages of the 200 pages of configurations and was feeling rather good about his progress. But the little voice inside of him was saying something different. There were no emails from Bill during the day. There were no emails from Ted. There were no emails from the Butler team. Something did not feel right, so he decided to call Bill on his cell.

"Hey, Bill, this is James. Have you had any contact with the Butler team today?"

"No, I have not. But I did not have any reason to call anyone. I am still working on the additional network configurations with Blue Point Hosting."

"OK. It just seems funny that no email or communications came out of the office today directed toward us."

"Give them until Tuesday. I am sure they are just busy with all the acquisition stuff."

"Are you going to be ready for next week?" James asked.

"Come hell or high water, I'll be done by Friday," said Bill.

"I will be done on schedule as well. I want to do some light testing on Thursday and Friday if that is possible."

"You will definitely need to wait until at least Thursday."

"Why is that?"

"We have to run the compiler utility once we are done. If it blows up, we could have a problem."

"Bill, don't forget I have to run the import of the posting rules. That is one of my last steps, and that one must be done before you run the utility program for the compiler."

"Well, can't you run that now?"

"I need the numbers for the chart of accounts, and Paul Meadows is AWOL."

"Shit, you better rattle his cage on Tuesday," Bill yelled into the cell phone.

"That's why I am having this conversation with you."

"OK. Let's give them until Tuesday and then go to Ted for a push."

"Sounds good. I'll follow up with Paul and then Ted bright and early on Tuesday. Thanks, Bill." The cell phone went dead on Bill's end.

I guess we were done, James thought to himself. Enough progress for one day. Time to play with the Westies.

Chapter 26

James was hoping that Tuesday would be a better day for the Butler team. Since he was still three hours behind Coraopolis, he could set off the alarm bells with Ted if it was warranted. As James got to his computer in the casita and turned it on, there was a bunch of email traffic in his inbox. An email from Paul Meadows on the numbers for the site, department, and chart segments. An email from Nina Charles on the customer terms and customer files. An email from Mary Thomas on the vendor terms and vendor files. James had plenty of work, and now he felt overwhelmed.

James responded to Paul's email first. After a careful review, he sent him a list of additional questions and set the file aside. James then looked over the customer files and again sent back some additional questions to Nina Charles. James then looked at the vendor files and again sent back some additional questions for Mary Thomas. This process of back-and-forth was a normal situation; it usually took three return trips between the consultant and the business user. The goal was to get a flat file that was loadable into the new software and only perform the upload once. There were many more files to load, and cleanup of the data files was best done before the process was started.

Since the urgent files had been sent back to the Butler team for clarifications to the three users, James went back to the template to finish the configurations. There were seventy-five pages of items, out of two hundred, to be finished, and he needed to stay focused and stay on track. The Westies would not be a bother today because Lynn had them in the main house. She was working from home today too.

Just as James started to get going, the two faces appeared at the doorway. Champ and Abbey were wagging their tails and barking at him through the glass. So a break was in order early in the morning. The customer would not know James was playing with the Westies on company time, and this was an advantage of having a casita and a courtyard between that building and the main house. After a few minutes, the Westies got tired and then retired for a nap in the main house with Lynn. James went back to work on the configurations.

Just then the cell phone rang. It was Bill Hogan.

"Hey. I got a call from Ted MacDonald this morning. He was checking in with me and said that the office yesterday was having some internet issues and email was not going out."

"That explains why I did not get any emails from the team," replied James.

"Ted had said there was an issue with the local provider and it is now fixed. So he thinks."

"Bill, that is good to know. Do I need to call him to confirm?"

"No. He said to keep working and haul ass. He also said to call him if for any reason you're not getting the stuff from the Butler team."

"We are good on that. I just got emails from Paul, Mary, and Nina. The files I was expecting."

"OK. I'll leave you to it. I have to get back to the Blue Point Hosting issues. This is kicking my ass, and I am not happy about it," Bill replied and then hung up.

Again, Bill had just dropped the call. How rude he was sometimes. James knew that Bill's etiquette on the cell phone was lacking, but sometimes you need to know who you're dealing with. Sometimes Bill was crude, brash, and downright vulgar. But as a friend James would not trade him in for a million dollars.

James went into the remaining configurations and finished by lunchtime. He was proud of his work and would use the balance

of the afternoon to go over the template and the Butler configuration document. This would be his first order of business on
Monday next week. The document was two hundred pages, and
a review by the Butler team was one way of getting them hooked
into the system and thinking that this was now their system, that
they owned it and knew how it was constructed. Ted would be happy to get the team engaged and to see that a knowledge transfer
was happening from the consultants to the Butler team.

After lunch, a review of the configuration document was in order before any load files would be opened. The two-hundred-page
document for the Butler Energy Corporation was now ready, and
James could move on to more pressing issues.

The Nina Charles customer and customer terms information
was revised and sent back to James. He completed a quick review
of the base files from the team member, reformatted them into a
template file, and then used the paste-insert feature to populate
the database to complete the upload process.

The Mary Thomas vendor and vendor terms information was
revised and sent back to James. He completed a quick review of
the base files from the team member, reformatted them into a
template file, and then used the paste-insert feature to populate
the database to complete the upload process.

The Paul Meadows site, branch, and chart numbers file was
revised and sent back to James. He completed a quick review of
the base files from the team member, reformatted them into a
template file, and then used the paste-insert feature to populate
the database to complete the upload process.

James sent an additional email to Paul Meadows to ask which
general ledger accounts needed to be activated. This process to
generate the actual GL accounts was the next step for Paul to confirm. Once this was done, more decisions would need to be made
by the team for next week. Paul had responded and said he did

not know what was being requested of him. James had said the combination of site and branch and chart had to be activated as a string of values so that currency transactions could be done in the ledger. He asked James to just set up the minimum accounts for now. James knew what that meant and said he would take care of it. An autogeneration utility was used to set up the base income statement and balance sheet accounts, and James guessed at the values. This would be placed on the review file for next week to discuss with the team.

There was one last thing to do before the day finished. Now that the AR, AP, and GL files were loaded, it was time to import the posting rules into the company code BEC for the version of the software that was on the database. These forty-three rules controlled how the transactions behaved and operated in the software platform. Once imported, all the rules had to be activated by turning them on as active in the database. This was where it became a nightmare if the version of each of the rules needed an update. Once in a while, the rules became stuck and needed a nudge on the revision tab to change the effective date.

James started the operation to import the rules, and after one hour, it was finished. No issue was encountered, and all forty-three rules appeared to be active with a current version file. A quick check of the rules by opening each one up and checking the revision tab revealed one rule was still not active. A nudge on this rule was done, and the active flag was green. If for any reason a rule was not working, the transaction would not work and a system error would be displayed, which would prevent the user from finishing the process. All the rules were now active.

This was a good second day away from the client, and James felt good. It was time to knock it off for the day. *Always end on a good note*, he thought.

Chapter 27

The system was ready for testing, and James was going to put it through the paces. There would be additional setups necessary as the testing went on, but this was a normal way to flex the database without breaking it. The intention would be to run some transactions through the AR, AP, and GL modules and measure the results for what configs needed to be reviewed and changed. Since this was Thursday, James had set aside a full day to run the system checks, starting with the general ledger.

A journal entry was prepared and entered using a couple of accounts with a minimum dollar amount. It failed to post due to a GL control account not being set up. Once the GL control was established, the debit and credit side of the transaction worked, and James could move on.

Next up was a miscellaneous invoice transaction. This was to test the billing function for a customer named Abbey, a fake set-up for the test. The invoice was processed and failed due to a GL control not being set up. The GL control account was established, and the transaction was now passed and posted to the GL. The cash receipt transaction was processed as the back-end part of the miscellaneous invoice, and this failed as well. The control needed to be set up, and once this was done, the transaction was posted to the GL.

Next, a dummy accounts payable invoice was processed with the fake vendor named Champ set up for a test. The vendor invoice failed. The GL control account needed to be established and was set up. The transaction was now posted to the GL. The payment transaction was processed as the back-end part of the vendor invoice and failed as well. The control needed to be set up, and once this was done, the GL results were posted.

The GL control issue would need to be discussed with the team next week. There were about one thousand different controls that could be set up by any one business, but only a handful would be needed to run the company. This would be on the agenda for Monday.

The system test was going well, and James was happy with the results so far. The base system for the Butler Energy Corporation would be ready by Monday. He was now breathing with a little bit of relief. There was always a feeling that the setups for a new company would go off the rails and require a ton of rework. But using the template approach of always keeping a copy-by version had proven to be a winning strategy for the consultant.

* * *

Charlotte walked into Ted's office with a cup of coffee.

"Thanks, Charlotte. You didn't have to do that."

"I just wanted to make sure you had some caffeine this morning."

"Hey, don't forget you volunteered for dinner with me and Rick Cook tonight."

"Did you need me to make a dinner reservation?" Charlotte asked.

"Yes, thank you. Can you make it at the Pittsburgh Chop House next to the Pittsburgh International Hotel? The one on Old Mill Road near the airport."

"Any reason you want that restaurant?"

"They have great steaks and seafood," replied Ted. "I need you to help me sway Rick Cook into accepting our offer to buy his company."

"So this is a heavy-pressure sales job?"

"Well, not really. I just need a beautiful woman to get the deal done."

"Are you using me, Ted?" Charlotte asked.

"Well, you're gorgeous, and I have seen the way men turn to jelly when they see you."

"Thank you for the compliment."

"You will get a nice dinner out of the evening."

"Should I be asking for a raise here or a bonus?"

"I will talk to Tim about that. Please can you assist me? I need to close this deal," Ted pleaded. "This deal was thrown at me by Tim, after all."

"Fine. I'll go to dinner with the two of you."

"Make the dinner reservation for seven p.m. I'll let Rick know to meet us there."

"Will do," said Charlotte as she walked out of his office. *Ted is using me as a shiny object to get the deal done. I need to get something out of this arrangement.*

* * *

The Pittsburgh Chop House was a high-end steak and seafood house and a genuinely nice place to have dinner. Ted was hoping to get Rick down from a $60 million ask price to $50 million. Otherwise, there was not going to be a deal.

All three arrived right around the 7:00 p.m. in the restaurant lobby. Charlotte had on her signature red dress that was just spectacular. The dress showed off her 34-28-32 hourglass figure to perfection. Ted could see that Rick was staring at Charlotte already.

"Hi, Rick, glad you could make it for dinner," said Ted.

"You know, Charlotte, You are even more gorgeous outside the office," commented Rick.

"Why thank you, Rick," replied Charlotte.

"Shall we go inside?" Ted motioned to the hostess. "Table for three under MacDonald."

"Right this way." The hostess directed them to their table.

"So, Rick, have you given our offer any more attention?" Ted asked.

"Well, yes I have," replied Rick.

As the waiter came by, Rick stopped talking. "I am Ricardo, your waiter tonight. Can I get you all a round of drinks?"

Charlotte said, "I'll have a Malbec, please."

Rick said, "I'll have a Gentleman Jack and Coke with a lemon twist."

Ted said, "I'll have a Gentleman Jack and Coke with a lemon twist also."

"I really think the business is worth sixty," Rick said.

"Butler is willing to pay you fifty," Ted replied.

The waiter returned with the drinks, and all were silent for a moment.

"Can I take your dining selection tonight, or do you need more time?" Ricardo asked.

Charlotte said, "A garden salad with ranch dressing, the petite filet medium well, and a baked potato. Thank you."

Rick said, "A garden salad with Thousand Island dressing, the porterhouse medium well, and a baked potato."

Ted said, "And I'll have a garden salad with ranch dressing, and the surf and turf special with a baked potato as well."

"Very good. I'll put your order in," said Ricardo as he took off to put the order into the POS terminal.

"Why do you think your business is worth sixty instead of fifty?" Ted asked.

"I just do," replied Rick.

"You only made $100,000 after taxes last year," said Ted. "Butler is willing to pay you fifty, and that's it."

Just then the salads were placed on the table and the conversation dried up. Rick and Ted did not want anyone to overhear their conversation. Charlotte was playing the eye candy and being quiet.

"What do you think, Charlotte?" Rick asked.

"I was just invited to dinner. I am not getting in the middle here," she replied.

The conversation changed to food, sports, news, and other topics for the rest of the evening. Just after the dessert, Ted ordered a second round of drinks and tried to steer the conversation back to the deal. Rick was not biting. Almost at the same time, Rick and Ted said they would be right back. They were headed to the bathroom for a little relief from the meal. Charlotte sprang into action. She had a vial of Viagra and one of Valium, and she mixed both into Rick's drink. This was an experiment for her to see if she could get a rise out of the guy's libido and knock him out at the same time. Ted was not getting anywhere with Rick on the number, and she knew the evening was just about over. Rick and Ted returned, and Charlotte could not resist conducting a little experiment.

"Did the two of you behave?" Charlotte asked.

"Of course we did," replied Rick.

"So, Rick, can we close this deal at fifty?" Ted asked.

"No, we can't. But how about you meet me in the middle, say fifty-five?" Rick asked.

"I can only go to fifty," replied Ted.

As Rick was finishing his drink, he was feeling the effect of the alcohol, or so he thought. "I am feeling a little lightheaded; I am going to go to my room."

"Sure. I'll take care of the check. Charlotte, can you help Rick get to his room?" Ted asked. "I'll see you all in the morning."

"Let's get you to your room," Charlotte put her arm around Rick's and walked him out of the restaurant.

The hotel was right next door, so Charlotte walked with Rick across the lobby and into the elevator bank. "What room are you in, Rick?"

"Room 310, on the third floor."

In the elevator Rick was getting a little bit frisky with Charlotte. She was curious whether it was the Valium or the Viagra working; perhaps it was both. But she knew something was going on. They got to room 310, and Rick pulled out his key card. As they made it through the door, his hands were all over Charlotte's body. She knew this was going her way. She led him to the bed, and as he sat down, he went for the back of her dress. His fingers were unzipping her before she could get to her purse. Her dress fell down to her ankles, and Rick commented, "I wanted you the minute I saw you in the office."

Charlotte was just standing there in her bra and panties, and Rick was the aggressor. But then she pushed him onto the bed and started to remove his clothes. He did not object and was rather quiet for a minute. After she took his pants off, she could see that Rick had a stiffy from the Viagra and her mix of the two drugs had worked. He was both docile and hard as a rock. She would not need the extra toys that were in her purse, but the Sabre stun gun was placed on the nightstand just in case. She took off her remaining clothes and placed a mask on her face, then mounted Rick. She pulled out her cell phone and took a couple of pictures with the mask on. This way her identity would be hidden and she would have plenty of ammunition against Rick. The cell phone was placed back in her purse, and the mask was removed.

She whispered into his ear, "The deal is fifty, right?"

"Ted said it's fifty-five."

"But you will do it for fifty, right?" Charlotte asked once again. But this time she squeezed him by the balls. She played pogo stick with his hard-as-a-rock penis.

"The deal is fifty, right?" she asked once again.

"OK. Fifty it is," Rick replied.

Charlotte rode him hard for a few more minutes and enjoyed every minute. Then it was time to get off and get out of there. As she left, Rick was recovering from the Valium and starting to come around.

"Don't forget we have a deal at fifty, right?" Charlotte asked. "I'll send you the pictures after you sign."

Charlotte gathered her clothes, got dressed, and exited the hotel. She knew that Ted would have to give her a bonus on this one. Shaving off $5 million on the deal had to be worth something. She was determined to get it. *Or Ted will be making a reservation at the local cemetery.* Just a passing thought. One she couldn't share with Ted.

Chapter 28

The final testing of the Butler Energy Corporation database was going to be completed on Friday away from the client site. James needed to poke around the system using the credentials from Blue Point Hosting that Bill had provided. A working script document would be prepared and tested that could be distributed to all users once they got started. This would be a coordination effort with the Blue Point Hosting team and Bill and James as the Butler team. Since the user base was only a handful of employees, this would be easy to manage. The system required an administrator or super user, and this was going to be Bill Hogan and James Crowley for now. Eventually this identity would be taken on by someone in the Butler team, but no one was available at this point.

James was in the casita early on Friday, and poking around the database was a breeze. There were one hundred customers loaded, and they looked OK. But there were four customer names that caught James's interest: Argonaut Corporation, Anco Corporation, Challenger Corporation, and Falcon Corporation, all of whom had the same billing address. *Could this be just a coincidence or possible duplication?* James thought. Either way he would ask the Butler team to review on Monday.

There were five hundred vendors loaded, and they looked OK. Again, there were four vendor names that had the same billing address: Argo Enterprise, Aspen Enterprise, Eagle Enterprise, and Monitor Enterprise. This would be placed on the list for the Butler team to review and possibly scrub once again.

The customer terms list and the vendor terms list looked OK for now. More values would be added to the table as the customers and vendors requested different terms and conditions. The general ledger accounts also seemed OK at first glance. Since the controller Paul Meadows had asked that they add the standard accounts, this would expand and explode as the accountants got into the system. But for now, the numbers appeared reasonable.

James would send an email to Ted MacDonald with the skinny list of users to confirm access and security for the Butler team members. This list would include the following: Tim Murphy as the CFO, Ted MacDonald as the vice president of information technology, Charlotte Webb as the executive secretary, Paul Meadows as the controller, Shirley Moore as the accounting manager, Nina Charles as the accounts receivable manager, Karen Rodgers as the accounts receivable analyst, Mary Thomas as the accounts payable manager, Barron Roberts as the president of Barron Trucking, and Jean Roberts the controller of Barron Trucking. A total of ten initial users needed a Blue Point Hosting account and an Enterprise Software Corporation user account. Then there would be a follow-up call to Bill Hogan to inform him that he was going to be the point of contact for Blue Point Hosting and James would handle all Enterprise Software Corporation accounts. This way there would be a division of labor on setups and a double check for security purposes. This decision would be relayed to Ted MacDonald when he was on site next week.

The cell phone rang, and Bill Hogan was on the other end.

"Hey, James. I got all the Blue Point Hosting loose ends tied down. The database is now secure for us to demo to the Butler team," said Bill.

"That's great, Bill. Right on schedule," replied James.

"How did you make out with the company configurations?"

"All done, including a preload of customers and vendors from the Barron Water Hauling Corporation."

"So we are ready for the Butler team on Monday?"

"We are right on the accelerated schedule," said James. "There are some data issues, and I'll need to bring that up with the team on Monday."

"What kind of data issues?"

"Looks like there are four customers and four vendors with the same billing address."

"Sounds like bad data."

"I'll have the team look at it next week. For now, it's done, and I am not making any more uploads."

"Sounds good."

"Hey, Bill, can you be the administrator for Blue Point Hosting accounts? And I will be the administrator for Enterprise Software Corporation accounts?"

"Sure, but we need to turn this over to a Butler team member ASAP."

"But who? We can have this discussion with Ted MacDonald on Monday."

"OK, I have a few more things to do today, so talk with you later."

"Thanks, Bill. See you in Coraopolis on Monday, in case I don't talk with you later today," said James as the call ended.

* * *

The paperwork for the Cook Salt Water Removal Corporation acquisition showed up in Ted MacDonald's email early Friday morning. Rick Cook had signed the deal and agreed to be bought for $50 million, which was the price Ted MacDonald had on the table last night. Ted wondered what had happened to Rick. Did he come to his senses, or was he just playing hardball? Either way, the deal was done and he could move on.

Charlotte walked into Ted's office early and dropped off a cup of coffee on his desk.

"I thought you might be needing this today," said Charlotte.

"Thanks, Charlotte. Guess what I got in my email?" Ted said.

"What are you talking about?"

"Rick Cook signed for the $50 million purchase price. I just got the email confirmation and the acquisition paperwork signed by him."

"That's great. You owe me a big bonus."

"What?"

"I convinced Rick last night it was in his best interests to take the $50 million. I also told him that you were going to walk away unless he took the number," explained Charlotte.

"How did you convince him to take $5 million less?"

"You don't want to know. What you do need to know is that I saved the company $5 million, and I would like a big bonus for my efforts."

"I'll talk with Tim to see what we can do."

"You're very welcome. Once in a while, you need to take one for the team."

"Thanks again, Charlotte," Ted said as she walked out of the office.

* * *

James decided to call Ted and do a check-in with him. Ted picked up his cell right away.

"Hey, James, give me some good news. I am on a roll today," said Ted.

"I just wanted to let you know we are on schedule for the demo on Monday in the Coraopolis office," said James.

"That is good news, and I am happy you are letting me know."

"Is that list of users OK? I did not get an approval from you on the ten accounts in my earlier email."

"I thought I responded to you on that already," said Ted. "But yes, I approved the ten people on the list."

"Thanks. I'll make sure their credentials are good for Monday," replied James. "Can I ask one favor? Can we start the demo on Tuesday? I would like to go through the template of two hundred pages of decisions that were made with the team on Monday."

"Sure, we can use Monday for the database review and then hit it hard on Tuesday."

"That is the plan."

"That sounds like a perfect plan, James."

"I told you the team of Bill and James would make it happen."

"You two are doing a fantastic job. Keep it up, and see you on Monday at eight a.m. sharp," said Ted.

"Thanks." The cell phone went dead.

Bill knew he had earned his money this week. He was ready to do a demo on the system after just a few weeks of work—this was the fastest turn-on in his history as a consultant working with the software.

Chapter 29

It was Friday afternoon, and the work week was almost over. Charlotte was anticipating her date with George Wilson on Saturday. This was compliments of Nina Charles. She had agreed to be fixed up because there was never a good man around when you wanted to go out. Nina had seen George around the office building and could not understand why a single guy like him had never run into Charlotte. She fixed Charlotte up with George but got her permission before the date was put together. George was an architect and had an office in the building next door to the Butler Energy Corporation offices. Nina was going to get these two together and play matchmaker once again as she always enjoyed the blossoming of an office romance.

* * *

"Hey, is your date on with George for Saturday," Nina said to Charlotte in the break room.

"Yes, the date is set for Saturday just like you suggested," replied Charlotte.

"Have fun with George. He is a great guy, from what I have heard of him."

"We are having dinner at his house. He claims to be a good cook and will be preparing an Italian dish for dinner."

"Dinner at his house? That seems to be a bit forward for a first date."

"Yes, I know. But he promised me a home-cooked meal instead of a restaurant-served dinner," said Charlotte. "I will see how his cooking skills are, and if they are not up to par, I will bail on him and leave."

"I did check this guy out; he seems to be a really nice guy," said Nina.

"Well, I reserve judgment on any new date that wants to impress me with a home-cooked meal."

"OK, Charlotte, I have to get going. Have fun on Saturday."

"I will try to do just that," Charlotte replied as she left the break room.

* * *

It was Saturday night, and Charlotte did not know what to wear. This was going to be a date at George Wilson's house, and she was not sure how attractive she wanted to appear. If she wore the blue dress, no cleavage would be exposed. If she wore the red dress, her signature, lots of cleavage would be presented. She settled on the purple dress that showed off her figure nicely but with only a hint of cleavage.

* * *

She drove over to George's house right at 7:00 p.m. The house was located on the outskirts of downtown Coraopolis on Old Tanner Road. Charlotte was saying to herself, *This dinner better be a good one, or this guy is toast.* She was not familiar with driving to see the guy. She was accustomed to having the guy pick her up and drop her off. But if the date went poorly, she could just make up an excuse that she had a headache and leave.

She parked her car in the driveway and went up to ring the doorbell. George answered the door with an apron on and immediately apologized.

"Sorry, the dinner is not ready. But please come in. Just give me a couple of minutes."

"Were you trying to have the dinner ready at seven?" Charlotte asked.

"Yes, I am preparing chicken marsala and pasta. I hope you will like it."

"That is one of my favorite dishes, George. How did you know?"

"I kind of asked Nina about what would be appropriate for a first date, and she said anything Italian," said George. "So I took a shot, and since I like chicken marsala, I rolled the dice."

"You did good. Can I help with anything?"

"Yes, you can open the wine," replied George. "A bottle of Malbec is in the fridge being chilled."

"I can open it and pour us some refreshment."

"Please help yourself; the glasses are on the counter."

The date was progressing nicely, and George was a perfect gentleman. The chicken marsala was done to perfection. They each took turns talking about their jobs and their family and then some sports. All the conversation was light and airy and not too deep into their backgrounds. A second glass of Malbec was poured during the dinner. Since the glasses were so large, only one glass was filled.

"This one is empty. Do you have another bottle?" Charlotte asked.

"Yes, it's in the fridge. I put three bottles in there just in case."

"I'll get the second bottle." Charlotte proceeded to the kitchen.

That was his opportunity to spike her wine glass. He pulled out a roofie capsule and opened it into her wine glass. The glass was swirled around to dissolve the drug so that she would not notice the white powder in the red wine. It was a bit of a gamble to try this on the first date. George had done this so many times in college, and he never got caught. He knew that in about thirty minutes, he would have about three hours to do what he wanted to her, and she would not even know what hit her.

Charlotte came back from the kitchen with a second bottle of Malbec wine and started to open the bottle. She was having trouble opening the foil on the bottle, and George offered to open it.

"Let me get the foil cutter from the kitchen," George said as he walked out of the room.

This was Charlotte's opportunity to spike George's wine glass. She had read before the roofie drug was a date-rape drug and seven to ten times more powerful than the Valium capsules she had been using on the vendors to get her 7 percent deals. This was her chance to experiment on George and possibly add a new method to her arsenal.

George opened the wine and did a generous pour into the large wine goblets to top off both glasses. The spiked wine was emptied by both George and Charlotte, and then the table was cleared of the dishes. George started to wash the dishes, and Charlotte helped to rinse and dry. Once the dishes were done, they sat down on the couch.

"More wine, George?" asked Charlotte.

"Well, sure."

George poured two more full glasses of wine, which emptied the second bottle of Malbec. It had been about thirty minutes since they had both drunk the drug-laced wine. They were both starting to feel the effects of the drugs running through their bloodstream. They both said that the wine was pretty strong.

"I am feeling really tired all of a sudden," said George.

"I am feeling a bit tired as well," said Charlotte.

They both feel asleep on the couch with their clothes on, sitting next to each other.

* * *

About three hours later, they both woke up still on the couch. Charlotte was wearing something on her wrists. She recognized what it was. George was wearing something on his ankles. He recognized what it was. They both seemed to remember placing the cuffs on each other but didn't really remember the details.

"What happened?" Charlotte asked.

"I was about to ask you the same question," replied George.

"Were you trying to take advantage of me?"

"Were you trying to take advantage of *me*?"

"We seem to have tried to take advantage of each other tonight."

They both took off the cuffs from the wrists and ankles and exchanged them.

"I think we both had too much wine to drink tonight," said George.

"Let's just call it a night and forget about what just happened."

"Agreed, let's just call it an evening."

Charlotte got up from the couch and walked toward the door.

"Are you OK to drive?" George asked.

"Yep, I am fine. Thanks for the interesting evening." With that, Charlotte left the house.

As she drove home, she thought about what went on at George's house. *He tried to get me, and I tried to get him. We crisscrossed each other and negated the effects of the drug. Did he use the same stuff I used?* George did not tell her this, and she was not going to ask. She now had several powerful ways to seduce and subjugate a man: Valium, Sabre Stun Gun, and roofie capsules were now all part of her bag of tricks.

Chapter 30

James arrived at the offices of Butler Energy Corporation early on Monday. The flight in on Sunday afternoon from San Diego was just a milk run and nothing exciting happened. He had a number of setup items to check before the team was present. The main conference room would be his base again, and he just helped himself to the facility.

A few minutes after James arrived, Charlotte walked in on him.

"I brought you a carafe of coffee, and the fruit and donuts will be here shortly," she said.

"You did not have to do that Charlotte," James commented but was thankful for the offering.

"Ted said to reserve the conference room for you and Bill the whole week and to provide snacks and beverages."

"The team will appreciate the sugar buzz, and I can use the food as a bribe to keep their attention on the tasks at hand."

"I'll plan to bring in a tray of sweets and several carafes of coffee during the day. There will be cookies in the afternoon, around two p.m., if that's OK?"

"You're wonderful, Charlotte. I am very much appreciative of your offering of food, coffee, and now sweets."

Charlotte began to rearrange the cords on the conference room table, and that's when James noticed something: her wrists had red marks around both of them, as if she had been tied up. He was going to say something to Charlotte but left it alone. *This is none of your business. Just shut up.*

Just then Bill strolled into the conference room, and James was now distracted from looking at Charlotte's wrists. He could see that Bill was goggle-eyed at Charlotte and knew this was trouble. Charlotte was wearing a see-through cream-colored blouse that accentuated her beautiful breasts and a light-blue bra that made her look so pretty. A leather skirt showed off her fabulous legs. It was going to be a handful to keep Bill's mind on the job and not on the executive secretary today.

"Play nice this week," Charlotte said as she left the conference room.

"I would like to play nice with that one," said Bill.

"You're a horny shit. Can you keep it in your pants this week, or am I going to have to move this demo to an off-site location?"

"No, I am good. She is just such a beautiful woman, and I still can't understand why she doesn't have a boyfriend or a husband."

"Let's get started this morning. The Butler team will be here in a few minutes."

James started to go through the agenda with Bill at the five-thousand-foot level. The order-to-cash cycle would be done first. The purchase-to-pay cycle would be done second. The general ledger cycle would be third. The inventory cycle would be ignored for now unless someone asked about it. The manufacturing cycle would be ignored as well.

"Does this sound like a good approach?" James asked Bill.

"You really know how to do demos," replied Bill.

"Damn straight. I have been doing this for twenty years, shithead. You know this is my strength."

"I know. You stay functional, and I stay technical."

"You need to remember that when the questions are flying around this week and the team starts to gang up on us, I'll do the answering, and if I look to you, then you can answer the question. Sound like a plan?" James said with a stern look on his face.

"Yeah, I know," replied Bill.

"You do remember the furniture gig we had in 2008?" James asked. "I cleaned up a lot of the crap you left on the table with that client, and then you took off."

"Yes, I remember. I will not do that again."

"I am counting on you this time."

A few minutes later, the Butler team started to stroll into the conference room, right on time at 8:00 a.m. There was only a handful of team members: Ted MacDonald, Paul Meadows, Shirley Moore, Nina Charles, and Mary Thomas. This was the core group that Ted said were the intended recipients for now. They seemed eager to see what the demo was all about since none of the employees had any experience with the Enterprise Software.

There was some uncertainty about how the week was going to proceed, so the schedule was discussed first. Meetings would be held from Monday through Friday from 8:00 a.m. to 10:00 a.m. and then reconvene from 1:00 p.m. to 3:00 p.m. This was a preset schedule that James and Ted had worked out in advance. It would give the members a chance to work their day job outside of the planned meeting times. The exposure to the new system would make them think about how they are using the current system and encourage them to ask questions about improvements to the future business process.

"Before we begin, I would like to ask Ted to make some opening comments for the week," said James.

Ted stood up in front of the group in the conference room and made a few remarks. "James and Bill have configured the system for the future business process of the company. It is now your responsibility to review and ask questions before we put the final configurations in place. That is what this week is all about. So ask questions this week. This is a learning curve for all of us."

"Thanks, Ted. I would like to demo three processes this morning: the order-to-cash cycle, the purchase-to-pay cycle, and the general journal cycle. You can ask questions on each, but let's try to get through them one at a time before you interrupt. I want to give you a flavor of how this software treats the entire cycle, and then we can go through the positives and the negatives. Are we all OK with the format?" James asked.

"So what if we have questions?" Controller Paul Meadows asked.

"By all means ask the consultants the question," replied Ted.

"Agreed. Bill and I will do our best to answer the question," replied James. "OK. Are we ready to get started?"

There was no response. It was as if the crickets could be heard chirping outside.

James started the presentation on the overhead projector. The order-to-cash cycle was put through the paces. A sales order was processed, a shipment was done, the invoice was prepared, the cash remittance was applied, and then a few reports were reviewed. Bill was careful to talk about four personnel that were needed to process the transaction through the entire cycle from start to finish: an order person, a shipping person, an invoice person, and a cash application person. A lengthy discussion started just after finishing the transaction. The whole team commented that they didn't have four people to do all that processing. Bill knew that this was going to be a major hurdle to resolve.

"Let's put this one on the issues list," said Bill. "This will be a project list item that we need to address before we turn the system on and do any of the conversions."

The subject of segregation of duties was the real issue here, and James knew he hit a home run. He could see that Ted was nodding his head that the discussion was right to the point.

"Can we put this on the issues list and move on for now?" said Ted once again.

"Sure can," replied James.

The team continued to pepper James and Bill with more and more questions on the first business process. The entire two hours was filled up with the demo and the follow-up questions. The ten o'clock hour came, and Bill announced that they were done until 1:00 p.m.

"We are adjourned for now until the afternoon session," said James. "I'll stick around to answer any questions, but you are all free to get out of here and get some real work done."

"Let's take a break for now. See you all at one p.m. for a review of the next business process," said Ted as he dismissed the Butler team.

Ted stayed behind with Bill and James to ask some follow-up questions.

"So do we really have an issue here with personnel?" Ted asked Bill.

"Well, you kind of do," replied James. "Your staff is thin, exposed, and really can't cover the security risk here. You should have four people completing the cycle for the order to cash with adequate security protocols in place. If you don't, you could have a collusion issue or a break in the segregation of duties."

"You know, I did not tell you this, but we need to be SOX compliant," said Ted.

"You were saving that morsel for later?" James asked.

"We will need to address this issue."

"Your auditors will put this item on the SUD list."

"SUD?"

"Significant Unexplained Discrepancies is usually what the auditors call it," replied James.

"Shit, that's a bad thing?"

"Yep. You're in crap if you get that one from the auditors."

"Let's highlight it on the issues list for now, and we will address it later."

"I will label it a high-priority item for now," James said as he circled it on the whiteboard.

At this point Ted left the room and Bill and James were by themselves to work on loose ends and emails. Bill knew that in any project like this, where the team members were not used to an integrated system, a review and home for all of the touchpoints needed to be addressed. Both Bill and James could remember when in a prior project there were not enough personnel, which resulted in a collusion issue. They were both worried that this could happen once again and someone would pay the price for poor controls. A strong recommendation would be made to Ted to manage this risk and document the decision taken by this team. This was a just-in-case and a "cover-your-ass" (CYA) approach for the consultants.

The consultants made it to the lunch hour with no one asking any more questions about the first process reviewed with the team.

"Hey, Bill, do you want to go get some lunch?" James asked.

"Let's go to the bagel shop down the street. They make a great sandwich, and it's quick so we can get back by one," replied Bill.

"Then let's get out of here."

Chapter 31

James and Bill were back on the project in the conference room at the Butler office and ready to tackle the next process after lunch. The original gang of Ted, Paul, Shirley, Nina, and Mary arrived right at 1:00 p.m.

"Thanks to all for showing up. I guess I did not scare anyone away. That's a good thing," James announced to the group. "Are there any outstanding questions from this morning, or can we move on to the next process?"

No responses were received from the group, so James moved on to the next process. He was thinking that they had either not paid attention or were too stuffed from lunch to digest the morning's results.

"If you have questions, please speak up," said Ted. "This is going to be your system. The consultants will not always be here to hold our hands." The group was shocked by that statement from Ted.

James started the presentation for the purchase-to-pay process. A purchase order was prepared, a receipt was received against the same purchase order, an invoice was matched to the transaction, and then a payment was processed to pay the vendor. James again talked about all the team members that would need to be involved to do their part of the transaction. Just after the demo of the transaction was completed, the team erupted in questions.

"We don't have four people to handle the purchasing transaction flow," Paul Meadows blurted out in an obvious comment.

"You need a buyer to prepare the purchase order, you need a receiving person to receive the goods, you need an invoice person to process the invoice match to the vendor, and you need a check to pay the vendor once the transaction is finished," James said.

"We can combine a few of the positions, right?" Ted asked the consultants.

"That is a good point, Ted. You can collapse some of the responsibilities and assign a few of the rights to one or two people on your team," said James. "But you will run into a SOX compliance issue if you are not careful."

"We can get a waiver on some of the SOX compliance issues," said Ted.

"Yes, you can, but you open yourself up to more scrutiny and more reviews that will need to be done if you go down that path."

"Let's put this one on the issues list for now."

"I can do that." James wrote the issue on the whiteboard and added a high-priority notation to it.

The rest of the afternoon was used to go through several different what-if scenarios related to purchasing goods and services for the Butler company. A full two hours was used to hash out the purchasing process, and no other topic was discussed.

"Well, it's almost three p.m., and we need to close this topic for now," said James. "I am sorry we only made it through one more process, but it was extremely important that we had a rigorous discussion on this topic. I did not want to leave any unopened issues and really wanted you all to understand how the system works."

"Let's cut this discussion for now," said Ted. "If there are more questions, let's hold them for the next session, on Tuesday morning."

The group disbanded from the conference room. Ted stayed back until they all left.

"How do you think today went?" he asked.

"I think Bill and I opened your team up to thinking about their new system and they are overwhelmed," said James.

"Is there a risk they will not get it?"

"That's why you hired us, Ted. We will make sure this doesn't happen," replied James. "You entrusted us to make sure we perform a knowledge transfer to your team so they can run the business with the new software."

"Thanks for that assurance, James," replied Ted.

"We have done this before. This is not our first rodeo," Bill chirped in.

"Thanks. You two seem to have everything under control," said Ted. "Let's have dinner tonight after work."

"We can do that. Bill and I will meet you after we finish up here."

"I'll meet you two at the hotel bar at six. We can go back to Frank's in downtown Coraopolis for Italian food," said Ted.

"Sounds good. That restaurant was great," said James.

The rest of the afternoon, Bill and James answered emails and added a few items to the issues list based on the questions that had come out of the first day of demo meetings with the Butler team.

They both knew that Ted had something planned for them tonight and it was going to be a liquid dinner at that. Drinks at the hotel bar. Dinner at Frank's. Drinks back at the hotel bar. The fun would start and end with a Gentleman Jack and Coke. The only sure thing was that James would wind up with the restaurant bill and the boys would have a hangover on Tuesday.

Chapter 32

James and Bill were back at it on Tuesday morning bright and early. They both arrived just before 8:00 a.m. with a hangover. Ted had had his way with them last night. There were drinks at the bar before dinner, then dinner at Frank's, then several nightcaps at the hotel bar compliments of Ted MacDonald. He liked to drink Gentleman Jack and Coke with a slice of lemon and could do it all night long. The boys were not used to a client drinking them under the table but needed to get hardened up because this was going to be a normal occurrence with Ted.

Right on schedule Charlotte walked into the conference room with a carafe of coffee and announced that the fruit plate and do-nuts would be there shortly. She was wearing that red dress once again. Her cleavage was exposed for the whole world to see, and James was sure that Bill would be a problem today.

"What the heck happened to you two?" Charlotte asked. "You both look like shit."

"Ted took us out for drinks and dinner last night," said James. "We went to Frank's."

"That is my favorite place," replied Charlotte. "Ted can drink, and it appears that he again got the best of you two."

"We are both dragging today," said James. "You wouldn't hap-pen to have any aspirin with you, Charlotte?"

"I probably have some in my purse. Let me bring you both a couple." She proceeded to get her purse and hand each of the boys two aspirin.

"This will help. Thanks," said James.

"You're very welcome. You need to watch out for Ted and take it slow next time. I have seen him drink many vendors under the table, if you know what I mean."

As Charlotte was leaving the conference room, she stopped to chat with Nina, who wanted to get filled in on how the date with George Wilson had gone.

"Morning, Charlotte. So how was your date on Saturday?" Nina asked.

Charlotte motioned to Nina to come over to the corner of the conference room so no one could hear them talking.

"Well, it was an interesting evening," said Charlotte.

"Fill me in on all the details."

"I thought you said George was a good guy?"

"What happened?"

"He tried to take advantage of me after dinner." That's all Charlotte wanted to tell Nina. She did not want to let it slip that she was trying to take advantage of George as well.

"He did what?" Nina raised her voice.

"Yep. We fell asleep on the couch, and I knew something was wrong."

"You should have called the police." Again, Nina raised her voice.

"I yelled at him, and we just called it an evening. I will not be going back there for a second date."

"I am so sorry to have set you up with him."

"You could not have known, Nina. Don't worry about it. Nothing happened."

"The next time I see him, I am going to give him a piece of my mind."

"Please just leave it alone. He will get what is coming to him one day," said Charlotte. She was thinking that now Nina would be an ally of hers and maybe cover for her in the future if she was needed.

The Butler team arrived right at the eight o'clock hour, and two new members showed up: Barron Roberts and Jean Roberts from the Barron Water Hauling Company.

"We are going to review the journal entry cycle this morning. Are there any questions from yesterday?" James asked.

Several of the team members were not with it this morning, and no questions or comments were asked. James proceeded to the next part of the presentation.

"You start with a group header, then you pick the period that defaults, then you add a line item. The account number is selected, and then you add an amount to the entry. That's it. This is a simple process to complete."

The presentation only took fifteen minutes, and then there erupted a series of questions from the team. The group asked about repeating entries, standard entries, reversing entries, template entries, and CSV entries. James had advised the group that the software was capable of all of them and he could demonstrate them if they provided some examples. A list would be prepared and set up for the afternoon session.

After an hour of good discussion, James wanted to go over the configuration document with the team. This was the next item in the project plan and consisted of about two hundred pages of setups and decisions that were made; a review needed to be confirmed by the Butler team. Some suggestions by the team were made, and the changes were carefully documented so that they could be reflected in the database after the meeting. This took them to the ten o'clock hour, and the group was then disbanded.

"See you all at the one p.m. session," said James.

As the group left the conference room, Ted walked over to James and Bill to have a little chat with them.

"How are you feeling, boys?" he asked.

"To be honest with you, Ted, like shit," said James.

"Me too," said Bill.

"You two need to harden up a little bit. I seem to have drunk you under the table," said Ted.

"You did indeed," said James.

"You both demonstrated that you can take it and show up the next day to do your job. So I give you credit for that," said Ted. "Nice job today."

"Thanks. We are going to have to keep an eye on you, Ted," said James.

"We are going to get along just fine, *boys*," said Ted.

The rest of the morning was spent on emails and cleanup. The team had provided a list of journal entries they wanted to see in the demo for this afternoon. James had to prepare some setups to be ready for the finance team's request, which took the balance of the morning to finish.

"Hey, Bill, you want to go and get some lunch?" James asked.

"What I want is for this hangover to stop," replied Bill.

"Let's go get lunch, and you will feel better."

"Sounds good. Can you drive this time?"

"Sure."

The consultants left the building for a much-needed lunch and a break from the Butler environment. The morning had been a struggle to get through, and they both agreed no drinking on Tuesday evening. If Ted wanted to go out, he would go out alone.

Chapter 33

The afternoon session on Tuesday was a bit of a mixed bag of items. The agenda had journal entry scenarios, GL controls, posting rules, MICR check processing, and a vendor/supplier review scheduled. All the participants from this morning's session were there in the afternoon as well.

James started the meeting by asking a question of the team assembled in the conference room. "How has the presentation been so far?"

He looked for a show of hands to tell him if he was on track. All the members raised their hands in unison.

"OK, based on a show of hands, we are good to go," said James. "You all asked about journal entry scenarios, so let's take care of this one next."

James went on to demo the journal entry process using standard entries, recurring entries, template entries, and CSV entries. These sample items were given to him earlier for review by the team and were set up in the database late in the morning.

"As you can see, the Enterprise Software package can handle all the types of journal entries that you asked about. Did I hit all of the requested types?" James asked the team. No one said a word.

"OK, let's move on, then," said Ted.

"We can do that," replied James.

"The next topic is GL controls. These are methods to control the transactions. You can have upward of five-hundred-plus different types. You need at least four to run the system. You assign general ledger accounts to these controls, and then the transactions will display the result in your general ledger account. I will prepare a list of these, and each of you will have some input on how best to use them. A typical control for, let's say, the accounts receivable account would be the AR control. This will debit the receivable account by customer and credit the sales account for the other side of the transaction. We will need to set aside a full two hours for this topic later in the week," said James. "Can we do this on Thursday, and then we can decide who needs to be there?"

"Pencil it into the schedule, James," said Ted. "I want the team to invite anyone who needs to review this topic. This also includes anyone who may have input on the topic. Let James know by end of day on Wednesday who will attend."

"Thanks, Ted," replied James.

"Can we talk about the check process?" Mary Thomas asked.

"That was my next topic," said James. "The Butler company has two choices here. You can use preprinted checks with the check number and the MICR already printed on the stock form. You can also use the plain paper with the check number and MICR controls built into the font through a report style. There are advantages and disadvantages to both."

"We prefer the preprinted check stock with the check numbers and MICR already on the special paper," said Mary.

"As long as you order this check stock from Enterprise Software Corporation's business partner, they guarantee the form to work with no issues," said James. "If we use blank paper and need to program the report style and mess with the MICR printing, I will need to add three months to the project plan."

"We don't have that kind of time," said Ted. "Mary, can we go with the preprinted stock for now?"

"Yes, we can use preprinted stock for now," replied Mary.

"There is a lead time on this item. So can I make a suggestion?" James asked.

"What is that?" Mary said.

"We need to order the check stock this week so we can do some testing with the live forms. Mary, can you and I have a separate meeting on this sometime this week?"

"Sure. How about Friday morning?"

"Yes. I'll get the specifications sheet from the business partner so we can prepare an order for Friday," said James.

"We are almost out of time this morning," said Ted. "Is there anything we need to cover, or can we break loose?"

There were no objections by the team, and the group left the conference room.

"Don't forget we have a one p.m. session for later today. See you all then," James shouted to the group.

* * *

Frank Browning showed up unannounced at Charlotte's desk around 10:45 a.m. Tuesday morning.

"Hi, gorgeous. Is Ted MacDonald around?' Frank asked.

"Good morning to you, Frank. What's up?"

"I was in the neighborhood and wanted to know if Ted needed anything from the Enterprise Software Corporation. I was also curious about how the implementation was going," said Frank.

"Ted will be out of a meeting in a couple of minutes. Do you feel like waiting?" Charlotte asked.

"Sure. You're wearing that same red dress when we first met," said Frank.

"A girl only has so many dresses to wear, and I do like the color red."

"Did you get my check in the mail?"

"Yes, I did. Thanks."

"Can I ask the same question as before?"

"What question was that?" Charlotte turned and looked him in the eye.

"Do I get a return trip?"

"Is there another seven points on new business?" Charlotte asked and returned the glance. "I told you before this was a negotiable item."

"I am working on Ted to buy more licenses, and that will create more business. Can you assist me?"

"Well, I guess we can have some fun tonight. Are you staying at the Palmer Hotel again?"

"Yes, I am. The same room as last time."

"I'll see you in the lobby at six thirty. Is Frank's restaurant OK for a seven o'clock supper?" Charlotte asked. "I can make a reservation."

"Thanks. That would be wonderful."

"Let me go get Ted from his meeting."

* * *

The afternoon session on Tuesday was going to be an open forum for questions and answers. The group had reassembled in the conference room with the same core team of Butler employees from this morning.

"I have one more topic I need to discuss with you, but before I do that, I would like to open the floor up for questions," said James.

"We have a couple of questions related to the financial reporting and what is available in the current package," Paul Meadows said.

"I had this on the agenda for Wednesday, but if you would like to talk about it now, let's do it," said James. "You have the standard reporting in the package. You can also buy a third-party bolt-on product that is an Excel version on steroids. There is a third choice, too, a complicated SQL package that requires programming and coding."

"What comes with the package with no additional costs?" Paul asked.

"The standard package can be used to generate financial statements, and if you're reporting is not too complicated, it could work for you nicely," said James.

"Can we see an example of the standard financial reports?" Paul asked.

"This is on the Wednesday schedule for discussion. I will need some parameters from you and anyone else who has input on this item," said James. "Then I can set up a sample report."

"We can give you those details," replied Paul.

"Thanks, Paul. Can we get together later, and you can give me some information on this?" said James.

"I'll give you a sample of a report later in the day," replied Paul.

"The only other thing I have for this afternoon is to discuss some vendors and customers that seem to have the same billing addresses in the Barron Water Hauling company data. I just need someone to review these four customers and vendors to determine if they need to be converted," said James.

"I can do that," said Jean Roberts. *Oh shit. Did this consultant find those items?* she thought to herself.

"OK, if there is nothing else, then I will leave the remainder of the session open to questions," said James. "Ted, do you have anything else to review?"

"No, I don't. An open session for the remaining afternoon would be fine," said Ted. "Let's break for now and get some real work done. You two are doing a great job. Thanks to everyone for attending today."

The group broke up early. All the participants were in a hurry to get to their day job. The rest of the afternoon was quiet, and both Bill and James were left alone to get some work done. No one came back to the conference room during the afternoon, which they thought was strange. *Is the team not engaged, or are they overworked?* James was having those thoughts once again.

* * *

Charlotte met Frank at the Palmer Hotel, and they drove over to Frank's for dinner. A wonderful dinner was had at the restaurant, and there was no real conversation, only chitchat. Frank drove back to the hotel with Charlotte. She was trying to anticipate what Frank's next moves were going to be.

"Are we having a nightcap?" Frank asked. "My place?"

"Sure. I thought you would never ask," replied Charlotte.

As they entered Frank's hotel room, Charlotte noticed a bottle of Chianti chilling in the beverage container.

"That is my favorite," said Charlotte.

"I remembered it from the last time we had dinner," said Frank.

"So what are we doing tonight for the return trip?"

"I kind of liked what you did to me last time."

"I can do a repeat performance. The same way or something different?"

"Just like before."

Two glasses of Chianti were poured from the chilled bottle. They toasted to each other and clinked glasses. Charlotte unzipped her red dress and let it fall to her ankles. She helped Frank out of his clothes and then straddled him on the bed. She grabbed her purse and pulled out the toys. Frank just lay on the bed and watched as Charlotte started to cuff his wrists. The Scarlet Couture Bond to Surrender Cuffs were placed on his left and then right wrist. The fun chains were pulled out next. Each bedpost was wrapped with one, and they were laid at a forty-five-degree angle. A lock was used to attach the fun chains to the wrists. The Scarlet

Couture Spreader Bar was attached to his ankles. The fun chains were connected with a lock to the ankles.

Now that Frank was fully restrained, Charlotte removed her bra and panties. It was time to mount and ride Frank once again. She had had her way with him once before, but this time felt different.

"Hey, you forgot the chocolate syrup and whipped cream," said Frank.

"Yes, I forgot," replied Charlotte. "How can I make it up to you?"

"Open the drawer of the nightstand."

"You remembered." Charlotte grabbed the bottle of chocolate syrup and squeezed it onto her breasts. The whipped cream was sprayed on top of the syrup. She pressed her breasts into his mouth so Frank could lick the sweetness off of her.

"Charlotte, you're amazing." The blond beauty with an hourglass figure was on top of him for the second time. How lucky could one guy get?

"Just make sure I get the seven points on the next deal," replied Charlotte.

"You will. You just need to get Ted to buy more licenses."

"I can take care of that."

As Charlotte finished riding Frank, she took off the toys and released him from the bound position.

"Thanks, Charlotte, for a memorable evening." Frank started to put his clothes back on.

"You're welcome, Frank. It was fun as always." Charlotte did the same and left the hotel room.

Chapter 34

The morning meeting was going to be jam-packed with a review of the financial report's functionality. Paul Meadows the controller had provided a few sample reports to James the day before. He was sure that the full two hours on Wednesday would be filled with questions and multiple threads of related issues. James was ready for this day. He even relished the battle with the finance team. After all, he had been a CPA before getting into the information technology business. He had learned from his past dealings with accountants and IT guys that neither one could cross professions. The accountants could not translate the business requirements to the IT guys, and the IT guys could not understand what the accountants really needed. This was an opportunity to reinvent himself and create a sought-after consultancy that produced an exceptionally good living.

James did the ceremonial routine and asked the question to the Butler team that was assembled in the conference room for day three.

"Are there any questions from the prior two days? No questions this morning? I guess we are on track to move to the next topic."

"Were you able to use those samples I provided yesterday?" Paul asked.

"Yes, I have built three skeleton reports in the database for our review this morning," said James. "They will not be exactly the way you need them due to a lack of financial transactions in the system."

"Will they provide us a model to evaluate?"

"They should provide you with enough to make a decision as to whether this will fit your requirements or not. Let's get started."

James went through a balance sheet, an income statement, and a simple general ledger report. All three reports required creating a report style and then adding a row set and a column set to each of the samples. The reports were displayed on the screen for all of the team members to review. There were numerous questions on how to create them and who would be doing this for the Butler company.

"I have compiled reports for prior clients with the requirements provided. I can then produce the reports for you or train someone to do this. The financial statement generator process is what is used to produce static reports in the database. It is your call on how to proceed with this item. I just want you all to know that I am a CPA by trade and can do this for you. Keep in mind that the initial outlay of time is an investment, and it can take a few hours to create, test, and finalize each report. Again, it's your call."

"Let me think about it for a few days. We really do not have the resources to dedicate to that function right now," said Paul.

"I can assist you as long as I have time. It would be subject to my boss—uh, Ted—approving," replied James.

"I am sure we can work something out," said Ted. "James, can you put it on the issues list for now?"

"I sure can," replied James. "This is a normal evolution of any business that needs financial data to report on the performance of the business. Initially the consultant provides the service, then it transitions to a subject matter expert, and then an accounting in-house employee takes over the maintenance of the reporting."

"Thanks for the explanation," said Ted.

The full two hours was used to demo the system's capability related to the standard financial reporting package. No other topics were covered.

"Our time is up, so you are all free to go," said James. "Any comments or concerns?"

"I think we are good," said Ted.

"See all your smiling faces back here at one p.m.," James announced as the meeting broke up.

Ted stayed back with Bill and James after the team left.

"Do we have any issues with the financial statement reporting?" Ted asked.

"No, there is no issue. It's just a resource and a training task on the project plan," replied James.

"Can you cover this deficiency for now?" Ted asked as he looked directly at James.

"I can't help you two. That's not my cup of tea," said Bill.

"Yes, I can cover that item, Ted. But it could be a lot of hours depending on the finance department's requirements," said James.

"Let's keep this with you for now, until further notice," said Ted.

"I can do that," replied James.

"If this becomes a bigger animal than expected, you will need to let me know," said Ted.

"Trust me, Ted, I'll let you know if the finance team takes advantage of my skills."

"I am counting on that. I have a lot of things you need to help me out with. I have been tasked with growing the IT organization, and you can see we don't have any resources currently."

"You mean the IT team is you, Bill, and me?" James asked.

"For now, that is the plan. A lean IT staff. And of course Blue Point Hosting, but they are a contract situation," said Ted.

"You do realize that this could be more than the forty hours per week you were expecting?" James asked.

"I am OK with that. Until I hire someone, you have a green light to bill in excess of forty per week. Just give me a heads-up so I know."

"I will do that on a routine basis every week," said James. "You are my boss and my client, after all."

"I am going to have Charlotte set up a dinner with the four of us for Thursday evening at seven at a restaurant in downtown Coraopolis. I assume you both can make it?" Ted asked.

"Sure, we can make it. But who is the fourth?" James asked.

"Tim Murphy, the CFO," replied Ted. "He wants an update on how the project is going."

"We can do that. Is there an agenda to follow, or is he after something?" James asked.

"No agenda. He just wants to have a casual dinner with you two to see if his money is being well spent," said Ted.

"We can handle that. Right, Bill?" James asked.

"No problem. We will be there," replied Bill.

"OK. Plan for seven p.m., and I'll let you know where we are going later today," said Ted as he left the conference room.

James knew that this meeting with the CFO was going to be a little bit tricky. The consultants would have to be on their toes to make sure they did not say anything negative in any way. A meeting with the boss's boss was always defensive to start, until you got to know him. You had to be careful about what you said and what you did not say. James knew his contract extension could be riding on this dinner.

Chapter 35

The conference room was filled with the bright and smiling faces of the core team on a Wednesday afternoon. James started the meeting promptly at 1:00 p.m.

"I am glad to see you all back for more fun," he said. "We have a big one on the agenda for today. This topic is GL control accounts for the Butler company."

"What are you talking about?" asked Mary Thomas. "Do I need to be in this meeting today?"

"Well, you all need to know about what they are and how they work," said James. "The GL control accounts regulate how the transactions go into the general ledger. So, Mary, you will need to tell me where you want the AP transactions to go. Nina, you will need to tell me where the AR transactions need to go. Shirley, you will need to tell me where the bank transactions need to go. There are optional controls as well, and we will discuss them as I ask you all a series of questions."

The next two hours was spent with the team going through the complete list of controls and for whom and/or if they needed to be set up. The team was assigned homework, and it would need to be completed before the system was turned on. James requested that the information be returned by next Friday at the latest; the team agreed to the deadline.

There were no other planned topics to go through for the balance of the Wednesday session, so the team was cut loose a little bit early. James thanked the entire team for their active participation and announced that for the rest of the day, the consultants would be available for one-on-one sessions if they were needed. Ted also thanked everyone for attending and said he had to run to another meeting.

After the Butler team left the conference room, James turned to Bill and voiced his concerns.

"The Butler team did not really understand the concept of these control account setups and how powerful they could be for managing the business."

"James, this has happened on each engagement you and I have been on over the past decade," said Bill.

"I know we are going to have to hold their hands on this topic. You and I will need to discuss this with Ted, maybe later in the afternoon."

"Why don't you just give them the ones we need, and we can do the rest?"

"You're right. I will plan to send them the templates with the accounts they need to plug in; that way I know we will be done. If they want to slice and dice the data later, they can add more or differentiate the accounts," said James. "That way we are not waiting on them. Instead, they are waiting on themselves for the different coding."

"You have done this more than me," said Bill.

"I will advise Ted that this is the course of action we are going to take. I'm sure he is not going to care about it and that he will be happy we are thinking in advance about what they need."

"Agreed."

Nina strolled into the conference room a little while later.

"Hey, you got a couple of minutes?" she asked.

"Sure, what's on your mind," replied James.

"I did some digging on those four customers and four vendors with the same billing address information."

"I thought that Jean Roberts was taking that on?" said James.

"She was, but I also looked into the data for those records."

"What did you find?"

"All four customers and all four vendors had a lot of activity this year, and then all of a sudden they were all zeroed out about a week ago. All of them have the exact same billing address."

"Is that a normal transaction process, to bring the balances to zero?"

"It just seems really strange on these accounts."

"Do you still want me to bring them over and activate them in the new system?" James asked.

"Let's wait to see what Jean says about them," said Nina. "I still would like to have them come over in the conversion load file even if they have zero balances, if that is OK with you."

"We can bring them across in the automated load. Converting four customers and four vendors will only take a couple of seconds to perform. No big deal."

"Thanks. Keep them on the list for now," said Nina. "Jean will not be running the business once the Barron company is purchased. I am sure they will find a job for her within the organization, but her responsibility will most likely change."

"What about the GL control account setup for the AR function?" James asked. "Are you OK with just one account for now?"

"Yes. I am good with the one control account," said Nina. "Will the receivables subledger balances agree to the account in the general ledger?"

"The accounts receivable aging report will be the sub ledger to the account balance in the general ledger. The totals of the report will add up to all of the customer balances on the report. This is the design of that control," said James.

"Perfect. My AR balances will tie out to the GL balances because of the controls."

"Right, that is exactly how this works. You seem to be the only Butler team member that gets it. I thought I was talking Greek to the team earlier today."

"You two don't know it, but we are all overworked here," said Nina. "They have us going in so many directions, and we have no staff to get all this stuff done. I am glad you both are here. You can help us out, possibly, by pushing back on the management for more bodies."

"We will do our best to address that during the project," said James.

"Thanks." Nina left the conference room in a hurry.

Trouble in paradise, James thought. Maybe Nina was onto something that needed a more careful review by the Butler team.

Chapter 36

The fourth day of the demo was really a wind-down day for James and Bill. They both knew after this week a whole lot of ideas would be placed into the Butler team's brains about what-if questions. Then the arguments of "the system needed to do this and the system needed to do that" would play out. James knew the pattern, and he would guide the team in the right direction to accomplish the goal of going live. He would need Ted's ear, though, and would beat the drum on what the best practices were and how the Butler company should adopt them. James always made recommendations for the client; sometimes they would take them, and sometimes they would not. He was reasonably successful in getting his way because, after all, this was why the client paid the consultants the money. The experience of making the mistakes before and not making them with the current client was the by-product of the consulting agreement.

The group had assembled in the conference room for the fourth day. All the core members were in attendance, including Barron and Jean Roberts. Charlotte had provided several carafes of coffee just as before. The fruit plate and donuts were always a welcome site and did not last long. Charlotte did her best to drop off the offering of food and silently slip out of the meeting. James could see that Bill had his eyes focused on her as she entered and exited the room. The light blue dress she had on was showing off her 34-28-32 hourglass figure to perfection. He even caught Ted taking a look at her as she was moving around. James did notice that her wrists appeared to be back to their normal color; the redness that she displayed on Monday was gone. What had happened to her was a question for a later date and time.

James opened up the meeting the same way as before.

"Are there any questions from the prior three days?"

Before anyone could answer, Ted stood up and made an announcement. "I just want to tell everyone that we officially have our first and second acquisitions. The Barron Water Hauling Corporation and the Cook Salt Water Removal Corporation will be part of the Butler company starting April first this year. The purchase agreements have been finalized, and we will need to make definitive plans to acquire the assets of both companies. These two divisions will become wholly owned subsidiaries of the Butler Energy Corporation. We will need to convert them onto our new software system."

"Thanks for that bit of breaking news," said James.

The group was shocked at the announcement. This meant that even more work had been placed on this team by the management of the Butler company. One could see it in their eyes. There were no questions raised by the group to James.

"Moving right along," said James. "I have one topic for review this morning. This is on the security menus and how they work. Once we get through this one, the rest of the day will be an open session."

A sample responsibility was set up in the database. A fake user account for Abbey Crowley was activated and associated with the accounts payable menus only. James pretended to sign in using the Abbey Crowley user account and showed the team how the menus were now displayed. This user could only see one of the thirty modules based on this change.

"How did you do that?" Shirley Moore asked. "We will need to segregate the responsibility by role because we will be a SOX-compliant company."

"You set up the roles and then associate those roles to the menu structure," said James. "You will then assign the roles to the users in the system, and then they get to see whatever is assigned to the role. You need to be careful to assign the right role to the right user."

"What do you mean 'the right role to the right user'?" Paul Meadows asked.

"I'll give you an example," said James. "You would give the role of setting up the vendor to one user. You would give the role of processing an invoice to a different user. You would give the role of running a check to another user. In all cases, you would never give two of the roles or three of the roles to the same person."

"I get it," said Paul. "This would be a classic case of collusion, and the user would be able to cover their tracks."

"That is exactly right, Paul," replied James. "Since you will need to have controls in place for the segregation of duties test by your auditors, you want to have strong security measures in place."

"Is this a standard feature in the software we bought?" Ted asked as he looked at James.

"There is functionality to do this in your package," said James. "You have to decide how you want it set up. You can set it up by roles or security groups, or even limit it down to a single business object. It all depends on to what level and how far down the rabbit hole you want to go down."

"Put this item on the issues list," said Ted.

"I can do that," replied James. "I have extensive knowledge on the topic, and I can propose a solution for you. I would just need to ask a couple of questions and get some input from the accounting team before I could put forth a solution."

"If we have a discussion meeting, can you get it done right away?"

"I could get it done next week. It should be set up and tested before we have any training so as not to confuse the user.

"I am glad you mentioned that," Ted said as he turned to James. "Can we start doing training next week?"

"That's a tall order. We have not finished the configurations and the MICR check process.

"But we can start training?"

"We can train on what we have so far and then modify the training as we go. It's not the most ideal of situations, but it can be done."

There was a sense of panic in the eyes of the Butler team that James could see. The shit was just getting piled higher and higher, and there was a genuine rush to get this system turned on.

"Let's talk about this later," said Ted. "Can you put it on the issues list? Then we can move on to the next topic."

"Sure," said James. "Other than that, I have no more topics this morning. Can I cut you all loose?"

"Let's break for now. We need some time to do some planning and a review of the issues list by the IT team."

The group broke up and left the conference room after Ted's comments.

"Hey, can we have a planning session this afternoon?" Ted asked. "Just the three of us?

"Sure. I'll block some time after one p.m.," said James. "Will you be available later today?"

"Afternoon will be fine. We need to have a plan before we chat with Tim tonight at dinner."

"Where is dinner, by the way?"

"Charlotte made a reservation at Peter's Steak House in downtown Coraopolis for seven. It is at the corner of Main Street and Ninth Avenue."

"This dinner is just the four of us?"

"Yep. Just the four of us."

The afternoon session was left open, and none of the Butler team showed up. James and Bill just kept their noses to the grindstone and worked the issues list. They expected Ted to show up for the meeting he requested, but he was a no-show as well. James knew that the dinner tonight with the CFO would be more of an uncertainty since there had been no preparations made. They would be shooting the shit with Tim, and they both had to be careful. Their contract extension with the Butler Energy Corporation could go down in flames if they said something wrong. James had been counting on the prep meeting with Ted this afternoon.

It was nearing the dinner hour, and still there was no sign of Ted. James did not hear that the dinner was off, so he assumed they should meet the two executives at Peter's Steak House as planned.

"Hey, Bill, shall we head over to the restaurant?" James asked.

"Still no sign of Ted. Let's just go. If they don't show up, we will have a nice steak dinner at their expense," replied Bill.

* * *

James and Bill arrived at Peter's in downtown Coraopolis just before seven, and there was no sign of Ted and Tim. Just then James's cell phone buzzed. Ted had texted they were running a few minutes late and asked if they could get a table at the restaurant. James sent him back a text message to confirm that they were already at the restaurant and would be waiting for them.

"Hey, Bill, I just got a text message from Ted," he said. "They will be at the restaurant in a couple of minutes. They are running a little bit late."

Tim and Ted showed up almost thirty minutes late.

"Sorry about that, guys. We were finalizing a deal for some water-hauling trucks, and the meeting went later than expected," said Ted. "We were purchasing ten trucks with the option of ten more when the vendor tried to play hardball with us."

"It's all straightened out now?" James asked.

"The vendor saw it our way," said Tim. "He wanted to get a commission on a lower purchase price rather than a commission on nothing."

Just then the waiter came around to the table. "My name is Fred. Can I get you gentlemen some drinks?" He handed them the menus.

Tim ordered a Gentleman Jack and Coke with a twist of lemon.

"That sounds good," said Ted. "Bring us four. Is that OK with you two?"

James and Bill just nodded their heads in agreement with Ted.

"So I have heard a bunch of nice comments from the team about you two," said Tim. "Ted has also filled me in on the results so far. He also said you're doing the training next week and then the conversions and turn-ons the following week."

James was stunned by the comment. "Well, we have a very aggressive schedule since the two acquisitions will be on the system the first of the next month," replied James. "It's tight but doable if we all pitch in."

"I'll take that to mean there is no slack in the schedule," said Tim.

"That is exactly right," replied James. "We are looking at a lot of hours in the next three weeks."

Just then the waiter brought the drinks. "A Gentleman Jack and Coke with a twist of lemon for all," he said. "Should I give you some time to look at the menu?"

"Give us a few minutes," said Ted.

"I need to know if you are going to pull this off, gentlemen," Tim said as he looked directly at James and Bill.

"We can get it done," said James. "This is what we do best."

"That was the right answer," replied Tim. "I was just trying to see if you two cracked."

"I can assure you, Tim, that we will not crack," said James. "Your team is another matter, though."

"Oh. What do you mean?" Tim asked.

"The Butler team appears to be spread a little bit thin," said James. "They have a lot on their plates, and they seem to be skaters on thin ice."

"They will stretch and not bend," said Ted. "We have pushed them before, and they took it then with flying colors."

"I am going to ask a favor here," said Tim. "You will need to help us evaluate all the core team members as they go through these two businesses we acquire. I want you two to keep a watchful eye on them and alert Ted or myself on how they are progressing."

"We can do that," said James. "Our specialty is matching people to the process using this software. We pride ourselves in crafting value through joint discovery."

"That is an interesting motto," said Tim.

"We adhere to the principle for every client," said James. "Bill can confirm what you ask as well."

Bill nodded his head in agreement.

"Let's order dinner," said Tim.

The rest of the evening was spent talking about an array of topics and never once circling back to the Butler team. Tim had said what he had to say, and he was now comfortable with James and Bill as their consultants, confident that they would get the job done.

Chapter 37

Charlotte knew she needed help and had asked a friend for a recommendation. A Dr. Natalie Parker was given as a name who could talk with her and maybe lend some assistance and even straighten her out. Her sexual conquests were fun but not very meaningful. When you factored in the seven-point commissions with a night of bondage, it was kind of a chore for Charlotte. But the feeling of emptiness was still inside her, and she needed to talk with someone. A steady boyfriend was really what Charlotte was after, but there were no good men out there. The idea of trying to have some fun with Ted or Tim had been thrown out by her a long time ago. Her mommy always said, "You don't crap where you work," and she remembered the phrase.

Charlotte arrived at the office for an 8:00 p.m. session with Natalie. Her specialty was psychosexual behaviors, and she had treated many patients in her ten years in the business. Natalie stepped into the waiting room, where Charlotte was reading a magazine. She was the last patient of the evening.

"Charlotte, hi. I am Dr. Natalie Parker."

"Hi. I am Charlotte Webb."

"Please step into my office, and we can dispense with the formalities," said Natalie. "You can have a seat on my couch."

"Thanks."

"So how can I help you today?" Natalie asked.

"Well, a friend spoke highly of you and then recommended that I come and see you."

"You don't have to tell me who that person is," replied Natalie. "I would like to thank them for the referral, but that is fine."

"Can you help me with my man problem?"

"What type of problem is it?"

"I can't seem to get close to any guy for any type of physical relationship."

"A beautiful woman such as yourself must have a lot of guys drooling to date you," replied Natalie. "You're a stunning young woman with a gorgeous figure."

"You're just saying that to make me laugh."

"You are, Charlotte. You're a beauty. Let me guess what your figure is? You're a 34-28-32, I think?"

"That is correct."

"What is wrong with those numbers?"

"Well, I can't seem to get close to a man, unless it's for a one-night stand."

"What happened with the last one-night stand, if you don't mind me asking?"

"Well, we had consensual sex in his hotel room. I put cuffs and chains on him, and he was completely bound to the bed."

"Was the man happy with the arrangement?"

"He enjoyed it."

"Did you enjoy it?"

"Well, kind of."

"Was it that you had to control and/or subjugate him?"

"Yes. I was once on the bottom, and I did not like it,"

"When was that, if you don't mind me asking?"

"It was in college a few years ago in my dorm room, on a Saturday night," said Charlotte. "I was having drinks with a guy on a first date. Then I just woke up a few hours later. The guy I was with said I fell asleep. But I knew something was wrong. I was not wearing my panties, and I kind of felt wet."

"Did he slip you a drug of some kind?"

"I did not know, and I could not be sure. I just could not account for the two hours I was asleep with the guy. I could not prove I was date-raped, and I did not report it to the campus police."

"Charlotte, I am so sorry about your unfortunate experience with this guy. Has it helped that you talked with me tonight to unburden you from this incident?"

"Well, yes. It has helped to get it out and share it with a stranger. Everything we say here is not to be shared with anyone?"

"That is correct," replied Natalie. "All conversation is privileged communication between doctor and patient. Why do you ask?"

"I was just wondering."

"Our hour is up for now. Do you want to schedule another hour next week?"

"Let me think about it, and I'll get back to you," said Charlotte.

"Sure thing," replied Natalie as she showed her to the door.

"I'll call you later if I need to schedule another session."

As Charlotte left the office of Natalie Parker, she knew that a lot of what she was doing was not going to be revealed to the shrink. There was only a certain amount of information she was willing to share with Natalie. The dumping of a body would be one of those tidbits of information that would qualify as a topic to be silent on. If revealed, this would cross the line of the patient and doctor confidentiality threshold. Charlotte was sure that Natalie would be compelled to report it to the police. *So for now, mum's the word*, she thought.

Chapter 38

The morning session on Friday was all that was left of the demo week. The only topic that needed attention was the MICR check processing, and James had requested Mary Thomas to take care of it first thing in the morning. The group of Butler core team members had assembled right at eight o'clock in the conference room. Charlotte had done her thing with the coffee, fruit plate, and donuts. She was dressed down in blue jeans because it was casual Friday, which was a new policy adopted by the company. James knew he would not have to worry about Bill getting sidetracked by the way Charlotte looked today.

"This is the final day of the demo process," said James. "We have shown you all how the system works and will plan to do training next week. The outstanding issues have been updated on the list, and it will be circulated. The one priority issue is the MICR check process, and I hope to take care of that one with Mary this morning."

"Is there anything we may have missed?" Ted asked the group.

No one raised their hands or even said a word. James knew Ted was strong-arming the core team into submission and did not want to say anything.

"If there is something we missed, please think about it and tell me later or on Monday," said James. "There is always something that gets missed, but Bill and I have been doing these implementations for over twenty years and we would be surprised if we missed something critical."

"When are we getting together to go over the MICR check issue?" Mary asked.

"Right away," said James. "If there are no objections, you are all free to go. Bill and I will be here until noon, and then we have to catch our respective flights back home."

"I have a couple of meetings this morning, but I would like to touch base with the two of you around eleven a.m. if you have time," said Ted.

"That should not be a problem," replied James.

The team took some of the fruit and the donuts and headed out of the conference room. There was a look of exhaustion on the faces of some of the Butler team members as they left. James knew that they were ridden really hard this week and they were glad it was Friday. They all were looking forward to the weekend.

"Mary, are you ready for me?" James asked. "I have the form from the business group on the requirements for the MICR check stock. Can you look it over?"

"Looks like the ABA number and the account number are the only two critical items on the form," said Mary.

"That is correct. The other things on the form are optional, and really you just need to pick them."

"How fast can they turn this around?"

"They can return this to Butler in three to five business days. I know it is a little bit tight, but they guarantee the form will work with the standard check processing if ordered through the business partner."

"So we will not be able to test it until Friday of next week?"

"I know it is not ideal, but I am not too worried about the possible delay."

"Well, if we can't pay the vendors on the new system, then there is going to be a big problem."

"Trust me, we will get this ironed out."

"Is that all you needed me for today?"

"Yep. You're free to go back to work."

"Thanks," said Mary. "Safe travels to you if I do not see you later this morning."

The morning dragged on, and none of the Butler team members returned to the conference room for any follow-ups. This was a quiet time that James and Bill enjoyed so they could get some real work done. The issues list had fattened up during the week, and James knew it was going to be a struggle to get it cleaned up next week. Ted had thrown at them the topic of training next week in last night's dinner conversation with Tim. James was really not happy about the accelerated schedule and how Ted was making changes on the fly. The client was always changing the schedule, but this time James was really concerned about the timeline. Ted was an aggressive manager with the schedule. James was going to tell him that at the 11:00 a.m. meeting.

Ted popped into the conference room at eleven sharp.

"Hey, I only have a minute," said Ted. "Sorry to have dumped that training thing on you with Tim at dinner. Things here are getting a little crazy."

"I just want you to know the training next week will be a little bit light," said James. "We don't have everything set up, and we don't even have the checks."

"You guys can pull this off. Right?" Ted asked. Bill and James nodded. "I'll make it up to you both, for the effort," Ted added. "We will be talking about the third acquisition sometime next week."

"Another company purchase to go on the system that's not finished?" James asked.

"I told you, we are moving fast at Butler," said Ted.

"You're going to need some more IT staff."

"I am working on a couple of requisitions as we speak."

"We are going to need some time to stabilize the software as soon as we go live. A period of thirty days is customary."

"We can talk about that next week. Listen, I need to run to another meeting. Safe travels, and you both are doing a wonderful job for Butler."

"Thanks, Ted," they said in unison as he ran out of the conference room.

James turned to Bill and just shrugged his shoulders. *What the hell did we just stumble into?*

"Cha-ching," replied Bill as he returned the glance.

Chapter 39

Mary had put in for a requisition to hire an AP analyst to help backfill her department. The business was starting to grow, and she just could not keep up with all of the vendor-related functions that needed to be completed. With the two acquisitions coming online and with the new system, this was her opportunity to add some staff to her department. The accounts payable department consisted of one person, Mary Thomas. The new hire would make two people and would give Mary some breathing room for cross-training and a vacation.

Mary's phone rang on Friday afternoon, and she could see it was the HR manager on the display.

"Hey, Mary, your candidate is in my office and ready for the interview," said Tracy Meyers, the human resources manager. "Do you want me to bring her to your cubicle or put her in the conference room?"

"The conference room is empty," said Mary. "Bring her there, and I'll meet you there in two minutes."

"Thanks," Tracy said as she hung up the phone.

Patty Gray was one of three candidates for the position of AP analyst 1, and they preferred the person to have some experience in similar positions. She had the necessary experience with a prior employer who for some reason had let her go: she had worked for several years as an AP clerk with the Coraopolis Administration Corporation.

Patty was shown into the conference room, and Mary was already there waiting for her.

"Mary, this is Patty Gray," said Tracy. "She sent in a resume for the accounts payable analyst 1 position. Here is a copy of her résumé for you to review with her."

"Hi, Patty. I am Mary Thomas, the accounts payable manager here."

"Nice to meet you."

"So you are applying for the accounts payable analyst one job?"

"That is correct."

Mary started the interview with Patty and grilled her about everything on her résumé. The meeting lasted about an hour. Mary was feeling really good about this candidate. She had a lot of experience for the position, and her salary requirements were in the ballpark of what Butler was willing to pay. Mary had two other people being considered for the same job, but they were not as strong as this one.

"So if we offered you the job, Patty, when could you start?" Mary asked.

"I am not working at this point," said Patty. "I am unemployed right now. I was downsized at my last employer, and so I could start within a week."

"That is terrific news. Let me talk with Tracy and get back to you on Monday."

Patty did not want to explain to Mary that she was fired from her last job. The company had made it a quiet downsizing decision and given her six weeks' severance. They did not want to make it public that Patty was stealing from the company right under their noses by falsifying invoices and processing checks to a vendor that did not exist. They offered Patty an exit package if she kept her mouth shut and then just let her go. The software system at her prior employer did not have a lot of checks and balances to catch the game that Patty was playing. The accounts payable clerk was able to process phony invoices to a phony vendor and then get paid on those invoices, which were submitted to a lockbox that Patty controlled. But these details were not going to be shared with Mary by her or her prior employer. Any reference call to that employer was not going to be answered; they wanted to avoid being sued by any prospective employer. The Coraopolis Administration Corporation was just trying to wash its hands of the recently severed Patty Gray.

Patty was escorted to the door after the interview, and she started to think about recreating the game all over again. She knew this was a start-up company and there were not enough hands to take care of all of the transaction controls needed to manage the business. The only issue was convincing Mary Thomas that she was the one they needed to hire for the position. She had expressed her strong interest in the company and that this was a good fit for both parties. She would have to wait till Monday when Mary touched base with Tracy and they compared notes on her as a candidate.

Patty did not know but the other two candidates had dropped out of the running. They had been offered jobs with other companies and they were no longer available. She was the only candidate left standing, and Mary was desperate to hire someone to help her out: she was tired of doing everything by herself and needed help. The help she would request could prove a ticking time bomb that would explode once the scheme surfaced.

* * *

Later in the afternoon, Mary got a chance to talk with Tracy. They both agreed that if her references and last employer checked out, an offer would be sent to Patty on Monday. Mary had pleaded with Tracy to find her some help. She was burned out and was thinking of quitting if this help was not provided. For her part, Tracy knew that Mary was overworked and on the edge. She was doing the best she could to find qualified candidates but had no luck for quite some time. Patty Gray was the only one that fit the bill. So for now, she was the one they would add to the accounts payable team.

Chapter 40

This was a rare case of working on a Saturday for Ted MacDonald. The weekend was reserved for golf with the boys and errands with the wife. On this occasion Tim Murphy had asked Ted to accompany him to a site visit of a possible acquisition. The company was Metairie Pipeline Corporation, located in Greenwood, Louisiana. This business was in a salt water disposal vein of the energy sector and was thought to be for sale. Tim had done a little research on the business but needed to see it in person and on the ground. The location was right in the East Texas Oil Field, just on the west side of Louisiana. The business consisted of a battery of twenty holding tanks and ten injection wells. A pipeline of fifty miles was also part of the company structure. The pipeline served the oil patch in Louisiana and Texas and terminated in the Greenwood battery tank farm. The farm processed the salt water and then sent it to the injection wells for final disposal. The company was grossing around $50 million. That was all the information Tim had that was current.

Tim's plan was to meet with the owner on a Saturday and get a tour of the facility and then maybe inquire about the financials. The latter would only happen if he felt that the acquisition was a good fit and could add value to the Butler company.

Tim and Ted arrived at the office of the Metairie Pipeline Corporation in Greenwood around 9:00 a.m. on Saturday. They were met by the owner, Duncan Bailey.

"Good morning, gentlemen. You must be Tim Murphy," said Duncan

"Yes, I am, and this is my colleague Ted MacDonald," said Tim.

"Nice to meet you both. Would you like a tour of the facility?" Duncan asked.

"That would be most helpful," said Tim.

The next hour was spent walking around the facility to understand the salt water disposal business that Duncan had built over the last ten years. The pipeline had five entrance ports upstream that led to the retention pond that was the final collection point for the battery. The salt water was then pumped into the massive storage tanks at the Greenwood facility for further processing. The tanks were used to drain the salt water by gravity to a series of pipes that channeled the wastewater into one of ten injection wells. The pipeline, tanks, injection wells, and retention pond had sophisticated water-monitoring equipment that was managed in the central office at this facility. It was known as the main control center. This is where the hub of activity was, and Ted was really interested in getting a better look.

Duncan was proud of his business, and he was the sole owner. This fact was really important for Tim because he would only be dealing with one person if he liked what he saw.

The site visit was over, and the three of them sat down in Duncan's office.

"So what did you two think of our facility?" Duncan asked.

"Your business seems very well suited for the disposal of salt water for the oil drillers in this area," said Tim. "Have you given much thought to expanding?"

"Well, I have, but that takes a lot of money and a lot of time," replied Duncan. "It took me ten years to get where I am."

"What if you had a partner like Butler Energy Corporation to expand the pipeline and maybe build a second and third tank battery farm?" Tim asked.

"That would be nice, but as we all know, an expansion takes a lot of cash. Are you interested in some sort of deal here?"

"We might be interested. We would like to see your financials before we put something forward. Can you provide them to us next week so we can have a look?"

"I can get you a package of my company's income statement and balance sheet sometime next week, if that's OK?"

"That would be fine. I can have my team take a look and give you an opinion on whether we could maybe cut you a deal on your business."

"Well, I don't know if I want to sell it."

"If your numbers are OK, we will give you a package. We will also leave you in control as the president, with an earn-out clause and an employment contract."

"I would remain in the business?"

"We would want you to stay for as long as you like. Good people are extremely hard to find in this business."

"Let me get you our financials for last month, and you can review it with your team," said Duncan. "Then we can talk some more, or I can come and visit your office next time."

"That would be a good idea," said Tim. "You can see our side of the business and see if you can picture yourself being a part of the Butler brand of companies."

"Brand of companies?"

"You would be a wholly owned subsidiary of the Butler Energy Corporation. We would purchase your company and absorb it into the Butler company. We are building a big company, and you can be a player in the future of this publicly traded entity. This could be a wonderful opportunity to grow and expand the business. We will all get wealthy on the expansion."

"Give me the weekend to think about this?" Duncan asked. "I'll get you the numbers next week."

"Sounds good," said Tim. "You already have my number. Just call my executive secretary to coordinate the submission. Her name is Charlotte Webb, and she will take care of the receipt of those documents."

"Thanks, Tim."

"Consider a visit to our office in Coraopolis, Pennsylvania."

"Let me think about it."

Tim and Ted left the office and were feeling fairly good about the site visit. This business would be a complementary one within the Butler family, and if the price was right, this could prove a doable deal.

Duncan had to think about the deal hard, though. He was skimming the oil residuals from the salt water disposal business into his personal account and not reporting it as revenue in his Metairie Pipeline Corporation books. A little bit of a sleight of hand, sure, but this was his gravy train, one he might not want to give up if the business was sold. A lot of his personal toys came from the side business. This was something he did not want to share. The real business did not make much money in its operations, but a big payday could be in his future if he sold it. This was a real dilemma. The weekend retrospection would determine whether he would send the documents to Tim.

Chapter 41

James was back in Coraopolis on Monday after flying in on Sunday night once again. Bill was with him in the conference room, and like clockwork Charlotte strolled in with a carafe of coffee. She was wearing a purple dress with a V-shape front to expose her gorgeous body. The dress was cut high above her knees, exposing her shapely legs. It was going to be trouble for Bill to keep his mind focused on his work. As Charlotte was about to exit the conference room, James could see that Bill was staring at her.

"Something wrong?" said Charlotte as she glanced at Bill.

"No," replied Bill. "Has anyone told you that you look gorgeous today?"

"Not yet. Thanks for noticing."

"Thanks for the coffee," said James.

"I did not order the fruit and the donuts today," said Charlotte. "When were you planning on doing the training this week?"

"We will be doing the training on Wednesday and Thursday," replied James.

"That's what I thought. I have booked you a conference room at your hotel, down the street. Tim informed me late Friday that the board of directors will be meeting in this room Wednesday and Thursday. So you can't use it."

"The whole Butler team will need to be notified of the change," said James.

"I can take care of that. Again, Tim told me about this late on Friday, and I just made you and your team an alternate meeting room arrangement."

"Thank you, Charlotte. I was not aware of the BOD meeting."

"It was something that came up over the weekend. All the directors need to attend and decide on something that's going on."

"Is it another acquisition?"

"I have no idea. All I heard is that I needed to clear this room for the meeting and find your team a new one."

"I appreciate you thinking about us, and thanks in advance for all your help in getting this arranged."

"I'll take care of you two and the team. I was thinking that we should arrange for breakfast, lunch, and snacks in the afternoon. Sound good?"

"That sounds wonderful. Can you set it up for nine team members on both days?"

"Can you confirm the number and the names?"

"The attendees should be Tim, Ted, Paul, Shirley, Nina, Karen, Mary, Bill, and myself."

"I'll finish up the arrangements based on that list," said Charlotte. "I'll follow up with an email letting them all know that there is a change in venue and give them directions."

"What about the hotel billing?"

"Ted told me to tell you to put it on the expense report and submit it to me like normal."

"It is going to be a big bill for two days of meeting rooms and food."

"Does your credit card have enough of a limit to charge the expense?"

"I should have sufficient room on my credit card, but I may need to get the expense report processed quick."

"I can take care of that."

Shortly after Charlotte left the conference room, Ted popped his head into the conference room.

"Did Charlotte tell you about the change in arrangements?" he said. "I need the conference room for a BOD meeting on Wednesday and Thursday."

"Yes, she did," said James. "Is there something going on that I should know about?"

"I can't tell you about the meeting. If and when I can, you will be the second to know. Are you two ready for the training sessions this week?"

"We will be ready by Tuesday afternoon," said James. "We need Monday and Tuesday to finish up the configurations and training setups."

"Sounds good. Just make it happen. I may have to bounce in and out of the sessions if my schedule permits."

"So you and Tim will not be attending?"

"I am going to have to play it by ear."

"Do you want us to reschedule the training sessions?"

"No, keep the schedule as is. Just do it off-site at the hotel. We need to get the team trained and ready to go."

"We will do our best. Bill and I will handle the two days of training like normal. A special issues list will be logged during the two-day session. Then we can give you the update on Friday."

"That sounds like a good plan," said Ted. "The Friday morning will be a recap for Tim and myself only. Thanks."

"You will then be able to determine if the team is ready to go live with the system or if we will need to perform a follow-up training session," James added.

Ted nodded, then left the conference room. Bill and James went back to work.

Chapter 42

The scheduled training sessions were going to be in the Butler conference room at the home office. The BOD meeting had forced James and Bill to change the location and meet in one of the bottom-floor hotel conference rooms off-site. One of the smallest conference rooms was booked for the nine attendees. A benefit of the hotel arrangement was that coffee, snacks, and lunch would travel to the Butler team and a solid two days of training could take place without interruptions. James had to worry whether the projector was going to be adequate to present to the group. He always had an extra HDMI cable because he had been burned on a prior engagement. The room would prove to be a cozy arrangement and would give James an opportunity to witness the team in action on their keyboards and assess just how good they really were.

It was now 8:00 a.m., and all the Butler team members arrived literally at the same time. The trainees consisted of Paul Meadows, Shirley Moore, Nina Charles, Karen Rodgers, Mary Thomas, Barron Roberts, Jean Roberts, Bill Hogan, and James Crowley. Tim Murphy and Ted MacDonald were nowhere to be found and considered optional.

"Good morning, everyone," James said to the group. "We will be served coffee and breakfast sandwiches in the morning. We will have lunch brought in around noon. We will have snacks in the afternoon. I hope this is satisfactory for all?"

The attendees were all shaking their heads in agreement as they grabbed a beverage and some food.

"One more thing," said James. "We will be in this room today and tomorrow all day. The bathrooms are down the hall. Thanks."

The first order of business was for James to display to the team how to get access. The URL was placed on the screen: bluepointhosting.com/customer/login. The credentials for each of the employees were their first initial followed by their last name. They were then instructed to change their password immediately. This would allow them access to the software that had been purchased. All attendees were able to get logged in, and the meeting went on without a hitch.

An explanation of the security menu was given to the group. The software contained thirty modules, and based on a few guesses from James, they would only see around three or four on their computer screen. If more access was needed, James would update their individual profiles as needed. This was going to be a managerial decision that had to be made by the controller Paul Meadows or the accounting manager Shirley Moore.

The menu structure was explained in great detail. Each of the modules had a setup folder, an operations folder, and a reports folder. James displayed all the folders to the group and then proceeded under the fake Abbey Crowley account. Each of the users logged in and started to move around the screens. Bill and James walked around to each of the laptops displaying Enterprise Software Version 10.0 to verify that everyone was on the same page.

The customer setup process was next. James had been told of the current setups and did not like what he had heard. So this was his opportunity to bring the Butler team to the twenty-first century.

"How many customers do we have in the first company we are going to convert?" James asked the team.

"There are a little over one hundred customers of the Barron Water Hauling Company," said Jean Roberts.

"How many have the same billing address with multiple ship-to addresses?" James asked.

"We have several customers with at least ten different locations," said Jean.

"So for each site and customer, you have a single customer record set up?"

"That is correct."

"This software will accommodate multiple ship-to locations to a single customer bill-to location," said James. "So if we collapse them into the new structure, how many customers will we end up with?"

"Maybe twenty different customers is my guess," replied Jean.

"The new software will accommodate up to four thousand ship-to sites to a single customer. This will streamline the customer billing process and significantly reduce the number of customers needed as we go forward."

"This new method means we need to completely rework the customer conversion file."

"If you adopt this best practice, then yes, the file will need to be scrubbed before I load it for conversion."

"When do we have to make this decision?"

"I would say this week. I'll place this item on the issues list. Can someone look at the second acquisition's customer list as well?"

"I can look at the customer base for the Cook Salt Water Removal Corporation," said Nina Charles. "I'll let you know what I find."

"Thanks."

James proceeded to display the setup features of the customer and the many attributes that could be used. This was a full hour for the team and was extremely important for everyone to understand. A break was warranted, based on all the looks that he was getting.

"OK, we are at the top of the hour," said James. "Let's take a break for about ten minutes in case you all need to catch up on any emails or urgent matters this morning."

* * *

James started the training session back up with the sales order process. He reviewed customer order processing, shipment, and invoicing. A review of the second method was done with a miscellaneous invoice. All of the participants were looking strangely at James, as if they would never use the sales order for anything.

"We will use the miscellaneous invoice and not have a need for the sales order," said Shirley Moore. "I can't think of any time we would use the SO in our business."

"Are you sure?" James asked.

"What benefit would we get out of using the SO instead of the misc. invoice?" Paul Meadows asked.

"You will have visibility of your customer orders and the backlog of all your outstanding services if you use the SO process," said James. "The misc invoice is an after-the-fact invoice for customers. This is referred to as a *lazy man's invoice.*"

"If no one objects, let's go with the misc invoice for now," said Shirley.

"I'll put a placeholder for this on the issues list," said James. "I really think that the Butler company should use the SO process in the future. This is a best practice, and you should adopt it going forward. You will also get the benefit of the checks and balances within the process. But that is just my opinion."

James moved on to the invoicing process and then the cash applications process. There were no surprises for the group here. The discussion took them to the next break.

"We are the top of the hour, so it is time for a break," said James. "We will reconvene in about ten minutes, if everyone is OK with that. Bill and I will stick around to answer any questions that have not been answered, with the exception of a bio break. Thanks, everyone."

* * *

The group was back together, and James was determined to finish up the sales order process. Nina Charles had other intentions.

"Can we discuss what is available for the credit manager functions?" she asked.

James went through the handful of reports and credit terms that could be used for customer balances, including alerts and reminders that were available out of the box. The system was rather robust for managing the balances owed to the company, and James knew that Nina would be pleased with the choices.

"You will need to review and poke around with what is available, Nina," said James. "The system has a lot to offer."

"Can I set up a dummy customer and play with it?" Nina asked.

"Sure. You can use the fake customer I have already set up, or you can create one for yourself. The fake customer is Abbey Crowley, which is the name of my female Westie."

"If we put a customer on hold, will we be able to stop the finance team from extending them credit?"

"The SO process is tied into the credit mechanism," said James. "The misc invoice process is not. So you all have a decision to make here."

"Thanks. Let me play with this a little bit."

"Take a look, and if you have questions, let me know."

James had gone through the order-to-cash process and was getting ready to push on to the next topic when a question was raised.

"Can we practice some of these transactions?" Shirley Moore asked.

"We had the eleven a.m. hour set aside for the order-to-cash hands-on practice exercises," said James. "Since we are ahead of schedule, we can jump to that right now. Shirley, you can place an invoice in the system for goods or a service. Nina, you can then process a check received from the customer, and then we can see all the touch points you have to make in the system to get it through."

The rest of the morning was consumed with practice by the group, and James was happy to bounce around between trainees to help them put their fingers on the keyboards. The real-time practice would reinforce the experience and complete the knowledge transfer from teacher to student. James was happy with the progress this morning.

Right around noon the hotel staff brought in lunch, and it was time to take a break. James had announced that the food had arrived and said if any of the team members needed to break away, they were welcome to do so.

"We will reconvene at one p.m. Bill and I will remain in the room in case anyone needs any assistance. Thanks, everyone. We made a lot of progress today."

* * *

Meanwhile, the BOD meeting was going on at the offices of the Butler Energy Corporation. The meetings were set to be over two days in the main conference room at the same time as the training meetings. Charlotte was doing her absolute best to keep everything organized, coordinate the catered meals, and respond to the special requests of the members. They were a bunch of overpaid babies that liked certain food and a lot of tender, loving care. Charlotte wore her beautiful red dress, which she knew would drive the board members crazy and soften them up. This tactic worked on almost every man she came in contact with. They were jellyfish in her hands.

Tim and Ted were presenting their three-year plan to the board over the next two days. This plan was a road map of acquiring ten companies within one system and thereby saving 60 percent of the cost of the administration process to run the business. The plan also included doubling the businesses acquired to create a $500 million public company. If achieved, this plan would make Tim and Ted very wealthy. They had a lot riding on the meeting and could not be bothered with the training sessions for the new system.

Charlotte had been exposed to all of this sensitive communications between the board and Tim and knew of the plan being presented. She was privy to this nonpublic information and wanted to make sure that a piece of the pie was hers if she played her cards right. She had to be careful about how the game was played; it would require finesse so as not to attract any attention.

* * *

James started up the afternoon meeting with the usual language. "Any questions from this morning? Is there anything we need to review, or did we miss something?"

There were no questions raised by the team. James decided to push on to the purchase-to-pay process.

"The purchasing module will be handled by which team?" James asked.

"We really don't have any purchasing staff in the office," said Paul Meadows.

"Who does the buying now?" James asked.

"We just call up the vendor and tell them to send over what we need," said Shirley Moore.

"Will the Butler company have buyers?" James asked.

"We are all kind of buyers," said Mary Thomas.

"I am going to have to put this on the list as an internal control issue," said James. "A SOX-compliant company will require a buyer, or you will fail the auditor testing process."

"You're correct, James," said Paul. "We need to hire a few buyers for our company to segregate the functions."

"Is it in the plan to do so in the immediate future?" James asked.

"We will need to check with Tim Murphy," replied Paul.

"Well, then let's go through the purchase-to-pay cycle," said James.

An explanation of the buyer, the purchase order, the receipt of the order, the invoice match, and then finally the payment of that PO was completed.

"We are not using purchase orders right now," said Mary Thomas. "I think we should be using them in the future."

"I think you will need to adopt this best practice," said James. "The buyer buys the goods from the vendor. An employee will receive the goods at the site where they arrive. An accounts payable person will then match the invoice to the receipt once received. There should be three different people to process the transaction and keep your controls strong."

"This is a big hole for us," said Paul. "We may have to table this topic for now. Can we skip the purchasing process for now?"

"Sure," replied James. "Let's just go through the invoice to payment portion of the transaction."

The next hour was spent going through the accounts payable portion of the invoice matching for Mary. There were no surprises in how this worked, so there were not a lot of questions. James did go through the features for setting up the vendors and the available options that the team could use.

"Since there are no more questions and we are at the end of the hour, let's break for ten minutes," said James. "We will reconvene at two ten."

* * *

The team got back together after the short break. James had on the agenda conversions as the next subject.

"We are going to start the discussion on what needs to be converted," said James. "There were no remaining questions from this morning, so let's move on."

"Do you have a recommendation as to the best practice?" Paul asked.

"Yes, I do," said James. "I'll give you my two cents, and then you can tell me what you would like. Customers are usually converted as long as they have a receivable balance. Vendors are usually converted if they have activity from the prior twelve months. Inventory is usually converted where there is activity in the past two years and/or a balance on the report. Your business does not have any inventory, so no conversion activity is planned. Payroll is handled through a third party such as ADP and does not need to be converted. There is no manufacturing, so no activity is planned. The general ledger balance sheet accounts will be converted. That is the way I see the Butler company for now. Did I miss anything?"

"Damn. You're good, James."

"Did I miss anything?"

"Why do you not want to bring over the accounts payable balances?" Mary asked.

"There is no value in bringing over the vendor payments due," said James. "The accounts payable aging of the vendors needs to be burned down to zero anyway. Why convert it and pay it off when the transactions did not start in the new system? You want the accounts payable transactions to start and finish on the same platform."

"So how do we 'burn them off,' as you say?" Mary asked.

"You have one last check run just before you go live," said James.

"But they will not all be due to the vendors at that time."

"You can release them in the mail as necessary. If you're paying inside of thirty days, the checks will be disbursed within the next month. So you really should not have an issue."

"That actually makes sense," said Paul.

"There is less admin for the AP team if you run a final check run at the conversion date," said James.

"What about the general ledger balances?" asked Shirley.

"The Butler company is buying the assets and liabilities at a point in time," said James. "The income statement is zeroed out on day one. I don't care about the prior business results under the old system."

"That is a good point," said Paul.

"One other thing to think about," said James. "The conversions must take place just prior to the start date of the new entity. This is usually the weekend or a forty-eight-hour window when no transactions can take place in the new system. I have a conversion program that will help me convert the AP and AR stuff, but this needs to be in a Microsoft Excel file or a CSV flat file."

"Can I provide you the customer file ahead of time?" Nina asked.

"Yes, you can," said James.

"I can provide you the vendor file ahead of time as well," said Mary.

"Anything you can get me ahead of time would be appreciated," said James. "If you send any files to me ahead of time, though, please keep in mind that you will need to do a delta file. This would be for vendors or customers you had to add to the old system and you wanted to bring across to the new system."

"We can do that," said Mary.

"We are coming up to the top of the hour," said James. "Let's take a ten-minute break and reconvene around three twenty, if that's OK with everyone?"

The group got up to stretch their legs just in time to see the hotel staff bring in a plate of cookies and candy with refreshments. This was perfect timing for the afternoon break.

* * *

The gang was assembled once again for the final hour off-site at the hotel. James was ahead of schedule, and he knew he had fulfilled the timeline of topics to cover.

"Are there any questions about the material so far?" said James. "No questions? I don't believe it. You all must me tired of me talking today."

The group laughed, and one person said, "*You're a good teacher.*"

"Thanks for that bit of reassurance," said James. "I have done this before."

"About twenty times," shouted Bill.

"What about the logo for the Butler company?" Nina asked.

"You sent me the logo file last week," said Bill. "I have developed a report style for the AR invoice form already with the logo on it. I can default it to the standard report if someone can approve it."

Bill took over the presentation and displayed the AR invoice form with the Butler logo in the top right corner.

"That looks correct," said Nina.

"What about the Butler check?" Mary asked.

"Did the check stock get here so we can test it?" James asked.

"Not yet," replied Mary.

"They guaranteed three business days," replied James. "I am hopeful that they will arrive on Thursday. We just ordered them last Friday."

"It is right around the four o'clock hour," said James. "Are there any more questions or open items from today? It looks to me like you all have had enough for one day. Am I right?"

The heads nodded, and no one said a word.

"If no one objects, let's call it a day," said James. "The first day of training is in the books. Thanks, everyone. See you all here on Thursday at eight a.m."

The group was dismissed for the day.

Chapter 43

The second day of training for the team had the same group of nine employees. Ted MacDonald had stopped by the room just before 8:00 a.m. to ask a few questions of James and Bill while they were alone.

"So how did the first day of training go?" Ted asked James.

"I think it went well," said James. "We started an issues list of items that need attention, and we would like to review them with you if there is time?"

"I only have about thirty minutes. Then I have to go back to the BOD meeting around eight thirty to get ready," said Ted.

"Do you want to package all the issues into the Friday meeting with Tim?" James asked.

"That would be fine," said Ted. "That way you two can give us both the update at the same time."

"I will hold everything for Friday and accumulate any more issues from today. Thanks," said James.

As the trainees started to arrive, they all noticed that Ted was already in the room. He announced that his presence would be brief because there was another meeting that he needed to attend at the office.

"How is the training going so far?" Ted asked the group.

They all kind of nodded their heads in agreement. No one really gave Ted an answer.

"Are there any questions from yesterday's session?" James asked.

"Since Ted is here, we need to discuss the purchasing situation with him," Paul said.

"What purchasing situation are you referring to?" Ted replied.

"We don't have a purchasing team or buyers for the business," said Shirley. "Are we planning on hiring a team?"

"I don't know the answer to that one," said Ted.

"The software that you bought has a best practice of using buyers with purchase orders," said James. "The transaction flow would be a purchase order followed by a receiving transaction and then an invoice match by the finance team. Three people would need to be involved to complete the cycle."

"I'll need to review this item with Tim Murphy," said Ted.

"The software is based on that purchase-to-pay cycle with buyers," said James. "This is a best practice in the industry."

"We will review the item with Tim on Friday morning," said Ted.

It was 8:30 a.m., and Ted had to excuse himself from the discussion: his presence was required at the BOD meeting down the street, and he did not want to be late. His future was riding on the delivery of the three-year plan.

"Let's get started," said James. "The next topic is journal entries."

James went into his presentation on how to create a journal entry. He started with the header and then added a line with the account and amount one needed. This process only took a few minutes. He then asked the group who would be involved in these transactions.

"I think that Paul, Nina, Mary, and I will be the only ones to prepare the JEs," said Shirley.

"I have sliced this module into its own security group, and it will only be associated to a user that you will identify," said James. "All other users will not even see this on the menu structure on their computer."

"So they will not know it exists?" Paul asked.

"The security group menu allows me to hide it from them," said James. "The module is still in the system. It is just hidden in the background. If you tell me to allow someone access, I can give it to them in three minutes."

"How does that work?" Paul asked.

"I can update a profile change to the user account," said James. "The affected user just has to sign out to allow me to make the change and then sign back in. I will be looking for someone in the finance team to manage or control who is allowed access."

"I think that Shirley would be the right person for that," said Paul.

"I can take care of the approval process," said Shirley.

"Please keep in mind that as we add users and allow or deny users access, it will become an SOX compliancy policy," said James. "I believe you need a review procedure in place to perform a monthly monitoring of this."

"Who is the monitor in the company?" Shirley asked.

"That would be whoever approves of the general access to the system," said James. "It is usually a few people in the accounting department that meet on a monthly basis."

"Can you add that to the issues list?" Paul asked.

"I'll make a note of it," said James. "Let's take our first break, if you don't mind? It's now nine thirty, and we will reconvene in ten minutes, at nine forty."

* * *

After the break James started to go through the financial report designer function. This was a standard function in the software that allowed the users to create financial statements. A careful explanation of column sets and row sets was given to the team.

"You mean there are no standard reports already built into the system?" Paul asked.

"There are no reports built in," said James. "The system does not know your chart of accounts."

"So we have to build them?" Paul asked.

"I have said before that I can help you with that task," said James. "But this is something that an accounting team member should learn how to do and maintain going forward. I do not want to be your long-term report writer."

"Our needs currently are very simple," said Paul. "Can you create and maintain this for now? Until we can figure something out."

"Yes, I can assist you," said James. "I'll need to review with my manager Ted, though."

"Can we go back to the customer ship-to issue from yesterday?" Nina asked.

"Are we done with the financials report writer issue for now?" James asked.

"Can we revisit this later?" Paul said.

"Absolutely," said James. Then he asked Nina, "Now what was your question about the customer ship-to issue?"

"I got a chance to look at the customer base for the Cook Salt Water Removal business," said Nina. "There are about five hundred customers with a single ship-to for each. If we collapse the ship-to sites for the customers, we would have eighty unique customers. So a customer like Chevron has one hundred wells that a truck could be dispatched to. All the wells are billed to a single Chevron location."

"That means that the customer file for Cook has to be scrubbed for the conversion to take place," said James. "Can I count on you, Nina, to perform the collapse function here?"

"I can take a crack at it but would like a second person to review it before you load it," Nina said.

"I can help you out with that," said Shirley.

"We can have it loaded the same way as it is now," said James. "But then you will need to clean it up later after there is a transaction against it. I would recommend you do it before I load the file. This is a best practice."

"Sure, we will clean it up before we give it to you, James," said Nina.

"OK, we are at the top of the hour," said James. "It is ten fifty, and we will reconvene at eleven, if that's OK with everyone?"

There were no objections, and the group broke for a well-deserved bio break.

* * *

"The next hour is a practice session," said James. "Bill and I will walk around the room to answer questions and help you with anything you would like to work on."

Bill and James split up and watched as the students tried certain screens. There were questions on what this or that did, and they got answered as fast as Bill and James could reply. The group appeared to have learned a lot in the last day and a half, and James was happy with the progress.

"Hey, can we go over the check process?" Mary asked.

"Did the checks arrive?" James said.

"They were delivered yesterday to the office," said Mary.

"Right on schedule," said James. "Three business days as promised. Can we do this on Friday in the office? I need to know which printer you are going to use, and we do not have a printer here in the conference room."

"First thing on Friday," said Mary.

"Yes, right after my meeting with Tim and Ted," said James. He went on, "Does anyone need assistance this morning?"

No hands were raised, so James and Bill took a breather and just walked around the room watching the students on their keyboards.

The hotel staff brought in lunch right at the noon hour.

"OK, it's lunchtime, everyone," announced James. "Bill and I will hang around during the lunch hour to answer any questions. Thanks."

The group dispersed, and most left the room for a well-deserved break. Some members came back for the lunch, and some just left the building. James knew that the training was going well but there were other forces at work here, namely that the work was not getting done and the emails were piling up.

* * *

It was just after lunch, and the group reconvened. James had on the schedule to talk about the cleanup that had to be done for next week prior to the conversions.

"So are we going to run the accounts payable to zero in both the acquisition companies?" James asked.

Jean Roberts and Mary Thomas nodded their heads in unison.

"Yes, we decided that bringing over the vendor balances did not make sense," said Paul.

"What about the vendor information?" James asked. "Will Jean and Mary be able to get me a file on the last twelve months of vendor activity?"

"That should not be a problem," said Mary as Jean just nodded.

"How about the customer files?" James asked.

"The Barron customer file will need a little bit of cleanup, but I don't see any issues," said Jean.

"The Cook customer files I may need some time with," said Nina. "I am not really familiar with them, but they may need some cleanup as well."

"Both companies will need to be collapsed into the new customer format," said James. "The multiple ship-to sites should make it easier but require you to massage the file. We did decide to go to this best practice method of setting up the customers?"

"We had an internal meeting on it," said Paul. "We are adopting the new setup method for customers."

The balance of the hour was spent going over the data file for the customer attributes that would be required in the conversion file. Since the software that the two companies were currently using was primitive, the new system was going to be a huge improvement.

"OK, we are at the top of the hour," said James. "You all know what that means: break time. See all your smiling faces back here in ten minutes."

* * *

The two o'clock hour came, and the group reconvened.

"Any open issues that need to be logged so far?" James asked.

"We are doing the checks back at the office on Friday?" Mary asked.

"I did not forget about you, Mary. You and I will personally test the process using the real check stock." James then went on, "The rest of the afternoon is for practice. Bill and I will perform one-on-one sessions for anything you have questions on that was not covered. Please keep in mind that the inventory and manufacturing modules were not included in this training. We are not using them as of now."

"Will we need them?" Paul asked.

"Only if you're planning on acquiring a manufacturing business," said James. "I think you have what you need for now."

No other issues came up in the afternoon. The team looked fully expended and in need of some rest.

"We are approaching the four o'clock hour, and you all look tired," said James. "Was the training session helpful? Did we get you all educated on the new system? OK then, let's call it a day."

"When are you and Bill coming back?" Paul asked.

"We will be in the office on Friday with Tim and Ted, and then we will be off-site next week," said James. "We will be working on the conversions of the customers, vendors, and the accounts receivable balances for the two companies. We can be available by phone or Webex next week in case anyone needs us. Bill will be on Eastern time, and I will be on Pacific time."

"I want to say thanks to you and Bill for doing this training with us," said Paul.

"You're very welcome," replied James. "Thank you all for the opportunity to learn all about the Butler organization. Bill and I look forward to working with everyone as you grow and acquire more businesses."

Chapter 44

Bill and James were both back in the conference room on Friday morning. The training sessions held off-site on Wednesday and Thursday went very well. James was happy with the success and the progress that the Butler team exhibited, even if Ted did not see them in action. He felt that he had earned his consulting money this week.

Charlotte walked into the conference room and asked, "Do you boys want a carafe of coffee for this morning's meetings?"

"That would be nice," said James. "We have a meeting with Tim and Ted this morning to go over the outstanding issues list."

"I don't know if you are going to see Tim," said Charlotte. "He has a few things on his agenda, and a meeting with you two was not on the schedule. There were some developments from the BOD meeting on Thursday that he has to take care of."

"Do you know if Ted will be joining us this morning?" James asked.

"I did not see your meeting on his schedule," replied Charlotte. "I'll take another look just in case he updated it after the fact."

"We are just going to have to play it by ear," said James.

As Charlotte left the room, James noticed that Bill did not even look in her direction. He was staring at his computer screen and did not look up. Fortunately, Charlotte was dressed down in jeans and a satin blouse that did not show off her body. She was rather plain and unattractive today.

"What are you starring at?" James asked.

"Sorry, I was watching a YouTube video on golf swings," replied Bill.

"You did not even notice that Charlotte came into the conference room and left."

"This video shows how to improve your swing by fifty yards," said Bill. "What was she wearing today?"

"Never mind," said James. "She wanted to know if we wanted coffee."

"Yes, please," said Bill.

"I already answered for the two of us," said James.

A few minutes later, Charlotte walked in, dropped the coffee off, and exited the conference room.

"Thanks, Charlotte," James shouted as the door closed.

The nine o'clock hour came and went. Neither Ted nor Tim joined the boys in the conference room to discuss the issues list. James knew something was up. He went over to Charlotte's desk to find out where they were. She informed James that they were still off-site in a meeting; she could not say anything more.

James knew that his catch-up meeting with Ted MacDonald was not that important. So it was time to shift gears. He went over to see Mary Thomas and ask if they could test the check process. She needed a few minutes and would come and get James when she had a break in the action.

The testing process of the check stock was not going to take too long. The checks were going to work or not. It was that simple. The Butler team would have an answer in just a few minutes. Mary came into the conference room shortly thereafter.

"OK, I am ready to test the checks," said Mary.

"Let's go to your desk, and you can show me the printer that you plan to use," said James.

As they walked over to Mary's desk, James grabbed his computer. He knew the final setups were not done.

"Now, Mary, we need to set up the bank account," said James. "The control account needs to be created as well, and then they need to be linked together in the new system."

"How often do we need to do this?"

"Just once. Let me show you how this works. Can you provide me the ABA number and the Butler account number?"

"Sure. Let me get a canceled check."

James walked Mary through the process of setting up a bank account in the system. A control account for the Wells Fargo account was set up as well. A linkage record was made to connect the two parameters together on the bank screen.

"Where do we set the check number?" Mary asked.

"You do that on the first check run," said James. "We will create a batch of checks and select a vendor to pay. I will use only one check for now so we can void it later. The payment process using a new batch record for MT0301 will be created. A selection of one vendor will be grabbed to include in this batch record. Let's set the check to 6001, which is the first check in the batch, and print the check. We need to place the blank check 6001 paper stock in the printer tray right side up."

"That's it?"

"We just have one more step, and that is to hit the process button. Then watch the check print. Here we go."

James launched the process button for a single check, and the printer next to Mary's desk started to spit out the check. Check number 6001 was preprinted and ready for review.

"So how does it look?" Mary asked.

"Look for yourself," said James.

The check was made out to Wells Fargo Bank in the amount of $1.00. The ABA number and the Butler company account number were preprinted on the check stock. The date printed was the current one, and all the rest of the information looked fine.

"This looks like a normal check," said Mary.

"Can I ask one favor?" James asked.

"What's that?"

"Will you go to the bank and have them review the check to make sure the MICR printing is correct and that the check will scan through their card reader?"

"I can do it on Monday."

"Thanks. If the bank signs off on the card reader, then we are good to process checks."

"What happens if it fails?"

"Let's not go there for now. There is one more thing that we have to perform in the system. If the check run is OK, then you post the batch."

James walked Mary through the final step of the process to post the payment batch MT0301 to the general ledger. Once this was done, the batch disappeared from the screen. This completed the process. The general ledger now had the debits and the credits for the transaction displayed.

"We are done for now," said James.

"You will walk me through this process a few more times?" Mary asked.

"Yes, we can test it some more until you're comfortable with the full process."

James left Mary and went back to the conference room to see if Ted had made an appearance. Still no Ted or Tim. They were still off-site, and it was getting late in the morning.

Charlotte walked into the conference room around 11:00 a.m. and announced that Tim and Ted would be delayed and not able to meet with James and Bill this morning. They would catch up with the consultants next week, and they had asked her to wish them both safe travels back home.

"I guess we are on our own for the rest of the day," said James.

"An easy Friday," replied Bill.

An hour later the two consultants were headed for the airport to catch some lunch and a plane home.

Chapter 45

The BOD members were presented with a plan to grow the Butler Energy Corporation to $500 million over a three-year period. Each of the five board members was going to contribute $5 million into the venture as a non-interest-bearing loan. Once financing was secured, the initial contribution would be paid off and an equivalent amount of stock for an additional $5 million would be granted to each contributor. This was a sweetheart deal, and the members were salivating at it when it was explained to them.

The president of the company, Jerry Evans, had joined the two days of meetings and had approved the three-year plan as presented by Tim and Ted. It was agreed that all participants, regardless of status, would put up $5 million personally. This totaled $40 million of their own money to be invested for a short period of time. The board members questioned how risky this deal was, and the answer was a surprise. Tim explained that the assets of the companies being acquired would cover their portion of the loan and the bank loan with room to spare. This was music to their ears.

The other part of the deal was the stock issuance. This was the reason that Jerry, Tim, and Ted were at the Wells Fargo main office in downtown Coraopolis. They were there presenting the plan to the investment bankers who were going to back the initial public offering. The Butler company was already doing business with Wells Fargo, and now was the time to get in deep with the bank. The plan with the bank was to borrow up to $100 million, establish a line of credit up to $100 million, and issue stock in the amount of $200 million. The stock issuance was to be done in the next couple of months and was conditional upon a third business being acquired and implemented on the new software system. This conditional requirement was a bit of an unwanted situation, but Jerry agreed to it. An additional wrinkle was added by the investment banker. The eight members that contributed five million in loan proceeds would be granted convertible stock, but they could not be exercised or sold from one-year after being granted. This was one more item that Jerry did not like but was a conservative strategy put forth by the bank to protect its loan to the Butler company. This was of course agreed to by the president, and the deal was signed.

The bank would release $100 million to the Butler company next week, and this was the green light to get the third acquisition done. The initial public offering would be started and could take three months to complete. This was going to be set up for release in the second quarter of the year. The line of credit was established and would only be tapped once the first loan was completed.

The meeting with the Wells Fargo investment team was a success. Jerry was incredibly happy with the presentation and the outcome of the $100 million loan. He had had a prior experience with Tim and Ted and had leveraged that relationship in this new venture with the Butler company. They were old friends, and the prior business had also made them a lot of money. He was so happy the three amigos were back together and looked forward to the road map for the future.

"Let's go celebrate at my club today," said Jerry.

"What did you have in mind?" Tim asked.

"How about a round of golf on me?" replied Jerry.

"That sounds great," said Ted. "Let me call Charlotte and let her know that we will be in an afternoon meeting and do not want to be disturbed."

"Just tell her that we are going to play golf at my club," said Jerry.

"You're right, I can do that," said Ted. "Charlotte is extremely trustworthy, and she is an asset to the company. By the way, I need to talk to you two about a significant bonus for her."

"What kind of bonus?" Tim asked.

"Well, she helped me with the negotiations with Rick Cook," said Ted. "The guy was stuck on fifty-five million, and she got him down to my target of fifty million."

"How did she do that?" Jerry asked. "Or do I not want to know?"

"Well, we went to dinner, and she helped him back to his hotel room one night," said Ted. "The next morning his paperwork was on my desk at the fifty-million-dollar number."

"Do you think she bonked him to get to your number?" Tim asked.

"Well, let's just say I am not going to ask her about it," said Ted.

"How much should we give her?" Jerry asked.

"I think it needs to be a sizeable number," said Tim. "Since Rick was stuck at fifty-five million and the reduction was five million, she needs to get a big six-figure bonus."

"Would a hundred grand be enough?" Jerry asked.

"I think that would be appropriate," said Tim.

"I agree," said Ted. "She made this happen. Whatever she did that night."

"I guess we should use her in a different capacity," said Jerry.

"What do you mean?" Tim asked.

"We should call her our 'closer,'" said Jerry.

"She is an extremely attractive woman," said Tim.

"Why is she still single?" Jerry asked.

"I don't know," replied Tim. "But she drove the board members crazy in that dress she wore."

"She did indeed," said Ted.

"OK, so we agree that a hundred grand is the right number?" Jerry asked.

"I think that would be fair," said Tim.

"You two take care of it next week," said Jerry. "Take her out for a nice dinner and hand her the check."

"What should we call it?" Tim asked.

"Call it a finder's fee," said Jerry.

"We will take care of it next week," said Tim. "This will build her loyalty to the Butler company. Good people are hard to attract and retain."

"You better keep her on our side," said Jerry.

"Understood," said Tim. "We will take care of it next week."

"What about those two consultants?" said Jerry. "Are they working out?"

"It is funny you mentioned that topic," said Ted. "I have nothing but praise for them. James and Bill will also need to be rewarded for their efforts. I need them as an integral part of our three-year plan."

"Do we have a contract on them?" Jerry asked.

"Yes, we have a six-month contract on both of them," said Ted.

"I think you better sign them up for a year and give them a raise if they are working out," said Jerry.

"I'll take care of it personally next week," said Ted.

"Now can we go play golf?" Jerry asked.

"You're the boss," said Tim. "Let's go hit some balls."

Chapter 46

Jean Roberts was working on the customer file to be converted for the Barron company. She had to restructure the current customer file extracted from the current system to the new-system way of doing things. One customer could now have multiple ship-to sites. This final file produced from the massaging operation ended up with twenty unique customers with numerous ship-to sites. Jean was careful to make sure that the four companies the Barrons were using were not contained within the conversion file. They were carefully plucked from the extract file. This customer conversion file was now ready to be sent to James for conversion purposes.

* * *

Nina Charles was working on the customer file to be converted for the Cook company. She had experience with conversions before in a prior company so was familiar with the process. You performed an extract file from the current business, dumped the result into an Excel file, and then massaged the customers to put their information into a loadable file for the new system. The final resulting file of five hundred customers was boiled down to eighty unique customers with multiple ship-to sites. This conversion file was now ready for James.

* * *

Mary Thomas was responsible for the Butler company and the Cook company vendor conversion files. The extract files that she was able to create were a straight dump from both companies.

Two files were prepared and readied for submission to James for conversion to the new system. Mary had to do little massaging of data because the vendor extracts were straightforward. The multiple-ship-to issue really did not exist for the vendors.

* * *

Ted arrived at the office early on Monday morning and stopped by Charlotte's desk.

"Did the financial information for the Metairie Pipeline Corporation come into your email this past week?" he asked.

"I don't recall seeing anything from them," replied Charlotte. "Who would have sent in the information?"

"The owner, Duncan Bailey. I'll give him a call today and see if he is having cold feet with sending us his numbers."

"I did recheck my emails, and I did not see anything from a Mr. Bailey."

"Thanks. I'll need to nudge him a little bit just in case he is not interested anymore."

"What do you mean 'not interested anymore'?"

"I'll tell you, but you need to keep this quiet," said Ted. "We want to buy his company but need his numbers to evaluate the possible acquisition."

"So that is where you two went last Saturday."

"Yep, we were in Greenwood, Louisiana, checking out his company. We took a tour of his business and liked what we saw."

"Are we buying this company?"

"If his numbers are in the relevant range, this could be our third acquisition."

"Mum's the word."

"By the way, Charlotte, can you join us for a dinner on Wednesday evening?" Ted asked.

"Sure. What's up?"

"We need to discuss some business ideas with you."

"Where should I make the reservation, and what do you have a taste for?"

"How about Frank's, that Italian place you like?"

"That is my favorite place for Italian food."

"Then let's go there."

"I'll make the reservation right away," said Charlotte.

* * *

James was working from home on Monday and was occupying the casita the whole week. A rare week in the home office. Lynn was happy since she was traveling this week. She would be in the Pasadena area, driving up on Monday, staying the week, and then driving back on Friday afternoon for her client. James would be babysitting Abbey and Champ by himself. He would have an easy week and was planning on getting the initial conversions done for the Barron company and the Cook company.

Late in the day, he finally received the first conversion file from Jean Roberts. The second one came in from Nina Charles almost within the hour. Later in the day, Mary Thomas sent in the two files for conversion for the vendors of the two acquisitions. James had plenty of work and needed to get it done within the next day.

James was planning on working to convert the files he had received but thought to call Ted and see if he wanted to catch up before he got started. He was not successful in contacting Ted, though. All he got was his voicemail. So he left a message and moved on.

The first conversion file, received from Jean, was converted into a customer file upload template and run through the data conversion process. The twenty customers took less than a minute to upload, and the records per minute (RPM) was displayed as twenty with no errors. James could not believe this error report.

The second conversion file, received from Nina, was converted to a customer file upload template like before. The file uploaded in four minutes, and again there were no errors. The RPM displayed twenty for the Cook company.

The third conversion was for the Barron vendor file. An upload template was prepared and run through the conversion process. Since there were five hundred vendors, this one took a little bit of time to process. The file was processed, and an error report was produced. There were no errors in the completed file, and the process took twenty minutes to complete. The RPM was twenty-five.

The fourth conversion was for the Cook vendor file. An upload template was prepared and run through the conversion process. Since there were only 250 vendors, this one took just under ten minutes to complete. The RPM was twenty-five once again.

James had managed to process all the planned conversion files on Monday. *What am I going to do for the rest of the week?* he thought. He would worry about this on Tuesday when he checked back in with the Butler team. For now, it was time to get the bike out for a ride through the canyons of Fallbrook. The Westies would not mind if James went for a ten-mile ride as long as he was not late for dinner. He left the Westies in the casita and took off for an early evening ride.

Chapter 47

Charlotte opened her email on Tuesday morning, and there it was: an email from Duncan Bailey with two attachments. One was for an income statement with the FYE 12.31.2023 and the balance sheet with the same dates. The documents were for the Metairie Pipeline Corporation business; she knew that Tim was waiting for this information. The email was forwarded to Tim, and the documents were printed as well. Charlotte knew that Tim would want them printed and sitting on his desk before he came in. She could not resist looking the documents over very carefully.

The Metairie business had grossed $35 million the previous year. The owner had taken a salary of $250,000. The business made $50,000 after taxes. There was $20 million in debt on the balance sheet. One other item that got her attention was the hunting expenses of $100,000. This seemed an odd line item on the PNL. If she got the chance, she would ask Tim about it. All in all the business really did not make much money, and Charlotte did not know why Tim was so interested in buying it.

One fact that Duncan Bailey left out was that his fleet of ten trucks were all over fifteen years old and were constantly being repaired. There were so many miles on the trucks that within a year, a massive cash infusion was going to be required to keep the fleet running.

"Hey, Charlotte, did we get that information from Duncan Bailey?" Tim asked as he strolled into this office.

"I forwarded you the email and printed the documents," said Charlotte. "They are sitting on your desk."

"You're wonderful. Thanks a bunch."

Tim looked over the printed documents from Duncan. The numbers appeared to be low as far as profit, but with single-owner businesses, you always have to dig deep to get the full story. The hunting expense stuck out like a sore thumb; he would need to question Duncan on that item. There appeared to be a few dollars to be made on the salt water disposal business, but an expansion would be the ticket to really make it profitable.

"Do you have a few minutes?" Tim called Ted on the phone.

"Sure, what's up?" Ted asked.

"We got the numbers from that business we visited last Saturday."

"I'll come right over to your office. Just give me a minute to get some coffee."

Ted joined Tim in his office, and they started to dissect the financial numbers. The documents presented a business just struggling to stay afloat. The debt load of $20 million seemed really high for a disposal business. But the tank farm and trucks made it an intensive-capital-equipment-driven business.

"Did you look at the trucks when we were there?" said Tim.

"Yes, I did," replied Ted. "The trucks seemed really old."

"That was my thought exactly."

"We would need to buy more trucks once we bought the business."

"That's what I was afraid of what you were going to say."

"At one fifty a truck, that would be an initial kick of one and a half million to upgrade the fleet."

"So what do you think the business is worth?"

"We have been using the one-times sales number, and that is probably appropriate here. So thirty-five million?"

"That is what I was thinking as well."

"We should take a run at this guy with an offer of twenty-five million and see where it goes."

"That's a good idea," replied Tim. "Can we try to get him up here next week and make a pitch to him?"

"I can take care of the invite," said Ted. "Should we use 'the Closer' on this deal? Just kidding."

"That would probably cost us another one hundred thousand dollars."

"Not a bad finder's fee for our bombshell."

"Let's hold on to that thought," replied Tim.

"OK. I'll try to set up an appointment with Duncan here in the office next week," said Ted.

* * *

James was back at it in the casita on Tuesday and looking over the converted customer file from Jean Roberts. He noticed that there were four missing customers in the file: Argonaut Corporation, Anco Corporation, Challenger Corporation, and Falcon Corporation. These were the companies he had noted previously. He thought this was odd since they had activity in the current year. *Why wouldn't they be converted?* James thought to himself. He wanted to ask Nina Charles to take a look at the converted file, so he sent her an email with the attachment. Maybe she could shed some light on the topic.

James went back to the converted vendor file for the Barron company, received from Mary Thomas. The vendor file did contain the four that were noticed earlier in the review. Argo Enterprise, Aspen Enterprise, Eagle Enterprise, and Monitor Enterprise were all contained in the conversion file and were in fact loaded into the new system. Something appeared out of place, but James could not put his finger on it.

A follow-up to any conversion was to send the converted files back to the sender for one last review. The customer file for the Barron company was sent to Jean. The customer file for the Cook company was sent to Nina. The vendor files were sent back to Mary. A lengthy email was forwarded to Ted as well to let him know that the conversions did take place and he was engaging the user community for a final review. Everything was on schedule, and James was going to have an extremely easy week remote from the client even though he was over two thousand miles away.

James had received an email from Ted and was advised that the team had said the two days of training was a complete success. There was no need for a follow-up meeting on that topic. Ted did ask that he work the issues list this week and finish the conversions; he would catch up on the following Monday when he was back in the office. That meant another trip to Coraopolis needed to be scheduled. The flight back and forth between San Diego and Coraopolis was just over twenty-four hundred miles, and James was racking up a lot of frequent flyer points. Still, the Sunday departure from San Diego to Pittsburgh coupled with the Friday return was getting to be a real chore; James was looking forward to the end of the six-month engagement. The money was good, and he was not ready to throw in the towel for a local assignment just yet. He would let the Butler company engagement play out and ride the gig for what it was worth.

Chapter 48

The Butler team had responded to the request by James to review the postconversion files in the new system. The Butler customers loaded were approved by Jean Roberts with no changes. The Cook customers loaded were approved by Nina Charles with no changes. The Butler and Cook vendors were reviewed and approved by Mary Thomas, again with no changes. James could not believe he was that good on his loads. The Butler team might have been asleep at the switch. So he decided to do a 100 percent record comparison review of what was sent to what was loaded independently of the team. He spent two hours and found no errors from the loads. His confidence was high, and he felt like this could be put to bed.

A separate email from Nina was received in regard to the four customers that were not loaded from the Barron company. Those four problem customers were not in the file that Jean submitted, per Nina. She requested that they be added back to the load and that Jean not be told about the reload. James's thought this was odd, but he complied.

* * *

Tim called Duncan Bailey Wednesday morning and requested a meeting in the Coraopolis office for next week. Duncan agreed to meet with the Butler team the following Wednesday. Tim requested that Charlotte send Duncan the details for his visit and make the arrangements at the Butler company's expense for the meeting. He would plan to fly up in the morning and spend about six hours with the team, then fly home later that same day. At that point Tim would spring the offer of $25 million for his business. This of course was the bottom end of the range, and he knew the offer would be rejected. But it was a starting point to see how desperate Duncan Bailey was to get out from under the twenty million in debt he had on the books.

"Hey, Tim, are we still on for dinner tonight?" Charlotte asked as she walked into his office.

"Absolutely," said Tim. "Did you make the reservation?"

"I did—seven p.m. at Frank's for three. Ted, you, and me. Any changes to that number?"

"Nope. It is just the three of us. We will meet you there."

* * *

Shirley walked into Paul's office; she needed to talk with him.

"Hey, Paul, we have some credits in our Wells Fargo lockbox account that I do not recognize," said Shirley.

"What kind of credits are you referring to?" Paul asked.

"There are five deposits each in the amount of $5 million from the board members. Do you know anything about this?"

"I am not aware of any agreement for that number. We will need to ask Tim Murphy about them. Just record them as loans for now until we can get to the bottom of it. I'll talk with Tim and get you an answer."

* * *

Just after lunch Paul saw Tim in the conference room and waved at him to get his attention.

"Hey, Tim, do you have a minute?" said Paul.

"What's up?" Tim asked as he stepped into the hallway.

"We received five deposits from the board members today and don't know what to do with them."

"I meant to talk to you before this happened. Sorry, that was my mistake. There will be eight payments of five million each coming into our account this week."

"Eight payments?" Paul asked. "You mean there are three more expected?"

"Yes, there will be three more: Jerry Evans, Ted MacDonald and I will be depositing five million each into the Butler account as part of the deal we worked out with the Wells Fargo Bank."

"Should I record these as loans to the company?"

"For now, mark them as loans. We will have to restructure them into convertible stock loans later. I'll get you more details after we get all the paperwork completed."

"We'll set up eight separate general ledger accounts for each of the payments."

"That would be fine. One other thing: keep an eye out for another deposit; this one is from Wells Fargo."

"How much are you expecting?"

"The proceeds will be for $100 million," said Tim. "It is to be used to fund the two acquisitions later this month."

"We will definitely keep an eye out for that one."

"There will also be a line of credit for $100 million. This is only if we need it."

"I am glad I caught you this morning."

"Sorry, I meant to catch up with you on this. Things around here have been a little bit crazy. I'll ask Charlotte to get you all the agreement information on this deal."

"Thanks. Appreciate the heads-up."

"Please let Shirley know about the deposits. Keep this information quiet and do not share it with your team. This is not public information, and we do not want it to be released until later. You will need to practice a bit of discretion here."

"I'll take care of it," said Paul.

"Did you get a chance to cut that check I asked for on Monday?" Tim asked.

"The one to Charlotte Webb for $100,000?"

"That is the one."

"It was cut and is sitting in my desk drawer under lock and key. I'll go and get it."

"Thanks."

Paul returned with the check in a plain envelope and handed it to Tim.

"What are we classifying this as?" Paul asked.

"Record this as a bonus to Charlotte Webb and keep it quiet," said Tim. "Understand?"

"Got it."

* * *

Tim and Ted had arrived at Frank's Italian Restaurant in downtown Coraopolis just before 7:00 p.m. to have a nice dinner with Charlotte. She did not know why the meeting was happening, but she could not pass up a meal at her favorite place. She planned to stop at the house for a quick change. The yellow dress with just a bit of cleavage but with a high line up her thigh was the one she would wear tonight. She had often received compliments on the dress and knew that men would be turning their heads to get a look at her.

Charlotte arrived promptly at 7:00 p.m. at Frank's. The restaurant was half-full of patrons having dinner. Tim spotted her at the door and waved her to their table. Charlotte walked past several tables of men, and she felt the looks and smiles they were all displaying. Both Tim and Ted got up to seat Charlotte at the table.

"Thank you, gentlemen," said Charlotte.

"You look beautiful," said Tim.

Ted just smiled and went to sit down. Charlotte was just smiling at both of them.

"We have a bottle of chilled Chianti; are you ready for a glass?" Tim asked.

Three glasses of Chianti were poured and then raised for a toast.

"So what did you two want to talk to me about?" Charlotte asked.

"Let's just order dinner," said Tim.

All three ordered a different specialty and enjoyed every bite. The conversation was lighthearted, and shoptalk was not on the agenda.

Then when the dessert menu came out, the group ordered three tiramisus. Just before dessert, Tim reached into his jacket pocket and pulled out a plain white envelope. He handed it to Charlotte.

"This is a token of our appreciation," said Tim.

"Thanks for your efforts on the Cook deal," said Ted.

Charlotte opened the envelope and was speechless.

"This is very generous," she eventually said.

"You earned it," said Tim. "You helped Ted close the deal on the way to our second acquisition."

"Well, I just pitched in where I was needed," said Charlotte.

"How did you do it?" Tim asked. "Never mind. I don't want to know."

"I just used my charm," said Charlotte. "A lady never tells."

The desserts arrived, and the table was quiet. They were all enjoying the tiramisu and sipping on a strong coffee. That is where it ended. A profitable evening for one Charlotte Webb a.k.a. the Closer

Chapter 49

Tim was in the office early on Thursday morning. He had to update the five board members on the conditions that the banker put on the agreement. They were not going to be happy with a one-year hold on the stock. The investment guy wanted a two-year lockout, but Jerry settled on one year instead. The board members would be stuck holding on to the stock for one year after the initial issuance date. There was one more condition that was not within their control: Butler had to acquire a third business prior to the stock issuance. This was another condition that the investment guys placed on the deal. All this information would be carefully crafted into an email and sent to the board members later in the day.

Charlotte strolled into Tim's office to bring him a cup of coffee.

"Hey, I just wanted you to know that Duncan Bailey confirmed for next week," she said. "Duncan arrives at the Pittsburgh airport on Wednesday morning and leaves on Thursday morning. He is staying at the Palmer Hotel down the street."

"That works out perfectly," said Tim. "Can you set up a dinner for Wednesday evening?"

"Sure can. What about the Pittsburgh Chop House down by the airport?"

"That sounds good. Duncan is probably a steak kind of guy."

"Who is going to the dinner party?"

"Make a reservation for four people. Duncan, Ted, you, and I."

"Do you really want me there for this meeting?" Charlotte asked.

"Absolutely," said Tim. "You're our new 'closer.'"

"What?"

"We need to soften this guy up, and your beauty will keep him distracted."

"This guy is married. So I am just going to be the eye candy to persuade him to take a low figure for his company?"

"That is the plan. Business is a rough game."

"I am learning a lot from you and Ted about the topic."

"How about if I get you a raise? An executive secretary with executive benefits?"

"I won't turn down a raise as long it is on the up and up."

"Consider it done," said Tim as Charlotte proceeded to walk out of his office.

***

A request from Mary Thomas to James Crowley was made to set up a new employee, Patty Gray. She had accepted the position of AP analyst 1 and was starting in the office next Monday. A Blue Point Hosting account, along with a user account in the Enterprise Software, would need activation. She would be limited to the AP module for now. Mary asked for James's personal assistance in training her on the new system. This was an odd request, but maybe Mary did not feel comfortable enough to train her team members just yet. But it was part of the consultants' overall responsibilities and would be offloaded to the employees just as soon as possible. James responded to Mary that he would carve out some time next week to complete the training.

* * *

Ted made a phone call to James early on Thursday morning. The time was 11:00 a.m. Eastern, 8:00 a.m. Pacific.

"Hey, James, this is Ted. Do you have a few minutes."

"Sure. What's up?"

"I need to run something by you and see if you're interested."

"What is this about?"

"You and Bill are doing a fantastic job, and we would like to extend both of you," said Ted. "The contract extension would be for one year."

"A year?"

"I know this is not the normal way of doing things, but we feel that good talent is hard to find. When you find it, you need to reward it."

"Thanks for that vote of confidence," said James.

"Oh, by the way, your new number will be $125 per hour," said Ted.

"That is very generous. Have you talked with Bill Hogan about this?"

"No. You're the first. If I can get you to sign, then Bill will agree to sign as well. You two are a well-run team."

"Do you want me to send you a new set of paperwork?"

"I'll have Charlotte draw something up and forward it to you for a signature. Are you in?"

"Yes, I am in. Thank you very much—we will deliver for you and the Butler team."

"I am counting on it."

The phone went dead, and James placed it on the desk. He started to jump around the casita like a two-year-old with a piece of candy. Abbey and Champ were looking at him and not sure what was going on. James immediately got on the phone and called Lynn to tell her the news. She was ecstatic for her husband.

A few minutes later, Bill called James and shared the news of his phone call from Ted. He was also happy to sign up for a one-year agreement. He did the math on 2,000 hours at $125 per hour and came up with a gross of $250,000 for a one-year gig.

"So what do you think?" asked Bill.

"I am going to sign up for the year," said James.

"This could be the goose that laid the golden egg."

"Let's not get ahead of our skis on this?"

"I know. But the money is going to be fantastic."

"Remember in good times, put some away," said James. "You never know when the lean times will come along."

"You're such a smart-ass."

"No. I am just a realist."

"Next time we get together, we need to celebrate."

"Agreed. We need to celebrate our good fortune."

"Talk to you later," Bill said as he ended the call.

Chapter 50

Mary Thomas was reviewing the cash requirements report for this week with Paul Meadows in his office. Every Thursday the routine was completed so that the vendor checks could be released by Friday. The envelopes would be stuffed and then dropped off in the mailbox late in the afternoon. This would allow the Butler company to float on the money for a three-day window. This was a common practice, and all the vendors knew it was going on. The earliest that a vendor would cash a check would be Monday, and Paul knew it.

"Hey, Paul, here is the cash required for this week's check run," said Mary. "The total is $150,000 for all the vendor checks."

"That is a light week," said Paul.

"Next week's total will be larger," Mary said. "We need to put a deposit on those new trucks, and we will need about one million dollars."

"We did get twenty-five million from the board members this week. We have two big outlays for the acquisitions at the end of the month."

"How are we going to cover that?"

"I forget to tell you: I had a conversation with Tim yesterday. He said that a line of credit was established, and a one hundred-million-dollar loan was coming this week."

"I did not see anything yet this week."

"Keep an eye out for it."

"I can do that," said Mary. "So this check run is approved?"

"Yep. Go ahead and run the checks."

Mary left his office and went to start the process. The software they were using was antiquated, and it took three times as long as it should have to process the checks. The new system would cut this process down to fifteen minutes; Mary couldn't wait to ditch the old method. She postdated the checks to Friday and processed the batch. After the checks were printed, the stack was proofed to the summary and handed to Paul for signature. Then the batch was returned to Mary and placed in a locked drawer for distribution on Friday afternoon.

* * *

Ted MacDonald was in the office of Tim Murphy. They were going over the schedule of the two acquisitions. Both companies were going to be purchased in an all-cash deal, the Barron Water Hauling Corporation for $50 million and the Cook Salt Water Removal Corporation for $50 million. The date was April 1, just ten days away.

"Do we have the money from the bank?" Ted asked.

"They said it would be here by Friday," replied Tim. "I asked Paul to let me know as soon as it gets credited to our account."

"Did you put your five million in yet?"

"I was planning to do it on Friday."

"I already scheduled my transfer for Friday."

"Do you know if Jerry put his contribution in yet?"

"We all agreed that Friday was the deadline," said Ted. "So he has one more day if it hasn't been completed. By the way, I took care of the consultants yesterday. I signed them up for a one-year agreement at the $125 rate we discussed before."

"Did they agree to the extension?"

"They both were delighted with the new arrangement. They are still cheaper than the alternative."

"Even at the new rate?"

"They're at least $100 per hour below what the other guys wanted. The best part is that we control them, and they are one hundred percent exclusive to Butler."

"That is a good deal," said Tim. "You just have to manage them."

"They are professionals, and I think they will work out nicely. We may want to consider converting them to employees at some time down the line."

"That is an excellent idea. They would be loyal to you and Butler and the three-year plan. You are going to have to reward them on the road with some perks," said Tim. "Nice dinners and maybe some golf outings?"

"Not a bad idea. They are big golfers so that fits really nicely in my wheelhouse."

"We both love golf. Let's plan an outing at Jerry's club. Just the four of us. I don't think Jerry would mind."

"That's not a bad idea," said Ted. "I'll plan to do it in April after the go-live date and if they perform."

"That sounds like an excellent reward for those two."

"I'll take care of it and ask Jerry to approve."

"What about the staff?" Tim asked. "Are they ready to handle the new system and to put two newly acquired businesses on the platform?"

"I think it is going to be a little bit rocky. The team needs to get their feet wet and make some mistakes. They need to grow into this situation. Most of this team has done this before. The only wild card is the new system."

"Why is the system the stumbling block?"

"None of them have used this one before. But the ace in the hole is that James and Bill are seasoned professionals. They will bend to meet the gap that our people may break."

"Good point," replied Tim. "So the $125 bump up is rather a cheap hedge against the team falling apart."

"Yep," said Ted. "And there's something else I think we need to consider."

"What's that?"

"I think we should announce to the team that there will be bonuses paid after this initial round of acquisitions. Sort of like a thank-you for all the hard work in launching the business on the new platform."

"I think that is another great idea. We should run it by Jerry and see what he thinks."

"You're the CFO. We need to infuse them into the Butler family."

"What about Charlotte?"

"If she wasn't our executive secretary, I would put her in the sales department," said Ted.

"She would be able to sell ice cubes to an Eskimo."

"She would sell them the dammed fridge as well."

"Should we use her on the Metairie deal next Wednesday?"

"Absolutely."

"It may cost us another hundred."

"If she can shave off another five million, then another bonus of one hundred is peanuts."

"Hey, I am late for a meeting. I have to run."

"We can catch up later if needed," said Ted.

As Ted left Tim's office, he thought, *We are using this beautiful woman to advance the business of the Butler company for profit. The company is getting the best of her, and she needs to be compensated for all her hard work.* Tim took it upon himself to go to the human resources manager and find out what her current salary was.

* * *

After lunch Ted had his planned conversation with the human resources manager. He found out that Tim had hired Charlotte Webb last year at an annual salary of $50,000 as an executive secretary. She was out of college three years ago, and her qualifications were strong. For what she was doing, the salary should be at least $100,000. Ted made a note to himself and was going to have a conversation with Tim later in the week. Charlotte Webb was priceless, after all.

Chapter 51

Nina Charles was processing Friday's lockbox deposits late in the morning and noticed that there were four extra deposits. There was a $5 million ACH deposit from Jerry Evans, one from Tim Murphy, and one from Ted MacDonald. The Wells Fargo Bank had also deposited a wire in the amount of $100 million. She was not sure what to think of all this newfound money. Rather than call the bank and ask for an explanation, she marched into Paul Meadows's office to run it by him.

"Hey, Paul, do you have a minute for me?" Nina asked.

"Sure, what's up?"

"We have some strange activity in the Wells Fargo regular account. There appear to be four mystery deposits that I don't recognize."

"Let me guess: three five-million-dollar deposits from Jerry, Tim, and Ted and a bank deposit of one hundred million dollars."

"How did you know that?"

"Tim told me about it yesterday. I meant to catch you up, but something else came up."

"Are you going to take care of the booking to the ledger?" Nina asked.

"Yes. I'll take care of it. One hundred and fifteen million in total. Right?"

"That is the exact number."

"We need one hundred million to buy the two companies next week. The acquisition date is April first. So the loan came in right in time."

"I'll leave this in your hands," Nina said as she left Paul's office.

Paul sent an email to Jerry, Tim, and Ted advising them that the Butler company acknowledged their deposit in the amount of $5 million each. Included in the email was the fact that Wells Fargo Bank deposited $100 million today as well. The bank had forwarded the loan agreement to Paul. The loan was a one-year balloon, and the rate was 8.5 percent, right at the current prime rate.

All the parties to the arrangement had complied with the deal so far. The board had done their part. The executives had done their part. The Wells Fargo Bank had done its part. All the proceeds were deposited in the regular checking account one week before the acquisition date of April 1.

* * *

James was in the casita with Champ and Abbey. Not much was going on. The configurations had all been completed, and there was no more training for any of the Butler team members. It was kind of a quiet day before the shit would hit the fan next week. The acquisition date was April 1, and that meant working the next weekend amid a twelve-day-straight on-site trip. Lynn was not happy about this, but that was how the consulting gig sometimes worked. She was traveling those same two weeks and would have to take care of getting the Westies to the sitter Sunday night and picking them up on Friday for two straight weeks.

James was planning on going for a ride through the canyons after work as long as Lynn got home in the afternoon. She was driving down from Pasadena to Fallbrook and was usually home by 4:00 p.m. This allowed James to pass the puppies to Lynn and go riding. The weather was nice and sunny, and the temp was ideal. A ten-mile ride was a nice way to spend a Friday afternoon. The Trek racing bike he had purchased just a few weeks ago was such a pleasure to ride. Lynn thought it was an unnecessary toy. But James bought it anyway.

* * *

Charlotte had decided to make a follow-up appointment with her shrink for next week. She did feel that talking with Natalie Parker had helped her get some of the pain of that incident in college off of her chest. Another session could maybe do her some good, and then just maybe she could have a normal boyfriend experience.

She had a date tonight with Phil Reynolds, whom she met at the downtown Coraopolis farmers market last Saturday. Phil was helping his father sell vegetables and she just struck up a conversation with him. They had a lot in common and were drawn together by a few common interests. Charlotte asked Phil if this was his real job, and he politely said no. He was just helping out to keep the family farm operating by moonlighting at the market. His full-time job was assistant chef at Frank's Italian Restaurant.

Charlotte was going to meet Phil at Frank's on Friday night at seven. She had a good feeling about the date and thought it was worth a chance. She would drive over to the restaurant, have dinner with Phil, and her plan was when the date was over, she would leave by herself. This would be just about dinner and nothing else. There would be no entanglement and no other evening activities. If the date went well, then maybe a second one could be arranged. Charlotte was determined to take this really slow, just in case this guy was a keeper.

Charlotte arrived at the restaurant right at 7:00 p.m. Phil already had a table in the back corner—a quiet and cozy little alcove where they would be left alone. Phil waved to Charlotte, and she walked right over to the waiting gentleman.

"Hi, Charlotte, glad you could make it."

"You know that this is my favorite restaurant," said Charlotte.

"That's a bit of good luck for me."

"I would like to think that it's because of my culinary talents."

"Well, you're doing a good job. The food is terrific."

"I have a good chef that taught me everything I know."

"Wait a minute. If you're here at the table, then who is in the kitchen?"

"That would be Momma Frank. She is the best Italian chef I know. She brought over her grandmother's recipes from Italy back in 1940, when she landed here in America."

"Tell her not to change one item on the menu. They are all perfect."

"Come with me. You can tell her yourself."

Phil brought Charlotte into the kitchen, where Momma Frank was creating her specialties. The aromas were pleasing to the nose as the door to the kitchen was opened.

"Momma Frank, this is Charlotte," said Phil. "She said your food is excellent, and she wanted to complement you on your recipes."

"Thank you, Ms. Charlotte," said Momma Frank. "I am glad you enjoy my cooking. I am going to make you my specialty: Do you enjoy lasagna?"

"Yours is the best in town," said Charlotte.

"You two get out of here," said Momma Frank. "Go drink some Chianti, and I'll make you my specialty. Out, out, out."

Phil grabbed Charlotte by the hand and ushered her back to the table. After all, they had been instructed to get out of Momma's kitchen and wait for a special dinner. Phil poured two glasses of Chianti, and the two of them just talked. The conversation was going well. Charlotte felt her guard was going down. *Could I like this guy?* she thought to herself.

Momma came out with a huge plate of lasagna, along with spaghetti and meatballs, for each of them. The presentation of the plate was perfect.

"Momma Frank, you have outdone yourself," said Phil.

"This smells wonderful," said Charlotte. "You really did not have to do this."

"A friend of Phil is a friend of the family," said Momma. "Enjoy, you two, and take home whatever you don't finish."

"Will do," said Charlotte.

The rest of the evening was spent devouring the food and drinking Chianti. There was a little bit of conversation; Charlotte was just enjoying the evening. There was no room for dessert, so after dinner the evening was over.

"Can I see you again?" asked Phil.

"The evening is still young," said Charlotte.

"I have to go back to the kitchen."

"You're working tonight?"

"Yep. I was just taking a break for you."

"You are so sweet," said Charlotte. "Call me for a second date, and I'll take you out."

"That's a deal. I am sorry to rush you, but I have to get back to the kitchen."

"Go." Charlotte gave him a kiss on the cheek.

"I'll call you next week," said Phil.

Charlotte left the restaurant and was in heaven. She had just met a guy that was wonderful, warm, friendly, funny, and dedicated to food. *Did I just score the perfect guy? Pinch me—I need to wake up.*

Chapter 52

James was in the conference room once again. It was 8:00 a.m. on Monday, and the whole gang was there. This time Tim Murphy and Jerry Evans were in attendance. This was Ted MacDonald's meeting. James knew to let Ted speak for the full fifteen minutes and only comment on the project if asked to do so.

"Let me start out by saying thank you to all who are here in today's meeting," announced Ted. "It is because all of you have contributed to this project and have dedicated a part of your lives to helping the Butler company achieve success. Our acquisition of the Barron company and the Cook company will start us on the road to a bigger and brighter future. James will lay out the schedule in just a couple of minutes. Tim, did you want to say a few words?"

"Thanks, Ted," replied Tim. "I would also like to express my deep gratitude for all of your efforts. We know that this has been rough on a lot of you, and we are going to reward you all. We have one more push to get this done, and then we can look to the future. There will be bonuses next week after the go-live date as a thanks from the Butler company to you all. Jerry, did you want to say a few words?"

"I'll try, but you two have already done that for me," said Jerry. "All I can say is thanks and we will be planning a big party when this is over."

The group erupted in loud clapping and cheering. The decibel level could be heard down the hall, where Charlotte was on the phone. She was wondering what was going on and rushed into the conference room.

"Is something wrong?" she asked.

"Nothing wrong, Charlotte," said Tim. "Jerry was just doing a bit of cheerleading."

"OK. I'll go back to my desk and *man the phone*," said Charlotte.

"Please do," said Tim. "Thanks for covering for us. We will not be long."

Jerry turned the presentation back over to Tim.

"We received the financing from the bank on Friday," said Tim. "The loan agreement is in place. The board members have stuck their neck out with five million dollars each, and we are ready to go. Now we need to deliver as a team and make this happen."

Tim looked at Ted; he knew that the spotlight had shifted to his team now. The new software system was expected to be the glue that held all the future companies together as they gobbled them up.

"This meeting is a short one for the entire team, and as we said, James will be laying out the schedule later today," said Ted. "The planning meeting will be at one p.m. James will send out the invites. Thanks again, and let's make this happen. You are all excused for now."

Jerry had motioned for Tim, Ted, Bill, and James to hang back and let the group leave. He had something to tell them.

"I would like to personally thank the four of you for the great job you're doing on this project," said Jerry. "A reservation at my club has been made for Tuesday afternoon to play golf. I would request that you enjoy the afternoon and have a little bit of fun before the conversion weekend. Thanks again for all of your valuable contributions to the Butler team."

Bill and James could say nothing but thanks.

"Are we OK on the schedule if we sneak away for an afternoon?" Ted asked James.

"I think we can squeeze in a round of golf," said James. "The Tuesday schedule has room because it's kind of a holding anyway."

"A holding?" Tim asked.

"We are waiting for things to happen," said James. "This week is still kind of prep for the event. Until the April first date, the consultants are kind of just hoovering around the users and putting out fires."

"You guys are working the weekend?" Tim asked.

"Yes, we are," said James. "Will the office be open Saturday and Sunday, or should we set up a room at the hotel?"

"I'll need to check with Charlotte to see if the management group allows access to the building over the weekend," said Ted.

"What we have done in the past is reserve a conference room at the hotel and then request that the team go there for the weekend activities," said James.

"I think that is a good idea," said Ted. "Can you set that up with the hotel and announce it in the one p.m. meeting?"

"Let me go ask Charlotte," said Tim. "She knows about the management staff here."

Tim left the conference room and went to visit Charlotte. After a short time, he returned.

"Charlotte said this place is locked up tighter than a drum on the weekend," said Tim.

"James, can you go back to the Palmer Hotel and make the necessary arrangements immediately?" Ted asked.

"I'll walk over there right now," said James.

* * *

James walked down to the Palmer Hotel, which was just about a block away from the office. It would have taken longer to drive than walk. It was a nice day, and some fresh air was very welcome. James arrived at the business office and inquired about available conference rooms. The manager said that they had several available and he could take his pick. This next weekend represented a rare situation in which nothing was going on at the hotel. James secured the Palmer Room for Saturday and Sunday for the team. The manager would add the charge to his bill and was happy to oblige. James requested breakfast food, coffee, lunch, and sweets available for both days for a capacity of ten people. This way the team would come to James and not the other way around. The manager would take care of the requests and was happy for the business.

James finished the arrangements and headed back to the office. The sun felt so warm on the skin that he was tempted to stay outside awhile. *Got to get back and manage this team,* he thought to himself.

Chapter 53

James sent out the email invitation Monday morning to the entire team. He wanted everyone at the meeting at 1:00 p.m. for a planning session. His goal was to run through the schedule and tell them that they were expected to work this weekend. James and Bill had done these activities before with at least twenty clients in the past twenty years. They would hear every excuse in the book for the team not working the weekend. But every conversion and go-live project he had done in the past required a weekend regiment to tie up loose ends before the first day of business, which was slated for Monday. The successful projects had that two-day window of slack time to button up issues and resolve fires. He was going to demand it from them and gently tell Ted it was absolutely needed for the success of the project.

It was now 1:00 p.m. on Monday, and the team started to arrive in the conference room.

"Thanks, everyone, for attending this planning session for the conversion and go-live event," said James. "This week will be spent closing the two businesses up on their old systems. The month end of March will be the old system, and the month of April will be on the new system. We will be working the weekend, Saturday, and Sunday, at the Palmer Hotel, in the Palmer Room. We have it reserved for two days. Until your area of the business is cleared, you will be expected to work on the weekend."

"I know it is a sacrifice to work on Saturday and Sunday, but we need your assistance to get this done," said Ted. "Your area will be cleared by James and Bill, and when you're done, you will be released."

"What does that mean, 'released'?" Tim asked.

"An example would be customer billings for Nina," said James. "A final AR aging report will be needed from the Barron company and the Cook company in a CSV file so I can convert it. It will be converted into the new system, and then the beginning balance of the AR aging report in the new system will be signed off. This signifies that the old business has been closed and that the new business can start up on Monday."

"Are you going to give us all instructions?" Paul asked.

"Yes," said James. "You all will need to schedule some time with Bill and myself between now and Wednesday to determine the specifics of your area that need preconversion activity, conversion activity, and postconversion activity. This will all be summarized into the project plan, and it will be printed and hung up on the door of the conference room at the Palmer Hotel."

"Why would you do that?" Paul asked.

"The project plan is the key document to running this conversion and go-live event," said James. "I will post the plan on the wall so everyone can see it and know in a minute's glance where we are. If a line item is highlighted in yellow and marked as checked on the list, it will be considered done, and Tim, Ted, and Jerry can assess how we are doing at any given minute."

"Jerry Evans—our president—is going to work the weekend?" Paul asked.

"Yes he is," said James. "He has a vested interest in the success of this project. This was reviewed with him and approved."

That last statement was a bit of fluff by James, and Ted looked at him kind of funny.

"Please coordinate with James," said Ted. "We want every opportunity to be successful, and these guys have done this before. They know what they are doing."

"Bill and I have done dozens of projects successfully, and this really is a best practice when it comes to converting an old business to a new business," said James. "We will clear you as fast as we can. Sometimes the Sunday work is just a couple of hours reviewing and buttoning up some last-minute items. You all want the conversions to be rock solid and be able to run the business Monday morning with no lookbacks."

"What is a lookback?" Tim asked.

"If we convert the AR balances and we find that the customers accounts are wrong, we have to reload the invoices. This is called a lookback. If a customer has five invoices and owes us $10,000, we don't want this line in the sand to shift. The ending number from the old system must match the beginning number in the new system. It is sort of like balancing your checkbook. If March thirty-first your balance is $1,000, then the April first balance should be $1,000. Does that make sense to everyone?"

There were a lot of nods and yawns from the team.

"Ladies and gentlemen, we are paying for James and Bill to steer us on this journey," said Ted. "Listen to their advice and suggestions."

"I am sorry if I sound like a broken record," said James. "I have seen clients make the same mistake over and over, and this is not for the Butler team. We want you to be successful the first time."

"My father had a saying: *Measure twice and cut once*," said Ted.

"You're exactly right, Ted," said James. "We don't want you all to make mistakes that are not necessary. If we do this right the first time, then everyone has an enjoyable experience with the go-live event."

"So when should we talk with you?" said Shirley Moore.

"Any time in the next forty-eight hours," said James. "You all need to have your activities on the project plan. I will review all the line items that are assigned to you and when they need to be done. This project plan list will control all the items that need to get done before, during, and after the conversion process."

"So pencil in a slot of time to go through the project plan with James and Bill," said Ted. "We need to have every activity on the plan so we can run the Butler company next week on the new software. Thanks, everyone. We are adjourned."

The team members hung around and started to request slots of time for impromptu meetings with James. He was happy to reserve blocks of time for each one as they left the conference room.

"I think that went well," said James as he looked at Ted.

"There are a couple of them that look like a deer in the headlights," said Ted.

"We will bring them around. We need to have the conversion project plan filled out so they know what has to be done and when. Then they will follow the schedule."

"Do you see them working Sunday?"

"If they do, it will be for only a short period of time. Most users will bust their hump on Saturday so they do not have to work on Sunday. The second day on the weekend is in case something really blows up."

"That is comforting to know."

"By the way, what about Blue Point Hosting?" James asked.

"I'll need to call them and request Saturday and Sunday on-call services," said Ted.

"I think that would be a good idea," said James. "They are our nerve center, and we should have them on speed dial in case something blows up and we need to do a backup."

"I'll call them as soon as I get out of here and see what their SLA is," said Ted, referring to the service level agreement.

"I think we are moving right along," said James.

"Keep the train on the track," said Ted as he left the conference room.

Chapter 54

Mary Thomas was the first team member to review the conversion activities list with James in the conference room on Tuesday morning. She was a bit of a worrywart and wanted to make sure her area was covered.

"Good morning, Mary," said James. "How are you this morning?"

"I wanted to be the first one in here today. I am concerned about our strategy to convert these payments to vendors on the new system."

"I thought we agreed that we were not going down that route?"

"How are we going to do it, then?"

"Can I make a suggestion?"

"Sure, any advice would be appreciated."

"If we do not have to get off the old system for the accounts payable function, then why don't we just run it out over a four-week period in April?" James asked. "You would process checks under the old system each week and then journalize the number into the new system as a debit and credit entry."

"That sounds like a good idea."

"It would require you to set up another AP trade account, like maybe 'AP Trade Old,' on the new system. Then you would journalize the number of the checks being processed for that weekly check run."

"Let me think about that option."

"Why don't we discuss it with Shirley and Paul and see what they think?"

"That's a wonderful suggestion."

"The only problem you will have is that you have two feet in both systems," said James. "You will need to be incredibly careful with where you are running the check processing. You could have an old check run the first week and a new check run in the same week."

"I can manage that," said Mary. "I am the only one running the checks."

"Then you should be fine. I can write up the activities using this method, and that will make it easy for you to wrap up the old company."

"So do I have to work on the weekend?"

"Probably not. As long as you can button up the AP function for the Barron and Cook companies and get to an ending number with accruals, you should be good."

"Can I accrue into the old companies if a bill comes due after the date?"

"Yes, you can. But you have to process it as old business against the newly created accrual account. This is a bit tricky, and you will need to be careful."

"I can take care of that," said Mary.

"Then I would suggest you talk with Paul and Shirley and tell them what you want to do, and I'll write it up accordingly."

"That sounds like a good plan for my department."

"Do you want to have a meeting with those two, or are you going to take care of it?"

"I'll go talk to them and let you know," said Mary as she left the conference room.

"Thanks," said James.

* * *

Nina Charles was the next team member to come into the conference room to voice her concerns. She wanted to make sure she had all of her planned activities on the list for the weekend party.

"Hi, James. Are you ready for me?" Nina asked.

"Yep let's take care of your area," James replied. "You have provided me with the customers for the Cook company, and they have been converted already. You will need to close the old system and process all of the cash through Friday. Then provide me a closing accounts receivable aging report as of the end of the month. A CSV file will be required with the new customer ID numbers under the new format. Remember, we collapsed all of the multiple ship-to sites under one unique customer."

"I have done this once before, so I am a little familiar with the process."

"Fantastic. You and I will have an easy time with this. So when on Friday will you have a final AR aging for the Cook company?"

"It will not be until at least three p.m. Eastern time."

"Can you coordinate the final AR aging for the Barron company with Jean? I assume you will be managing both companies in the new system?"

"You are correct. Jean will have nothing to do with the customer base, and I will be responsible for both companies."

"So I will put your name on the conversion project plan for both companies for the conversion activities?" James asked.

"Yes, please do. I'll manage Jean on this point and let Paul know the decision we just made."

"OK. You will be down on the list to provide me a final AR for the Barron and Cook companies. I'll convert them into the new system. The postconversion AR lists will be sent to you for a blessing and a sign-off, and then you can be released."

"So I have to work the weekend?" Nina asked.

"If I were you, I would plan it that way. You really want the AR opening balances in the new company on the new software to be solid."

"I'll plan to be at the hotel Saturday and Sunday."

"It's in your best interest to be there. If something has to be reviewed and fixed, it will be up to you."

"What happens to cash that gets in after the date?"

"The new cash is the property of the new owner and the would-be Butler company. So it is extremely important that you process all of the preacquisition cash to the seller company. Please keep in mind that the deal as I know it is a purchase of assets, which includes the AR balances."

"You are correct," said Nina. "That is what was explained to me as well. What about those four customers that Jean did not include in the customer file?"

"I added them into the Butler company as you requested."

"Thanks. I have a funny feeling about those four records."

"I am in agreement with you. I can't put my finger on it just yet, but something is a little bit off."

"Do you have everything from me for the activities on the conversion list?"

"I believe your area is complete, and I'll review it with you once it has been updated on Wednesday."

"OK. I'll just stop by sometime on Wednesday."

"I'll be here all week. Thanks in advance for all your help on this. I'll try to make the process easy and painless for you."

"I appreciate it," said Nina as she left the conference room.

* * *

Late in the afternoon, Shirley and Paul arrived in the conference room together and unannounced.

"Hey, James, do you have a few minutes for us?" Paul asked.

"Sure. What's up?" James asked.

"We want to talk to you about the general ledger stuff," said Paul.

"I have the opening balance sheet numbers for both the Barron company and the Cook company as part of the postconversion activities," said James.

"We don't have any preconversion or conversion activities?" asked Shirley.

"Both of these companies are purchases, right?" James asked.

"That is correct," said Paul.

"And I am not loading the prior income statement activity, correct?"

"You are one hundred percent on the money," said Paul.

"So I need your general ledger numbers sometime in the next thirty days," said James. "I would prefer to have them before your first month end if possible."

"You will get the opening numbers in the first week," said Paul.

"I have a placeholder on the conversion project plan for the Barron company and the Cook company on these two items," said James. "But this is not a time-sensitive item. You have some room to get it to me. You will need to give it to me in a CSV file with the new account code combinations. Will Jean Roberts be giving me the Barron numbers?"

"We will take care of both of them, no problem," said Paul.

"So can I put your name on this activity?"

"I'll deliver both of these items to you when it is finalized."

"Are you two going to show up at the hotel over the weekend?"

"We will be there," said Paul. "We need to support the team and make an appearance." Shirley just nodded her head in agreement.

"Thanks," said James. "Did you get a chance to talk with Mary on the AP decision we made?"

"Yes," said Paul. "I am good with the suggestion you made."

"It just requires a separate AP trade account to be set up."

"I'll take care of that," said Shirley. "Separating the old AP from the new was a good suggestion."

"I have used this approach before, and it proved to be invaluable," said James. "It will keep the preconversion AP frozen and identified for burnout. This way if the value of the AP turns out differently, then a residual can be paid to the former owners."

"I did not really think about that one," said Paul. "That is a good point."

"Let's just say *I have seen this story before.*"

"You're good at what you do," Paul said as he left the conference room with Shirley in tow.

James had it on the list to update the conversion project list by the end of the day on Tuesday for all of the team's activities. He was right on track now that all the team members had discussed just what was expected of them for the next couple of days. All of the pieces to the puzzle were being aligned and falling into place. James was feeling really good about the progress but was always weary of something being missed. For now, though, the i's were dotted and the t's were crossed.

Chapter 55

It was Wednesday, just three days away from the conversion weekend, and James was feeling a little bit of heat. He had finished the conversion project list of all the tasks and items that needed to be documented. There was a resource assigned to each of the line items in the plan, including those assigned to him. Each of the team members floated into the conference room to review the assigned list of action items, and there were minor changes and some additions. James was happy to make the adds and get a confirmation from all involved that he had everything covered.

Late in the morning, Ted wandered into the conference room with a stranger.

"Hey, James, I want you to meet someone," said Ted.

"Good morning, gentlemen," said James. "What can I do for you?"

"I just want to introduce you to Duncan Bailey," said Ted. "He is the owner of Metairie Pipeline Corporation in Greenwood, Louisiana."

"Nice to meet you," said James as he shook Duncan's hand.

"James is running our conversion project onto a new software platform for the two companies we are in the process of acquiring," said Ted.

"Sounds like a large project with a lot of moving pieces," said Duncan. "When are you acquiring the companies?"

"We will place two companies on our system on Saturday of this week," said James. "They will be operational on Monday if all goes well."

"He is kidding, of course," said Ted.

"Sorry, just a little bit of humor," said James. "We will be running the two new businesses on the new software Monday morning bright and early."

"Well, congratulations and the best of luck," said Duncan.

"Thanks," said James. "I have done over twenty of these, and they all have some wrinkles. But the Butler team is prepared for all contingencies."

"That's good to know," said Duncan. "You really sound like you know what you're doing."

"James and Bill are the best in the business," said Ted. "They are on an exclusive contract with the Butler company. If you join the Butler team, you experience them as well. Thanks, James, and sorry for the interruption."

"No problem," said James. "We are tracking to the plan, just wanted you to know."

Ted escorted Duncan out of the conference room and then introduced him to Charlotte.

"Charlotte, do you have a minute?" Ted asked.

"Good morning to you too, Ted," said Charlotte. "Who do you have with you?"

"You may know him," said Ted. "You spoke with him on the phone."

"You must be Duncan Bailey," said Charlotte.

"That's me," said Duncan. "It is nice to put a face to the voice."

"Charlotte is the executive secretary to Tim Murphy," said Ted.

"I take care of Ted as well," said Charlotte.

"I wish I were not married," said Duncan. "You're gorgeous."

"Thank you," said Charlotte as she started to blush.

"Charlotte, we will be in my office for a little while going over a few things," said Ted as he closed the door.

"Did you get the numbers I sent you and Tim earlier?" said Duncan as soon as they sat down.

"Yes, we did," said Ted. "There was one item in your PNL that we were curious about."

"What's that?"

"You have a hunting expense for over $100,000. Can you shed some light on this expense?"

"Sure. As you know, the oil patch is a bunch of good old boys and they all like to drink, hunt, and shoot at things. This is where I entertain them and some of our employees."

"What do you hunt, if I may ask?"

"Mostly wild turkey and wild boar, with an assortment of handguns and rifles. It is a lot of fun, and a good time is always had by the customers."

"So would this be part of the purchase if we bought your business?"

"That's negotiable," said Duncan. "I kind of like that twenty-acre hunting farm. It has been in our family for over fifty years."

"That is definitely something we could talk about. But what do you think your business is worth?"

"You get right to the point, don't you?"

"We did not bring you here for no reason. We are interested, at the right price."

"What are you offering?"

"Well, we think your business is worth $25 million."

"That is a very low offer. The business is worth at least $35 million."

"You have $20 million in debt on the books," said Ted. "You pulled out a salary of $250,000, and your net profit was only $50,000."

"The business is still worth at least $35 million," said Duncan.

"You did not include any information on your trucks," said Ted. "We figure based on the expenses on the PNL that these ten trucks are at least fifteen years old. We would be willing to double your salt water capacity and provide ten brand-new trucks."

"That's an interesting development," said Duncan. "But what else would I get?"

"We would let you stay on as president with a bigger salary, a noncompete agreement, and an earn-out agreement while we double and possibly triple the business. You could stand to earn some big bucks as the Butler company takes all the risks."

"Let me think about it for a little bit."

"Sure. We will put it on paper and can send you an offer later this week."

"You guys don't waste any time."

"We are putting a premier business together into a $500 million enterprise. You could be on the ground floor of this opportunity."

"That sounds really good. Let me think about it."

Ted continued to entertain Duncan and introduced him to everyone at the Butler organization, including Jerry Evans. At the end of the day, Duncan was full of information. The Butler company wanted to buy his business and add it to the portfolio of wholly owned subsidiaries. But Duncan was still a little bit turned off by the low $25 million offer.

* * *

It was well after six o'clock and time to call it a night. Ted had done his best to sell the Butler company to Duncan, but he could see he was getting nowhere.

"Did you want to freshen up?" asked Ted.

"I would like that," said Duncan.

"We have a reservation at the Pittsburgh Chop House a few miles from here at seven."

"Can you pick me up at the hotel down the street in a couple of minutes?"

"Sure. I can pick you up around six forty-five, and we can drive over."

"Sounds good," said Duncan. "See you then."

* * *

Ted picked up Duncan from the hotel, and they drove over to the Pittsburgh Chop House.

"I hope you like steaks," Ted said.

"That's my favorite," said Duncan.

At the restaurant Tim Murphy and Charlotte Webb were already seated waiting for Ted and Duncan to arrive. Ted waved at the front door, and Tim motioned them over to their table.

"Glad you made it, Duncan," said Tim. "You know everyone here,"

"You're even more beautiful here in this restaurant than in the office," said Duncan. "How do you keep all the men away, Ms. Charlotte."

"Easy," said Charlotte. "They are all married."

"Let's get some drinks," said Tim.

A round of Gentleman Jack and Cokes with a lemon twist for the men was ordered. Charlotte had a glass of Chardonnay. A second round of drinks for the men had arrived before the waiter took their dinner orders. The conversation turned to marital status: all three men said they were married with children.

"I have two children," said Duncan. "A twenty-five-year-old, Bruce Greene, and a twenty-two-year-old, Carl Bailey. Bruce is my stepson from another marriage."

Charlotte got quiet all of a sudden. Could the Bruce Greene that Duncan Bailey mentioned be the guy she went out with that night in college? The guy that date-raped her. Charlotte would need to slip in some questions to find out.

The subject shifted back to business late in the meal, and that is when Tim asked Duncan, "So what do you think about our offer?"

"Ted said it was twenty-five," said Duncan. "I think the business is worth thirty-five."

"You only made fifty thousand after taxes last year," said Tim. "Your trucks are fifteen-plus years old, and you have twenty million in debt."

"I still think the business is worth thirty-five," said Duncan.

"I want you to think about it," said Tim. "Did Ted explain the other perks?"

"Yes, he did," said Duncan. "Let me think about it?"

The waiter cleared the table and asked if another round of drinks would be needed; they all said yes. Charlotte excused herself to go to the bathroom. When she came out, she saw all three headed for the restroom. This was her chance to spike Duncan's drink.

She got back to the table and pulled out a vial with two crushed-up Valium. She casually grabbed Duncan's drink and dropped the powder into it. Carefully she stirred it to dissolve the white color to a murky color; now it was not noticeable. *It's payback time, and I am going to get a payoff for what the son did to me back in college.*

The men returned from the restroom and decided to order dessert. Charlotte knew that the effects of the Valium would take maybe fifteen to thirty minutes to set in.

The desserts were finished, the bill was paid, and now it was time to leave. Just then Tim got a call from his wife about something that happened at home; he was to come home immediately. Since his wife dropped him off at the office, Tim had no way of getting home. Her car was still in the shop being repaired from an earlier accident. Ted offered to drive him home in a hurry.

"Charlotte, can you drive Duncan back to the hotel?" Tim asked.

"Sure," said Charlotte.

As Charlotte and Duncan left the restaurant, she noticed the Valium was starting to take effect. Duncan was a little frisky and wobbly. She knew the stuff was working.

"Where did you say your two boys went to school?" Charlotte asked.

"Carl went to Ohio State, and Bruce went to Penn State," said Duncan.

She now knew that Bruce was the one that had assaulted her.

This should be worth another one hundred thousand dollars. Time to put her plan in motion.

The drive to the Palmer Hotel only took a few minutes. They used the side door so no one would see them enter the building.

"Why don't you come up for a nightcap?" Duncan asked.

"You're married," said Charlotte.

"I won't tell if you won't tell," said Duncan as he pawed at her chest.

"Well, maybe just one."

As they got to his room on the fourth floor, Duncan almost fell down. She helped him into his room, and he did not need another drink. He fell on the bed and was just about passed out. This was her opportunity to spring her plan into action.

She took off his clothes and threw them onto the floor. The toys came out of her purse and were laid out on the nightstand. The fun chains were fastened to the four posts of the bed. The cuffs were fastened to Duncan's wrists and legs. The locks were fastened to the fun chains and then the cuffs. A ball gag was placed in his mouth and fastened around the back of his neck. This way he could not yell out and attract any attention. The hard part was next. She put on a mask, took off her bra and panties, and mounted Duncan. She took several pictures of her in the mask naked and having sex with him in unflattering poses. Charlotte was determined to get payback tonight from the father for the sins of the son.

Just then Duncan started to come around. He was mumbling, but the ball gag prevented the sounds from coming out. Charlotte loosened the gag just enough so she could make out what Duncan was saying.

"What do you want?" Duncan asked.

"Sell your company to Butler for thirty million, or I send these pictures to your wife."

"Please don't do that," mumbled Duncan. "I'll do anything you want."

Charlotte removed the ball gag from his mouth and let him repeat the words once again.

"Do we have a deal?" she asked.

"We have a deal for thirty million. Can I keep my hunting club?"

"If you're a good boy, I'll let you have that."

"I never really liked the business anyway."

She rode him hard until she was satisfied that her fun was over. When she was finished, she bounced off of one Duncan Bailey, the bound victim. She put on her clothes and was ready to exit the hotel.

"Hey, you can't leave me like this," Duncan said.

"You're right," said Charlotte.

She pulled out the Sabre stun gun and pushed the two electrodes into his stomach. Duncan flopped around for a few seconds and then passed out. Charlotte had to work fast. She removed the fun chains, locks, and cuffs from Duncan and put them all in her purse.

It was time to make a hasty exit from the Palmer Hotel. *Another one hundred grand earned from Tim and Ted.*

Chapter 56

Mary ran the cash requirements for this week's check run on Thursday. This was going to be the last run on the old system before the acquisition date. Any accounts payable balances left-over would have to be run in the old system and journalized into the new system after the acquisition date of April 1. The total amount of this week's expenses were $100,900,000.00. There were a few unusual items in this batch of checks. A check in the amount of $750,000 made out to Peterman Trucking for the deposit on ten new heavy-duty water trucks. A check in the amount of $25 million made out to Barron Roberts for one half of the Barron Water Hauling Company. A check in the amount of $25 million made out to Jean Roberts for the other half of the Barron Water Hauling company. A check in the amount of $50 million made out to Rick Cook for the Cook Salt Water Hauling company. The balance of $150,000 was for normal vendor purchases.

The batch of checks was printed and delivered to Paul on his desk early in the morning. It was Paul's job to review and sign the checks before they could be distributed. Since Paul had signing authority for up to fifty thousand, Jerry Evans needed to sign the second line or the check would bounce.

Paul signed all the checks except the four that were above his limit. He took them in hand to Jerry's office.

"Jerry, do you have a few minutes?"

"Sure. What's up?"

"I have four checks that need your signature as well as mine. There are two checks for the Barron company, one check for the Cook company, and one check for Peterman Trucking."

"We need to get these checks out on Friday afternoon and no sooner. Barron, Jean, Rick, and the trucking vendor need to pick them up in person from your office Friday."

"I can call them to make the arrangements."

"Thanks for taking care of this," said Jerry as he signed the checks and handed them to Paul. "Please call me just before you hand-deliver these."

"Are we having second thoughts on all of this?"

"No, we are not. But just in case, I want you to get a verbal yes from me Friday afternoon. Understand?"

"I hear you loud and clear," said Paul as he left his office.

The four signed checks would be locked up in Paul's desk for now. A phone call would be placed to the four recipients to meet him in his office late Friday afternoon to pick them up.

* * *

Tim had been working with Charlotte to put the offer paperwork together for the Metairie company on Thursday morning. The offer letter was written up with the number of $35 million along with the other documents: the NDA, the noncompete, and the exclusive employment contract.

"Tim, did you mean to put the thirty-five number on the offer letter?" Charlotte asked.

"Yes, that is the right number," said Tim. "Ted and I discussed it, and this business is worth $35 million."

"Well, I have it on good authority that Duncan Bailey will accept $30 million and if we let him keep his hunting club, that's all it will cost us."

"How do you know that?"

"I was with him last night, and I got him to agree to the $5 million reduction," said Charlotte. "Again, if he gets to keep the hunting club."

"How did you do that, Charlotte?"

"A lady never tells. I think it is worth another one hundred grand."

"Charlotte, you really are our closer," said Tim. "A hundred grand for a $5 million reduction is a steal."

"I am glad you think so."

"We are going to have to be a little bit careful how we pay this one to you. The payment may cause some suspicion from our auditors when they look over the books. How about you set up a company that you own, and we pay that company the money?" Tim asked.

"That sounds like a really good idea. I'll call it Taylor Enterprises. Taylor was my mom's middle name."

"That sounds like a wonderful company name. I'll call our legal department and ask them to start the paperwork for you."

"Thanks. I would not know how to do that."

"I'll take care of it personally."

"Thanks again," said Charlotte as she gave him a kiss on the cheek.

"You're lucky I am married. I would be all over you."

"Thanks for the compliment. But I have a boyfriend."

"I thought you were not dating?"

"I am not. He just doesn't know he is my boyfriend."

"Beautiful women like you are a puzzle, and I will never be able to figure you out," said Tim. "Let's get that paperwork out today to Duncan Bailey and strike while the iron is hot."

"You got it. I'll send it to him in just a couple of minutes."

* * *

James was back in the conference room all day on Thursday. Not much was going on. But the hallways were terribly busy with the Butler team trying to button things up for the last two days of business on the old systems. James could only think that the team was so busy with work that they had forgotten about working the weekend. He sent out a project meeting request for Friday morning to all of the team. This would be the very last meeting before the conversion weekend. If there were any members with their hair on fire, this is when it would be found.

The email went out to the entire team for a proposed fifteen-minute meeting on Friday at 8:00 a.m. sharp. The subject line was "Project Readiness." A bounce back from Jerry was received that he could not attend. All the other team members accepted quickly. James was set for now.

Ted strolled into the conference room where James and Bill were working.

"Hey guys, I just wanted to let you know about a recent development," said Ted.

"Don't tell me it's another acquisition," James asked.

"How did you know?"

"You had that look on your face."

"My face gave it away?"

"Yep," said James. "You are like a Cheshire cat with a grin from ear to ear."

"You guessed right, James. We have a third acquisition in the hooper for May first. So please keep in mind that we have to push these two over the finish line and quickly."

"Can you tell me anything about it?"

"No. Once the owner has accepted, I can tell you both a lot more about the business. Until then just keep it to yourself."

"We will keep it quiet," said James.

* * *

Later in the afternoon on Thursday, the paperwork came back from Duncan Bailey to Charlotte. There was the signed offer for

$30 million, just as she had said. There was also the stipulation that the hunting club would stay in the Bailey family and not be part of the sale. This would be acceptable to Tim and was just like Charlotte had predicted.

"Hey, Ted, we got the paperwork back from Duncan already," said Charlotte.

"We did?" said Tim. "That was fast. Did he reject it?"

"No, we got the deal at the $30 million amount. And Duncan is asking for the hunting club to be excluded from the deal."

"That is exactly the way you said it would be. How the heck did you do it? Never mind. I don't want to know."

"That's OK, I am not going to tell you. And you're going to take care of that one hundred grand to Taylor Enterprises?"

"I'll promise you the hundred," said Tim. "That is the least the Butler company can do while saving $5 million. I would have gone up to the $35 million if Duncan insisted."

"Well, you can tell Jerry to put the savings somewhere else. Maybe you and Ted should get a bonus?"

"That's not a bad idea," said Tim.

* * *

Charlotte had an appointment with her shrink Thursday evening at eight. Dr. Natalie Parker specialized in psychosexual behaviors, and she felt that Charlotte was one messed-up woman. This was only her second appointment with this patient, and she already knew there was a deep resentment of men—the experience she had had in college had scarred her. Natalie was certain she could help.

Natalie had Charlotte as her last patient for the evening and found her in the waiting room right at 8:00 p.m.

"Hi, Charlotte. Step right into my office."

"Thanks for seeing me so late."

"So how have you been this week?" Natalie asked.

"I met a wonderful guy last weekend; he was a complete gentleman."

"Was this a date?"

"I thought it was a date," said Charlotte. "His name is Phil Reynolds, and I met him at the farmers market the prior weekend. We went on a date Friday night at Frank's in downtown Coraopolis. The night was going so well, I was kind of pushing for a little bit more. That's when he said he had to go back to work. He took a break from working to have dinner with me and then dumped me, kind of."

"How did it make you feel?"

"Well, it was nice. I was pursuing him. After the meal I gave him a kiss on the cheek, and he left to go back in the kitchen. I told him to call me for a second date and that I would take him out for dinner."

"Sounds like he was a real gentleman."

"I was in heaven. I can't wait for a second date. I just want to jump all over him."

"Slow down," said Natalie. "You will want to let this develop into solid relationship. Don't rush it."

"I know," said Charlotte. "I want a good guy. Not like the guy I had last night."

"What happened last night?"

"I slept with a work customer to get a bonus."

"Did your boss ask you to do this?"

"Well, no. I kind of like doing it because if I sleep with the guy, he sells his company to my employer and then I get a big bonus."

"So this is sex for money?"

"Kind of. There is a bit of an adrenaline rush when I do it. I seduce the drunken man, chain him to the bed, and then take advantage of him for money."

"I think you are trying to compensate for what happened in college," said Natalie. "That experience was so traumatic that you blocked it out and now you are trying to get even with every man you encounter."

"You maybe right. I am kind of a hot mess."

"We just need to get you into a loving relationship."

"Maybe Phil can help me with that."

"I would take it real slow here. He sounds like a real keeper, and you don't want to throw him away. Play it slow and try to develop this one."

"I will try."

"Our time together is up," said Natalie. "Do you want to schedule another session or leave it open?"

"Let's leave it open for now," said Charlotte. "Thanks, Doc. I'll try to take your advice."

"You're very welcome. Look forward to seeing you next time. Remember, take it slow."

"I'll try." Charlotte left the office with a smile on her face, thinking about Phil.

Chapter 57

Friday morning was the make-or-break moment for the team. James had the whole group of players in the conference room at exactly 8:00 a.m., and he was delighted they were there. This was his opportunity to take the wheel and steer the car to its final destination. For the next three days, the team would be beating to his drum and following his schedule on every line item from the conversion project plan.

"Good morning, everyone," said James. "I'll make this brief. Tim or Ted, do you want to say anything before I get started?"

"Yes, I do," said Ted. "We are almost at the finish line, so if anything comes up that you can't handle, raise your hand; Tim, James, Bill, or I will need to resolve it quickly."

"Thanks, Ted," said James. "Tim, did you have anything else on this?"

"All I can say is thank you to all who have made the effort to pull together and get this thing done," said Tim. "There will be a bonus payment in next week's checks as our way of saying thanks once again."

"The conversion project plan has been updated," said James. "On the wall is the printout of all the things that need to happen over the next three days. You are welcome to review it at your leisure today and let me know if there are any missing steps. Otherwise, this same printout will be on the wall in the Palmer Room of the hotel for us to complete over the weekend. I will highlight an item with a yellow marker and check it off when it is completely done. If an item is started and taking some time to finish, it will be partially highlighted and a percentage will be noted in the right margin. That is really all I have to say for now."

"You and Bill will be at the Palmer Hotel all day Saturday and Sunday?" Ted asked.

"That is the plan for now," said James. "Your areas will be cleared and completed over the weekend, and then you will be released. When you're released, that means that all the action items on the plan that are your responsibility are complete. You are then ready to start running the business on Monday morning."

"Thanks, James, for that bit of clarification," said Ted. "Remember, everyone, James is now in control of this project. Please coordinate with him over the next seventy-two hours."

"Bill and I will be in the conference room all day today if anyone needs anything," said James. "Please come and ask for assistance if there is a roadblock in your area. We are all in this together."

"Let's get back to running the Butler company," said Ted.

The crowd left the conference room, and Ted nodded to James in approval. He knew he had hit the mark and was ready for almost any situation.

"Nice job, James," said Ted.

"Short and sweet and to the point," said Tim. "Thanks."

"Bill and I have been around the block on these types of projects," said James. "We enjoy doing them and look forward to building the Butler business."

* * *

Tim and Ted were in Ted's office and started to discuss the Charlotte situation.

"Tim, I think we need to do something for Charlotte," said Ted.

"You mean the second hundred grand we need to pay her?"

"In addition to that. I think we need to bump up her salary."

"What did you have in mind?"

"She is at $50K, and we should bump her to $100K."

"I was thinking the same thing," said Tim. "She is worth every dime."

"Agreed," said Ted.

"I'll take care of it with the HR manager. We are also going to help her set up a company for the second one hundred grand finder's fee, for the Metairie business."

"Is this a side deal or something?"

"I suggested that she set up a company so we can pay her the finder's fee that way. I will help her by asking the legal team to get it rolling."

"I am sure that our auditors would frown upon us paying $200,000 to an executive secretary."

"That's what I am afraid of," said Tim. "That's why we need a company setup and controlled by her. She came up with the name Talyor Enterprises."

"That's a nice name."

"Charlotte picked it after her mother's middle name."

"That will work," said Ted.

* * *

Mary walked back into the conference room; she wanted to talk with James after the meeting alone.

"Hey, James, I have had a couple of new vendors since I gave you that file last week," said Mary. "Can I add them to the new software?"

"Yes, you can. You remember how?"

"Can you shadow me while I do it?"

"Absolutely. Do you want to do it at your desk?"

"That would be terrific."

James and Mary went to her cubicle. He watched her go through the process of setting up a vendor with all the pieces on the new system. She received an error message when the record was being saved.

"Mary, did you remember to associate a terms code to the vendor? You're getting an error message, and the system will not let you save the record until you do that one step."

"Yes, I forgot," said Mary. "They are a net-thirty vendor."

"Pick the terms code from the drop-down. Then try to save the record."

"That worked. Thanks. I forgot that step."

"No problem. Now add the next one, and I am not going to say anything."

Mary added the next three vendors with all the setup pieces that were necessary. She did not receive any error messages.

"I think I am good for now," said Mary. "Thanks."

"Anytime you need something, you know where I am," James said, thinking to himself, *If this is all I have to worry about, then this conversion will be easy.*

James went back in the conference room. Nina was sitting in there waiting for him.

"Hey, James, can I add a new customer into the system?" she asked.

"The system is ready for you to do just that. Is this a new customer that was not in the file you gave me last week?"

"That is correct. I need to add this one to the new system. I just wanted to check with you if it was OK to do so."

"You're good to go. Do you need assistance setting it up?"

"I can take care of it. If I need you, I'll yell."

"Please do," said James.

It was getting close to noon, and no other fires were burning. So James and Bill decided to go get some lunch.

"What do you have a taste for today?" James asked.

"How about Chick-fil-A?"

"Sounds good. Time to take a break."

* * *

Early Friday afternoon Paul placed a call to Jerry Evans. He had these four checks in his desk, and they were burning a hole in it. He had never handled a check for $50 million and wanted it and the other three out of his office. The four recipients for those checks would be arriving after 1:00 p.m., and as Jerry had asked him to do, Paul was calling him for confirmation.

"Jerry, how are you?"

"Fine. What can I do for you?"

"You wanted me to get a verbal approval before I released these four checks."

"Give me a few minutes, and I'll meet you in your office. Stay put. I'll be right down."

Jerry hung up the phone and went down to see Tim, then grabbed Ted.

"Gentlemen, are we good to release those checks for the Barron company, Cook company, and the trucks?"

"There are no issues with releasing the checks," said Tim.

"OK, let's go down to see Paul," said Jerry. "He has the four checks in his desk."

As the three men strolled into Paul's office, he pulled the checks out and placed them on the desk. They were signed by Paul and countersigned by Jerry already and had today's date.

"Last chance to stop this," Jerry said.

"We are good to go," said Tim and Ted as they nodded in agreement.

"Let them go," said Jerry. "When are they going to come and get them?"

"Between two p.m. and three p.m. today," said Paul.

"On second thought, give me those checks," said Jerry. "When these folks come to get them, send them to me. I want to personally hand them over."

"Here you go, Jerry," said Paul. "They have been literally burning in my desk since yesterday. Sort of like a hot potato, if you know what I mean."

Jerry took the checks and headed back to his office. He was convinced that something could be obtained by hand-delivering the checks to the recipients that would benefit the Butler company. A sweetener of some sort for his team or maybe a party at the seller's expense. Either way he wanted to extract something from them and was bound to get it.

* * *

Later that day the first to arrive was Peter Hamilton from Peterman Trucking. Jerry held the check in his hand.

"So what are you going to give my team for giving you the business?" Jerry asked.

"What would you like?"

"What can you provide?"

"I have a budget for stuff like this," said Peter. "I can provide a booth at the Pittsburgh Penguins hockey game with food and a full bar for a night."

"That sounds great. Put us down for an evening and let me know when." Jerry handed him the check for $750,000.

"Thanks for your business," said Peter as he placed the check in his breast pocket and left Jerry's office.

* * *

Shortly after Peter left, Rick Cook arrived. Jerry held the check in his hand and was waving it in front of Rick.

"So what are you going to give my team for giving you this business?"

"What would you like?"

"What can you provide?"

"I don't know what to provide, but I am willing to give your team something."

"What about a two-night stay at Disney World for all our core members with all expenses paid?"

"You mean, like, airfare, lodging, meals, park tickets, et cetera?" said Rick.

"Exactly. Like, one trip for each of the fifteen employees and their spouse," said Jerry. "All at your expense."

"That is a little bit extravagant, but I may be able to do something."

"Can I put you down for it?" Jerry asked as he waved the check in front of Rick.

"Well, OK. You guys will earn me a lot of money as we expand the business."

"You can count on that. We are going to double your business, and you will still be the president."

"I'll take care of it," said Rick. "Fifteen employees and spouses and two nights at Disney World, right?"

"Those are the numbers. Make if for June or July of this year."

"I'll work on it after the check clears."

"Then we have a deal," said Jerry as he handed him the check for $50 million.

* * *

Jean and Barron Roberts were the last ones to arrive at Jerry's office; by this point it was late in the afternoon.

"So what are you going to give my team for the sale of your business?"

"What are you talking about?" Barron asked.

"It's customary for the seller to provide something to the team as a gift."

"What do you have in mind?"

"A nice gesture for all their work to integrate the acquired business onto the new software would be most appreciated," said Jerry. "They are also going to grow the business and double it while you both are still in management. So how about a big party at a sports event where you two pick up the tab? A booth at the Pittsburg Pirates baseball game some evening in the summertime would be nice."

"What do you think?" said Barron as he looked over to Jean.

"I guess we can do that," said Jean.

"This would be a good thing to do for my team," said Jerry. "After all, they are kind of working for you two."

"You're right," said Barron. "They will help us to make our numbers, Jean."

"OK," said Jean. "I'll pick up half of the bill."

"I will pick up the other half," said Barron.

"Then we have a deal," said Jerry as he handed them each a check for $25 million.

As the Barrons left the office, they felt they had been extorted by one Jerry Evans, but they had agreed to the deal anyway. A big check was still a big check.

Jerry Evans was a master at getting something from people. He knew when to lever the payment of the purse to what he wanted. After all, his team was going to pay for the acquisitions, and he wanted to get something for them personally. These gratuities would also solidify his hold on the team and make them extremely loyal to Jerry, Tim, and Ted.

* * *

The afternoon for James and Bill in the conference room was uneventful. The Butler team was scrambling to get all the things buttoned up under the old systems, and their assistance was not sought out for the rest of the day. James knew that the real test would come on Saturday morning, when the shit hit the fan. For now, it was a quiet afternoon and one to enjoy for as long as it lasted.

Chapter 58

James was the only one that arrived at the Palmer Room early on Saturday morning. It was around 8:00 a.m., and the coffee and pastry service had just been dropped off by the hotel restaurant staff. He hoped that the food and beverages would entice the team to come early but would have to wait and see if this approach worked.

Bill joined him in the room a few minutes after eight; both consultants were having coffee, chitchatting about what to expect in the next forty-eight hours.

"You know, James, this is a pretty easy conversion project."

"Yes, I know. But I am not telling Ted that. I want him to think that this is tough and that we are going to earn our money."

"We will earn our money. No doubt about that."

"There will be shit that we have to take care of," said James. "That third acquisition in one month is going to be stressful for you and me. I was hoping to take a week off for vacation, but that seems like a pipe dream."

"I think all vacations are off for a few months. Let's just hope this gravy train keeps cranking at least for a little while."

Midmorning, Nina stopped by. She had the two customer files to be converted.

"Hi, James. I have the accounts receivable files for the Cook and Barron companies," said Nina. "I just need to touch the files up and code them with the new customer IDs, and then I can provide them to you for conversion."

"So what are the numbers I am looking at for the two companies?" James asked.

"Give me a second, and I'll give you the exact numbers. The Cook company has 85 customers with an AR balance of $8,100,000 and 8,123 invoices. The Barron company has 25 customers with an AR balance of $6,800,000 dollars and 6,200 invoices."

"So the Cook company is carrying about two months' sales in the AR amounts," said James. "The Barron company is carrying about one and a half months' sales in the AR amounts."

"That sounds about right."

"The AR balances over thirty days is a killer to small businesses. You are becoming the customers' banker, and I really don't like that metric."

"I am in agreement with you, James. I like my number to be no more than a thirty-day amount in AR."

"You are going to have your work cut out for you once we convert these businesses and get going. You do know that the oil patch is a good-old-boy network.

"I was warned about that by Tim and Ted."

"So you know what you're stepping in," said James.

"You mean horseshit?" Nina asked.

"No, I mean *bullshit*."

"I'll do what I can. If I don't like it, there is always something else I can do."

"You always have options, yes."

"Give me about an hour, and I'll finish up the files for you."

"Take your time," said James. "I'll be here all weekend."

Mary walked into the conference room and looked at the conversion project plan taped to the wall. She had five items on the list and informed James that they were all completed now.

"Mary, you finished all your action items?" he asked.

"I just wanted to make sure that I was done and that you could release the accounts payable department."

James went to the wall and highlighted Mary's items with a yellow marker. As he read the line items aloud, Mary reiterated, "Yep, that's done."

"Looks like you're the first department to be done," said James. "I guess you can go home. Are you sure you're ready for Monday?"

"Well, I have ten more vendors that we added to the old system this past week."

"Then you should add them to the database today. Can you add them this morning? Then you really will be done and ready for Monday."

"Sure," said Mary. "I'll add them right away."

Tim and Ted bounced into the conference room.

"How is it going this morning?" asked Tim.

"We are underway and on schedule so far," said James.

"Good. Stay on schedule," said Tim.

"If you're off schedule, please call me right away," said Ted.

"Hey, James, do you have a minute?" Nina asked.

"Sure," said James. "Do you have that file for me?"

"I am going to send you the Cook file," said Nina. "Are you ready to convert it?"

"Send it to me, and I'll work on it immediately. Is the control 85 customers with a total of $8,100,000 still?"

"That's it," said Nina.

James received the Cook accounts receivable file and converted the data file to a conversion file. He added a reference field ID and added "COOK" as the value. The upload process was run, and the file took forty-one minutes to process. The RPM was two hundred; it was as expected. There were no errors in the file, which gave James a warm and fuzzy feeling. The accounts receivable aging report was run, and it was an exact match to what was provided by Nina. The converted file was forwarded to Nina for review and sign-off.

Nina sent James the Barron file for conversion. She coded the newly created customer ID numbers to the customer account balances. James took one look at the file added a customer reference of "BARR," converted it to a data conversion file, and then uploaded the file. The upload process took just under thirty-one minutes with no errors received. The RPM was also two hundred, as expected. The accounts receivable Aging report was run, and the results of twenty-five customers with a total balance of $6,800,000 were displayed. This converted file was sent to Nina for review and sign-off.

Later in the morning, a flood of Butler team members arrived, and the first stop was the breakfast table for pastries and some coffee.

"Hey, Paul, did you ever decide on the site ID numbers for Barron and Cook numbering in the general ledger?" James asked.

"No, we did not," replied Paul.

"Can I make a suggestion?"

"Sure. What do you recommend?"

"What if we use 000 for the Butler balance sheet designation, 105 for the Barron balance sheet designation, and 110 for the Cook balance sheet designation?"

"I see where you are going with this, and I like it. Can you set it up?"

"I sure can. Just remember when you submit the general ledger numbers to me, they will need to be coded this way."

"I can take care of that," said Paul. "I am curious, why would you want to separately identify the acquisitions balance sheet numbers?"

"If you ever sell a subsidiary or division, you will need to know which numbers belong to which site. I have seen a scenario where a company bought something that didn't integrate well and a few years later it was sold off."

"That is a very good point. That is why you're doing this for us. You know better."

"Well, I just like to think *I have seen this picture before*, if you know what I mean," said James. "One other thing to think about is that the general ledger accounts will need to be generated before we upload the values."

"I can take care of that also. Shirley and I are on the hook for that piece, with your help, of course."

"Of course."

Just about everyone had checked in this morning with James. He was happy that all the participants were in the room eating, drinking coffee, and most importantly, working.

"Hey, James, looks like your plan is working today," Ted said.

"Yep, looks like everyone listened to my talk and is here. Even Charlotte showed up to help out, even though she has nothing on the plan. She always brightens up the room. I don't see Barron or Jean. Did we lose them?"

"They both got their checks yesterday, from Jerry: $25 million each. Maybe they are hungover?"

"That would not surprise me," said James. "What about Rick Cook?"

"He got his check for fifty million yesterday, so I would not expect him to show up here either."

Just then Jerry Evans showed up in the conference room.

"Hi, everyone, looks like we are having a party," he said. "I have an announcement for everyone."

"OK, quiet down, everybody," said Ted.

"I have some good news for all of you," said Jerry. "Peterman Trucking will be providing us with a booth at an upcoming Penguins game. The Barrons will be providing us a booth at an upcoming Pirates game. Rick from the Cook company will be providing you all with a two-night stay at Disney World this summer."

The whole room erupted in cheers and clapping. As the room quieted down, Jerry continued, "While you all were working, I was squeezing something out of the sellers for us to enjoy as a team. This is just my way of getting you some fun stuff after this is all over."

The chants of "*Jerry, Jerry, Jerry*" were heard down the hotel hallways.

"OK, let's quiet down, everyone," said Tim. "Can we get back to work?"

James pulled Ted aside. "Does that include Bill and me?"

"I'll find out," said Ted.

The day progressed right on schedule. The action items on the conversion project plan were getting completed, and no real road blocks were encountered. James was releasing the Butler team members throughout the day, and when done, they left the conference room as fast as possible. Charlotte and Ted stayed most of the day even though they did not have any items on the list. They were there for moral support, and James was happy they were.

It was now after 4:00 p.m., and James was seeing mostly yellow items on the wall.

"Do you guys need me for anything?" Charlotte asked.

"You can get out of here," said Ted "You have been wonderful today."

"I am just trying to do my part," said Charlotte as she left the room.

"James, do you have anything left for me to do?" Ted asked.

"No, I don't have any open items for you," said James. "You were kind of on standby with Blue Point Hosting just in case we needed a backup."

"Then I'll see you both here on Sunday," said Ted.

"Sounds good," said James. "I think we can wrap this one up for today."

"Go have a nice dinner on Butler tonight," said Ted as he left the conference room.

"Thanks," said James. "We will do that. And a couple of drinks too." He turned to Bill and continued, "It's time to leave. Are you ready to quit for today?"

"Yes, I have had enough for today," said Bill. "We are in good shape for Sunday."

"We do not have much to do on Sunday. Look at the wall. The conversion project plan is almost all covered in yellow highlighter."

"Do you want to go play golf?"

"You're so funny. We have to be here even if we don't have to be here."

"I know. Let's go have some dinner."

"OK," said James. "I am hungry all of a sudden."

Chapter 59

James was the first to arrive at the Palmer Room bright and early, around 8:00 a.m., Sunday morning, and Bill was nowhere to be found. He tried to log into the database for the Butler company and received a system network error; it seemed the access to the network was not working this morning. James's thought that his computer was acting up, so he did a reboot and tried once again. No luck. This appeared to be a Blue Point Hosting issue.

Bill arrived a few minutes after 8:15 a.m., and James gave him the business.

"Did you sleep in today? Just kidding."

"I slept in a few minutes, no big deal."

"Can you try to log into our database? I think we have a problem."

"Give me a minute, and I'll boot up my laptop," said Bill. "Hey, *Houston, we have a problem.*"

"I thought this was too easy," said James.

"I am receiving a network connection issue. Is this the same thing you were receiving?"

"I was getting a 401 Unauthorized Access error when trying to log in. Are you getting the same thing, or is it different?"

"Nope, I am getting that same error. I'll need to call the Blue Point Hosting team and see what is going on."

Bill called the emergency number for Blue Point Hosting. He identified himself as the admin for the Butler Energy Corporation with the company code of BEC. After a few minutes, he reached a technician working on the issue. It seemed that a blade from a single server had overheated due to an air-conditioning failure and the server had stopped working. They were attending to it now, and no further information was available. A request from Bill to the technician was made; he would be called back as soon as the server could be restarted. Bill relayed the information to James, who was not happy.

"So what the hell are we going to do if the Butler team comes in here today?" James asked.

Around 9:00 a.m. Ted showed up in the conference room for his morning coffee and pastry.

"How is it going this morning?" he asked.

"We are down, and they are working on the issue," said James.

"How long have we been down?"

"Since eight a.m. or earlier. An air conditioner unit broke down at Blue Point Hosting this morning. Bill has been on the phone with them several times this morning."

"So are we operational?"

"No, we are not. We are dead in the water. I only hope the backup was done last night. I requested a special backup for after hours Saturday night, and I was getting a little bit of pushback from Blue Point Hosting's team."

"In hindsight that could have been a very good call."

"If they listened to me and completed it."

"When will we know what is going on?"

"They told Bill an update would be given in about thirty minutes, so around nine thirty."

"OK. They better have something for us, or I am going to be yelling at their president," said Ted.

Right around 9:30 a.m., they called Bill and advised him that the system was back up and operational. The team at Blue Point Hosting also confirmed that a backup of the database was completed at 11:30 p.m. on Saturday evening and that they had restored the database to that point in time this morning. The outage was nine an a half hours in total. This information was repeated to Ted.

"Thanks for that information, Bill," he said. "I am going to talk with our account representative on Monday. Our SLA was one hour during the week and two hours on the weekend. They will need to have some explanation for this, or I will be going shopping."

"It's your call if you want to ream them a new one," said Bill.

"The system seems to be back up," said James. "I just logged in, and we are operational this morning."

"If anyone asks, *boys*, do not say a word," said Ted. "This is just between the three of us. Understand?"

"Mum's the word," said James as Bill nodded in agreement.

"Can the two of you check the database and see if we lost anything?" Ted asked.

"If they did a backup late Saturday night, we should be fine," said James. "But we will check and let you know."

Bill and James reviewed the database by looking at the time stamps; this revealed that the last series of updates were done around the 5:00 p.m. timeframe, by James. So it appeared that there was no loss in data or configurations. The users would never know what had happened. This would be a secret of the IT team. Ted was informed and was happy that James's smart action of performing a backup at the end of the day saved their bacon. The users would not have to rework the lost activity due to the line item on the conversion project plan. James could now highlight the backup activity.

"The database appears to be fine," said James. "There appears to be no loss of data or configs."

"That was a good move," said Ted. "Was that step on the plan?"

"Yes sir," said James. "I have been burned by this once before, and I caught holy hell for it."

"You definitely saved our skins on that line item."

"Just doing what you paid me to do. Watching out for the client is part of the job.

"I'll make it up to you boys."

Just then Charlotte walked into the conference room. She was wearing a pair of jeans and a cream-colored blouse with a silver belt. Her figure was a beautiful hourglass shape; she was just a plain drop-dead gorgeous woman.

"Don't you have something better to do with your Sunday?" Ted asked.

"I just stopped by to see if you needed anything," said Charlotte.

"Well, not really," said James. "But since you're here, can you try to log into the database?"

"Sure. What do you want me to do?"

"Just try to get access to the Butler Energy Company instance and move around the screens," said James.

Charlotte used her credentials to log in and had no issue. She navigated between screens with ease and seemed to be fine. This was a relief for James.

"Thanks, Charlotte," said James. "We just wanted to make sure a user could get into the system after the backup was done."

"You're very welcome."

James watched Bill as Charlotte proceeded to the coffee and pastries table. He was staring at her like so many times before.

"Hey, Bill, you are drooling."

"Sorry. That woman just drives me nuts. She is the most gorgeous woman I have ever seen in the world."

"OK, I get it," said James. "Button the lip and get back to work."

"Sorry about that."

"Are we expecting anyone from the team today?" Ted asked.

"It is kind of optional at this point," said James. "If you look at the wall there where the conversion project plan is, the color is mostly yellow."

"So we are ahead of schedule," said Ted.

"I would say we are on schedule."

"If nobody surfaces by noon then, shut it down and send out an email to that fact."

"We can do that."

"Charlotte, let's get out of here," said Ted. "The boys have it under control."

"I like these two," said Charlotte. "They seem to know what they are doing."

"You're a good judge of character," said Ted. "I am so glad we found them and they're on our team," he added as they left the Palmer Room.

The noon hour came, and no Butler team members had shown up. This was the signal to send out an email saying that the conversion was a success and that we are ready for business. James knew that the next morning, Monday, was the final test. For now he could relax and enjoy the moment.

Chapter 60

April 1, Monday, was the first day on the new system, and two companies would be using the software from the Enterprise Software Corporation. The Cook company and the Barron company would be wholly owned subsidiaries of the Butler Energy Corporation, and their names would cease to exist.

James planted himself in the main floor conference room bright and early before anyone had arrived. Charlotte saw him there and brought a carafe of coffee just like before.

"I think you're going to need this today," she said as she poured him a cup of coffee.

"Thanks," said James. "You didn't have to do that."

"I like taking care of my men." Charlotte gave him a kiss on the cheek. "Tim, Ted, Bill, and now you are all my men."

"Charlotte, you know I am married?"

"Yes, I know. All the good guys are married. But I can still take care of you, can't I?"

"Sure, I don't mind you fussing over me."

She kissed him on the other cheek and brushed her boobs against his chest.

"Charlotte, if I didn't know better, I would say you were flirting with me."

"Just a little. You do like me, don't you?"

"Charlotte, you're the most beautiful woman I have ever seen," said James. "Your figure is a perfect eleven on a ten-point system. Your personality is wonderful, warm, funny, and very affectionate."

"Thank you for those compliments. But you're married, right?"

"Yes I am."

"Well, you can't blame a girl for trying. You passed."

"What do you mean 'I passed'?" James asked.

"Ted and I had a bet that I could turn you on," said Charlotte. "Ted lost, and I won."

"You won?"

"Yep. I told Ted that you were a really good guy and that I couldn't turn you. He lost, and I won."

"What was the bet?"

"A dinner at a restaurant of my choice."

"Did you make the same bet with Ted on Bill?"

"No. We both know he can be corrupted. I have seen out of the corner of my eye how he looks at me and stares."

"You figured him out."

"I had him pegged on day one."

"Then why do you keep doing it to him?"

"It amuses me. I get a kick out of it."

"I will never ever be able to figure you women out. You all are like an unbreakable enigma machine."

"Keep trying," replied Charlotte. "We enjoy the attention." With that, she left the conference room.

James was thinking to himself that Charlotte was a real strange woman. *If she ever finds a boyfriend, he better have big balls to hang on to, or she will cut him up and feed him to the wolves. She is trouble with a capital* T.

Ted drifted into the conference room and went right to the carafe of coffee. He grabbed a cup and walked toward James.

"How are we doing so far this morning?" he asked.

"You lost, and Charlotte won," said James.

"So she tried this morning?"

"You owe her a nice dinner."

"How is the user community doing?" Ted asked as he shifted the subject away from the bet.

"The system is up, and everything seems normal this morning. It has only been a little while, though, and I have had no customers yet."

"Let's call an emergency meeting for nine a.m. and ask everyone to attend."

"I'll send out an email right away."

James sent the email as requested. All team members were required to attend the 9:00 a.m. meeting with the IT team. There were no excuses for not attending, per Ted. The meeting would be in the conference room and would only be a few minutes.

Right at 9:00 a.m., everyone packed the conference room.

"Looks like we have everyone," said Ted. "I asked you all to be here for a few minutes. I want to thank everyone for your efforts over the weekend and for showing up this morning. We are up and running on the new platform with the Barron company and the Cook company, as scheduled. If you have any issues or need assistance, please see James or Bill in the main floor conference room this week. They will log any issues as they come up. Thanks. Now get back to business."

Jerry hung back in the conference room and let everyone leave the room. When he had James, Bill, Ted, and Tim together, he closed the door.

"I want to thank you guys," said Jerry. "You pulled it off."

"Did you have any doubts?" Tim asked.

"No, I just wanted to personally thank you all," said Jerry. "I have seen some really bad conversions. They were ugly. This one seems to be going really smoothly."

"Jerry, can I speak frankly here?" said James.

"Sure, go ahead."

"We are really not going to see any real fires until Wednesday, which is day three," said James. "That is when the shit will hit the fan if it does. Then it will moderate on day four and day five. If we did our homework, and I think we have, on Monday of next week, you will be able to gauge how the project went."

"Thanks for that bit of honesty," said Jerry.

"I say that because of my prior experience with this software," said James. "The users build up a tolerance until they can't take it anymore. This generally happens on day three, four, or five. That is when reality sets in and the user can't cut it or throw their hands up for help."

"So I should hold on to the congratulations until next week?" Jerry asked.

"I will feel more comfortable if we can get through five business days of transactions with everyone signing in and out," said James. "I will plan to visit with everyone in the office each day and take an in-person poll on how they are doing. Sort of the pulse of the community."

"I like that," said Jerry. "Where did you get this guy, Ted?"

"I am glad he is on our team," said Ted. "Let's get back to running the business."

The executives left the conference room, and Bill and James were all alone. There were no real fires the whole day: with the exception of log-in and user account access issues, nothing really happened.

* * *

Charlotte received a phone call from Peter Hamilton late Monday afternoon.

"Hi. Is this Charlotte?" he asked.

"This is Charlotte."

"This is Peter Hamilton from Peterman Trucking. I have a check for you but don't know who to make it out to?"

"You can make it out to Taylor Enterprises."

"OK. I am going to be in the Pittsburgh area on Thursday," said Peter. "Can I give it to you then?"

"Let me check my schedule. It just so happens that I am free on Thursday."

"Can we do a round trip at the Pittsburgh International Hotel at seven p.m.?"

"You want another night like we had before?"

"That was nice. Can we go again but add a twist? I'll have your finder's fee check."

"Sure. Let me know your room number later in the week," said Charlotte. "Thursday at seven p.m. Meet you there. Oh, and next time use my cell phone number and not my work number."

* * *

Monday ended as quiet as James expected. The next day would probably be different. But only time would tell.

Chapter 61

The second day of the go-live event for the Barron company and the Cook company had yielded very few issues. The user community was using the system, customers were being billed, and a few vendors were being paid. All normal events for a growing company. James was surprised that there were no hair-on-fire moments. Everything seemed so calm and quiet. *When is the other shoe going to drop?* he thought.

"Hey, Bill, I am going to make the rounds of the Butler team," said James as he left the conference room.

His first stop was at Nina's desk to see how she was doing. Her answer was she was fine, and James moved on. His next stop was at Mary's desk to see how she was doing. Her answer was she was fine, and James moved on again. He thought he would try Shirley next. Again, no issues reported; everything was normal. He bounced into Paul's office and asked how he was doing.

"Hey, James, how are you?" said Paul. "I am working on finishing up the opening general ledger balances for the Barron company as of the April first numbers. I am coding them using the GL string like we talked about on Saturday. You will have them in a few minutes."

"Thanks. I'll upload them immediately," said James. "Everything else going OK?"

"No issues to report as of now."

James returned to the conference room and relayed what he had found to Bill. He was as surprised as James was and did not know what to think of it. They had done a good job of configuring the database and done a good job during the two days of training the Butler team. But nobody was that good. There had to be something they missed. There had to be issues that needed to be logged and fixed.

An email came into James from Paul with the attached general ledger opening balance sheet numbers for the Barron company. James converted them to an upload file and then processed the complete file. A few minutes later, a trial balance report was run and compared to what Paul had submitted. They were an exact match to the input file. The report was sent to Paul for a review and sign-off.

Around 10:00 a.m. the system went down. James started to receive emails from the users saying they could not access the URL to the Blue Point Hosting site. James fired off a company-wide email saying they would investigate immediately and all users should sign out and wait for instructions. James asked Bill to call Blue Point Hosting to find out what had gone wrong. Within five minutes the Blue Point Hosting team had found the error and said a blade had overheated on the server and their instance would be rerouted to a different blade. The system was back up and only down for ten minutes during the morning. James sent out a company-wide email saying the database was now available and apologizing for the delay.

Ted came into the conference room and said, "Guys, I saw the email traffic that our instance was down and now back up. What can you tell me?"

"The Blue Point Hosting team said that a blade overheated and they had to reroute our server traffic."

"This is twice in three days," said Ted. "I think I am going to have a chat with the rep today."

"Ted, I am going to log this as an issue and put your name on it for now," said James.

"That is fine. Put my name as the owner."

314 | Chris Bryda

"Will do."

Shirley and Nina walked into the conference room and announced that they had a problem. There were ten customer invoice
ladies at the Cook and Barron companies that needed immediate
access and training. It seemed that these ten employees had been
missed in the initial training rollout. Shirley and Nina would take
care of the training, but they needed access and user accounts at
Blue Point Hosting. James agreed to set them up provided he had
their names and email accounts. Shirley would forward the list so
he could work on it immediately.

The list provided from Shirley was set up in the Enterprise
Software Corporation and the Blue Point Hosting systems. James
scheduled a 1:00 p.m. meeting for all ten employees via a Webex
to walk them through the log-in procedures. He also sent out an
email to all ten employees and advised them that their accounts
had been set up in advance of this meeting and if they wanted to
try and log in, they could do so.

The 1:00 p.m. Webex was held, and all ten new users were
online. James walked through the URL credentials for them, and
there were no questions. At the end of the Webex, James offered
to do a one-on-one session if anyone needed any additional support. The online meeting lasted only fifteen minutes, and Shirley
thanked him in the meeting. Shirley and Nina could now proceed
with the training.

The rest of the day was quiet; no other issues came to the attention of Bill or James. They both thought to themselves that the
team might be underreporting any issues they are having by not
raising their hands. Perhaps they were struggling to figure something out but then getting frustrated and doing nothing about it.
This would set up a typical blowup day on Wednesday. At least that
was what James was thinking.

Chapter 62

This was the day that James had been dreading: the third day of go-live projects always proved to be a long, tiring, and eventful day. Right on cue Charlotte came into the conference room with a carafe of coffee. Both Bill and James were there this time. As she said good morning, she just could not resist.

"Good morning, Charlotte," said James. "Thanks so much for the coffee."

"You're very welcome," said Charlotte as she gave James a kiss on the cheek.

"Are you trying to get me in trouble with HR?" he asked in a hushed whisper.

"No. I am just messing with Bill," she replied as she left the conference room.

"Hey, are you two an item?" Bill asked.

"No. Charlotte is just trying to be friendly," said James.

"Well, I wish she were more friendly with me."

"I don't think she is in your league. She is a cougar disguised as a mouse."

"It could be a hell of an evening."

"Can we get back to work?"

Just then Shirley burst into the conference room with her laptop and an AR issue.

"Hey, can you help me out," she said. "I have a batch of customer invoices that will not post. There should be twenty-five invoices, but there are only twenty-four and I cannot get a batch edit report to print."

"Let's take a look," said James. "Can you get out of the batch number and let me know which one it is?"

"I am out of the batch now," said Shirley. "It is AR invoice batch SH040324."

James went into the batch and looked at the error code. An out-of-balance condition existed on the last invoice. The invoice number twenty-five had an invoice number with a blank line item. This invoice was deleted and there were now twenty-four invoices and in balance. The edit report was run, and the total batch could now be displayed for a user review.

"I'll get out of this batch," said James. "Take a look and let me know if this is OK."

"I can get into the batch now," said Shirley. "The edit report is displayed, but will the batch post?"

"Save your edit report first, then try and post the batch. One other thing you should know is when you post, the batch will disappear from the screen, so make sure you save it somewhere."

Shirley exported the batch of twenty-four invoices to a file and then posted the batch. The system allowed her to perform the function, and then the batch disappeared from the screen.

"How did you do that?" Shirley asked.

"I just knew where to look and how to troubleshoot the error message," said James.

"Thanks. I am sure I'll be back for something else," said Shirley as she walked out.

"No problem. I'll be here until Friday noon."

As Shirley left the conference room, Nina was coming in.

"Hey, James, do you have a minute?" she asked.

"For you, anytime," said James. "What's up?"

"We put this new customer in the system, but the system put them on hold," said Nina. "What is wrong with this customer?"

"There is nothing wrong here," said James. "The system automatically places the customer on hold the minute you create one in the AR module."

"Well, that is a dumb thing. Can we get it changed?"

"This is a standard feature for the software. I could put it on the list for a mod review, but don't get your hopes up. This will not be a priority item. We need to go through a period of stabilization first before we tackle business process method changes, or BPMs for short."

"Who do I have to talk to get it changed?"

"I'll review it with Paul and Ted."

"Thanks." Nina left the conference room with her laptop in hand.

Just as she exited, like clockwork, Paul walked into the conference room.

"Hey, James, can you spend a minute with me?" he asked. "In my office?"

"Sure," replied James as they proceeded to Paul's workstation.

"I was working on the Cook file, and all the accounts are not working," Paul said.

"Did you generate them in a range or individually? Show me what you did."

Paul displayed the general ledger account generation process and went through the steps. As he did this, James noticed that he used the single account generation process instead of the range process.

"Let me show you how to do the range process," said James. "You go to the chart of accounts and then hit the auto generate button at the top. The screen is displayed, and you select the range function. For the parameters, you use site 110-110 for Cook, department 000-000 for the balance sheet, and chart 0000-3999 for all balance sheet accounts. The one series is for assets, two series is for liabilities, and three series is for stockholders' equity."

"I did not do that."

"You need to be really careful here. The range we put in will auto generate an account for 110.000.0000 through 3999. I think you only have 100 balance sheet accounts, so that's all this will generate. But if you put in 0-99 for all three segments, you could auto generate thousands of general ledger accounts."

"We don't want to do that," said Paul. "We should restrict this function for other users."

"That is your call. I could restrict this using the security group feature or a BPM."

"What's a BPM?"

"It's a business process method change that requires programing. We really are not entertaining modifications to the software. I have strict orders from Ted that we are to use the software in the standard format and that there has to be a compelling reason for a mod."

"I'll talk with Ted about it."

"Absolutely," said James. "The security group for the general ledger setup can be hidden from all who don't need it. This is something I can change in the next fifteen minutes with your approval."

"You have it, and do it."

"Send me an email so I can log it and review it with Ted."

"Thanks. You will have it before you get back to the conference room."

The email from Paul was sitting in the inbox, and James logged it on the issues list. A review with Ted would be done before any modification was turned over to Bill to start on.

"You have a customer waiting for you, James," Bill said as he pointed toward Mary, carrying her laptop.

"What is up, Mary?" James asked.

"I can't get the check payment batch for some vendor checks."

"Show me what you did."

Mary went through the process of creating a payment batch with the initials MT040324 and then selected the vendors button, and nothing came up. James was puzzled.

"Show me that one more time but slowly," he said.

Mary went through the process once more. When she went to hit the selection criteria option, she blew through the screen and got nothing once again.

"I know what you did," said James. "Go back to the selection criteria option. Hit the drop down and select thirty-five days out, or May 8, 2024."

"Why do I need to do that?"

"The software is terms driven. You're trying to select a payment today for something that the system thinks is due in thirty days, or net-thirty, right?"

"Yes. We just entered some invoices this week that we have to pay right away," said Mary.

"Are these invoices due upon receipt or due within one day?"

"Yes, they are due upon receipt."

"Can we go look at what their terms code is?" James asked.

Mary looked up the vendor in question, and the terms was net-thirty days.

"So you may want to have a terms code of zero days or one day so you can pay these vendors quick."

"We put everyone on net thirty days. Even you and Bill are net-thirty."

"You may want to change that. Bill and I are due on receipt per our contract."

"I will need to go through the file and make some changes to the vendor file immediately," said Mary. "We have utility bills that are due in seven days, and they will just shut us off if we don't pay on time."

"Mary, I suggest you review the vendor file right away so this situation does not come up. Do you need assistance in setting up new terms' codes, or are you good with doing it by yourself?"

"I can do it. If I have an issue, I'll be back."

"Where have I heard that before? That was a line in a movie with Arnold Schwarzenegger."

"*Terminator*," said Mary as she walked out of the room.

"Yep, you know your movies," said James.

Late in the morning Ted stopped by for an update on the project.

"So how is it going today, boys?" he asked.

"It has been all James this morning," said Bill.

"Oh," said Ted.

"He means that all the issues we have had this morning were functional," said James.

"Did you take care of them?" Ted asked.

"They were managed. Shirley had an unbalanced batch, Nina had a customer on hold, Paul had a missing general ledger account, and Mary had a check selection issue."

"So they're resolved?"

"They made it to the issues list with a status of closed," said James.

"Like I said, it's been all James this morning," repeated Bill.

"Fantastic," said Ted. "I got a hold of our rep this morning at Blue Point Hosting. He said that they were in the process of moving Butler onto a brand-new server and they were using the old one temporarily. They thought that they had a little more time, but they were mistaken."

"Did you rip them a new one?" James asked.

"I certainly did. They broke the SLA that was promised, and the rep said it would not happen again. I advised him that if it did, we would go shopping."

"He knows what that means," said James.

"No one likes to lose business. Especially in that line of business. The name of Blue Point Hosting will be tarnished to the point no one will hire them."

"I will cross that issue off the list," said James.

"You can for now," said Ted. "But I am a little bit skeptical here. Bill, I want you to go down there Thursday and check out the hardware and physically look at what they are doing."

"I'll call them later today to set up a time," said Bill.

"Are there any other fires today?" Ted asked.

"We seem to be treading water today, and the boat is not sinking," said James. "I told you before, day three is the tough one."

"Keep going, boys," said Ted. "Resolve the issues as they come up and keep the users happy."

Ted had another meeting to go to and was off like a shot.

* * *

Charlotte received a text message on her cell from a number she had not recognized. All it said was *Room 507 at 7:00 p.m. Thursday, same place as before.* She figured it was Peter and he had her seven points. This was one encounter she was going to enjoy physically and financially.

* * *

The rest of the day for Bill and James proved to be an uneventful snooze fest with no additional issues being logged. Bill had set up the appointment with Blue Point Hosting for Thursday morning, so James would be by himself holding down the fort on day four.

Chapter 63

Just as James entered the conference room, Paul was pouring himself a cup of coffee.

"I hope you don't mind," said Paul. "I helped myself to the coffee that Charlotte just brought in."

"No problem," replied James. "What's on your mind?"

"I'll only need a minute of your time. I finished the Cook file last night and wanted to make sure you got it and can work on it first thing today."

"Were the general ledger accounts there in the system, or did you have to create some new ones?"

"The general ledger accounts are all there. I double-checked them to my Excel file, and only one was missing. I added that stray account, so you should be good to upload the file now."

"Give me about thirty minutes. I'll work on it first thing this morning."

"Thanks." Paul left the conference room in a hurry. He was late for a rare early morning meeting.

James checked his email for messages that were urgent and found none. They all could wait. He took the Cook file and converted the Excel file into a load file for the system. Once compiled, the file was uploaded into the software using the data conversion program. The processing duration was only three minutes, and James was a happy camper. He ran the trial balance for the Cook company and did a quick comparison to the conversion file; all was correct and in balance. This would be sent to Paul later in the morning for review and approval. James was hesitant to send it too quickly to him as completed. He did not want the users to get things too fast.

"Should I take a number, or can you serve me next?" Shirley asked as she walked in to see James.

"What's up?"

"I am getting an error message that says, 'Valid fiscal period is required.'"

"What were you trying to do this morning?"

"Just enter a few invoices into an AR batch."

"Show me what you are looking at on your laptop," James said. As she did, he went on, "The third invoice in your batch has a date of March 31, 2024, as the receipt date. This is not allowed in your batch. That date is outside the April month. The months of January, February, and March of this year were never opened up for transactions."

"I get it. It is date sensitive."

"Yes, it is. The open period allows you to transact invoices currently. This is one way of keeping stray entries from hitting the books. There is another way, and that is using the feature of the 'earliest apply date' function."

"Did you show us that feature in the training session?"

"No, I did not," said James. "You can set any of the six modules by date to stop users from putting in transactions to a closed period. It is sort of like a closing schedule before you shut the period down."

"Can we talk about it later with Paul?"

"When you're ready to go over it, let's put it in the mix. I'll place it on the issues list to discuss next week."

"Thanks for fixing the invoice," said Shirley as she exited the conference room.

Nina walked into the conference room with her laptop in her hands.

"Help," she said.

"What do you have this time?"

"I have an AR invoice batch that is out of balance by one cent. The edit report is out of balance, and I do not know what to do with it."

"Show me the group that you were reviewing. Open up that third invoice in the group."

"The invoice item has a decimal with a .495 number on the line."

"Do you have pricing with a third digit to the right of the decimal point?"

"Yes, we have some pricing like that."

"This is a rounding GL control issue," said James. "We never set this up in the system. Where do you want the pennies to go in the rounding of transactions?"

"We can use any-expense account like the bank charges number. I think it is 9998 in the chart."

"Hang on and I'll set this up."

An expense account called "rounding" was generated. A GL control account was created and linked to the 9998 account and activated.

"I'll need to confirm this account with Paul," said Nina.

"That is fine," said James. "The new rounding account is ready for you. Can you try to print and preview the edit report once more?"

"I'll rerun the edit," Nina said, then added, "It is in balance and looks OK to post."

"Can you run this by Paul so he approves of the general ledger rounding account we set up?"

"I'll talk to him later this morning."

* * *

Karen did not know who James was, and she had not taken part in the training session that had been held over the past couple of weeks. But she was told that he could fix the error she was having with the software.

"Are you James?" Karen asked.

"Hi. I am James Crowley."

"My name is Karen Rodgers, and I work with Nina Charles."

"What can I do for you?"

"I seem to be stuck in this AR batch."

"Can you sign out of the application and reboot your laptop? I'll look at this batch while you're doing that."

Karen rebooted her laptop and signed back into the application. The batch that she was in before was still showing "Account Locked" as the error message.

"Hey, Bill, can you unlock a user account on the admin console?" said James.

"Sure, give me a minute," said Bill. "Which user account?"

"That would be Karen Rodgers," James said, then explained to Karen, "Sometimes when a user gets stuck in a batch, the system will lock the account. The software provides a utility to unlock the account, but a system administrator has to do it in a separate place."

"She is unlocked," said Bill. "Try to get into the batch now?"

"I can get into the batch now," said Karen. "Thanks, guys. You're terrific."

"Any time. Just come on in," said James.

* * *

Two men approached Charlotte's desk late in the afternoon. They looked familiar, but she was not sure who they were.

"Can I help you?" Charlotte asked.

"Hello again. I am Officer Glowicki, and this is my partner Officer Piotrowski. We are investigating the death of Tom McFaden, as you might remember, and we need to see your boss Tim Murphy."

"Let me see if he is off the phone."

A few minutes later, Tim came out of his office and greeted the officers. "What can I do for you two?"

"We just wanted to let you know that we found the killer of Tom McFaden," said Officer Glowicki. "A guy by the name of Billy Jackson confessed to killing him. He said that he robbed him and rolled him down a mountain pass but couldn't remember where. We found Tom's cell phone on Billy, so we are sure he is the one who did it."

"So the case is closed?" Tim asked.

"We just wanted you to know in case there was anything you could add to this case," said Officer Glowicki. "Billy Jackson did not work for the Butler Energy Corporation?"

"That name is not familiar to me."

"Thanks for your time, and if you come across anything related to this case, give us a call."

"I will," Tim said as the two officers left his office.

Charlotte had heard every word that the officers told Tim. How could she be so fortunate that a drifter would find Tom's cell phone and get framed for his murder? That was a stroke of good luck, to be sure.

* * *

Mary had to prepare three check runs today: one each from the old AP system for the Barron and Cook companies and one from the new system for both. The cash requirements report for the three check runs was printed and placed on Paul's desk for approval.

All three check runs were approved, and Mary ran the checks. The stack of checks to be signed was then placed on the desk for Paul to sign. All three batches were signed and returned to Mary for distribution on Friday.

Mary started to thumb through the three stacks of checks, and that is when she noticed something wrong. The Barron stack was fine. The Cook stack was fine. The new combined company stack of checks had a problem, though. There were three checks on which she did not recognize the vendors: a check in the amount of $15,500 made out to Acme Chemical supply, a check in the amount of $16,600 made out to Aaron Gas Corp., and a check in the amount of $17,700 made out to Adam Services LLC. She pulled the supporting invoices for these three checks; all three had the same PO box number (321) and Coraopolis, Pennsylvania, as the city and state. There were no approvals on the invoices, so she knew something was wrong. A review of the system revealed that Patty Gray was the entry person on all three of these invoices. Mary was now alarmed that maybe one of her own had put in fake invoices for payment into the new system.

Mary grabbed the three checks with the supporting invoices and walked into Paul's office. She explained what she had uncovered. Paul called Patty to his office. A discussion with Patty Gray, Mary Thomas, and Paul Meadows on the subject of the three invoices was now under way. After a few minutes, Patty confessed to forging the three invoices.

"Why did you do this?" Paul asked.

"I needed the money," said Patty.

"You're fired," said Paul. "Immediately."

The three of them walked back to Patty's desk so she could get her personal effects and leave the building. Mary asked for her key card to the building, and Patty turned it over. She walked down the hallway to the front door and watched Patty as she left the building.

"I am all alone in the AP department once again," said Mary.

"Well, you will need to run another search for a new AP analyst," said Paul. "I'll let HR know what happened this morning when they get back from vacation."

"I'll need to void these three checks," said Mary. "I'll need to inactivate those three vendors as well."

"Go see James right away," said Paul. "Fill him in on the details."

* * *

Charlotte received another text message on her mobile phone. *Are we still on for 7:00 p.m. tonight at the same place?* She replied with a simple *Yes*.

Peter knew he was in for a night of fun with Charlotte once again.

* * *

Mary walked into the conference room just after lunch.

"Hey, James, can you help me void some checks?" she asked.

"Sure, is something wrong?" James asked.

Mary told James what had happened and that Patty Gray was fired on the spot that morning.

"Let me guess, she was able to enter invoices and enter checks?" James said.

"That is correct. You warned us about the proper controls needing to be put in place."

"This is referred to as growing pains in any new business," said James. "The opportunity presents itself, and people take advantage while you're not looking. This happens in every new business I have worked on over the years."

"Here are the three checks we need to void."

"You need to go into the AP application under the operations folder and select the void process. Then enter the check numbers, review the edit, and post the batch. That's it. It is quite simple."

"Can you watch me do it?" Mary went into the application and voided the checks with no issue. "Thanks," she said when the process was complete. "I have to get back to my desk. I am all alone once again in the AP department."

"Sorry to hear that," said James. "Take it easy and holler if you need help."

* * *

The rest of the day on Thursday was quiet. The firing of Patty Gray had spread through the organization like wildfire in the forest. The gossip was everywhere. There was little business going on during the day. As a consequence, Bill and James had survived day number four of the go-live event and were looking forward to going home on Friday. He had been in the Coraopolis office for almost twelve days, and he missed his wife and Westies.

* * *

Charlotte wore her signature red dress and brought all her toys in her purse. She made sure to bring the vial of three powdered Valium tablets this time. The Pittsburgh International Hotel by the airport was a familiar place to her, and it would be easy to go from the lobby to room 507 on the fifth floor unnoticed.

She knocked on the door. Peter was waiting for her. She had brought a bottle of Malbec with her, already chilled.

"You brought wine," said Peter.

"I thought we would have some to celebrate."

"I am drinking Gentleman Jack already."

"You know me, I like my Malbec."

"Let me get the wine opener from the kitchen," said Peter.

That is when Charlotte knew she had only a few seconds. The vial of three crushed and powdered Valium tablets was pulled from her purse and dumped in his drink. She stirred the glass and wiped her finger on the side of the couch. She pretended to have been stationary since Peter went to the kitchen. He would never know what hit him.

He opened the wine and poured a glass for Charlotte. They clinked glasses as a toast to a continued relationship.

"You like your whiskey, and I like my wine," said Charlotte.

"Here is your finder's fee," said Peter.

"Thanks," said Charlotte as she placed the envelope in her purse. "What's the twist tonight?"

"The twist is a going to be a card game. There are two decks of cards in my purse. Do you want to play?"

"What is the game?"

"It's a card game called Choices: Each participant selects from the deck of cards, and when two matches are made, the partner performs the action. So if I matched two cards with 'bodice' on them, you would put it on me. Or if you picked two cards with 'cuffs,' then I would put them on you."

"This sounds like fun," said Peter.

"You did ask me for a *twist* tonight."

"Yes, I did."

"Cheers and down the hatch," said Charlotte as she emptied her glass. "Another one, please."

"Wait," said Peter. "Let me catch up." He downed his Gentleman Jack.

The glasses were refilled, and Charlotte knew in about fifteen minutes he would be putty in her hands. She just had to stretch out the game so the Valium could take effect.

"Are you ready to play?" she asked.

Peter just shook his head in agreement. Charlotte went to take his clothes off and push him onto the bed. He helped unzip her dress, and it fell to the floor. She placed the two decks of cards on the nightstands.

"Now pick ten cards and place them on your nightstand face down in the order you will flip them up," she said. "I'll take ten cards and place them face down on the other nightstand."

"How many should I flip up?"

"As soon as you get a match, it's my turn."

Peter flipped up four cards and got a match: cuffs, fun chains, mask, cuffs.

Charlotte wrapped his wrists and legs with the cuffs.

She flipped up four cards and got a match: bodice, mask, chocolate syrup, bodice.

Peter placed the bodice around Charlotte.

He flipped up another card: fun chains.

Charlotte wrapped the fun chains around the four bedposts.

She flipped up two more cards: spreader bar, chocolate syrup.

Peter squeezed the chocolate syrup on Charlotte's lips and gave her a kiss by licking it all off with his tongue.

He flipped up another two cards: locks, locks.

Charlotte placed the locks on the fun chains and attached them to the cuffs. She could not have asked for a better progression in the game.

She flipped up two more cards: cuff, cuffs.

"Hey, I can't put them on you," said Peter.

"I'll put them on."

She placed a pair of handcuffs on his right wrist and her left ankle and then the other pair on his left wrist and her right ankle.

Peter could not flip over any more cards, but Charlotte could do it for him. She flipped over two more cards and got a match: ball gag, ball gag.

She placed the ball gag in his mouth and wrapped it around the back of his neck.

She then flipped over two more cards and got a match: mask, mask.

She put the mask on her face and grabbed her cell phone. This was the time to take more pictures and cement the business relationship between the two for the future.

Peter was starting to become dazed and docile, and Charlotte knew that the Valium was working. At this point she would ride him and put him away. She would have her fun and try to get a last rise out of him before she put him to bed.

Now that she was done, it was time to go. She worked quickly to take off all the toys and place them in her overstuffed purse. Peter appeared to be comatose, and she hoped that she had not killed him. A fitting conclusion to a profitable night.

Charlotte was just about to leave and could see that Peter was actually sleeping. She had gathered all her toys, put her clothes back on, and then checked to make sure she had the finder's fee in her purse. She opened the envelope. The amount had to be wrong: the check was only for $37,500, not $52,500.

That bastard changed the deal from seven points to five points. I should kill him. That is what Charlotte was thinking as she left the hotel.

Chapter 64

Friday was day five of the go-live event. James knew that in a couple of hours, he would be going home for a much-needed rest. The evening phone calls to Lynn were helpful but were hardly a substitute for seeing her smiling face. His Trek racing bike was collecting dust, and a long ride was in the cards. A walk with the Westies was also on the agenda. But before he could get on the plane, a few more hours would need to be spent with the Butler team.

"So how did it go at the Blue Point Hosting office yesterday?" James asked.

"Fine," said Bill. "They had moved our instance to a new blade on a new server like they said, and I hope we don't have any more issues with them. The server they were using was over ten years old; I wouldn't trust it with two nickels."

"If it happens again, Ted is going to come down hard on that team."

"He should. He is paying big bucks for the hosting services, and they need to adhere to the SLA as agreed."

"What time is your flight out today?" James asked.

"One thirty. So, I need to leave here by noon."

"I'll be gone by the same time."

Right on schedule Charlotte walked into the conference room with a carafe of coffee.

"Morning, boys," she Charlotte. "I brought you some wake-up juice."

"Thanks," said James. "Are you going to mess with Bill this morning?"

"Absolutely," said Charlotte as she gave James a peck on the cheek and left the room.

"Dude," said Bill. "She did it again. That's two days in a row. You two are an item."

"She is just messing with you."

"Well, she is doing a good job," replied Bill.

Mary walked into the conference room and was looking for James.

"What's broken this morning?" he asked.

"I just have a question for you. The Wells Fargo Bank is requesting that we use an electronic file process called Positive Pay. It is some sort of process for heavy volume check processing that they want us to implement."

"The software we are using has this feature built in. There is some configuration and testing that needs to be done first before you can use it, though. I do not have time to push this forward, so I'll talk with Ted and put it on the project list for now."

"How much time will that take to turn on?"

"It could take about four to six hours, plus testing time. We will need to get the bank specifications on what they require before we even get started."

"I'll work on it next week," Mary responded. "In case I don't see you, safe travels back home."

"Thanks," said James. "If you need something over the weekend, call me on my cell."

* * *

There were no other team members who sought assistance from Bill or James.

Ted stopped by late in the morning and got an update from both Bill and James just before they headed for the airport. There were no pressing issues that needed to be resolved, and Ted was one happy camper. The software was working as designed; no major "showstoppers" were hanging over their heads. James had informed the Butler team via email that if they needed some assistance over the weekend, they should call him on his cell. He would not be monitoring his email unless called. Ted was grateful for the after-hours service touch. James knew that you always had to take care of the client, even on a weekend.

There would be no calls from the Butler team this weekend, though. They were all tired and would take the two days off.

Chapter 65

James was all alone in the conference room on Monday. Bill had a plane issue that he was dealing with and would arrive later in the morning. Charlotte walked in with the coffee and wondered why James was all by himself.

"Do you need some company this morning?" she asked as she brought him some coffee. "Where is Bill?"

"He was delayed due to a mechanical issue on his plane," said James. "He will be here as soon as possible. Coffee would be nice."

As Charlotte poured a cup of coffee, she gave him a peck on the cheek like before. James didn't think anything of it and knew that she was just messing around once again.

"Care to go around?" Charlotte asked and then pressed her boobs up against his chest.

"Charlotte, you're flirting again."

"I just can't help it. I take care of my men."

"I'll remind you again, I am married."

"You passed," said Charlotte. "Again."

"Don't you have a boyfriend?"

"Kind of. He still doesn't know it."

"Well, please tell him and stop fussing over me."

"I know. I just can't stop it," Charlotte said as she left the room.

Jerry, Tim, and Ted walked into the conference room as Charlotte was exiting. Their look was a serious one, and James thought that maybe he was in trouble.

"Gentlemen, what's up?" James asked.

"How is the team this morning?" Jerry said.

"All is quiet on the project scene," said James. "I need to answer a few emails but nothing out of the normal for day six."

"Congratulations on a successful launch of the first two businesses," said Jerry. "Where is Bill?"

"Thanks, and he is delayed due to a plane issue."

"Well, we want you to travel with Ted and Bill to Greenwood, Louisiana, next week to preview our next acquisition," said Tim.

"When are you planning on gobbling up another business?" James asked.

"Our target date is May 1, next month," said Tim. "We are doing our due diligence over the next two weeks."

"This is not public information," said Ted. "We have to go there and stay quiet about it."

"You guys don't waste any time," said James.

"Can you and Bill be ready for this?" Jerry asked.

"The real hard part of this implementation was standing up the instance and getting the hosting service," said James. "The next on-ramp for a business takes considerably less time. There are just configurations and any deltas that the business has that we did not turn on or don't know about."

"That is good news," said Jerry. "By the way, the four of you are playing golf on Tuesday afternoon at my club. Make sure you clear your schedule for this."

"Thanks. That is very generous," said James.

"Your time on the course is billable," said Ted.

"I don't know what to say," said James. "I will let Bill know when he gets here."

"It is just our thanks for both of you doing a bang-up job on this implementation," said Jerry. "Ted will give you the details later today."

* * *

Later in the day a meeting was scheduled in Jerry's office with the Wells Fargo brokerage team. The broker had waived the third acquisition requirement and was preparing the underwriting for the Butler IPO. The placement offering was going to raise $200 million or 10 million shares at the offering price of $20 per share. The restrictive covenant of the loan repayment was removed. The board would be paid in full for the $5 million loans provided to Butler early that month. The bank would receive a $100 million loan repayment on the original loan amount previously issued. The board members would also be granted $5 million in stock once the loans were repaid, and the stock was issued. The board members would make a 100 percent profit on the deal if all went well. The IPO was set for May 1 of this year.

* * *

A mechanical issue and then a crew out-of-hours issue had plagued Bill's morning flight from Indianapolis International Airport to Pittsburgh International Airport.

"I see you finally made it in," said James.

"Just in time for lunch," said Bill.

"Let's go eat. I have a few things to share with you this morning. Or should I say this afternoon."

"Do I hear a bit of sarcasm in that tone?"

"I am just giving you shit," said James.

* * *

Lunch at the local Chick-fil-A was going to be a long one. James had to fill Bill in on the events of that morning. The thank-you from Jerry. The golf event scheduled for Tuesday at Jerry's private club. The Greenwood trip next week for the third acquisition. These were wrenches in the stabilization of the current software plan.

"We get to bill them for golf?" Bill asked in shock.

"That is what Jerry said."

"This is the goose that laid the golden-egg client."

"We really need to stabilize this software before we add a third one onto the platform," said James.

"We can handle it for now."

James was worried; he always was the realist of the two. This was a situation where a vacuum was being created and they needed some extra bodies to support the team while working on acquisitions. This would be an issue to take up with Ted. James had asked about a help desk ticketing system before but was blown off due to a lack of staff. After the third acquisition was completed, it would be time to resurrect this request.

* * *

The rest of the week at Butler proved to be a quiet time. The team had settled into a routine. A user would bring up an issue, and Bill or James would resolve it, log it, and mark it closed on the project plan. It was almost getting boring, if a consultant could call it that. James felt comfortable with where the Butler team was.

Now it was time for the next acquisition: the Metairie Pipeline Corporation in Greenwood, Louisiana.

Chapter 66

The IT team traveled through the Houston International Airport Sunday afternoon, then had a three-hour road trip to Carthage, Texas, to get to the hotel. Ted, James, and Bill would then travel on Monday morning to the Metairie Pipeline Corporation in Greenwood. This facility was a salt water tank battery operation that serviced the East Texas Oil Field area.

They arrived at the Greenwood facility right around 9:00 a.m. on Monday and were met by Duncan Bailey at the main office.

"Good morning, gentlemen," said Duncan. "Nice of you to come and visit us here in Louisiana."

"Thanks," said Ted. "I want you to meet my associates Bill Hogan and James Crowley, who will be working on the integration of your company into the Butler company software."

"Can you give us a tour of the facility?" said James.

"Sure," said Duncan. "Let's get out of the office and walk around."

Duncan spent the next hour with Ted, Bill, and James walking through the facility on an informational tour. Ted had seen and heard this before, and it was exactly the same story. The main thrust of the business all boiled down to dumping picked-up salt water from oil operators in the oil patches of Texas and Louisiana. Bill and James were well versed in this business and did not see any problems with the implementation. The dispatcher turned a phone call into a service agreement with the customers on the oil rig, a truck driver then picked up a salt water load, and then a miscellaneous invoice was prepared and sent to the customer. This process had no surprises and could easily be moved onto the Butler software platform. James had commented that there looked to be about twenty-five office workers that would need to be trained and get access to the system. Duncan later confirmed that number.

As they walked through the yard, they all noticed that there were truck parts everywhere. The trucks that were being repaired looked really old. Duncan kind of confirmed that the average age of the trucks was well over ten years. After the tour was over, they headed back to Duncan's office.

"So what did you think of my business?" Duncan asked.

"You have done a nice job building the business," said James. "Can you tell me, what is the life of the injection wells that you use to dump the salt water into?"

"We have ten injection wells ranging in age from three to twelve years old, and none of them have failed," said Duncan. "The flow rate slows down and we have to shift the salt water around, but they are still all active."

"Can I ask you about some of your financials?"

"Ask away."

"Can you tell me what your receivables and payables balances are currently?"

"The customer accounts are around six million, and the vendor stuff is around one million."

"That sounds like sixty days' worth of customer accounts and thirty days' worth of vendor bills."

"That sounds about right," said Duncan. "I can get you the exact figures if you need it."

"No, that's fine," said James. "I don't need the exact figures."

"Any other questions?"

"Nope, I think we are good for now," said Ted.

"Hey, I have a customer I need to run out and see," said Duncan. "Do you need anything else from me?"

"Go to your customer meeting," said Ted. "Can we hang around here the rest of the day and maybe talk with your accounting team?"

"The accounting manager is Terry Bailey, my sister," said Duncan. "Hey, Terry, can you come in here?"

"What do you need?" said Terry.

"Can you give these guys anything they need today while I am gone? They are from the Butler Energy company, the ones buying us out. Set them up in the conference room for now."

"Step this way, boys," said Terry as she escorted them to the conference room.

Terry was a wealth of information to the IT team. She was able to fill in the missing holes that Bill and James needed to complete the picture of the struggling Metairie Pipeline business. The company was in need of a serious cash infusion to grow the business and keep it afloat. The trucks were old and would need replacement. The good news was that Butler was picking the business up for only $30 million.

Duncan never returned to the office on Monday, and the boys left for the hotel at the end of the day. The IT team had obtained all the necessary information about the business and did not foresee any surprises in implementing this one onto the existing system.

Ted had missed a voicemail from Duncan. He had apologized and said something came up and he was not able to return to the office for any follow-ups. He would make himself available on Tuesday if Ted was still in town.

* * *

Ted decided that they would work out of the Metairie Pipeline office for the rest of the week. The consultants could handle anything that the Coraopolis office was having issues with while working on the Metairie configurations concurrently. The goal would be to get them ready to perform training for the twenty-five employees that were being absorbed with the purchase.

James had a conversation with Paul, and he agreed to use the site number 115 for the Metairie company. All general ledger accounts would be generated with the new numbers and established ahead of time. James had carte blanche on this item as Paul said he had no time this week to help. James would make some educated guesses on the configurations of this third company.

He received the list of current customers and vendors from Terry Bailey and converted both files into upload files. The customer file had to be reconverted to unique customers, which brought the number down from 1,100 to 600 with multiple ship-to sites. The vendor file contained 200 unique records, and no additional changes to the file were necessary. James added one change to both the vendor file and the customer file: a reference field of "MET." This was just in case someone needed some slicing and dicing of the data. Both files were uploaded in less than an hour. The list of uploaded customers was sent to Nina for a review, while the list of uploaded vendors was sent to Mary for a review. James would make the assumption that the AP payments would be burned in the old system by having four check runs after the acquisition date. The accounts receivable balances would be the only item that would be converted at the cut-over date.

The rest of the week in Greenwood was a bit of a letdown. After the initial rush of work on Tuesday and Wednesday, Thursday was rather dull and uneventful. The only real thing to worry about was how much was going to be in the accounts receivable balance when the books were closed. Ted had implied that the acquisition date was being moved around and could be as early as Sunday, April 28. That change would require the configs to be done by this week or next and for training to start next week. This was a bit of a messy schedule. If there was a project plan, you could throw it out the window.

Ted informed Bill and James that they needed to perform the training of the Metairie Pipeline employees next week and that their presence would be required back in Greenwood. Ted apologized to them both and said that he would make it up to them.

James had decided that the training materials that were used for the Butler team last month would be reused for the team next week. This way he would not have to create new documentation. The Metairie Pipeline would be a wholly owned subsidiary of the Butler Energy Corporation. He would personally set up the twenty-five employees based on what Terry Bailey said they all did for Metairie.

James sat down with Terry and obtained the list. A short meeting was held, and an explanation of each person on the list was reviewed. The email accounts and the exact names were added; James would create the user accounts and get Blue Point Hosting to set them up in the system on the back end.

James thought, *This was too easy a setup for a new business. Something is going to bite me in the ass.* That is exactly how the week finished out.

Chapter 67

James had traveled back to Carthage on a Sunday night once again. He had to get ready to train a group of twenty-five employees of the Metairie Pipeline on the new system. Ted had called him between flights to confirm that the acquisition date was Sunday, April 28, 2024. This left little time to finish up the configurations, train the new group of people, and get ready for the launch of the third business. Ted gave James many words of encouragement and praise. He said that the right person for this job was him. If anyone could do it, it would be the duo of James and Bill.

James and Bill arrived at the offices of the Metairie Pipeline company bright and early on the morning of Monday, April 22. Terry Bailey had reserved the conference room on the first floor for the training classes to be held on Monday and Tuesday.

There were three sessions scheduled for Monday: 8:00 a.m. for the customer service group, 10:00 a.m. for the second customer service group, and 1:00 p.m. for the third customer service group. The basics of setting up customer accounts and the billing function were the only tasks for these ladies. There were three groups of five ladies that Terry put together based on the work schedules. She did not want to have the current customers ignored for two hours while the ladies were in training. Terry felt it was important that the customers could get ahold of anyone from the customer service team at Metairie during the day and not have to leave a voicemail for service. Since the ladies that were attending the training sessions did not have laptops, James could only instruct them on how to do certain things. The shit would hit the fan next week, when the ladies actual went into the new system and performed the invoicing·or customer related work.

This approach was going to be a struggle. James and Bill would have to use Wednesday and Thursday for on-the-job training at each of the lady's desktop machines. The consultants would have to move from lady to lady and machine to machine for training reinforcement.

The Monday sessions went well, and no significant issues were raised from the three groups. There were questions about what the new system could do that the current system doesn't do. There was always the question of why they were converting to the new system, which James could not answer. He knew the reason for moving to an integrated system was to cut heads at the acquired business, and so he would not offer up any explanation. Indeed, one of the main reasons for going to the system was to cut 30 percent of the administration of running the business. That meant that any acquired business would lose up to 30 percent of its workforce. This was a business strategy that was baked into the cards of any purchased company. And this was a key fundamental of the Butler company's existence. You take ten companies and put them on one platform and wring out 30 percent of the admin of all the businesses you acquire to achieve cost savings. The whole of ten becomes more valuable than the pieces of the ten individually.

* * *

James and Bill decided to have a quiet evening Monday by having dinner at their hotel, the Hampton Inn & Suites, which offered a light dinner service with a full bar. The boys did not feel like driving around and were content on eating in and having a couple of drinks.

"So what did you think about today's training group?" James asked.

"I think they got it," said Bill. "But we will have to jump around to their desks to see that they made the leap on Wednesday and Thursday."

"That's what I was afraid of. None of the ladies have laptops. They are sitting ducks."

"You mean the technology has passed them by?"

"Exactly. When they gut that team, it will be an easy one to do."

"I agree with you. Those stupid bastards will cut the team in half."

"That group of fifteen will be reduced to five," said James. "The software they are using is terribly inefficient."

"I think that is why Ted and Tim picked this business."

"I wonder if the owner Duncan shared this with the employees."

"I really doubt it."

"He is just in it for his check. He will get a little bit rich on the sale and move on. The ladies will be left holding the bag when they get cut."

"This is how every one of our implementations has progressed."

"You and I seem to be at the center of this all. So are we good guys or bad guys?"

"We are good guys for the owners and bad guys for the employees."

"I would like to think that we *craft value through joint discovery*," said James.

"We are the modern-day ax cutters of the efficiency consultants," said Bill.

"You really think we are? Let's just have another drink and forget about it for a while."

"Sounds good."

"Another Gentleman Jack and Coke?"

"Sure, what the hell," said Bill. "We just have to walk to our rooms."

* * *

The Tuesday training sessions would be the cash collections group of ladies in the morning, followed by the payables ladies in the afternoon. There were three people in the HR department, but there were no changes there, so no training would be provided. The general ledger training involved just one person, Terry Bailey. Her training would be one-on-one at her desk sometime during the week.

There were no surprises during the day with the sessions, and James and Bill finished early. There were very few questions asked on how to do things. Plus, the ladies were not very talkative during the day. They just nodded their heads and said, "Yes sir" and "No sir."

* * *

Wednesday and Thursday were spent individually sitting with each of the twenty-five ladies to see what they did. An attempt to log in using their credentials and replicate on the new system what they transacted on the old system was explored. All of the employees were successful in accessing the new system, and the comfort level was adequate. But until the ladies went on the new system cold turkey, James would not know how good the training was.

* * *

Friday was a wrap-up session, and there was not a lot going on. None of the ladies came into the conference room in the morning; James and Bill thought that was strange. The official acquisition date was set for Sunday, so there was a little bit of an uneasy feeling in the air. James and Bill would be back on Sunday night and back in the Metairie office on Monday, April 29, which was the day after the acquisition date. They both knew that this implementation would be a little bit different than all the rest. This one was a baptism by fire, James thought. *Throw all the ingredients into the pot and turn up the heat to get it to boil.*

Chapter 68

Mary had prepared a check for $30 million payable to Duncan Bailey and hand-delivered the postdated check to Paul for safekeeping. The check would be signed by Paul and countersigned by Jerry Monday morning. It would then be picked up by Duncan at the Butler office at 8:00 a.m. the same day. This was the big payoff to Duncan for the purchase of the Metairie Pipeline company. It would be referred to as a wholly owned subsidiary of Butler temporarily until all the signage could be changed. The deal that was struck did not include the hunting club, and Duncan was a happy man his club would be private. The oil-skimming operation was going to continue until he got caught. A private truck would siphon off the oil from the holding pond, and the revenue generated would go directly to Duncan's bank account. Sooner or later the Butler company would figure this out. The gravy train would end, and it was just a matter of time until this situation was unwound.

* * *

James and Bill had arrived at the Greenwood facility of Metairie Pipeline, now called a wholly owned subsidiary of the Butler Energy Corporation, on Monday morning. The go-live event was underway, and both of the consultants knew it would be a little bit shaky. The twenty-five employees would have to transition to the new system cold turkey. James logged into the system to make sure the software platform was up and running, and it was. He then started to make the rounds with the ladies in the office. None of the team had logged in; they were just having coffee and donuts.

James returned to the conference room and sent out a company-wide email. He advised the ladies that he and Bill would be in the conference room and were available if needed. The consultants would make rounds as well to help anyone who needed assistance with the new system.

It did not take long until the chaos started. Right around 8:30 a.m., the ladies all asked for help at the same time. They had forgotten everything they were taught and had to be hand-held for the rest of the day. James and Bill spent more time at the workstations than back in the conference room answering emails.

Ted had called James on his cell and asked for an update. James had replied that they were treading water and starting to see some daylight. It would take the full day to get this team to start to be productive on the new system. The message from Ted was to hang in there and do what they could to push forward.

James and Bill were exhausted by the end of the day. Five o'clock could not come soon enough. The next hour would be spent answering emails and trying to get caught up. The day seemed to be a success, and the business was billing customers based on the pickups completed on Monday. A repeat of this chaos would not be a pleasant feeling, and they both hoped that Tuesday would be a better day.

* * *

Monday night at the restaurant and bar was a repeat of last week with one big change: Bill and James had dinner and only one drink, then went to bed early. This go-live event had burned them out, and they had to get ready for Tuesday. Sleep was needed; they both knew it.

* * *

The second day at the Greenwood facility was much better than the first day. James and Bill spent most of their time in the conference room and only ventured out to the bullpens of the ladies upon a request. The goal today was to let them sink a little and then let them ask for help. The approach worked, and the consultants were able to get ahold of the project as they pushed forward. The volume of unanswered email traffic was what they were dealing with. There were still other users back in Coraopolis asking for assistance, and they had been ignored on Monday due to the third business launch. The morning hours were spent catching up and treading water.

Ted called James on his cell and asked for another update.

"Good morning, Ted, what can I do for you?" James said.

"I just wanted to know how things were going."

"We seem to be leveling off this morning. The ladies are asking fewer questions and appear to be settling in."

"That is good news."

"Thanks. We need to get through the day on Wednesday for a good read on this bunch."

"Sounds like a plan. Keep me informed if anything happens or you two need something."

"Will do," replied James as he ended the call.

Terry Bailey provided James with the accounts receivable file to be converted late in the day. She apologized for the delay and said it was difficult to finalize the file. She had made several attempts from their old system to get the right customers with the right balances. This file was scrubbed and converted to an upload file, then processed. James added a reference of MET to the file in case of the old slice-and-dice issue. The final file converted was $6,050,000.00 in customer receivable balances. A review file was sent back to Terry Bailey, and a copy was sent to Nina Charles for a secondary review.

The rest of the day was one of firefighting and was typical of day-two activities. James and Bill once again made it to the end of the day unscathed. They were exhausted once again, but this time it came with a feeling of satisfaction. Dinner and drinks at the hotel were a welcome sight. This time the drinks were flowing, and they both were feeling a little carefree after pulling this one off. Only day three would tell.

* * *

Wednesday, day three, was the critical one. The users would make or break the system. They would throw up their hands or plain get it. The day was a little bit hectic but simmered down fast. Since the ladies were billers, after several hundred invoices, they got it. They became proficient in the process and had no trouble with processing their invoice groups. The real test would come later next week when the customers would accept or reject the invoices from the new wholly owned subsidiary of the Butler Energy company.

A call from Ted was received by James, and he passed along the good news to Bill. Ted was delighted and said the next time the two of them were in Coraopolis, there would be a celebration for this successful third launch.

Paul sent an email to James about the opening general ledger balances for the Metairie acquisition. There would be a delay in the numbers because Terry Bailey was having some issues with the old system. She had to compile the balances by hand. This file would not be ready until Friday at the earliest. This was not an issue; James said he understood. He had other fish to fry and was trying to keep up with his email traffic.

The rest of the day went smoothly, and James and Bill were surprised. The issues that came up during the day were all handled and managed by some simple hand-holding with the ladies. They knew that they were over the hump and could put this acquisition to bed. There would be a mini celebration for the duo of James and Bill tonight.

The next phase of this project was to stabilize the user community, and this message had to be delivered to Ted and Tim next week in Coraopolis.

Chapter 69

The second week after the Metairie go-live event, the team of James and Bill were back in the Coraopolis office. Their goal was to stabilize the user community and take a breather from all the emails they had received. There were now three new business units operating on the new software system. The three groups of employees were using a lot of the current licenses on the Enterprise Software, and the Butler organization would need to buy another block. This would be raised as an immediate issue to Ted at the Monday morning project update meeting.

Charlotte had brought a carafe of coffee into the main floor conference room for James and Bill, like she had done so many times before. She was dressed in a royal blue full-length dress that showed her figure off like never before. She was a gorgeous young woman.

"Can I mess with Bill today?" Charlotte whispered into James's ear.

"What did you have in mind?" he asked.

"Just watch. Did you have a nice weekend, Bill?" She brushed his back with her breasts and gave him a peck on the cheek.

"Uh, uh, yes I did," said Bill.

"You know, I have been messing with you these past couple of weeks."

"I thought you and James had a thing going on."

"No, it was just my way of taking care of my men. Are you one of my men?"

"I don't know what you mean," said Bill.

"You men are so easy to manipulate. You do know that I have a boyfriend."

"I would hope so," said Bill. "You're too beautiful a woman to be loose in this city. You would drive all the men in Coraopolis nuts."

"Thanks for the compliment," said Charlotte as she left the conference room.

Just then Ted strolled into the room with a huge smile on his face.

"You look rather happy this morning," said James.

"I am very happy," said Ted. "The Butler company is going public today, and we will be traded on the NASDAQ with the symbol of BEC."

"Congratulations to you and the senior management team," said James.

"Jerry, Tim, the board, and I are receiving a huge block of stock in the company, and our loans are being repaid in full. All the core employees are receiving a $25,000 bonus this week."

"Whoa, that is very generous," said James.

"You and Bill will be receiving a bonus as well. You will have to keep it quiet."

"You're giving us a bonus?" said Bill.

"A lot of the Butler organization's success at this point is due to the efforts of the two of you," said Ted. "The board agreed to a $50,000 bonus for each of you to show their appreciation."

"We are your consultants," James reminded Ted.

"That's another thing we would like to change."

"Oh, what did you have in mind?"

"Jerry, Tim, the board, and I feel strongly that you two should join us here at Butler. We all feel that the two of you would be a fine addition to the team as permanent employees."

"That would be a wonderful opportunity," said James.

"Before you say no," said Ted. "Hear me out."

"I am not saying no. I just want to hear the offer."

"A generous salary, quarterly bonus, and stock options. I will provide you the details later on in the week, after we put the package together."

"That sounds too good to pass up. What do you think, Bill?"

"I'm in," said Bill.

"I'll consider the package," said James.

"I'll have the HR manager get the details to you both by week's end," said Ted.

"We appreciate that," said James.

"Now get back to work," Ted said as he left the conference room.

James and Bill were supposed to have an update meeting, but the news trumped the meeting.

"What do you think, James?" Bill asked. "Are you going to stop being a consultant and become an employee once again?"

"I'll need to discuss this with Lynn."

"I am going to take the package."

"How is this going to work? I live in Fallbrook, California, and you live in Indianapolis, Indiana. Are we going to commute or work from home or a hybrid of the two? How is this going to play out?"

"We will need to see the package they come up with."

"Let's wait and see before we decide."

"Agreed."

"Now let's get back to work," said James. "We have some hungry users out there in three cities asking for assistance. Let's get them some service."

One of the last project items for Metairie was the general ledger balances from Paul. He finally got around to the final numbers and sent them to James for processing. The upload took five minutes to complete, and it was done. This was one of the last items for the Metairie company acquisition project plan. The Metairie ladies were fat, dumb, and happy billing the customers just like before but using the new software with no other significant issues. The rest of the users were really on their own and not bothering James and Bill.

* * *

Later that night Charlotte invited Phil over to her house for a home-cooked meal. Monday was one of the only days that the restaurant was not busy, and he could get the evening off. She was delighted to cook an Italian dish of spaghetti, homemade meatballs, and garlic bread for her new boyfriend. She wanted to share a meal with Phil at her place because she wanted him all to herself. The meal was a hit, and they both enjoyed the food, drinks, and good conversation.

At the end of the meal, Charlotte wanted more. They finished cleaning up the dishes, and that's when she jumped him.

"I want you so much," said Charlotte as she kissed him in an embrace.

Phil wrapped his arms around her and kissed her profusely, hugging her in his arms and caressing her lips. Charlotte started to unbutton his shirt while they were kissing.

"Charlotte, I don't know you that well," said Phil as he grabbed her hands and stopped her from unbuttoning his shirt.

"I want you tonight, here and now."

"This is too fast. This is just our second date." Phil pulled away from Charlotte's embrace.

"You don't like me?"

"I was raised to be kind, gentle, and courteous to all women. I need to get to know you better before we jump into bed together."

"I'm sorry. I jumped the gun a bit. All the right signals were there in front of me."

"I like you, Charlotte," said Phil, "but I need to get to know you better."

She had met her match for a change. A nice guy that didn't want to sleep with his date too soon. A nice guy that was kind, considerate, gentle, and courteous to Charlotte. The kind of guy that she had been looking for while being the Butler "Closer" all this time. *Maybe now Charlotte's web can be shut down for good,* she thought quietly.

* * *

Nina was reviewing the first monthly financial results with Shirley on Tuesday for the month of April, and there were some weird numbers for the Barron business unit. The financial results appeared to represent a company grossing $2.5 million per month, or $30 million per year, rather than the $50 million from the prior year's results. A further review of the four customers and four vendors with the same remit-to address revealed that Barron and Jean had control of these eight records. This information would be turned over to Paul for follow-up and possible legal action against both Barron and Jean.

A later discussion with Jerry would lead to no action being taken against Barron and Jean. The earn-out clause would be changed to such a high number that the Robertses could not make another bonus as punishment.

* * *

James and Nina were having a discussion on the billing results late Tuesday morning. This involved the Cook business unit. The new invoices with some of the same customers were being invoiced at 300 barrels, or 12,600 gallons, per load. There were 350 barrels, or 14,700 gallons, per load on the accounts receivable for the exact same service. James had surmised that the prior owner was fraudulently overcharging the customer base by 50 barrels per load for a long time. The real irony was that the trucks being used to service the customers for the Cook business were rated at a capacity of only 300 barrels per truck.

A later discussion with Jerry would lead to no action being taken against Rick Cook. The earn-out clause would be ratcheted up to such a high number that Rick could not make another bonus as punishment for the next three years.

* * *

A call came into Nina Charles late Tuesday afternoon about how to record the oil residual from the disposal pond at the Metairie business unit. A miscellaneous check had come into the office for $25,000 from the Metairie Oil Refinery. This was for skimmed oil for the month of April, payable in the first week of May. Nina would discuss the matter with Paul and get back to the biller once she determined if it was the prior owner's check or Butler's property.

Nina walked into Paul's office and reviewed the check with him. He was unaware of this operation at Metairie and called James. James had seen the pond for oil skimming operations while he was on site last month. It was later determined that Duncan did not offer any explanation for this little honey pot—his private piggy bank. James brought the new information to Ted, and he was shocked. This was another deception by a business owner to conceal a side business from the Butler company.

News of this got to Jerry and Tim; they were not happy. A subsequent meeting with Duncan revealed that it had been overlooked, and Duncan apologized for the item. His three-year earn-out clause was significantly changed as a punishment to make it harder for Duncan to make his numbers.

* * *

The employment package details arrived in both James's and Bill's email on Friday just before they were about to leave for the weekend. The salary was generous, the bonus schedule was huge, and the stock options grant schedule was extremely good. The two consultants had a decision to make, and the Butler company was expecting it next Monday. This life-changing event would take place when they arrived back on site in the Coraopolis conference room knee-deep in the next acquisition while supporting three newly acquired companies. Their status as consultants would hang in the balance.

James had to think hard about the decision over the weekend. The three recently uncovered anomalies had proven that once you implement a good system, if there is any hanky-panky using inferior systems, the real facts surface and become noticeably clear to the new owners. Sooner or later, the truth will come out in a fully integrated business software system.

Thank You

I would like to thank my wife Deborah, who is my greatest supporter, a source of inspiration, and one of my harshest critics. She often refers to me as Ricky even though that is not my real name.

Thanks to Shirley Moy for reading my first draft and helping me along the way.

Thanks to the boys for giving me a little push to keep going on Sundays. They always seem to have ideas and opinions on every topic while playing a round of golf.

Thanks to my fellow golfers at Willow Creek Golf Course for being receptive to my babbling about *The Traveling Consultant* while I was writing it.

A special thanks to the team at Palmetto Publishing for getting this second book off the ground. Aaron Brewer and Weston Richards, you guys are terrific.

Milton Keynes UK
Ingram Content Group UK Ltd.
UKHW031919041124
450744UK00017B/307/J

9 798822 963399